The Awakening of Navi Septa

Book One

The Keys of Wisdom

By Linda Williams

CheckPoint
Press

THE AWAKENING OF NAVI SEPTA
BOOK ONE: THE KEYS OF WISDOM

ISBN-13: 978-1-906628-31-4

PUBLISHED BY CHECKPOINT PRESS, IRELAND

CheckPoint Press
Books With Something to Say..

CHECKPOINT PRESS

DOOAGH

ACHILL ISLAND

WESTPORT

CO. MAYO

REP. OF IRELAND

WWW.CHECKPOINTPRESS.COM

The Awakening of Navi Septa

Book One

The Keys of Wisdom

A Fantasy of Reality

by Linda Williams

This book is humbly dedicated to the memory of Her Holiness
Shri Mataji Nirmala Devi, who has given humanity
the awakening described in this trilogy

CONTENTS

Part One - Escape from Teletsia

The First Key

The Second Key

The Third Key

Part Two – The Light of Sasrar

PROLOGUE

I was clearing out a trunk the other day and found some of my old diaries. I opened one and began to read.

'My name is Asha Herbhealer. I am a girl of fourteen and I live in Teletos, the capital of our beautiful but wounded land of Teletsia. Like all true Teletsian families - you can pick us out by our honey-brown skins, blue-black hair, green eyes and aquiline noses - we have our pride, even if our freedom and wealth have long gone, stolen by the power hungry Sorcerers, as we call the 'High Priests' who rule our land these days. Nevertheless, we firmly believe that better days will come. We have been waiting for many, many years, but we do not give up hope.'

I turned over a few pages. They were blank, and I remembered what a terrible place Teletsia was then. I went to the medicine cupboard and took out a bottle of rubbing alcohol, dabbed some on one of the pages and within moments this appeared.

'Today was so important that I must put it in my journal, even though it is dangerous. I'm writing in invisible ink. I'll only put the solvent on to make it visible if it is ever safe to do so.'

That was the day it all started and this is what I wrote.

'Last week my cousin Lee and I were walking back from school – (he's always so strong and sensible) – and we saw something which made me feel faint and nauseous with horror, and to want to run away from this land – to escape – anywhere. In the street near our home was a Sorcerer, wearing his black cloak and a flat brimmed hat, talking angrily with a man who was desperately holding on to a boy of about eight years old. Then the Sorcerer waved his staff around, said a few words, the man burst into flames and within moments was reduced to a pile of ashes on the ground. The Sorcerer grabbed the child, who was in complete shock, picked him up and disappeared into a nearby building, which is one of the state run nurseries. I was shattered, and Lee calmed me, cheered me up and took me home, but I had nightmares for three nights after that.

'Why, oh why, do we have to live like this?'

This took me back to my childhood, when Teletos was a noble city, as long as you didn't look too closely. It stood on a number of islands at the mouth of a great river. Canals ringed the town and it would have looked like half an onion to a high-flying bird. Many other waterways crisscrossed these canals and on the islands were broad, tree lined avenues and narrow winding alleys. Each side of the avenues were residential buildings, old beyond the memories of the inhabitants, but built in a grand and solid style. Usually gardens stretched behind them down to the waterways.

Much of the city however, was in a deplorable state of decay and in need of repair. On the facades of many of the buildings were fearsome beasts carved in stone, especially atop the columns, drainpipes and doorjambs. Whether they had originally been put there to frighten away intruders, or whether they expressed the natures of the people who lived in the buildings, nobody dared openly ask. Certainly within the innermost ring of the city, the forbidden area – forbidden to anybody but the rulers of the land, the gruesome stone beasts with their quasi-human heads writhed in their thousands over the administrative buildings. The people who worked in them did look uncannily like the statues on their outsides.

The Sorcerers were supposed to look after the country for everybody to enjoy, but instead they dominated and controlled the rest of us, so they could get on with abusing the laws of nature and becoming ever more powerful. They encouraged everyone to indulge in anything which weakened them from the inside, like drugs and other addictions such as gambling: anything which did not threaten their authority. Many people lost the ability to know right from wrong and then could more easily be manipulated. The Sorcerers were masters of feats of illusion, black magic and hypnotism, and were backed up by the Specials - the Special Secret Police, who were vicious and sinister, and knew that physical torture was also very effective when tracking down dissidents and keeping the population cowed.

Teletsia and the Sea of Illusion

PART ONE

ESCAPE FROM TELETSIA

The First Key -The Root

This key expresses the power of the first subtle centre, at the root of the Tree of Life. Within us this is at the base of the backbone. Its qualities are innocence and childlike wisdom. On our world its country is Teletsia and its seat is the Temple of Support.

Ancient Teletsian manuscript (banned by the Sorcerers)

CHAPTER 1

AN INNOCENT PICNIC

A few days after we had seen the poor man reduced to ashes, Raynor Antiquarian, our friend, wanted to go out to an island near the city for a picnic, and knowing Raynor as I did, I suspected there was more to it than that. We sailed out of town in a small boat belonging to Lee, who is a couple of months younger than me and short and stocky. Like most Teletsians, his hair is black, but his sticks out like a brush. His manner is bright, his eyes are bright and he is very intelligent. I, on the other hand, am thought to be a hopeless dreamer, but that is a cultivated image, a protective outer shell. Lee's bright-as-brass outer self is something similar and there is a deeper Lee hiding within. He is always very protective of me, for which I am very grateful, because my father's work as a dealer in medicinal herbs often takes him away from home for long periods.

Raynor Antiquarian's father owns a bookshop where my mother works and I have known him for ever. Raynor, older than Lee and me, is tall and thin, has blue-black hair like us, but his skin is paler than Lee's or mine, perhaps because his grandmother came from a clan of mountain dwellers. Raynor has just gone to the dreaded Sorcerers' Academy. Its official name is the Teletsian Academy for Advanced Spiritual Study. Raynor's father knows why he has gone there, but many of his friends and relations have ceased to have anything to do with him. His slimy younger brother Mardhang is eternally curious as to why he has made such an unexpected career move. Mardhang is just the sort to become a Sorcerer, a real cockroach of a youth. Nevertheless it is Raynor: sunny, scholarly and shy, a kindly soul who would not harm any living thing, who is learning the dark arts and other cruel methods of keeping the rest of us under control. He lacks the smouldering, controlled defiance of Lee, but he has an inner determination, which is mainly directed towards his book learning, and he is brilliant at that.

On this day, as usual, Lee sailed the boat. He has tried to teach Raynor and me the basics of sailing but we aren't much good, so he usually takes charge. Whereas Raynor makes it his business to understand virtually anything written down Lee manages just as well with anything of a practical nature. They are

3

full of admiration for each other and very tolerant of me, who fails in both categories, most of the time. But we complement each other, and share a lot that even our parents do not know about. We have a deep mutual love and respect, and in this insecure city, where you don't quite know who to trust, it is great to have two close friends like this.

We left the large river and went up a smaller one that came out through the forest, and here we did help Lee row. There was an island in the middle of this river and from the water it appeared to be completely covered in trees and undergrowth. We hid the boat under some overhanging branches and walked up a narrow path to an open space we had discovered in its centre. The sunlight flickered through the tall trees above and flowers dotted the ground with pink sparkles of colour. We sat down and had some food and drinks I had brought along – curried fish, home made flatbread, salad, a fruit tart and a delicious fruit cordial made by my mother. The boys loved my cooking and I knew it would always make them both very happy.

Nog, Raynor's large dog, had come too. He had brown hair, a long tail and a rather serious expression. One ear turned down, the other up. Nog would be sure to bark if anyone had followed us onto the island. He liked having his stomach tickled and knew he could generally persuade me to do this. I made a fuss of him and fed him some leftovers, and thought enviously how simple his life was. Meanwhile Lee told Raynor about what we had seen the week before.

'Did I tell you about that man I saw in the street who had a set-to with one of the Sorcerers?'

'No, what happened?' replied Raynor.

'Asha was devastated, so I decided to find out more. I learnt yesterday that he was just standing up for the right to look after his children himself, and he refused to send them to the state nurseries.'

'You don't absolutely have to give your children to the state nurseries. What happened?'

'The Sorcerer reduced him to a heap of ashes.'

'That's appalling, but it happens all the time.'

'You know what else I heard they do to people who speak out against the Sorcerers? They take away their powers of speech so these poor folk can only grunt or bark like some animal.'

'That's an old trick.'

'I heard something even worse the other day. There's a village out in the country where the people were fed up with so many of them finishing up grunting like pigs and so on, and they organised a rebellion. When the chief Sorcerers heard about this, one went to sort it out with a whole lot of Specials - he did his chanting routine, there was a blinding flash and every villager in sight dropped dead.'

'Oh Mother Earth, when will it end?' I cried. Our family, like many in Teletsia, secretly worshipped the Mother Earth. To pray to her was forbidden, because the Sorcerers maintained that either everything in creation was an accident, or, if there was a creator, it would have to be fearsome and male.

'If I could devote my whole life to trying to solve the nightmares of this country,' said Lee, in a slow, deliberate manner, 'I swear, before our great Mother Earth, that I'd do just that.' Raynor and I agreed, and there in the beautiful woodland clearing, we each put one hand on the ground and the other on our foreheads to pay our respects to her as we repeated the oath. It was a sombre moment. Something in my closed, scared heart opened just a crack.

'It's time we trusted each other more deeply,' added Raynor. 'I wanted Lee to bring us here today, because we have to talk alone.'

'So, what are you really doing at the Sorcerer's Academy?' Lee challenged him.

'I'm a spy.' Was this the end for Lee and myself? I couldn't believe Raynor was about to betray us, he was almost a part of our family. He noticed the fear on my face, 'I didn't mean to frighten you – let me explain. The Sorcerers are always on the lookout for young people with exceptional powers. This is no news, but now that I'm at the Sorcerers' Academy I know the real reason for the state run nurseries. They watch the kids closely and if they show any qualities near to the powers of the Sorcerers they are hypnotised and brainwashed. That's something advanced students learn.'

'Have you learnt that yet?'

'No.' Raynor was short; not the right question to have asked. 'Let me go on. What I'm telling you is incredibly important.'

'Sorry.' Lee was rather in awe of Raynor.

'Really stubborn boys and girls are killed, and the parents are told their little one caught a fever and died. But because people have often given in to the hypnosis of the Sorcerers many of them do send their children to these nurseries. We three have escaped because our parents managed to get permission to raise us themselves. You know how delicate the situation is and how careful our parents are not to disturb them.

'My family is lucky to have the bookshop. The Sorcerers don't trouble us much, because they're interested in our ancient manuscripts and old books. They use us when they want to get hold of historical documents. It's an old book that I have to tell you about, but once I've told you about what we've found out, if anyone betrays us, we're all lost.'

'We live in Teletos and we know what happens,' said Lee.

'Raynor is at the Academy, Lee, and he probably knows far more than he's letting on.' Raynor looked pointedly at me and went on speaking.

'I've been helping my father at the shop this past year. When trade is slack on hot afternoons, dad sends out for iced sherbets and we disappear into the back room where nobody can hear us. Recently he let me in on some of our family secrets......'

'You sure it's all right to tell us?' interrupted Lee.

'Yes, he asked me to, because if anything happens to me, someone of our generation will have to take over my researches.'

'Researches?' I queried. Lee and I were in muddy waters here, because neither of us were the researching type.

'We secretly read our stock,' Raynor ignored my question, 'to try and find out anything that may one day help to free our country from these cursed Sorcerers. No one in Teletsia is taught the ancient language today, because ignorance is the easiest way to stop us thinking for ourselves.'

'We all know that,' said Lee ruefully. 'Well, anyone with any sense does.'

'Most of us in this country haven't a clue of what really happened in the past. The history we learn at school is utter fantasy, made up by the Sorcerers.'

'No wonder I find it so boring.'

'Now I'm going to tell you some of the real stuff.'

'From what your dad has found out?'

'Right. Plus he's been teaching me the ancient language for years and I can also read it pretty well.'

'So?'

'Grandfather Zack, and later on dad, have been working on this for ages now. As grandpa is now dead dad has decided to bring me into the secret. A lot of the ancient scrolls mention the writings of a great prophet who lived some centuries ago. He foretold what's going on today, or anyway at a time when there are all the same problems we've got right now. Years ago grandpa found a copy of this prophecy, but it was confiscated by the Sorcerers. He made some notes, which tell of a time when some young people will somehow expose them.'

'They'll be lucky! But I'd give a lot to be able to see your grandfather's notes.'

'I've got them here. I wish we could find these people the prophet talks about. If they're alive at the moment I'm sure we'd have a lot in common with them.'

'Maybe we're them,' I said hopefully.

'Oh, come on! You can't be serious,' replied Lee.

'They have to be somewhere,' I continued.

'You really think help is at hand? At long last?' said Lee.

'Could be,' Raynor agreed.

'Is that why you wanted to come here today?'

'Yes, of course!' Raynor smiled broadly, because this mattered so much to him. 'You'll have to listen carefully.'

'Go on, we will.'

'This prophet described a land ruled by black magicians who pretend to be priests, and who use all sorts of psychic forces to dominate and destroy people. It describes Teletsia exactly as it is today.'

'How can you be so sure?'

'It just feels so right. The only way the Sorcerers can be overcome is if people become at one with their spirit and then gain subtle powers. They must become consciously connected with the world-soul, the greatest force for good. A person's mind, feelings and body are a reflection of this. This is called the inner 'Tree of Life' and in a strange way it says it has shining, flower-like jewels on the trunk, which is like a golden thread. These jewels are always at certain specific places in people's bodies. For instance, there's one like a diamond in the forehead. All the different powers of creation are reflected within us through this. This Tree of Life must be awakened within people, and for that to happen, a group of young people, who are prepared to risk their lives for their country, will have to go on a long journey to find this wisdom and learn how to make use of the power it gives, and how to give it to others.'

'I don't understand much of this.'

'Don't worry, I didn't either to start with, but it's very important...'

While they were talking, the answer came to me. I had an ability about which I kept very quiet. It was just what the Sorcerers were seeking to discover, because it enabled me to see them for what they were – totally evil. When I put my attention on a person, I could see what looked like jewels on a golden thread within them, stretching from the bottom of the backbone up to the top of the head, like a celestial tree. This had to be the Tree of Life. If anyone knew my secret it could be the end for me, but hadn't Raynor already shown us he trusted us completely?

'The Tree of Life is easy to understand!' I blurted out.

'What do you mean?' exclaimed Raynor.

'The jewels and the golden thread: the Tree of Life. We've all got one.' This was the first time in my life I had spoken about this. Fear gripped me - what if the boys decided to denounce me? There were large rewards offered by the Sorcerers for information such as this. The rumours about what happened to people like me were awful. Lee picked up the flicker of terror on my face, but then I came to my senses – they of all people would never harm me.

'Try not to be afraid,' he implored me. 'Raynor's family has been struggling to understand this prophecy for generations. I swear to you that we won't hand you over to the Sorcerers or anything horrible.'

'Please tell us more. It could be vital,' begged Raynor.

'All right, if you promise not to tell anyone, not even my brother Derwin,' I began cautiously.

'Of course not! After all, he's only ten. He couldn't keep a secret to save his life,' Raynor was closer to the truth than he realised.

'It's like this, when I put my attention on the inner nature of a person, I see inside them what looks like a string of shining jewels on a golden thread. If a person is evil then these jewels are dull. Sometimes, in really bad people, like Sorcerers, they are like balls of writhing worms. The root of the tree, the bottom of the thread, starts at the base of the spine and goes up through the jewels. These jewels are always at certain specific places in people's bodies. For instance, there really is one like a diamond in the forehead. At the top of the

7

head, in you two and a few other people, there's a light like a flower.' I was committed now, so there was no point in holding back.

'Go on. At last we may be getting somewhere.'

'What I see is just like the prophet's description of the Tree of Life. People who are kind, joyful characters with some wisdom tend to have shining jewels within them - usually.'

'You're not very sure.'

'Sometimes even the best people's inner jewels look dull, when they've got some bad problem.'

'What about people who aren't like this: the vast mass who dance to the tune of the Sorcerers?'

'Oh, them? They vary. The ones who are greedy, cruel, insincere and so on have dark, dirty wheels of fire within them. There's another thing too. The way the jewels look at any one time and the way people are at that moment fit together perfectly. Like, if a person gets angry, the light in the forehead goes dim, and if a person says something hurtful, then the jewel in the throat doesn't shine for a time.'

'Are you saying people's characters are reflected in these jewels?'

'More than that. I reckon they're right at the source of a person's whole makeup, and it's amazingly useful. I can always make accurate judgments about people, but I have to keep it an absolute secret or I'd be taken off somewhere dreadful by the Sorcerers.'

'You're right there!' Lee stared at me and I knew he was seeing me in a very new way.

'Oh, and another thing,' I went on, 'you two nearly always have shining inner jewels and glowing flowers on the top of your heads.' Lee and Raynor looked very dubious. I couldn't blame them; I'd just come out with something very weird.

'You said nearly always?' Lee went on.

'Now and again, when you're in a gloomy mood, or angry, your jewels get dull, but it doesn't last, and your murkiest moments are much brighter than the Sorcerers' good days.'

'This is astounding! Why didn't you tell us before? No, actually, you'd have been crazy to tell us until you were sure we'd keep it secret. I've also got an unusual power, although it's not as dramatic as yours,' admitted Raynor. 'You may not be the only one the Sorcerers would like to get hold of. If I put my attention on the top of my head, it's called the fontanel - I feel complete inner peace and at that time I'm never distracted by any unwanted thoughts. When the Sorcerer who's trained to read minds at the Academy comes around to see if I have any subversive thoughts, he can't probe when I'm in this state.'

'How do you know?' I wondered.

'Because I loathe the place and all that goes on there, but when I go into this state, he just passes me by and says, "You're doing fine," so I know for sure the Truthsayer, as he's called, isn't reading my mind. When he gets to friends of mine who are also critical of the Sorcerers, he often looks serious. One of my friends was taken off and never seen again after one of these sessions.'

'I can do this too!' Lee was excited. 'I never dared say so, but I can be totally alert and inwardly still at the same time.'

'Like when?' asked Raynor

'I've realised that many of the classes at school are sessions in mass hypnosis, in that we're being conned into accepting the Sorcerers as our perfect lords and masters, but when I go into my secret pool of calm, no bent teacher can make me fall for those lies. Also, our teachers often try to get into our minds and make us admit to wrong things we haven't even done.'

'I've also stumbled on this pool of calm,' I added, 'but I pretend to be in a constant dream. You've got to play a few games to survive in Teletsia.'

'You had me completely fooled,' admitted Lee.

'Me too,' laughed Raynor, 'but this is all the more reason why we have to look after you and protect you.'

Soon after this we went home, but the seeds had been sown. We fully intended to be an instrument for the Sorcerers' destruction, even if we had no idea how.

CHAPTER 2

THE PROPHECY

Nothing much happened for some time after the visit to the island. Lee and I went back to school and Raynor returned to the Sorcerers' Academy. Now that we knew we had powers which made us 'subversive,' it was even more important for us learn more about the prophecy, to see if it could help us in any way. If we had been a few years older and a few years more crushed by the Sorcerers we would not have attempted the virtually impossible, but we were young and idealistic. Then, quite unexpectedly, there was another memorable day.

Lee and I were waiting for Raynor in the large hall of his house. It was a warm afternoon. It usually is in Teletsia, but this day was almost like summer, not the end of winter, and I was glad to be in the cool, flag-stoned hall with its high, beamed ceiling and small stained-glass windows. Mardhang, Raynor's brother, was there. I never trusted him, not only because his Tree of Life was dark, rotten and worm-eaten, but also because he was a sneak. On that day he offered us some cooling juice, and until I put my attention on his inner side I thought for one fleeting moment he might be improving. But no, the inner, subtle worms were still writhing. Ugh! I had to look away.

Finally, the door opened with its usual squeak. Raynor came in and smiled knowingly when he saw us. He was wearing the common dress for young men in Teletos: loose cotton trousers, a flowing shirt and a sleeveless overtunic. Nevertheless, his red and black clothes were the uniform of the elitist Academy, where future oppressors were trained. I noticed that whenever he came from there, his Tree of Life looked dull, but after some time with us the inner jewels would start to glow again. Outwardly it was Lee and I who looked drab in our earth coloured cottons, because bright colours were frowned upon in the everyday clothes of ordinary young people like us. We, even more than others, would never try to attract attention to ourselves.

On his back Raynor carried an old leather schoolbag. The way he smiled at us was a dead giveaway. Something was up. He put down his bag and gave Lee a slap on the back, and me a broad grin and an enthusiastic 'Hi Asha!'

He'd always been like a brother to me and I was touched by his warm affection. We were usually so reserved in Teletsia.

Mardhang was lounging on the cushions in the corner, reading. Raynor said 'Hello' somewhat coolly; Mardhang gazed vacantly at him and returned to his book in frosty silence. Raynor went to his room and changed out of his hated uniform, then rejoined us with his schoolbag over his shoulder. Together we went out into the garden at the back of his house to get away from Mardhang, who reminded me of some fungus that rarely saw light as he lay among the purple and brown cushions.

The sunlight hit us like a trumpet blast as we went out through the garden door. I loved Raynor's garden. It was colourful, aromatic and escapist. His folk needed somewhere like that, in contrast to all those musty old books and manuscripts they worked with. Some way from the house were a lot of evergreen hedges and a fishpond. We walked down the scrunching gravel path and sat on a stone bench near the pond. Flowerbeds on each side spilled out gaily-coloured blooms, red, orange, yellow, and fragrant herbs. Bees always buzzed around and today some brilliant blue butterflies flitted languidly from flower to flower. The heat made us, as well as the butterflies, lazy and a little careless. Behind and around us were the tall hedges, concealing us from view and anyone from us.

While Raynor looked into his bag Lee and I stood up and had a quick look around to make sure no one was listening who shouldn't. We didn't see anyone, but as we sat down a tornado in the form of Nog threw himself at Raynor. Nog was supposed to be the family watchdog, but he had been asleep and only woke up when he heard Raynor's voice. After greeting Raynor enthusiastically, with wet nose and wagging tail, he went to sleep again in a shady patch.

'So, what's it this time?' Lee asked Raynor eagerly.

'I've got it!'

'Got what?'

'The prophecy!'

'Isn't that incredibly risky?' I said nervously. I could see his fear in the inner jewel of his heart, which suddenly went dull.

'Yes, and I've only got it for the afternoon. I smuggled it out but I must take it back tonight.'

'I wish we could go somewhere safer,' Lee immediately made sense of the situation.

'We simply don't have the time,' Raynor took an old book out of his schoolbag. 'I went into a room in the library that is usually closed and noticed a book with the seal we put on all our stock. I realised this was the prophecy. This represents the true flowering of knowledge.' He pointed to a small embossed impression on the spine of the book, an open book with a flower growing out of it.

'We must be careful,' I had a strong feeling this was not the place to talk about this, 'I just hope Nog will watch out for us.'

'I'm sure he will,' said Raynor absently, scanning the book. He turned the pages, fascinated. 'From what I can gather, the young people who are to be the catalysts for change have to go on a long journey to a country in some mountains in the far north.'

'Any names given?' asked Lee.

'No. It just says, "Beyond the Great Sea." "In that land they will come to understand" - it's not easy to translate – "their true potential, that inner power which exists within every individual".'

'Mysterious gobbledygook. Any revelations today, Asha?' Lee looked hopefully at me. I shook my head.

'Listen, do you want to hear this or not?' Raynor was very much on edge and not his usual even-tempered self. Neither he nor Lee were being as cautious as they generally were.

'Yes of course, take it easy,' said Lee.

' "There, in that land, they will come to be at one with the force of creation. This powerful awareness will flow through them and help them to be instruments of change."'

'Do you really think the prophet believed this?' Lee was beginning to prickle against all the obscure language.

'He wouldn't have written it if he didn't,' I commented. 'It's telling us what to seek.'

'What do you mean?'

'Us? Seek what?' said Raynor. 'We're not these people the prophecy is talking about.'

'Even if we're only ordinary people, we must try to make this journey,' I was about to explain further.

'Great, so we just up and off across the world,' interrupted Lee, 'forget our families, forget the Sorcerers and their Secret Police, and on the way we just happen to come across a group of people who are putting the world to rights, who know exactly where they are going and why.'

'What I mean is,' I persisted, 'maybe it's an inner spiritual journey each one of us has to take.'

'It does tell you how to start,' went on Raynor. '"The journey must start from the Temple of Support. The temple has four great stones..".'

'I've heard of that place!' cried Lee, completely forgetting to keep his voice down. 'It's in the country, past Clatan. Have you learnt about it at the Academy?'

'Can't say I have,' replied Raynor.

'The local people say it's sacred to the Mother Earth.'

'How do you know?'

'I was staying out that way on holiday last year.'

'According to the prophecy, there are four large rocks in a square in the centre and a lot of smaller ones twisting around in a spiral.'

'That's it!'

'Listen to this,' Raynor continued translating, '"There are seven jewelled keys to match the seven jewels of the soul. The subtle centres of the inner Tree of Life match these actual jewelled keys".'

'Where on earth are we to come by them?'

'No idea.'

'Go on.'

' "The jewelled keys are effective in certain areas of the world. The seekers can open the inner doors of the spirit with them and can also use these magical jewels to help them get to the northern country."' Just then we heard the crunch of footsteps on the gravel behind us. Nog was awakened by someone standing on his tail, which had been lying across the path. Mardhang appeared, running round the corner of the hedge, pursued by a snarling Nog. I jumped up to shield Raynor as he pushed the book back into the bag. Lee lurched towards Mardhang to protect him from Nog, because Nog hated Mardhang as much as he loved Raynor.

'That wretched dog of yours nearly bit me!' complained Mardhang. 'Father should have the brute destroyed! It never attacks intruders, only me!' I looked away so Mardhang couldn't see me smiling and Lee also hid his amusement in a fake sneezing fit. We forgot that our freedom hung by a thread.

'By the way, I happened to overhear that you're going to the old stone circle beyond Clatan to look for some buried treasure. I'm your brother. You'd better not leave me behind.' We all knew that wheedling, threatening voice. While Mardhang was speaking, the inner jewels of his soul were horrible.

Our meeting broke up immediately. We arranged to get together again the following weekend at Lee's house, which was safer. Raynor's garden backed onto a canal and we left in Lee's boat that we had come in. Raynor managed to get the book back to the library without any problems, or so he thought.

Journal of Herzog, Scribe to the Most High Priests of Teletsia

I, Herzog, scribe to the most illustrious Lords of Teletsia, do hereby record the latest report of our trusted servant Mardhang Antiquarian.

Raynor Antiquarian assumed he had returned the prophecy without being seen. Mardhang Antiquarian made his way to the Administrative Quarter, disguised as a fishwife in a veil and carrying a basket of fish on his head. We always insist he comes in disguise. He came in by a servant's entrance and was given clean clothes, for their Supreme Holinesses the Priests cannot stand the smell of fish. They were waiting for him, wearing their black cloaks and red robes of office and sitting round a heavy wooden table in the Interrogation Chamber. This room has bare grey stone walls, a high, vaulted ceiling and small windows, so no one can try to escape by jumping out of them. Armed guards stand by the doors and many people have been condemned to death or torture in this room. Mardhang felt hemmed in and afraid, standing alone at the hub of the power of Teletsia.

'Speak, wretch,' said His Supreme Lordship, who has a thin, refined face like a death mask and wears his grey hair long.

'Raynor has deciphered the prophet's book,' began Mardhang in a quavering voice.

'Speak up, idiot!' ordered the Master of the Dead Souls, who is somewhat deaf due to his great age. He has a carved wooden ear trumpet, but it does not help him much.

'This Raynor must be a genius indeed, would that he was on our side,' said His Supreme Lordship.

'He will be, when we have captured and broken him, but first let him lead us to the jewels of power. Those we must have in order to prevent the prophecy from being fulfilled,' this was the Master of Mind Control. Few people can return his gaze, and when his deep dark eyes bore into anyone being questioned, they find it hard not to tell him the truth.

'He must also lead us to this prophesied group of young traitors,' continued the Head of the Special Secret Police Force.

'None of them must survive or Teletsia as we know it is finished,' insisted His Supreme Lordship.

'They will meet again soon, probably in the house of Lee Restorer's

family,' said Mardhang.

'Thank you for that information. Go and claim your usual reward. But remember, if you cease serving us, unending terror will fill your brain.'

Mardhang grovelled on the floor. 'Oh, and another thing,' the Master of the Dead Souls spoke once more, 'we will send a bat to spy for us next time Raynor meets his friends. You needn't try to follow them.'

'A bat, My Lord?' Mardhang picked himself up from his grovel.

'Yes, we force a human spirit which is under our control into the body of a bat. It spies on whomsoever we command it to. When the bat returns, we put the spirit back into its own human body and then it tells us whatever it heard while it was hidden in the body of the bat. We might transfer you into a bat, permanently, if you displease us.'

Some days later, in the early evening, we met in the rambling old palace which belonged to Lee's father. It had several floors, was built round a central courtyard, and behind was a larger yard with more buildings that had been converted into flats, as had the central building. There were gardens around it, including a walled rose garden at the back, and behind this was one of the larger canals. We went to the garret at the top of the tower in one corner of the courtyard. From here we could see the whole city built on many interconnected islands, with its canals, roads, houses and gardens. Teletos was near the shore and connected to it by bridges, and beyond was the broad river estuary, where ships from many countries always lay out in the deeper water. No one could hear us because Lee had locked the door from the inside and it was at the bottom of the long spiral staircase that led up to the little room. We sat on cushions we had brought up with us, because it was empty and not used.

'We didn't think of going to have a look at the Temple of Support, did we?' said Raynor.

'No, that was the one good idea we got from that horrendous brother of yours,' said Lee. 'He's a real pain. I'm sure you don't like to hear that, but it's the truth.'

'At least you don't have to live with him, that can be too much sometimes. It says in the prophecy that if a person is not humbly seeking wisdom on this journey, he won't get very far. Let's not worry about Mardhang too much at the moment.'

'I agree with you,' I added. 'Let's hope nothing, especially Mardhang, is going to stop us from all this seeking of wisdom and jewelled keys and temples.'

'By the way,' said Raynor, 'did you notice that my father has taken to growing large clumps of scented tulsi in our garden?'

'Yes, I did!' I laughed. 'What's it for?'

'I read in the prophecy that we can use the dried leaves, which as you know

15

give off a wonderful sharp smell, to protect us from evil people.'

'What do you mean?' asked Lee.

'It said, "Tulsi will nullify the destructive energies of negative beings, or even harmful spirits".'

'Sounds odd. Does it work?'

'Yes, it does. It saved me the other day. Here, Asha, take these leaves and sew them into little sachets and we'll wear them around our waists or something. We can't be too careful, because we'd be prime targets for the Sorcerers if they knew more about us.' Before I could tell Raynor I wasn't much good at sewing, he gave me a bag full of scented tulsi. Its strong smell filled the garret. I was just wondering whether I could persuade my mother to do the sewing job for me when a bat, which had been hiding in the rafters, suddenly flew terrified towards the glassless window, hitting itself in its haste. It was completely disoriented. We looked at it and each other, then went on talking.

'Funny about that bat,' continued Raynor, 'the other day a similar thing happened.'

'You mean your teacher flew out of the window?' joked Lee.

'Not far off. When I smuggled the prophecy out of the library at the Sorcerers' Academy, the old Sorcerer, who sometimes searches you when you leave, saw my bag. I thought for one terrible moment the game was up. However, I had by chance put some scented tulsi in the top of it. He demanded to see what was inside and made me open it. As I did, he smelled it, had a violent coughing fit, then ran back into the librarian's office shrieking and retching, as if he'd been poisoned.'

'You didn't tell us that. How did you get out?'

'I quietly left the library before the hullabaloo died down.'

'But scented tulsi has a lovely smell!' I said, and buried my nose in the bag full of it.

'Not if you're a Sorcerer,' observed Raynor.

'Or a bat,' concluded Lee.

We made plans to visit the Temple of Support near Clatan and the next day Raynor returned to the Sorcerers' Academy, armed as usual with scented tulsi.

Journal of Herzog, Scribe to the Most High Priests of Teletsia

The priests found no trace of the bat or the spirit possessing it. We assume a bird of prey caught the bat. We will have to go back to using Mardhang Antiquarian, who is doing well in this matter so far.

CHAPTER 3

THE START OF THE JOURNEY

Lee, Raynor and I had a short holiday from our places of education and wanted to visit the Temple of Support. My mother had a friend called Mrs. Starwise, an elderly lady with white hair and a wrinkled, kindly face. She was one of Lee's father's tenants and was a professional astrologer, and the week before we left I happened to see her. She warned me that there was something important in my stars, and also Derwin's: 'It's a very good time to start a project that could have far-reaching repercussions, but you'll have to be careful about dangerous negative influences which will try to come your way. It's a very rare line-up of stars and heralds great change.'

'It bears out what's in the prophecy,' Raynor said when I told him. 'It says, "The hopes of the very stars in the heavens are reflected in the minds and hearts of people on earth." I'd never thought of stars as having hopes, but that's what it said.

Before we planned to go into the countryside, Lee mentioned that we'd come up with a problem. We needed to borrow Lee's neighbours' pony trap. The neighbour was another of the tenants in Lee's family palace, and his family could borrow it whenever they needed it. However, Conwenna, the neighbour's daughter, wanted to come too and we couldn't really refuse her. Conwenna was a courageous little girl, with a shining Tree of Life, but she was even younger than my brother Derwin, so we weren't keen on taking her. She had a reticence about her, even more than us. We thought this was because her mother had died when she was very young. Her father was often away for his work and she had been brought up by her maiden aunt, a bitter and cold-hearted woman. Lee's mother spoke to him about Conwenna one evening.

'If you want to go camping on the plain near Clatan,' she said, 'I can't see why you don't want to take Conwenna.'

'It might be dangerous,' he objected. 'There are lots of snakes there, especially during this season, when it sometimes rains.' It was important that his mother didn't know why we were going. If she were ever questioned about this trip, the less she knew the better. The Sorcerers had many tortures to wring secrets out of people, and Lee would naturally never have wanted his mother to suffer on his account.

'I would have thought that Conwenna would know better than any of you about poisonous snakes. After all her father is a prospector and she sometimes goes on trips with him to the jungles and mountains for weeks at a time.'

'Yeah, I s'pose you are right, ma.'

Lee was concerned that this outwardly innocent camping trip might turn out much more serious, especially after I had told him what Mrs Starwise had said. If anything unexpected happened none of the parents would see any of us again, because the authorities were ruthless, but on the other hand it would not do to be too secretive about the whole thing and thus attract attention in that way. We were going to have to take Conwenna, because we really did need to borrow the pony trap.

My brother Derwin also wanted to tag along. He was a few months older than Conwenna and an acquaintance of hers, when it suited him. It suited him then and nobody could think of any good reason to stop him coming too. He and Conwenna were undoubtedly out of the ordinary, but because they were so young we had not let them into our secrets.

Something happened at my home too. My mother dreamed of a girl riding a white horse and wearing a blue cloak. She told my mother that we were going on an important journey where older people would be afraid to travel, but our innocence and courage would carry us through and we would be guided by many wise people. I had some trouble persuading my mother not to worry, but eventually managed to calm her down. I told Raynor and Lee and they took the omen very seriously, because we knew my family members had prophetic dreams.

Some days later we set out for the Temple of Support. At sunrise we were loading up the pony trap in the yard of Lee's large home. My mother was there and she took Raynor aside.

'Look after them, Raynor. This may be the start of what we've been waiting for, for so long,' she said, and he understood that she was referring to her dream.

Raynor was riding his father's horse; Derwin had borrowed a pony and Conwenna, Lee and I were in the pony trap with the camping gear and food. Conwenna was quiet and strong-minded – there was no way anyone was going to leave her behind. She was thin and wiry, like me, but had a shock of curly shoulder-length hair, whereas mine was longer, straight and tied back. Her expression gave away little of what was going on inside her, and her mouth was set and pursed. She didn't say much. Derwin was his usual enthusiastic self. He looked like Lee, short for his age and stocky, with straight hair. He had the strong nose of most of our people, and a cheeky dimple in his chin. Neither Derwin nor Conwenna had any idea why we were really going to the country. It was better they did not know, in case things went wrong.

We set out early and everything went well until we came to the great stone gatehouse just before the bridge onto the mainland which carried the western road. All land traffic had to leave the city via one of the bridges and we used this one when we took Nog for a walk. Although a few of the Sorcerers and Special Secret Police had carriages powered by coal, the horse was the main means of transport, apart from donkeys, mules, oxen and a type of camel in the mountain districts.

This was Teletos, the capital of Teletsia and you didn't just come and go as you pleased. We had the necessary passes to go to the Clatan district, but it was only when Raynor produced his badge which showed that he was at the Sorcerers' Academy that we were allowed out without being searched and questioned. Even so we had to wait a long time under the arches of the old gate. As was the custom, the gatehouse was covered with carvings of beasts with horrible expressions on their faces. Most of my friends thought these ones looked like Sorcerers but we were told they were there to frighten away unwanted intruders. As I was waiting, I noticed one that reminded me of Mardhang.

After satisfying the gatekeepers we crossed the bridge among the crowds of people on foot, on horses, in coal powered carriages and carts. We were just taking a look over the side of the parapet to see the boats and barges sliding along the smooth, dirty surface of the canal, and there, horror of horrors, on the further side of the bridge, we saw Mardhang.

He looked ridiculous and stood out even in this crowd. He rode a horse that he had hired for the occasion, wore the gaudy clothes of a town dandy and his hat had a great feather in it. Passers by laughed at him as he stood waiting for us. Mardhang insisted on coming too and told us he was wearing smart clothes because he intended to stay at an inn rather than camp in the open. I didn't believe him - he wanted to be noticed for some reason, and it wasn't one that would help us in any way.

While we were all arguing at the further end of the bridge, who should come bounding across it, weaving in and out of the people, vehicles and animals with the slithery skill of an eel in a hurry, but Nog. He panted to a stop and howled with joy at the prospect of a run. It was too late to take him back and he just wagged his tail stupidly when Raynor told him to go home on his own. He jumped in the back of the pony trap and promptly fell asleep, triumphantly. So our trip had begun, but not without problems.

We left the built up area on the mainland near the island city and began our journey through the farmland. It was one of those marvellous days when all nature was basking in the return of the warm and balmy weather we have for ten months of the year. I forgot the mixed feelings I had when saying goodbye to my parents as I watched, heard and even smelled the countryside around me, but nevertheless felt we might be away much longer than a few days.

Things became lively again when we reached the second village. We rounded the corner into the village street, rutted and muddy due to recent rain. Coming towards us was a farmer in a cart pulled by a team of at least six donkeys. It was piled high with wooden crates full of hissing geese and quacking ducks on their way to Teletos market.

Mardhang's horse couldn't take this at all. It reared up and bounded sideways into the village duck pond. The water was shallow and coated with green slime. Mardhang went in head first, after he and the horse parted company. He was soaked by his fall and the horse careered around the pond in its fright, trying to escape from the dreadful hissing monster, which had by now disappeared in the direction of the city.

At the side of the pond some yokels were commenting on the scene as Mardhang was helped back on his horse by Lee and Derwin. I couldn't help it, but my heart sang for joy when I saw Mardhang, stinking like a rotten fish, coming out of that pond. I overheard the yokels' comments.

'I reckon the parrot's fallen into a puddle!' cackled one antique chap, with a hoot of laughter as he leant on his walking stick.

'Right place for 'im too, and all his kind as well, says I,' put in another, not quite so ancient.

'If he's going to ride a handsome horse, he should at least know how to stay aboard it,' said a third.

'Ain't so handsome now; looks right bedraggled,' went on the very old man who had spoken first, chewing on his wispy moustache. 'Good horse though, to tip one of them Sorcerers' men into the slime. Wish we could put them all in there, eh?' he poked his elbow into the side of the old man sitting next to him.

'Be careful, Grandpa,' said the third one, 'that blighter could have you put away before your time, just for saying that. You know them Sorcerers and their mates.'

'I don't care; I'll be going soon enough. It's a rum world when an old boy like me can't even enjoy a good joke,' finished the very old one who then went stumping off, chuckling and pointing his stick at Mardhang.

Mardhang was furious. He rode off up the street ahead of us and told us to go on, saying that he would catch us up. We saw his horse tethered outside the office of the Specials. I was beginning to fear the worst about Mardhang.

After the incident of the duck pond, Mardhang sank into a silent, damp and rather smelly gloom and his horse was not quite so skittish. He threatened to go home but unfortunately didn't, so the journey continued. That night we camped by the roadside and Mardhang went to stay at a nearby inn. We thought nothing of it, only that he didn't enjoy camping or our company. It became very cloudy and rained hard in the night, so despite our tents we got quite wet. He rejoined us on the road the following morning and no longer smelled of stagnant pond as he had for most of the previous day.

Records of the Special Police, Noldi Village, Teletos Province

I, Constable Rasp, do hereby report the following:

Yesterday morning, Mardhang Antiquarian of Teletos complained that he had been mentally abused by three men, (named below) when his horse threw him into the village pond. Mr. Mardhang showed me his badge, proving him to be a Grade IV Informer for the High Priests. This type of abuse is treason when the plaintiff is so important. Offenders have no trial when reported by such a one, whose evidence alone is considered damning.

In the night I took my two assistants and we dragged the old men from their homes and drowned them in the same pond. It was a routine killing. Their families found them the following morning and no complaints were lodged.

We went on and by mid afternoon were nearing the part of the country where Lee's friends had their farm. He had written to tell them that we were coming and they had replied that they were looking forward to seeing us. Sure enough, where the lane from the farm joined the country road, there they were. The three of them had seen us on the far hill, from their farmhouse, and had come to meet us. There were a lot of 'hellos,' and Tandi Riverside embraced everyone. She was taller than me and I was immediately struck by her almost picture perfect face, her perfectly proportioned body and her long, thick hair – black like most people's in Teletsia. She had a warm, infectious laugh and smiled a lot – much more than me, who was always wary in those days. Her twin brothers Gwant and Mabron led the way up the hill, to their farmhouse. The lane went through fields where fat, contented cows grazed the lush grass, and fruit groves, heavy with scented yellow, white and pink blossom at this time of year.

These young farm people were healthy and sturdy and had something that was missing from us sons and daughters of Teletos. In the city, which was held in a gridlock by black-hearted Sorcerers, we were always on our guard. Out here the creeping, ever-searching tendrils of the evil rulers, always seeking to trap, entwine and suffocate our freedom, didn't seem so threatening. Mother Nature was the stronger. We could see this all around us in the shining green of the earth's spring clothing and the explosion of flowers decorating the gardens, meadows and riversides. Even the rich red of the soil, where the ploughs had turned the fields, was brighter and more alive than our muted world of grey city streets.

We followed Tandi and her brothers up the lane and Lee noticed that Mardhang was no longer with us. Raynor said he had gone to see some friends in the nearby town of Clatan. We were relieved that he had left us, even if only temporarily.

Tandi's mother prepared a meal and we ate and ate the home grown food. After we had finished our dessert of yellow springberries, delicious pale yellow berries found in the hedgerows, which tasted slightly sharp and were best with lashings of cream and sugar, Tandi took us to find someone Lee had met the previous year.

'Ahren is as wild as a hawk, but he's got a heart of gold,' Tandi had said when describing him to Conwenna and myself.

By a small river, in a thicket of tall bushes we met Ahren, who, Tandi insisted, knew the country around the Temple of Support well. At first we could not see anyone, but then, in the shadows under the overhanging bank of the stream, we noticed a boy slightly younger than Lee lying on his stomach, leaning over the water's edge with his arms in the water. He was oblivious of us and was trying to tickle a fish, that is, trying to catch a fish by gently tickling its sides, so it mistook a person's fingers for the flowing waters of the stream. Then it was thrown out onto the bank before it realised its fatal mistake. It needed much patience and very quick reactions and Ahren was a bit short on the patience.

The half tickled fish heard the human footsteps even if Ahren didn't, and it swam away as we approached. Ahren stood up and turned around to reveal a front covered in reddish dirt from lying at the water's edge. He saw Tandi, who was in the lead. Ahren was taller than Lee, although he was younger, and thin, as if all his growing had gone into his height. He had a small turned up nose, smiling eyes, a mop of curly, almost frizzy hair, and when one looked at him the words rebellious mischief came to mind.

'That's the end of that fish for today. Honestly Tandi, you'll never learn,' cried Ahren with a resigned grin. Nothing bothered him for long, however. 'Oh, hello! I didn't see the rest of you,' he called to us as we came out of the thick bushes. 'I didn't know you were coming today. When are we going to the temple? That's why you've come, isn't it?'

'You must be careful what you say,' Tandi cautioned him. 'Most people don't even know it is a temple.' We had previously decided that we would probably tell her more about why we had come, once I had checked on her inner Tree of Life. As soon as I saw her I realised she was another of the people who walked around with shining jewels inside them, even though they didn't know it.

'Hello, Ahren,' cried Lee from the back, 'good to see you again.'

'And you! I hope we are going to get into some real living soon!'

'So do I,' added Lee, 'but we've got to watch out for Raynor's ghastly brother. He's coming along too if we can't shake him off, so you must be very careful of him. We don't know whose side he's on, but I'm pretty sure it's not ours. Although what we're doing isn't exactly wrong, he could twist the truth and make things very difficult for us. So you've *got* to keep your mouth shut when he's around - right?' Raynor and I had also previously arranged that if, when I looked into Ahren's Tree of Life, the inner jewels were shining, I would give Raynor a nod and then Raynor would let him into at least some of our reason for being here. I took one look at Ahren and gave Raynor the prearranged nod. Fate was at work, because of the thousands of people in Teletos and the few I had seen on our way here, none of them had such vibrant Trees of Life as those of us standing together in the bushes of Tandi's farm.

'We want to go and see if we can find some clues as to whether it really is a temple,' Raynor took over. 'I've been doing a lot of research and we've come up with some awesome stuff. There might be some golden keys or jewelled charms hidden there, near the springs or those big stones in the centre. We're doubtful, because we got our information from an old book, and after so many years someone has probably already found them. Plus if they are still there we don't stand much chance of finding them just by doing the odd bit of digging. We think maybe the mention of the jewels may mean something else. It may be symbolic.'

Raynor had been sizing up Ahren as he was speaking and saw in him just the sort of person needed for a trip of this kind. Although Raynor could be quietly courageous and very determined, he sometimes lacked fire, and needed someone to push him into action. These qualities Ahren had in abundance, even if he could be hot-headed and utterly tactless.

'We'll leave early tomorrow morning, because it's a full day's journey,' said Tandi to Ahren. 'Meet us at the bottom of the lane after breakfast. Can you get hold of a horse?'

'Yeah, no problem. I'll borrow one of the milk-round horses from dad.' Ahren's father owned the dairy in nearby Clatan, a small and sleepy town. I must admit that when I first spoke to Ahren, as opposed to looking at his inner

Tree of Life, I found him very immature, considering he was almost as old as Lee and me. But then I realised that these country people were much more spontaneous and less suspicious than us from the city, and I shouldn't have felt so critical.

Tandi's brothers were not able to come, as it was their turn to look after the poultry. Their father was very strict about these duties being carried out properly. The milk-round horses were all in use, but Ahren managed to borrow an ancient racing pony. He found it at his uncle's abattoir, where it was about to be slaughtered for dog meat. As it had no other failings except old age and a mournful expression, he persuaded his uncle to give it a few days' reprieve.

CHAPTER 4

THE TEMPLE OF SUPPORT

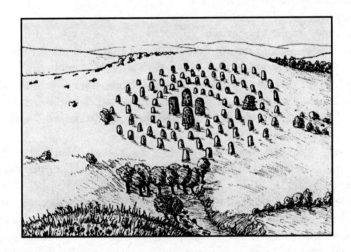

The seven of us set off through the winding country lanes the next morning and all day we slowly climbed to higher ground. It was getting towards sunset when we reached the plain and saw the great stones of the temple. It was still hot, even though breezy, as we approached them, standing like sentinels among the flowering bushes and long grass of this singing, rattling, sighing wildland. The sun was setting exactly in line with the two large stones which were aligned east and west. Lee noticed that the following day it would rise exactly in line with the western one. As we got closer the warm breeze died down and the noise of the plants being blown around stopped. Even the birds ceased their singing.

We paused and looked at the temple, and I sensed a great power emanating from it, as if something wanted to grow out of the three and a half circles of rocks dotted at intervals on the plain. These spirals of rocks surrounded the four vast megaliths in the centre. I experienced a feeling that was somewhere between power, joy and energy, and when I put my hands in the direction of the standing stones there was a cool and subtle wind blowing on my face and the palms of my hands. This was strange because otherwise the evening was still and warm.

The light was fading and we decided to spend the night in the little valley to the north of the temple where seven springs gushed out of the rock, in a clearing surrounded by some trees. We unhitched the pony from the trap and tied up the animals, after giving them food and water. Ahren made a fire and Tandi started to cook supper on it: chicken roast on skewers and baked roots, wild yams, similar to sweet potatoes. They were large and brownish and very tasty when baked in the embers. Just as we settled ourselves around the fire and began to eat, into the circle of firelight came Mardhang leading his horse.

'I thought I'd find you here,' he muttered. There was a chilly silence and then someone ventured a hello.

'Been here long?' he asked.

'Not very,' replied Lee curtly.

'Was it dark when you got here?' No one bothered to reply because our mouths were full of food. 'I asked, was it dark when you got here?' he repeated, this time looking directly and rather nastily at Conwenna. She didn't flinch but gave him a vacant smile. She appeared to be looking right through him. Could she see what I saw, or feel what I felt: the slimy, smouldering, sneaky essence of Mardhang?

'Sunset,' she said, and returned to her chicken. Mardhang didn't say 'useless brat', but you could almost hear him thinking it. He turned his attention to Tandi.

'Found anything interesting?' Mardhang tried a more direct approach.

'Such as?' asked Tandi and went on turning some wild yams in the fire as if unaware of the undertones of the question. She was expert at appearing to be a naive country bumpkin, when in fact she was highly intelligent and intuitive. With her sparkling eyes and pretty heart shaped face many people failed to appreciate her inner depth. They took her for a beautiful, unsophisticated farmer's daughter who longed for the finery and excitement of the big city. This was one side of her nature, but only a part of it. I noticed Mardhang looking at her and heard him murmur, 'Idiot female, I wonder if she can really be as stupid as she looks.'

'I've heard what you lot are up to these past months and what you're doing is deadly dangerous. This stuff is only for Priests.' He almost shouted, losing his temper. None of us said a word. Then he went on more quietly, assuming he had scared us. 'If you're going treasure hunting though, I could help to protect you from - from them. You know who I mean.'

'Mardhang, I'll soon be a Priest myself,' said Raynor. It was a bluff, because Raynor had no intention of becoming a Sorcerer. Mardhang scowled and Tandi innocently handed him a leg of hot chicken and a charred wild yam just out of the embers. He promptly burnt his mouth and fingers.

After we had finished, Tandi brewed a syrupy drink and we sipped it while sitting round the fire. Lee took out his flute and we asked Raynor for a song. It was his own composition, unpractised and clumsy in parts, but it came straight from the heart, a reaction to the stupidity of the Sorcerers' Academy, where the Sorcerers taught students to manipulate the almost perfect Teletsian climate for their own selfish ends. The poem was dedicated to the Mother Earth, so this wild countryside was the right place to sing it.

'Wreathed in an endless garment of white clouds, you hide your vast equanimity,

With your changing moods and seasons, you reveal your tender fragility.

You know to perfection your part, in the dance of the planets and stars,

When we learn how we travel with you, then perhaps we'll come to know ours.

How carefully, how delicately, you slowly form your great creation,

With man as the crest-jewel, mirror of all evolution.

But humans abuse your gift of free will and deny what they might become,

At a moment in time when mankind could in spirit be one.

While arrogant people disturb the living surface of your being,

Will you one day rise, throw off compassion and show us that in truth, you are all seeing?

One little shudder, some subtle rippling of your shimmering skin,

And there'd just be blue rolling ocean where our ancient country once had been.

So let us worship and respect you, and accept all your variety,

Not try to mould you and control you with our human notoriety.'

Mardhang found the song very offensive. He was clutching at the buttons on his jacket and shaking his head in disapproval. I heard him muttering under his breath, 'Subversive songs. Enough of this. There're better things going on over the hill.' Then he spoke out loud and announced that he was going for a walk in the moons' light.

I was concerned for a moment, but in the beauty of the night forgot his words and their possible meaning. I love our moons and tonight they were even more spectacular than usual. As we had been having supper, and later when Raynor and Lee were singing and playing, all three had risen and shone over the towering megaliths behind us on the hilltop.

The first moon to rise had been the small white, fastest moving Moon of Wisdom. Next had come the largest, the golden Moon of Good Fortune and the last to appear above the rocks of the temple had been the medium sized and slowest moving Moon of Compassion, fainter than the other two. I was sure the moons were connected with the qualities that their names suggested, but most people, cut off from anything of value in their culture, ridiculed the idea. The Sorcerers did not like to see correlations between the outer forces of nature and our inner selves. They liked everything split up into separate compartments so they could control everyone and everything more easily. The concept of a vast and sentient Mother Earth, and moons that could affect people's natures, terrified the Sorcerers, so Raynor said. He knew. He knew them all too well.

We looked in wonder at the majesty of the moons and something deep stirred within us. In contrast to the silent procession of the moons, we could hear the seven little springs, gurgling down the hillside with the spontaneous joy of a newborn baby. Nog, who had been off hunting for some extra dinner, now came and kept guard, growling periodically. He understood things like moons, and he probably also saw the Tree of Life in people, because he always judged a person's character so accurately.

We slept under the stars and moons. I had a dream. I was in infinite space and there was complete silence. Then there was a sound, a vibration that solidified into an enormous golden egg. From the egg came the wailing of a baby, and it cracked open. There was a blinding light and out came a young boy, sweet and innocent. He modelled a baby elephant out of the bare earth nearby and then breathed life into it. Next the boy and the elephant walked up the hill and when they were nearly at the top the boy crouched down and made signs in the earth, in the shape of a square.

A little golden key had appeared in the ground where he had made the signs. The key had a four-petalled flower on the end of it, set with orange-red gems. He picked it up and gave it to the elephant. The elephant held it carefully in its trunk and gave it to me.

In the next part of the dream the three of us stood back from the place on the ground where the signs had been made and I noticed that there was a definite impression in the earth where the jewelled key had been. The impression became a roaring vortex and out of it arose the great stones of the Temple of Support. Then everything became still and I saw a stream, the stream with the seven springs. The small boy pointed to it flowing north and said to me in a clear voice, 'That's your way, seeker. Follow it!'

The dream faded and I woke up. It was still dark, although I knew from the position of the stars that night was nearly over. For some reason I felt by my side, and there in the earth next to me, I could just see, by the faint light of the Moon of Compassion, a key, with a jewelled flower-shaped end, hung on a golden chain. Half asleep, I picked it up and put it round my neck, under my clothes. Then I dozed off again.

When I next woke up it was that time of grey light just before dawn, the coldest part of the night. Raynor was bending over Lee, who was sleeping on the ground beyond Conwenna, next to me. Lee was snoring and I whispered to Raynor, 'What's going on?'

'We've been followed by a group of Specials,' he replied, desperately anxious.

'Huh? What? You must have had a bad dream,' I mumbled.

'No, wake up Asha, or this might be the last time you do.' I looked at Raynor and with my inner awareness felt his fear, a hollow pain in the subtle centre at the level of his heart. Raynor, and indeed all of us, had plenty to be utterly terrified about. My heart began pounding and I felt as if someone was crushing me with a great rock. My worst fears were being realised. I looked in horror at him.

'What on earth are we going to do?'

'I don't know. I'm asking you,' he was almost shaking with fear.

'Why me?'

'Why not? You're the psychic one.'

'How do you know we've been followed?'

'In the night, I thought I heard voices and went to have a look. I went up to the temple and over the hill to the other side to where there're a few trees - scrubby ones, but trees. I kept low and crept from the cover of one tree to the next. I could hear the noise of men talking and laughing, and they sounded as if they were high on some drug. Eventually I saw them, some men drinking what I think was that new one, imported stuff - fermented juice. They were sitting around a campfire and soon they bedded down and went to sleep. I went closer and saw their red and black uniforms: Specials, for sure, and you know what they're like. At first I thought I'd come and wake you all up. It was too much of a coincidence to find them here tonight, way off the beaten track, the very same evening that we're here. Then I realised that if we let them know we're frightened we'd be playing into their hands.'

'So what did you do?' I was sitting up now and wide awake.

'Nothing. After the horror of the first minute or so, I remembered that there's no reason why we shouldn't be here. Our passes are good for all this area. Plus we have Mardhang with us. We don't know whether he's just being his usual tricky self, or whether he's in league with this crew. To begin with I was stunned. I just sat there alone, hiding, terrified. I couldn't think of anything, let alone do anything, but then I calmed down and came back here and tried to get some sleep.'

'Did you?'

'No way, I just tossed and turned and decided to wake you up.'

'What if they do find us digging for gold?' wondered Lee, who had now woken up.

'Hush, quietly,' I urged.

'Pretend we're digging for wild yams!' Ahren chortled loudly. He had woken up too.

'Do whisper!' urged Raynor. 'Or you'll wake the others. Don't you know these Specials are no joke? Murder and torture are their middle names.'

'Listen,' I suggested, 'let's go and have a quick look at the temple right now, before it gets light.'

As is often the case when I wake up in the night and then go back to sleep, waking reality and dream awareness got mixed up. I had forgotten I had the jewelled key around my neck. It had merged into being part of my dream, which had also slipped my mind at that moment.

'That makes sense,' whispered Lee. 'Let's go to that side of the temple,' he pointed to where the sun was rising over it, 'and we may see something useful. This morning the sun is going to come up just in line with the two big stones that point due east and west, of the central four. I have a feeling that we might get some clues if we watch carefully.'

The four of us silently left the camp. We managed not to disturb the others, who were still sleeping. We made our way up the hill and by the time we had reached the eastern side of the temple the sun was about to appear over the distant horizon of the plain. Out of the mists on the horizon came a vast orb, vague and golden coloured at first and then clearer as it shone free of the morning haze. We all turned to look at the Temple of Support before us on the hillside.

The first rays of the fully risen sun pierced the shadows, shone over the outer spiral of stones and struck the foot of the nearest of the four great megaliths. Something at the foot of the rock glittered gold and then all the stones also sparkled and shone with a warm orange glow - the glittering evidently came from some quartz or mica in the rock. In the morning light the next object to catch the sun's rays was the stream, dancing down the hill in its first moments of life as the water flowed from the seven springs beneath the northern side of the temple.

'Look! See how the sunlight shows up those, sort of like, elephant heads carved in the stones?' Lee pointed to some weathered outlines on the rocks. 'We didn't notice those before, did we?'

'I was going to tell you,' I began, 'I had this dream...' but stopped short because we heard the snort of a horse and a man's voice. We sank down in the long grass and crept behind a bush.

'If we want to catch these vermin red-handed the best plan would be to wait until they start digging for treasure, near the stones. He said they'd be there.'

'Oh no, Specials!' whispered Lee.

'I don't see why we have to go to all this trouble,' another voice answered. 'What with everything that informer boy told us and the stuff his brother took from that library: top-secret it was, and all those other things we know about them. These children have got to be the ones the Priests are looking high and low for. They may be young, but they're bound to be very dangerous.

'The mindbenders at the High Priests' Clinic for Traitors will deal with them. This lot will be as bright as boiled cabbages this time next week. They'll make good labourers and be fine for simple work. I might try and buy them when they've been treated. We'd get them quite cheap, because I'm sure a discount could be arranged if we took them all - we might do a little business together.'

'All right, steady on,' interrupted the other voice. 'Let's get today's job done first. We'll wait until they find some treasure, or something else of interest, and you can be sure they will, what with all their unnatural powers. Then they'll actually be committing a crime. They'll be - um? How does it go? "Molesting ancient monuments which are state property and stealing antiquities found thereon, which rightfully belong to the state." Then we can pick 'em up and the parents won't have a leg to stand on. And, what's more, they won't have grounds for complaint or public outcry.

'Let's sit tight and wait for them to fall into the trap. Plus, if they do find any treasure, us boys can cream off some nice pieces for ourselves. What do you say to that, eh? My head is agony from that new drug the lads brought last night. I'm going back to sleep for a couple of hours.'

'Me too,' said the other voice.

We crept away to a safe distance, horrified by what we had just heard. For some moments we stared at each other, wide-eyed and speechless.

'Our only hope is, is to do what the prophecy says,' Raynor stuttered.

'What's that?' asked Ahren.

'There's this group of people and they've got to make a long journey to the north,' Raynor's voice shook in fear. 'We'll have to try and do the same. Unless anyone has any better ideas?' We were silent. 'We haven't got a snowflake's chance in a volcano if we stay here. Ahren, I can't forgive myself for getting you into all this.'

'Forget it. I've been expecting trouble. I've been told off seriously, twice, by the Sorcerers' Inspector at our school now. Once more and I'm for the Clinic anyway. I can see our teacher is lying when he tries to bend our minds to make us think the Sorcerers are good, when I know they're as rotten as can be.'

Again it hit me that maybe we were the prophesied group. I fingered the key around my neck. Another coincidence? While we had been listening to the Specials I'd remembered it. As I felt the key I became unexpectedly courageous and confident, and recalled the words of the powerful boy in my dream. 'Look!' I said to the others. They were amazed when I showed it to them, and it still had specks of reddish earth in the cracks of the finely wrought leaves and petals.

'I've never seen such a beautiful jewel! Wherever did you get it?' asked Lee in astonishment.

'I had a dream about it. Then I found it in the earth by my side. In my dream a little boy gave it to me and told me what we all have to do.'

'Oh yes, and what's that?' Raynor sounded doubtful and desperate. I felt that way too, but went on speaking regardless.

'We have to follow the stream north, like it said in the prophecy.'

'Sometimes,' admitted Lee with a smile, 'I almost think of you as a boy. You're so in tune with what's going on.'

'That's because I'm a girl. Girls have more intuition.' My joke fell flat, like a stone in mud. 'What I'm telling you just might be the way out.' Somehow finding the jewel at this time, which fitted so exactly the descriptions we had read in the prophecy, made us all a bit less despondent about our slim chances of slipping out of the clutches of the dreaded Specials. The boys looked at it and as they touched it I could feel that same cool wind coming from it that I had felt the night before, coming from the temple itself. It gave them courage and even a sort of calm confidence. Ahren came up with a plan of action. He was a complete optimist and therefore our only hope.

'We're going to need horses and ponies. We've got to go fast, and this is rough country,' he began. 'We won't get far with the Specials on their large horses chasing us. We'd better take their horses with us, or at least send them packing. Then we might get away. The country is very empty north of here, until we get much closer to the sea, at any rate.'

'How far's that?' I asked.

'Not too far. People from home go to the port at the river's mouth on business and so on. I think it takes a day or two.'

We crept back to where we had heard the two men talking. They were both sleeping in a drunken coma with empty bottles by their sides - they didn't know the strength of the drug called alcohol yet. It was new to Teletsia then, although there were masses of other drugs on the market to knock you out, if that was what you wanted.

Six horses were standing sleepily nearby, hitched to trees with their saddles nearby on the ground. We carefully untied the horses, picked up some of their harness and led the animals stealthily to our side of the hill. The animals sensed we were friendly and were quite happy to be stolen. They didn't resist or make any problems at all. Ahren told us to hide them some way away from our own animals, 'we don't want them neighing at each other and waking everyone up,' he explained.

'Now is the tricky part,' Raynor whispered, as we came closer to our own camp. 'Mardhang came back late last night, smelling of that drink. Leave him to Ahren and me if he wakes up too soon.' Raynor and Ahren made various alternative plans for dealing with Mardhang, but were none too sure any of them would work. At this moment the whole project seemed a complete pipe dream to me, and although Ahren appeared to be courageous, was he merely foolhardy?

Mardhang was snoring under a tree some distance away. He rarely got up until midday at the best of times, so we hoped he wouldn't bother us for a while. Lee gently roused Tandi, Conwenna and Derwin and managed to explain to them in as few words as possible what was to be done. Our horses and ponies were to be led out of sight of the camp, so Mardhang wouldn't see them packed up and ready to leave. The pony trap was to have its wheels broken. As Lee did this job, I thought wistfully to myself, 'Conwenna's father is losing more than a pony trap; he's losing the very centre of his life, his only daughter.' It came to me that whether our plan worked or not, none of our parents would ever see us again, in all probability. This weighed heavily on my mind but I couldn't see any way out. We had to try and save our lives.

The Specials' horses, even those we did not need to ride, were going to come along with us for some distance and the same applied to Mardhang's animal. Only the bare necessities were to be packed, and camping gear and cooking pots were left around in a disorganised fashion, so that when Mardhang woke up he would think we had gone for a walk or something. Everything was nearly ready. It looked as if it was going to be an easy getaway when someone accidentally tripped over Mardhang and woke him up. Ahren went into action with one of the contingent plans.

'Mardhang, we've got great news!' he cried breathlessly, pretending he thought Mardhang was 'with' us. He continued in a bragging, boyish tone of voice, 'We've found the place to dig for gold! We went up on the hillside to look at the dawn and saw some gold glinting at the bottom of one of the four large stones.' Mardhang stood up, as quick as lightning.

'Really? Tell me more!' he demanded, wide awake and looking around anxiously.

'If you go up there now, very fast, the sun will still be shining on the gold. I'll be with you shortly and we'll do some digging before breakfast. Take this spade, it's a good one, I borrowed it from my dad. But don't lose it or he'll flay me!' After Mardhang had run off with the precious spade, Ahren continued, 'I'm not joking, he would flay me. But I guess that'll be the least of his troubles. He's tough, but he loves me. What will happen to him now? He's never been popular with the Sorcerers. He can't abide their corruption and they know it. Now he'll be in trouble just because he's my dad.' A few moments later Derwin came down from where he had been hiding behind some rocks, keeping watch over our comings and goings.

'This is it, folks!' he shouted excitedly. 'Mardhang has gone to the temple. I saw him start digging at the base of one of the big stones!' At the same time Conwenna and Raynor ran up and said the horses were ready.

'You're incredibly quick at this,' Raynor complimented Conwenna.

'I've had to be. Not everybody likes prospectors and my dad and I sometimes have to make a quick getaway to save our skins.'

'Let's go!' urged Ahren.

At this moment Derwin nearly ruined everything. Up to now he had thought it a great game, but suddenly the tension and terror in all of us engulfed him and he became so frightened that all he could do was to sit down and refuse to go anywhere. I knelt down by his side, took him in my arms and hugged him, telling him that I would do my best to look after him and I loved him very much, and didn't want to leave him behind. It didn't do any good, so I told him, as gently but firmly as I could, that I was going to try my best to escape and he had two choices: either he'd be captured by the Specials when they realised we'd pinched their horses and came looking for them, or he could come with us, and we just might escape. I felt awful being so hard on him, but it was a ghastly moment. His attachment to me was very strong, and finally he agreed to get on a pony and come, as long as I rode beside him.

'Hurry, you lot. My dad would have been way out of here by now. We're not in Teletos waiting for a donkey-bus. I'm leaving right now, even if you aren't.' Conwenna vaulted neatly onto her pony, showing her to be best prepared of any of us. She later admitted she was almost paralysed with fear, but she wasn't going to let anyone, least of all Derwin, know this. She felt dreadfully alone and vulnerable that morning, as she often did. Nevertheless, we were all mightily impressed at the smallest member of our escape posse, and quickly followed her as she headed her pony down the track to the north.

CHAPTER 5

ESCAPE

Each of us rode a horse or pony and the larger boys led the spare animals. Nog, who had been watching the events of the morning carefully, head on paws with one eye open, jumped up and lolloped after us. The camp was suddenly deserted. After we were out of sight of the temple we pushed our animals into a gallop and went as fast as the rough ground would allow. All of us had been able to ride, more or less, from an early age, but this flight for our lives through pathless country, leading the extra animals, was a test of anyone's skill and courage.

I wasn't so used to riding horses as I later became, but luckily mine, a stolen one, was very steady in his gait, otherwise I'm sure I'd have fallen off. We became good friends after a couple of hours, but to begin with I just grabbed his mane and hoped for the best. Tandi and Ahren handled horses with the graceful ease of professionals; Conwenna had had plenty of practice on her travels and Lee and Raynor rode well. Derwin, like me, was hanging on to his pony as best he could.

We kept close to the stream, which was gaining tributaries all the time and rapidly becoming a river. It was open country, with flocks of sheep and cattle here and there, and occasionally some deer or other harmless wild animals that ran away as we passed. Trees grew at the edges of the watercourse; otherwise the land was covered with a sea of grass, nodding flowers and a few thorn bushes. After some hours we abandoned the spare horses and only kept one extra as a baggage animal.

We went on until late morning and by then both we and our animals were very tired. We were looking for a place to rest and eat some food, out of the heat of the sun, when something made me glance behind. On the far horizon, in the direction of the Temple of Support I saw three or four brilliant flashes rise out of the earth and flare up into the cloudless sky.

A minute or two later there was a deafening clap of thunder; the animals broke out in a cold sweat and Nog cowered close to the ground, tail between his legs and whimpering. I felt a stabbing pain at the base of my backbone. I knew this was the seat of the lowest of the seven subtle centres of my soul and that it was somehow connected with the Temple of Support, on the level of the Mother Earth. This was written in the prophecy. A violent shiver went up my back. The light wind dropped, the world was hushed and even the birds and insects made no noise. Something was about to happen.

'There's an earthquake coming!' shouted Conwenna. 'Get away from those rocks and out into the open! Get off the horses. Quick!' she shouted, and as she finished speaking there was a rumble from the direction of the temple and it was upon us. There was a loud cracking, groaning, roaring noise and our whole world shook and heaved. The animals quivered in terror but stood still, not knowing which way to run. Rocks slid, trees collapsed where there was no ground to hold them up and the river disappeared with a great splash into a chasm which had opened not twenty paces from us.

The end of the rift was near where Derwin was standing with one of the Specials' horses that we had stolen. It reared and panicked as the ground sank beneath its feet and pushed Derwin onto the ground in its terror. When it had stopped struggling, we could all see its leg was broken and a ring of blood oozed where the limb swung loose. It tried to gallop off on three legs, the fourth hanging useless, but getting nowhere it stopped, its nostrils distended and head down, as if it knew it had no hope.

Like all of us, I was praying to the Mother Earth that the nightmare would end and I spontaneously clasped the golden key. The quaking died away and there was a deathly quiet, apart from the occasional loose stone coming to rest at the bottom of the valley. I took the key from my neck and held it up for everyone to see, the orange-red jewels flashing in the bright sunlight. As I did this all of us, including the animals, began to calm down, but around us was the contorted plain and valley with gashes and cracks in the red soil where the earth had split in its anger. Tandi and I ran over to where Derwin was lying in pain. Tandi felt the shoulder he had fallen on when the horse had pushed him over. I held him in my arms and tried to comfort him.

'It hurts a terrible lot,' said Derwin, clenching his teeth and trying to be brave.

'Can you move it?' I asked.

'Just about, but it's very sore - Ow! Please don't prod, Tandi!'

'Sorry, I'm trying to see if it's broken.'

'I don't think so. See, I can move it. If we could bind it up maybe I could ride.' The last thing Derwin wanted to do was ride, I could see that, but he knew that we would have to keep moving fast to have any chance whatsoever of escaping. We had no medical supplies, so Tandi discreetly went behind a bush and took off her petticoat, tore it into strips and made it into a sling. I was beginning to realise that she was brilliant in a crisis - cool and unflappable.

I was so worried about Derwin. How could we go on with him like this? How could we not go on? What if the Specials should appear over the brow of the hill? While I was thinking all these useless thoughts, doing nothing sensible, there was Tandi being practical. Next she asked if anyone could find any herbs growing round about which might dull Derwin's pain.

'There's one which is a type of flat ground cover, with white flowers that are out at this time of year. The leaves have a strong sour smell. My mother uses it when we get sprains and headaches. You might find some here.'

'I know the one you mean,' I said. 'There are two or three plants which might work.'

'We can't spend all day looking for them,' said Raynor. 'If we can't find anything to kill his pain, we'll just have to take him as he is.'

'Oh please, Raynor. We've got to do something to help him.'

I was desperate; all that mattered for me at that moment was my brother. Derwin was not some baggage to be bound up and carried along with us regardless of how much pain he was in. He was lucky. I was able to find a bunch of pink daisies which were as good, if not stronger, than the plant Tandi had talked about. I gave them to Raynor, who knew a lot about how to apply herbs as medicines. This was about the only useful thing he learnt at the Sorcerers' Academy. He squeezed some sap from the stalks and smeared it onto what was fast turning into a blue and swollen shoulder and told Derwin to chew some of the flowers as well. While Tandi bandaged him up and I held his other hand, Raynor told him about the daisy plant.

'The flowers taste awful but they'll dull the pain,' explained Raynor. 'Just chew them however much you hate the taste. They'll also make you very dozy, so you'd better sit in front of me on my horse, to make sure you don't fall off, for the next few hours.'

At this moment Ahren came up. He had been looking at the doomed horse.

'We'll have to kill him to put him out of his agony. I've learnt how to do it from my uncle. He's the local butcher, but I need you to hold him, Raynor, while I stun him. You're the only one strong enough.'

Raynor was in a great dilemma; he had a horror of blood and violence. Tending Derwin's wound was unpleasant but possible; but killing a horse was beyond him. He evaded the situation by saying that he had to look after Derwin, so Lee and Tandi between them had to hold it while Ahren did the deed of mercy. This involved not only stunning the beast but also stabbing it in the heart with Ahren's hunting knife to make sure it was well and truly dead. It was a nasty, messy job and even Tandi looked shocked when it was done. Her honey brown face, with its smooth and shining complexion, looked distinctly yellow for a short while.

Raynor's problem was that he didn't realise how brave he was. He had had the courage to walk into the Sorcerers' Academy, one of the most feared places in the country, and calmly borrow some of their most risky information. For more than a year now he had been playing an extremely dangerous role that could end in torture at any moment and yet somehow he couldn't bring himself to kill a horse. Not that I wasn't sorry for the horse, but compared to a Sorcerer - I don't know. Raynor sat by himself while the rest of us unpacked some food. Derwin was lying in the shade of a tree and also wanted to be left alone, so I went over and spoke to Raynor.

'I'm sorry I lost it with you just now,' I began.

'That's all right,' he replied, his head down.

'What's the matter?'

'Oh, nothing. Why don't you go and find yourself something to eat?'

'I'm not hungry.'

I knew what he'd said was a lie. During the past year, Lee, Raynor and I have worked out by trial and error that each inner jewel, or centre of the soul, goes with a certain emotion or group of emotions or qualities and we feel this in our bodies, collectively. For instance, when at this moment I sat with Raynor and put my attention on him, I felt a pain at the left side of my throat. Also, the inner jewels were dull within Raynor. Although Lee and Raynor didn't see the inner jewels of our souls like I did, they felt pain if there was a problem and a radiating coolness if there was a positive experience relating to that centre.

'Nonsense, there's something troubling you,' I tried to cheer him up. 'Don't you want to talk about it? I'm sure it's not that ghastly.'

'It's no good, I'm the oldest of us, but I feel so ashamed. Ahren is a simple kid from the country and twice now he's shown me up. I feel so useless, especially as your mother asked me to look after you all.'

'Raynor, forget it. It doesn't matter. Stop worrying about whether you can kill horses better than a butcher's nephew or not. What does matter is that we've got to be much further away from the Temple of Support by nightfall. I'm sure that earthquake came from there and I bet Mardhang had something to do with it.'

'It said somewhere in the prophecy that it would be very foolish to mess around with the Temple of Support, and that the earth herself might rise up and fight back,' added Raynor, coming out of his gloomy, self-critical mood. 'It didn't mean much when I read it, because I didn't see how anyone could do anything to those enormous stones.'

'Well, it certainly makes sense now,' said Conwenna nervously, coming to join us as an aftershock rippled through the ground like a wave through water. I looked at the blood red wounds in the rusty coloured earth, and thought we were lucky to have got off so lightly.

While we ate, Raynor told Tandi, Ahren, Derwin and Conwenna about the prophecy and the real reason why we had come to the Temple of Support. I was looking at their inner natures while Raynor spoke. Their inner subtle centres began to glow, the flower on the top of their heads began to flicker with the most beautiful colours, and I felt a coolness on my hands as I looked at them. Lee was watching me and gave a nod, as if to say, 'They're all right, we can trust them,' because he felt the sensations in his own subtle centres as clearly, if not more so, than I did, even though he didn't see inside people in the way I could. I caught Raynor's eye, nodded slightly, and he began explaining about our powers, and why the Specials wanted to get hold of us.

'Now I understand why there was an earthquake when the Specials tried to capture us,' said Conwenna. 'Mother Earth feels our inner centres, just as we feel each other's, and she must be trying to protect us.'

'Do you think she really cares?' asked Raynor, still somewhat despondent.

'Yes, I do. I haven't read the books, but I know nature. My father has taught me always to respect Mother Earth and to be truly grateful when she gives us the gold or silver nuggets we live by. I've been so cared for by her.' This surprised me. Not only was it the longest speech I'd heard from Conwenna, but she spoke with such conviction. 'I always wondered what you were up to with your meetings! I had a feeling you'd let me in on your secrets sooner or later. It's not all new to me,' she added.

'I can see that,' Raynor replied.

'We didn't want to make things dangerous for you,' said Lee weakly. In fact, we had thought her too young. She picked this up.

'I've had to grow up even quicker than all of you,' said Conwenna. 'I know Teletsia's sick and it's got to change. Don't know how though.'

She took life as it came from day to day, because she never knew whether her father would return from his present prospecting trip safely, or indeed at all. For her this was just another incident in an uncertain life. Also, despite the fact she had never, before today, shared her experience with anyone else, she found it easier than any of us to turn to that state of inner thoughtless awareness and peace.

Derwin was pretty drugged at this moment and so said nothing; at any other time he would definitely have added something, to keep his end up in front of Conwenna. We went on eating in silence. Then Raynor brought us back to the here and now.

'Do you have any idea where we are?' he asked Tandi, in an effort to take her mind off the events of the recent past. He assumed she had an easy, uncomplicated life, which we had just destroyed.

'Not exactly,' she replied. 'But I do know that after this plain, the country becomes more hilly and the river gets wider until it becomes a tidal estuary. Then there are some farms and the odd village. There's only one small town, a port called Plimpet which is at the seaward end of the estuary.'

'So unless people are actually searching for us, it's unlikely that we'll see anybody?'

'Hope not, don't you?' Tandi tried to hide her anxiety. She looked in the picnic bag to see what remained to eat. 'Anyone fancy the last of the cold yams?' she enquired tentatively.

'I never want to see another wild yam in my life,' grumbled Ahren. 'I've had enough in the last two days to last me a hundred years.'

'I know what you mean,' I laughed. 'Still, they're better than nothing.' We rested for a short while, after which the others left Tandi and me to clear up the food while they went to rearrange our horses. We had lost one and now had to move everything around.

'How bad is Derwin's shoulder?' I asked her.

'I don't know. We all tumble off and have falls now and again. But these sprains and bruises do take time to come right.'

'And time is what we don't have,' I groaned. 'It's bad enough having the responsibility of Derwin coming along with us at all, and now he's gone and hurt himself, I don't know how we're going to manage.'

'At least you have your brother with you,' said Tandi desperately. 'I pray the Sorcerers don't try to torture some non-existent information out of my two brothers as to where I've gone. Then there's the marriage problem. My family has been forced into accepting a proposal from a young lawyer who's well 'in' with the Sorcerers. If I refuse to marry him, or anything else goes wrong with the match, my family may be in deep trouble. What if he thinks I've run away from him? All because of my so-called beautiful face!'

'I'd be rather flattered if someone wanted to marry me because of my beauty. Not that there's any danger of that, with my thin face and bony body.'

'I'd swap with you any day. What's the point if I have to marry that lizard?' and she burst into tears. I could see it was the result of the earthquake, our flight and everything rolled up into one.

'In one way you're the most fortunate of all of us, because at least you *want* to escape from your lizard,' I said in the hope of cheering her up, and put my arm around her shoulders.

'Freedom from a lizard. Yes, you're right there,' she laughed through her tears. 'Yes, as of today, I'm free!' Raynor came over, surprised to see that Tandi was both crying and laughing at the same time.

'Are you all right?' he asked.

'Yes, I've suddenly realised that I am, very much so!'

Raynor mentioned that we were ready to move on. I saw his puzzled look and realised he had a long way to go in understanding people. He'd had a lot of lessons today, not one of them from a book.

Lee, Raynor and I had been aware that some upheaval might occur at any time after we had discovered the prophecy, but none of us imagined it would be so dramatic. Only Derwin was finding all this very hard. Despite the dose of daisies his shoulder hurt more and more. Until that morning the true horror of life in Teletsia had not been a living reality to him, because we had shielded him from a great deal that would have shocked him too much.

We travelled on and in the late afternoon we noticed a heavy fog come rolling across the plains towards us in a cool thick blanket. Raynor asked Tandi if it came from the sea.

'It may do. We can't be more than a day's journey from there. We came a long way this morning.'

'This fog is a blessing. No one will be able to see us now,' said Conwenna. 'Mother Earth has thrown the Specials off our trail with an earthquake and now Father Sea is going to help us with some fog.'

I felt that Conwenna thought we were much more important than we actually were. It seemed incredibly egotistical to presume that the very forces of nature would help seven desperate and virtually helpless young people in trouble with their evil regime. Lee agreed with Conwenna that the fog would hide us, if not with her other remark. He thought she lived in a child's fairyland, where a different reality held true.

'Another good thing about the fog,' he said, 'is that the Specials won't be able to do that light signalling. You know, they flash mirrors between the hilltops in code form when they want their friends to know something in a hurry. Let's go on while the fog hides us, because as we get nearer the sea there'll be more people around. Isn't that so, Tandi?'

'Yes, definitely.'

CHAPTER 6

STELLAMAR

As evening approached we didn't go so fast. We found a track, which led more or less north, towards the sea. Because of the fog, we couldn't see very far ahead. We were damp and cold from the water droplets, but grateful to be hidden from prying eyes. The horses and ponies became more and more exhausted, and we realised we were going to have to stop somewhere for the night. We were approaching more cultivated and populated parts of the country, and Tandi was sure that soon we would have to go through some villages near the port of Plimpet. So far, the path we were riding down only had the occasional farmhouse near it and we saw no one except some fishermen going home, when we approached the river.

We had been travelling along the same valley all the time and eventually camped in a wood by the now wide river. For supper we ate some sodden bread and damp cheese we had found in the saddlebags of one of the Special's horses. We made this sorry meal a little more exciting with some wild salad plants, which Tandi and Ahren picked in the water meadows between the wood and the river bank. We went down there as dusk fell to paddle in the river and wash ourselves as best we could, but even the lush riverside meadows, filled with colourful spring flowers, could not lift our spirits. The fog came down with a vengeance once the night fell and the moisture collected in large drops on the trees, which rained down on us throughout the night.

As we tossed and turned, lying on the ground with only thin blankets to cover us, no one wanted to ask the obvious question: how were we going to continue the journey when we reach the Great Sea? How were we going to get out of Teletsia - which we had to in order to get away from the Sorcerers?

We took turns to watch in case we had been followed, but nobody slept very much and we were wet, cold and tired the following morning. Not surprisingly, we all woke up from our snatched scraps of sleep very easily and quickly. Ahren gleefully told everyone that he had dreamed he was turning into a large sponge. No one laughed. Everyone was too stiff and too hungry. Derwin, not to be outdone by this country bumpkin, claimed he had dreamed that Nog was talking to him and saying that all humans were mad. Knowing

Derwin as I did, I think he was just trying to be as brave as he could over his shoulder and arm. He later admitted to me that he had hardly slept at all and his arm was still sore, and the dampness had made it worse.

The fog had gone and by mid morning we knew we were coming near to the sea, because the waters were becoming tidal in the river estuary. The tides were incredibly complex because of the three moons, and the mudflats of the estuary with a ribbon of water in the centre showed without a doubt that a tide was running. The river now ran in a broad valley between high hills, but the thick fog that had hidden us the day before was thinning out and the last wisps were being blown away by a rising wind.

We were following a dirt track by the side of the river and saw more and more farmhouses. We passed through a sleepy village, going slowly so as not to attract too much attention, but the few people we saw did not appear to be interested in us. We also saw some fishermen again, across the estuary, who glanced at us and waved, and earlier on we had made out the figures of people working in the fields. We had one or two rests during the morning, because we had put a good distance between ourselves and the Temple of Support. We entered a heavily wooded part of the country, the horses were making good progress on the firm turf of the track and we galloped round a bend, half concealed by bushes.

Then we met her. None of us even had the time to be frightened, because in order not to run her down we all had to skid to a stop. There she was in front of us, a figure on a white pony standing in the middle of the track, blocking the way where the bushes grew tall on either side. While slithering to a stop we saw the rider was a girl about the same age as Tandi, with a bright tawny coloured face, dark shining hair and piercing blue eyes. Over her light fawn robes she wore a blue cloak; her expression was open but at the same time very dignified; her glowing smile made her face even more radiant and friendly, but most importantly, her hand was raised in the gesture which means 'Stop!' Not that we had much choice in the matter, as she was barring our road.

When I put my attention on her inner nature I saw a string of shining jewels in her back, a shimmering flower on the top of her head, and felt sincerity. I looked at Lee and Raynor and we glanced at each other, because they had also felt her inner being. We agreed to do as she asked, even though on the face of it, we could easily have been opening ourselves for an ambush. Firstly, why did we not bolt for cover? After all, in Teletsia one learnt to suspect the worst. Secondly, Lee, Raynor and I were not overly sensible in moments of crisis and yet on this occasion we three acted confidently and in unison, and trusted our inner awareness. The mysterious girl beckoned to us to follow her off the road and once we were hidden she introduced herself.

'I'm Stellamar. You've got to stop riding along this road. Some of my father's fishermen saw you last night and this morning and sent me an urgent message. You're in great danger. Please trust me, and follow me. You've got to be hidden as soon as possible. It may already be too late.' She did not wait for us to reply. The greatest risk was whether we followed her into the deeper undergrowth, because if this was an ambush, that would be the place to spring it. But again Lee, Raynor and I spontaneously checked her inner being and nodded at each other. Something was attracting us to her.

A few steps ahead was a stream which flowed into the estuary, and our new guide led us down the edge of it. Here there were trees covered in creepers full of noisy birds, and monkeys which jumped from branch to branch chattering to each other. Half hidden in this jungly greenery was an old boathouse, surrounded by rushes that grew tall and thick out of the water. Here at least we were well hidden. The stranger dismounted and the rest of us did the same. Nog went up to her and licked her feet respectfully, then sat down nearby. He was panting from all this unexpected exercise and glad of a rest. The girl gave him a pat while Raynor watched with interest, knowing that he was always a perfect judge of character.

'The Sorcerers' Police are after you.' The word 'Sorcerer' itself marked her as a friend, because only those who faced the truth called our demonic rulers by that name. 'My parents and I can read their flashing messages. We've learnt their codes. This morning we discovered they're after a dangerous group of young people who they're sure are making for Plimpet. In case you don't know, that's the port at the mouth of this river here.' She looked at each of us in turn. A deep, knowing look. We were stunned, silent. If she had recognised us, what about all the other people we'd seen today?

'Somehow when I felt the tremors in the earth coming from the direction of the Temple of Support, I knew you would be on this road,' she went on. 'You do realise that the Specials are out in large numbers looking for you? And that you haven't a hope if you go near the port?' Despite this catastrophic news, the girl was so confident and poised that we began to feel slightly calmer as she went on speaking. 'You've got to avoid the port. Where are you going? And why?'

'We don't know exactly where we're going. We're fleeing for our lives. We only know we've got to go north,' replied Raynor, 'but now that we're near the seashore we don't know what to do next. We've got to get out of Teletsia, that's for sure. Otherwise we've had it. We thought maybe we could somehow - well, get hold of a boat - or something.' Raynor did not want to say so, but our plan, made hastily in the morning, had been to wait until nightfall and then to try to steal a boat in Plimpet. We didn't want to make a habit of thieving, having already stolen some horses, but we couldn't think of any alternative. Now, with this latest thunderbolt of news, we hadn't any idea how we were going to go on.

'I'm going to show you the best and only way out for you.' As she said this she was fingering a beautiful jewel around her neck. It was almost identical to the one I had found and was now myself wearing under my clothing.

While we had been in the dark wood on the previous evening, I had again told the others the full story of the dream and how I had come by the jewel.

Consequently when they saw that this girl had a similar one we all knew for certain that however mysterious she might be, she could definitely be trusted. She saw us looking at it.

'Yes, this jewel is the true emblem of our land,' she said wistfully. 'The land as it should be and will be one day, no doubt.' She smiled and went on, 'Before we go on, I've got a little surprise for you. We're quite safe here for a while. No one ever comes here except for the pearl fishermen, and they're all friends of my family. Can one of you take my pony, and you two come with me, please?'

A few moments later Lee and Ahren, who had gone into the dark boathouse with Stellamar, came out carrying heavy hampers. First she took a tablecloth out of one hamper and placed it on the ground, and then she spread out a marvellous meal for us. We were starving, and looking back I'm shocked at how much we gobbled and grab bed, and how much we ate. Stellamar took it as a compliment that we enjoyed the food so much. Or she was too polite to look horrified at our animal-like manners.

After we had finished Stellamar told us that her father was a dealer in a highly prized type of pearl, which was found in these northern Teletsian estuaries. The pearl fishermen had admired her family for generations, and would only sell their pearls to them, because her family protected them from the worst excesses of the Sorcerers.

At this point Stellamar noticed Derwin, who was leaning against a tree trunk and nursing his shoulder. By now just about everybody had tried to put him right, but it was still very sore and he was beginning to get tired of being examined, bandaged and made to chew unpleasant tasting daisies which made him feel sick and sleepy.

'Can you help Derwin?' asked Conwenna. 'He hurt himself during the earthquake.'

'Yes, for goodness sake, why didn't any of you tell me before?' said Stellamar.

'I told them not to say anything,' Derwin explained. 'I'm fed up with being poked and prodded.' Stellamar walked over to him and insisted on seeing his shoulder.

'What's happened? Let me see it,' she had him remove his tunic before he could protest. 'It needs sunlight. It's all cold and frozen up.' He warmed the bruise in the sunlight and the pain subsided slightly. 'It still hurts here, and here, doesn't it?' she went on, as if she, like the rest of us, had the same collective awareness which enabled her to share her physical feelings with another person, and another person's feelings with her.

'Yes.' Derwin watched with curiosity as Stellamar made strange signs in the air with her fingers just above his shoulder. Then she put her right hand towards his shoulder and her left hand towards the sun. At first he felt a penetrating heat, then a tingling, and then a coolness. The pain was gone, even though the bruise still showed. 'Whatever did you do? Thanks!'

'I used the power that is at the heart of all things. The heat you felt was the power of the sun driving out the problem, and the coolness that came over you afterwards was the natural flow of the Spirit of Life. It's everywhere, and you feel it as a cooling breeze. You've just got to learn how to use it, and then you can help each other with it. This is the living, all pervading power. You feel it as heat or coolness in your hands or bodies - it exists in the earth, sky, sun and every element. You have to use the world around you in a new way. If one of you gets hurt, you should put your right hand to the part that's been hurt and your left hands towards the earth, or the sea, or the sun, whichever you want and that element will help you. Somehow you're all awake to that: not many people are. But don't play with this gift, and don't use it to heal anyone except your little group. Always have reverence, and remember what power you are using.'

'What is that?' asked Raynor, almost cautiously.

'It's the power that moves the universe, that is itself beyond all movement and change,' answered Stellamar.

We were awed by this statement and wondered what was coming next. I got the same feeling as when Raynor had read out the prophecy to us. We had seen Stellamar using the power she spoke of and didn't doubt a word she said. After a moment or two the deep stillness passed, and Derwin could not resist telling everyone he felt fine. Stellamar, who had been meditative after her explanation of the healing process, smiled gaily and went on talking.

'Where was I? Yes, before we changed the subject I was telling you about my family. Our family house is on the bank of the river and it happens to be in a line of sight between two of the Sorcerers' signalling posts, so we intercept their messages if they keep on and on. If they do, we know they're important. This morning there were more signals than we've seen for a long time. They were frantic about something, the same message over and over again. It began as soon as the fog lifted.

'We decoded the message and it said that the Sorcerers were quite determined to catch a group of seven young people. They said this group had stolen some vitally important jewels, which belong to the High Priests. They had also made off with some of the Specials' horses, and had evil powers that had caused a serious earthquake. It killed some Specials who were guarding the stone circle near Clatan. The people they're looking for were described as 'Highly Dangerous Class One Traitors'. There are four boys and three girls and their descriptions are exactly like all of you.'

'Yippee, we're famous!' interrupted Ahren and then felt extremely foolish as the rest of us glared furiously at him.

Sometimes Ahren was too much. I prayed in my heart that perhaps he would eventually learn some sense. At first I thought it was the way of the country people, but Tandi was not at all like him, so it had to be just Ahren. At that point I thought Ahren had come into my life solely to teach me tolerance, but it was a hard lesson and so far I hadn't got very far with learning it, at least as far as he was concerned. Lee and Raynor shared my feelings. Later they told me that although they felt he was great at the rougher side of life, they dreaded having to be with him in polite, civilized company, like that of Stellamar. Town people in Teletos always felt superior to country folk, and I'm afraid we were no exception.

'Or infamous,' continued Stellamar, completely unperturbed by Ahren, 'but you're not alone. Anyone "aiding or encouraging these dangerous insurgents" is guilty of High Treason as well. So that includes me, doesn't it?'

'Should you be helping us?' I asked, concerned for Stellamar's safety.

'Yes. They can't touch me,' Stellamar reassured us. 'My father has some very powerful connections with the rulers of the neighbouring countries, and our pearls bring Teletsia an enormous amount of money. Consequently the authorities won't lay a finger on us as long as we don't criticise the Sorcerers too openly.' I felt this wasn't the whole story, but now was not the moment to ask for the rest of it. 'But for you, well, that's a very different matter. You must be out of their clutches very, very soon.' Stellamar paused and appeared to be weighing up alternatives in her mind, then went on, 'Let's go now. I'll show you how to get to the sea by a little known path. Once we get there, I'll have to leave you, but I'll give you all the advice you need to get out of Teletsia.'

I knew it was no accident that we had met Stellamar at this moment. While the boys helped her hide the hampers in the boathouse, I took her aside and unburdened my heart to her.

'I can see you're very wise, even though you're not much older than me,' I began. 'There's something I'd really like to ask you, if you don't mind.'

'No, of course not,' she replied, 'what's your name, by the way? I never asked.'

'People call me Asha. It means hope, which is about all we have at the moment, apart from your good advice.'

'Don't be too sure about that, you may have more assets than you think. What's your question? We don't have much time. I've got to try to get you out of here.'

'It's obvious that we're in for a mighty tough time even if you can get us out of Teletsia. From the start I wasn't keen for the two smallest ones to come on this trip. Now everything has gone so disastrously wrong, I don't know what's best for them. I wonder if it wouldn't be better to try and hide them in the mountains in the south of the country, beyond the jungles.'

'I know it's incredibly difficult to get there,' said Raynor, coming up behind us, 'but my grandmother comes from there, and once with that clan they should be safe.'

'You wouldn't have a hope of even getting back to Teletos. You don't realise how much the Sorcerers want to catch you,' said Stellamar. 'Our family has a copy of the great prophecy: seven young people on the run from the Sorcerers. What were you doing at the Temple of Support? Asha, you recognised my key. Do you by chance have one the same? And you Raynor, I think you know your history rather well. Am I right?'

'You are,' agreed Raynor.

'You must start fitting the pieces together, because if you don't you won't have a hope of escaping, and even so it's all very much in the balance. Even prophecies only give possibilities. You've got to leave Teletsia and you're all quite capable of it. Conwenna's one of your strongest members.' I wanted to ask Stellamar a thousand questions now that she was starting to make things clear but there was no time. Instead I continued with my original line of thought.

'I'm dead scared for our parents; there might be reprisals against them. Plus, even if we do manage to escape, they're going to be unbelievably worried about us. I mean, you know what usually happens to young people when they disappear?'

'As far as reprisals are concerned, I can't help your parents. But I have to go to Teletos next week to deliver some pearls and see about some orders. If you tell me where your parents live and how to get there, I'll go to see them and tell them what happens to you. You might be lucky. If you do get away it's just possible the whole thing may be hushed up.

'The Sorcerers are very strange. They're convinced that you caused the earthquake that did such widespread damage yesterday. They might assume that if they rock the boat any further by giving your parents trouble, you might in turn produce another natural disaster. The Sorcerers dominate, and are totally dominated, by fear. They're not at all like us.'

It was a weight off my mind to know there was a chance that our families might get some news of us.

CHAPTER 7

QUICKSAND

Soon we set off again. We followed Stellamar up the path by the stream, across the road and then up the rocky streambed further inland. We clattered up the stony rivulet, the animals splashing through the shallow water. Nog followed up the bank, seeing all this paddling as a waste of effort, especially when he had just begun a delightful snooze on a full stomach. Stellamar had given him the remains of the picnic and his belly was tight as a drum.

She led us out of the streambed onto an overgrown path parallel to the road and the estuary. It led through rough country and wound between windswept pines, which bent their tops away from the gales coming off the sea. The animals picked their way carefully so as to avoid the numerous holes belonging to rabbits, rats, snakes and so on. The exposed roots of the trees which poked through the sandy soil were another hazard and branches whipped back into our faces if we didn't keep a constant lookout for them. The ride went on for a long time, eventually dusk fell and later on two of the moons came up. Stellamar led us on and on without stopping, ever watchful. We struggled to keep up the pace, so tired that we tended to forget she was doing her level best to save all our lives. Eventually, in a thick pine wood which smelled of resin and with the wind howling in the trees overhead, Stellamar stopped.

'This is going to be dangerous,' she began, 'and this is where, to help you, we must part company. I'm going to ride down the coastal road to where the Specials may be waiting for you. To get out of Teletsia there is a causeway you're going to have to cross. It leads to an island a little way offshore. There's a place where the track to the causeway leads off the road along the coast.

'If a party of Specials is waiting to ambush you there, I'll try and keep them busy as long as possible by talking to them, and making use of the fact that I know some of them personally. Doesn't mean I like them, but at least they know who I am, and also that I often deliver orders of pearls to customers up the coast. They know they're supposed to guard people like me from dangerous bands of... eh... rebels?' Stellamar laughed. 'If you manage to reach the island you'll be safe for the time being because the Sorcerers and their police are mortally afraid of the place. It's got certain qualities they don't understand so they call it black magic, meaning forces they can't dominate. The island is the home of my great uncle and aunt, Lord Jarwhen and Lady Mercola: wonderful, free people.

'On the island there's a lighthouse in line with the causeway and as long as you keep that light directly in front of you, your animals won't lose their footing. Even if the tide is rising and the water starts to get deep, keep straight ahead and you'll be safe. Father Sea won't let any of you drown, that's for sure.' I was amazed that Stellamar used almost the same words as Conwenna had the day before. 'Now, you don't have much time if you're going to catch the low tide. But wait! There's one more thing that I have to tell you, - how to cross the band of quicksand.'

'What?' said Conwenna anxiously. The previous year her father had lost a mule in quicksand when it had been loaded up with samples from a prospecting trip, and he himself had barely survived.

'Yes, quicksand. Don't be afraid. This is your escape route. Remember, there's enormous power in the elements. The jewelled key you are wearing, Asha, radiates the power of the earth element in a very concentrated form. Provided your hearts and minds are pure, then the jewel will get you across the quicksand safely. The leader of your band must hold up the jewel so you can all see it.' She now turned to Raynor and said firmly, 'Raynor, this is you. At this time you absolutely must, all of you, keep right in touch with your inner state of peace and thoughtless awareness,' Stellamar continued, 'and you know you can do this by putting your attention on the subtle centre at the top of your head. It will work out, you see. If your attention is scattered all over the place or your intentions are not pure and sincere, you'll start to sink into the sand and then nothing can help you. But don't worry, you'll manage. Don't lose faith in yourselves and the power which has brought you this far.

'This path leads through the wood and out onto the sand dunes. Then there's a flat strip of quicksand. From there you might just be able to see the top of the lighthouse. After the quicksand there's another line of dunes covered with tall grass and bushes. If the Specials are there they will be at that particular gap in the dunes, because they'll try to stop you from reaching the beginning of the causeway, which is straight ahead of you. The bar of quicksand goes a long way up and down the coast but you'll have to cross it there because that's the place where the power of the earth element resonates best with the power of the jewel. That's the only part where the sand will support you.' Stellamar turned to leave us.

'It's a real pity you are not coming with us,' said Tandi.

'I must stay here, but in a way I will be with you. It's my heart's greatest desire that your journey works out. The hopes of so many hang on it, if they did but know. I have a lot to do here, now that you've activated the Temple of Support.' She smiled, said goodbye, then turned her pony and was gone before we could even thank her. She had given us much to think about and it was only later that we began to understand what she was saying on a deeper level. At that moment we were too busy trying to stay alive to reflect on anything.

Raynor knew he had a very big test ahead of him. He had to take the key and lead the rest of us across the quicksand. He also knew he had failed in his role recently and couldn't afford do so again. He asked me to give him the jewel. I understood what he was going through, because I knew both his strengths and his weaknesses.

'Good luck, you'll be fine. You see,' I encouraged him. He was holding the jewel and believed that it was one of the very jewels he had read about in the prophecy. For Raynor, something he had read about and studied was very real and powerful. Not only that, I could see with my inner eye that Stellamar had transformed him. He was dreadfully concerned at what lay ahead but at the same time had an intense feeling of excitement and exhilaration, and felt power in the subtle centre of his heart. This was new to him and I could see his heart centre was shining like a red star. He urged his horse on and we wound our way through the first line of dunes.

We could hear the boom of the surf in the distance and as we rode through the low hillocks the moons' light cast ghostly two-way shadows against the bleached white of the sand. Every now and again someone's eyes would play tricks on him or her. Each particularly strange shadow would turn into a waiting horse and rider: the rider wearing the flat hat and black cloak of the Special's uniform, but in reality these dunes were deserted and the shadows were just delusions.

Raynor had never in his life felt the power of the Mother Earth throbbing through him as strongly as at that moment. We reached the beginnings of the bar of quicksand, he checked the inner feelings of everyone in the group, and realised Tandi was very scared. She had matured greatly in these two days but was not as aware of her own inner powers as the three of us from the city. Derwin had enormous faith in me and Conwenna had been like us all along, if only we had known it. Ahren had the natural courage of a young lion. Raynor stopped and mentioned the fact that he was aware of Tandi's uncertainty to Conwenna, who was riding behind him.

'We must do what Stellamar said, to help her,' Conwenna said. 'What's the point of having powers if we don't use them?'

'What do you mean?' I asked her.

'We must pray to the Mother Earth to stop Tandi from feeling scared. She'll never get across the quicksand if she's like this. I've seen quicksand. Once you start to go down, the more you struggle and panic the quicker it sucks you in. She's got to understand that even things like quicksand can be our friend if we relate to the Mother Earth in the right way.'

It was becoming obvious that Conwenna was fairly in tune. I felt humbled, and gently explained to Tandi that the rest of us were feeling her fear and we could help her, so we could all feel better. We stopped behind a large sand dune and did as Stellamar had explained, this time using the power of the earth and the moons instead of the sun. I also had Tandi take a turn in holding the jewel close to her heart and as she did so its extraordinary power transformed her as it had Raynor. He saw Tandi smile and gave me a flicker of recognition, as if to say, 'We're ready to go.'

Just as we were about to leave the cover of the dunes for the flat expanse of quicksand, Raynor remembered Nog, who was trotting along at the rear of the cavalcade. After a few moments of discussion he was hoisted up in front of Lee and somehow balanced on the saddlebags.

Raynor was now at the edge of the sand, having left the last dune. The sand looked soft and smooth. He tried to put out of his head what Conwenna had said about quicksand and realised that 'trying not to think' and *trying* to be peaceful and serene was no good. Instead he held up the jewel so we could all see it and put his attention on the top of his head. Immediately all thoughts, fears and uncertainty left him and he knew he could set the necessary example of leader. It was not 'Raynor' in an egotistical sense, but he felt the power of the universal Spirit flowing through him, channelled by the jewel.

Something changed in him and he became mature. He sat straight in the saddle and the slight stoop he usually had left him. His head was held high and his fine Teletsian features – aquiline nose, high forehead and firm jaw gave him the appearance of confidence he felt more than ever before, when doing something active and not connected with his book learning. He went forward at the trot and held the jewel, glinting and swaying in the moons' light, in the long, sensitive fingers of his right hand. Not once did any of the horses' hooves start to sink and miraculously the sand held firm. As soon as we were through the quicksand Lee let Nog down to the ground. Nog was not perturbed by his ride and it was only when we reached the hard sand on the further side, and could already see the lighthouse winking in the distance through a gap in the second line of dunes that he became agitated. He disappeared into the dunes, howling.

'That's the noise he makes when the Specials are close by!' Raynor cried urgently, quickly putting the jewel around his neck for safety. 'Hurry! Hide, everyone - into the dunes - the opposite way to Nog!'

Within seconds we had all hidden behind the tall bushes and grasses. That is all except Raynor, for now came the real test, with no magic jewel to do it all for him. Raynor rode after Nog and stopped just after he had reached the end of the line of hillocks. The bushes rustled and the grasses whined with a hollow whispering sound in the night breeze and he went on cautiously so as not to be seen. Raynor could hear Nog hidden in the long grass somewhere nearby but could also hear the sound he dreaded most: the noise of men's voices questioning each other about the howl of the dog, or wolf, as they thought it might be.

Raynor knew he could calmly steal a forbidden book from under the noses of the Sorcerers and that he had held up the jewel and led his friends across a patch of deadly quicksand, but what faced him now was different. It was here that the wonderful self-confidence that Stellamar had instilled in him blossomed into reality. He was on his own. If he failed now there would be no tomorrow for any of us.

He could not risk a dash for the beach, as some of the senior Specials were armed with weapons which homed onto the target their owners singled out for them, and rarely missed. There were not many of these, because they were imbued with some sort of sorcery, but they were around. Raynor had seen them demonstrated at the Sorcerers' Academy Open Day, as a warning to the students not to consider defecting. Very nasty. He returned to where we were concealing ourselves and explained that there was a band of Specials waiting for us.

'I have a plan which might work,' Raynor ventured cautiously. 'If you hear the call of the dune owl three times in succession, about ten minutes from now, then make a dash for the causeway and I'll follow you. If you don't, wait a bit and make a dash for it anyway, but don't expect to see me again. Stay hidden for the time being and don't make a single sound.' Before anyone could protest he rode off to where he could hear Nog howling in the long grass.

As Raynor had ridden with me earlier, he told me a quotation from the old book. Along with what Stellamar had just said, he realised he could use his understanding of the prophecy to try to get us out of this latest confrontation: 'Do not be afraid to part with the key when the time is right. The keys are to open the doors to your soul. Anyone who hoards the keys for their value as jewellery; who fails to sacrifice them for this higher purpose, or if the keys fall into the possession of evil men, will see how they inflict destruction in the wrong hands.' He prayed hard to the Mother Earth to save him from these servants of darkness.

Raynor rode out onto the beach to where the Specials were waiting. They saw him and came towards him and at the same time as Nog bounded out of his hiding place. So far, so good, because Nog was an integral part of the plan.

'Stop, in the name of the Holy Protectors of the State!' This was the standard salute of the Specials, who were neither holy nor protective, just the opposite. 'Who are you and what is your business?' demanded the captain of the band.

'I've been rabbiting with my dog. I live some way up the coast,' Raynor nodded at the multi-purpose Nog.

'Makes enough noise for a wolf with all that bellowing,' complained one of the underlings.

'Seems strange that no one saw you,' continued the captain, slyly, 'we've got boys all the way up the beach tonight, telling people to keep away from the shore and dunes.'

'I'm sorry, sir, I'll go straight home. I was in the dunes, which is perhaps why no one warned me earlier that my dog and I were doing the wrong thing,'

Raynor replied in a servile fashion, which was what these demons liked. A year at the Sorcerers' Academy had taught him a thing or two about getting out of trouble with characters like these.

'You didn't by chance see a party of seven children on horses, with lots of jewellery and treasure, did you?' asked the cruel-faced captain, his eyes narrowing in concentration as he tried to mind-read Raynor, who knew this old trick and blocked the intrusion by going into his 'fortress of thoughtless awareness'. He put his attention firmly on the top of his head, on the uppermost jewel of his soul. It was difficult, because terror, like some unwanted creeper in a garden, kept trying to wind its way into his heart and then he could be pulled out into mentally vulnerable territory where this skilled master of the dark arts could have read his mind like a book.

Now was the moment for Raynor to spring his big surprise, the flash point of his plan. He felt the jewel under his clothing and brought it out for all of them to see. Having it visible and in his attention gave him inner strength and also made the Specials react very strongly, as he intended.

'Hey, cap'n, do you see that?' shouted one of the Specials and came up to him with a vicious looking knife.

This is what Raynor had hoped would happen and although he was tested to the utmost as far as his ability to stay calm was concerned, somehow, by the grace of the Mother Earth, he said, 'What do you mean? Is there anything wrong? This is the emblem of my family, and surely it is allowed, to wear one's family emblem?'

'No,' agreed the chief, 'but it happens to fit the description of one of the items we are seeking: stolen treasure. It's a beautiful piece of jewellery for a lad like you to be wearing. You must come from a rich family.' Raynor could see they were working up to asking for a bribe. They could always make up a crime to arrest him for and then ask for a bribe to let him off. Nevertheless, he was glad their minds were moving on these low levels.

'You know, I think I might be able to help you there. I happened to see something very similar to this, lying with some other gems in the sand back there. I left them because I was intending to report them at Plimpet Special Secret Police Office. I was going to tell you, but with respect sir, you did not give me a chance. If you would like to follow me, I'm sure I can put you on the right track.'

'All right, take us to them,' ordered the captain suspiciously, and told his men to let Raynor go free. Even so he could see at least one gun trained on him. He trotted ahead on his horse, back through the dunes towards the quicksand. As he did so the Specials were behind him on the narrow path and could not see what he was doing with his hand. He twisted the jewel around a piece of dead wood he had previously picked up for this purpose and held it under his cloak.

Finally he reached the edge of the quicksand. He asked them to wait so as not to disturb the sand and fortunately they agreed. Then he went into the middle and naturally did not sink; because his attention was fixed on the magically charged jewel in his hand. His life depended on the next few moments.

'Isn't he near the quicksand?' said one of the Specials.

'Could easily be, but if he gets swallowed up, that solves our problem, doesn't it?' answered his superior. 'But look you, he's not sinking, so it's got to be all right.'

Raynor turned his horse so it was between the jewel and the Specials and dropped the jewel and the piece of wood into the sand. From his saddlebag he took a small casket. It contained some valuable items he no longer needed, such as his student's badge for the Sorcerers' Academy, which had now become no more than damning evidence against him. He balanced the casket on the same piece of wood that held the jewel. Then he remounted his horse and walked back to the Specials.

'See that branch there in the sand? There's a jewel like mine on the sand and a casket as well. I'll bet there are some more jewels in it. Perhaps that's what you're looking for.' The key glimmered in the moons' light. It was shining and beautiful, and the Specials were all attracted to its beauty for very different reasons from those which had drawn us to its vibrant power.

Without a care in the world and full of greed, they galloped over the sand to what they thought to be a hoard of jewels. They jumped heavily from their horses, every one of them wanting to be the first to snatch the gem and open the casket. Raynor retreated to the edge of the dunes and called Nog over to him. He was close enough to the rest of us to give the call of the dune owl, but near enough to the quicksand to see that all went according to plan. We, from our hiding places, heard his call, rode out onto the beach and over the causeway towards the island at a gallop, a cloud of sea spray hiding us as we dashed through the shallow water.

In the dunes the Specials screamed in horror, fear and dismay; because in their hurry to be the first to get to the golden key they had forgotten to test the deadly sand, even the cautious one who had asked his chief about it. The more they floundered to escape the more quickly they sank to their doom. Although one or two of the horses managed to haul themselves to safety, the men, because of the urgency with which they had jumped from their mounts and the fact that their attention was totally taken up with the possibility of getting rich quickly, all sank without a trace. Perhaps the power that governed the jewel also had a hand in their downfall, because although quicksand pulls you down, it rarely engulfs you completely. Raynor wasn't sure what happened but he did know it was time to go, and to leave his homeland, probably forever.

He called Nog, who by this time really was hunting rabbits while the humans behaved so foolishly, and hurried out onto the beach and into the sea where the tide was coming in rapidly over the broad sand flats. The last thing he saw as he urged his horse into the shallow sea, and turned back to look in case he was being chased, was a small figure in a voluminous cloak with her long hair blowing in the sea breeze. She was seated on a white pony on top of the highest dune, waving at Raynor. Behind her shone the moon of Good Fortune, making a crown above and behind her head. Raynor never forgot the sight of Stellamar on the dune bidding him goodbye. He pulled Nog up onto his horse and set off into the sea.

Records of the Family of the Pearl Lords, Volume 189

As promised I, Stellamar, visited Asha's family. I met her mother at the bookshop belonging Raynor's father, Mr Kitab Antiquarian. I told Asha's mother that the seven young people had escaped from Teletsia. She was startled when she first saw me and explained that I looked like someone she had seen in a dream, who had given similar news. She told me that Asha sees the subtle centres inside people. I warned her that this could be dangerous; it was too near to the power of the Sorcerers. I am concerned for Asha if this is the case, but there is not much I can do about it now she has gone out of my sphere of influence. I hope her sincere desire to seek and know truth will help her to come to the right path, the middle road of awareness, and that she doesn't get lost through a desire to peep around the edges.

The key has done its work and has dissolved back into the elements from which it came. But in doing so, the very ground, the actual earth of Teletsia, has woken up. This land is now vibrating on a very different wavelength. Things are going to become more and more difficult for the Sorcerers from now on, while the rest of the suppressed population can expect better days, even though they are entirely unaware of it at this time.

Journal of Herzog, Scribe to the Most High Priests

I, Herzog, must record the following although it is not pleasant to do so. Those few of us who know what is important in Teletsia, because we are its chosen protectors, have cause for concern. It is possible that the seven dangerous rebels, all young people, who molested the stone circles near Clatan and caused a serious earthquake, might have escaped from Teletsia.

We fear that these may be the ones prophesied by the nameless one who claims to have foreseen our downfall centuries ago. It is probably nothing to worry about. We have had these false alarms before, but nevertheless it has been decided to send a number of search parties over the Great Sea.

A few days after the earthquake some pearl fishers near Plimpet came to one of our representatives there and said that they had found the bodies of seven young people answering to the description of the fugitives we are seeking. When we asked to see these bodies the simpletons told us they had buried them at sea, with stones in the shrouds so they would sink to the bottom. We do not know whether to believe them, because for some reason we cannot read their minds, even though, or perhaps because, they are illiterate and uneducated.

We have decided not to publicise the issue and not to arrest the parents. If it becomes known that the great prophecy may be about to be fulfilled we might have a revolt on our hands that even we could find hard to contain.

The Second Key

Creativity and Pure Knowledge

This second centre is situated in the lower abdomen within the human body. Its qualities are pure knowledge and creativity. Its seat on our world is our Isle of Creations.

From 'The Nature of our World' in the library of Lord Jarwhen

CHAPTER 8

HOT BATHS AND HOSPITALITY

After we had heard Raynor's owl cry the rest of us galloped our horses out onto the beach to where the causeway started. Once we could get to the deeper water any pursuers would not be able to see us so easily. The sea was choppy, on account of the wind, and we had to urge the horses and even slap them to get them to wade out into the deepening water. Ahren went first and then the other horses were not too afraid to follow. Thank goodness Tandi and Ahren were there, because we city kids weren't nearly as good with animals as they were, especially Ahren.

The beach shelved down gradually and I could see that the tide was running very fast. The causeway was firm underfoot and in the distance the lighthouse beamed out as a guide, but soon the water was swirling around the stomachs of the ponies and a little later even the largest of the horses. Then they began to swim and soon we were all soaking wet. Conwenna and Derwin were uneasy and shouted that they weren't strong swimmers and were afraid they would drown if they fell off. There was nothing we could do except urge the horses to swim on.

We looked back to the mainland, expecting at any moment to see a party of men bearing down on us with lethal weapons and I thought I could see Raynor entering the water. Every now and again we would come to a shallower bit where the horses would wade and we kept the lighthouse on the island directly ahead. The only noises were the waves, the wind and the heavy breathing of the horses. The cross currents became stronger and stronger and it seemed such a long way.

As time went on even the horses were beginning to gasp with exhaustion. Tandi and Ahren, in the lead, tried to look confident, but gave each other nervous glances as their animals began to flounder in the rising waves. I remembered what Stellamar had said about Father Sea not letting us drown and it may have been coincidence but at that very moment I felt my horse touch solid ground beneath the waves as the long beach began to shelve ever so slowly upwards towards the island. Then after a few minutes the smaller animals also started to wade again. Was I relieved!

We looked back and could just make out Raynor's horse some way behind, but still, strangely, no sign of pursuit, although it could have been it was too dark to see. I wondered what had happened to the Specials that Raynor had come across on the now distant dunes. We kicked the horses yet again to hurry them on; poor things, their sides were heaving and they had done us proud, and soon our assorted collection of people and animals scrambled, dripping, onto the stony beach. We waited to give Raynor time to catch up.

'I hope he's all right out there,' said Lee, who knew something about the sea and its moods. 'The tide and the wind are both rising. We got across just in time but I'm not sure about Raynor - he's got Nog with him as well.' Now and again Raynor disappeared from view behind a wave crashing on the beach between us and him, but then, just as we were starting to worry in earnest, the three of them, Nog, Raynor and the horse, appeared through the surf and reached the beach.

'Phew, that was a close one!' spluttered Raynor. 'Another few minutes and the water would have been too deep. And the wind! See the surf flying in the moons' light! Is everyone in one piece?'

'Yes, but where did you get to? What happened to the Specials? Did they just disappear somewhere?'

'More or less. Yes, that's about it,' Raynor was confused and nervous. 'Yes, they just dis - disappeared. I don't want to talk about it now. I'll explain later.' He walked away and I could see him retching behind a rock. I wondered if he had swallowed too much seawater during his swim. He was having a hard time but pulled himself together and walked back to where we were. Derwin had been so busy shivering that he hadn't noticed this.

'Where are the Specials?' Derwin asked Raynor.

'They...they...um... well, I had to throw the key away. I'm sorry Asha, but it was either the key or us. Let's sit down a minute. I'm feeling terrible.'

'Can't we go on?' Derwin persisted. 'I'm so cold and wet.'

'Derwin,' I said gently. 'Put up with it a minute. Whatever Raynor has done is very brave. He's most probably saved all our lives, yours included.'

'Derwin's freezing cold,' Lee came to his defence. I found him a blanket that was not too wet, having been behind my large horse's saddle and well protected by a waterproof cover. Tandi did the same for Conwenna. Meanwhile Lee asked Raynor, 'Can you tell us, or would you rather not?'

'I - I threw the key into the quicksand and the Specials went in after it and were caught and sucked in. The strange thing is, it was only too easy to try to kill them. I remember what my father once said, when he and his friends had been attacked by robbers on a lonely road and had been forced to kill two of them to avoid being murdered themselves, "When it's you or them, son, you don't stop to think about the moral side of it". Right now though, I feel sick. I want to make things better in Teletsia, not destroy people.'

'You have made things better. You've just saved us from the Sorcerers. I can't believe we're free,' said Tandi, her voice choking with emotion. She gave him a quick hug. Then she felt embarrassed and sat down on a rock and stared at the ground. Raynor started speaking again, somewhat too fast. He wasn't very good at accepting praise.

'It wasn't much to do with me. It was the key and the advice that Stellamar gave me, and I got the idea from the prophecy.' Raynor tried in vain to squeeze some of the water out of his clothes, and went on, 'I'm soaking and freezing. We all are, aren't we? Let's go over there, towards the lighthouse. I can see the causeway turns into a track and goes up under those trees.'

He nodded in the direction of a black hole in the moonlit wood below the blazing lighthouse. We led the horses across the beach, then went into the dark tunnel where the track entered the wood, up the hill towards the lighthouse. It finally dawned on me that we had left Teletsia, and if Stellamar was right were out of the clutches of the Specials, the Sorcerers and all the dark forces that controlled us, for the first time in our lives. Tandi had said it but it had taken time to sink in.

At that moment we had other problems. We were waterlogged and shivering and both Nog and the horses, not to mention us, were hesitant in the dark wood. We could hear the scary screeching of a number of birds, saw a lantern bobbing up and down, coming from the direction of the lighthouse and heard the footsteps of someone running towards us.

'That's enough, you lot, I've got the message! Don't have to go and frighten our visitors!' The carrier of the lantern shouted and amazingly the screeching stopped. Soon Lee and Ahren, in the front, saw a man on the track. 'Hello,' he began, peering at us by the light of his lantern. 'Who goes there in the darkness?'

We could now see that he was indeed a cheerful soul and wore a white cloak. What was odd was that he was surrounded by about ten very large peacocks, evidently the watchdogs of the island. Nog growled at them but stopped when Raynor held his collar firmly and ordered him to sit down. He liked chasing birds, especially big juicy ones. He whined but did as he was told.

'We come from Lady Stellamar,' said Raynor, making his way forward.

'In that case you'll be honoured in our master's house, that is, in the home of the owner of this island,' continued the man formally. 'Please follow me. I'm on guard tonight and will show you the way.' I got the impression he put on the formality when he heard the name Lady Stellamar. It was only when Raynor called her 'Lady' that I understood that she was a very noble person, even though she had been so friendly and easy with us.

He led us up the slope under the trees and when we reached the brow of the hill the woodland thinned out. Below us we could see land stretching away in the moons' light; the island was the crater of a very ancient volcano, long extinct. The inner part was covered with grassy meadows, woodlands, orchards and fields of crops. The people who lived on this island were more or less self-sufficient and had no contact at all with Teletsia.

Our guide had told us that further on was a large house, surrounded by cottages and farms. He returned to his post at the lighthouse and on his instruction the peacocks, who were far more intelligent than the average bird and flew ahead to direct us, so we got on our horses and followed them.

At last we saw the welcome lights of some cottages. Then at the end of a lighted avenue lined with trees and bushes, all covered with flowers which gave out heavy scents in the night air, we saw an impressive mansion with many gables, whitewashed walls and a tiled roof. The gravel in the front courtyard was also of a whitish colour and shone in the twinkling lights.

As we approached the peacocks screeched once more and servants came out to greet us. Grooms took the horses and Nog was also led away, looking mournful. Then we were led into the palatial home, and from being subversive rebels who were the scum of the earth we had somehow become honoured guests. We were shown to a suite of magnificent bedrooms with bathrooms, along with a living room for all to share. Waiting to greet us was a neat, grey haired lady that we presumed was the housekeeper.

'My name is Ma Ganoozal,' she began. 'The first place for you young ladies and gentlemen is a long, warm bath,' she said firmly. One did not argue with Ma Ganoozal.

'Oh - h, yes - s, p - please,' stuttered Conwenna, teeth chattering.

'Now dears,' she continued, 'the water comes from some hot springs hereabouts. It does smell like rotten eggs, but don't you worry, it's just the thing for chilled bodies and aching joints.'

We were all beginning to feel incredibly stiff after our marathon ride. We took turns in the bathrooms; Conwenna and Derwin first because they had been most affected by the cold. The water did indeed smell horrible as we poured it and bubbled and fizzed as well, but as Ma Ganoozal predicted, all our tiredness, aches and shivers were sucked into the healing waters and we felt like new afterwards. Besides, someone, probably Ma Ganoozal, had been most thoughtful.

Around the marble baths were shelves on which stood porcelain jars with plants and trees painted on them to show what was inside. The contents were also written on so no one could make a mistake; the boys chose 'Extract of Lemon Balm' or 'Oil of Scented Tulsi', while we girls preferred 'Nectar of Jasmine' or 'Attar of Roses'. We all smelled delicious after we had poured some drops of the scented oils into our baths.

Afterwards everyone except me sat in front of the log fire in the living room, dressed in long towelling robes from the bathrooms, toasting their toes and drying their hair. I went to the girls' room to look for something to tie up my hair and there was Ma Ganoozal with some brilliantly coloured silk dresses over her arm. I stood quietly in the doorway so as not to disturb her as she was lovingly laying them out, one on each of the beds. They had long sleeves and skirts, embroidered and beaded belts to match, and were the sort of dresses every girl would imagine the princess in the fairy tale to be wearing.

'Ooh!' I gasped, gaping at the beautiful clothes.

'Ah, there you are, dear,' said Ma Ganoozal, smoothing out some non-existent creases in one of the dresses. 'Where are your friends?'

'Warming themselves by the fire. Shall I get them?'

'No, dear. We'll put on your dress first and see if it suits you. If it doesn't we'll get you another.'

'Ooh,' I repeated. What can you say at a time like that? I had never worn such clothes, which shimmered like opals. 'Is this really for me?'

'Yes, and there're lots more besides. Now come here, there's a good lass.' Ma Ganoozal put me into a yellow and green gown as if she had been dressing her own daughter for her first grown up party. She brushed my dark hair, braided it most imaginatively, and then put a pretty copper and enamelled clasp in it.

'There, now you look a picture,' she said. 'I could have mistaken you for a family of drowned rats when you arrived. And those gloomy clothes, how ever did you smile in such dull rags? That dreadful country must be even worse than they all make out, forcing you young ones to go around in browns and greys.' None of us ever saw any of our old clothes again. It was somehow symbolic. 'Go and show your friends and tell them there are new clothes for everyone.'

'Thank you. The dress is beautiful,' I looked at the colours of my dress rippling in the soft golden light that permeated the whole house.

'Don't thank me - they're from the mistress of the house.'

'She must be very kind,' I murmured in a daze, and went to show the others, but as I went into the passage I could not resist having a brief look around before going back to them. I was grateful and delighted at the dress but there was so much else to take in all around me in the house itself that my appearance soon slipped my mind. Finally I returned to the room where the others were warming themselves and chatting.

'This is the most incredible house!' I exclaimed, coming into the room full of enthusiasm and as fresh as a newly opened rose, despite my long day.

'And this is the most fantastic log fire!' replied my brother in a cheeky fashion without looking round. 'Come and warm yourself; you don't know what you are missing.'

'Where did you get that glorious dress?' asked Tandi in complete amazement. She had turned round to look at me because I had sounded so excited about the house. I realised from her expression that she was somewhat envious. 'You're so lucky. I'd love something like that.'

'Girls always get all the good luck. Not that I'd want a dress like that,' commented Derwin, poking the fire as he smiled impishly at me. The kid brother approved mightily of his elegant sister. I smiled a secret smile at him, just between us two.

'Ma Ganoozal asked me to tell you that there are new clothes for everyone. If you lot were slightly more adventurous and went to your rooms you'd also find some nice things to wear. I don't know,' I teased, 'you're so un-enterprising sometimes.'

At this they all went and put their new clothes on. The boys had white silk tops and trousers with coloured cummerbunds; which looked very smart but made Ahren and Derwin, at any rate, feel decidedly odd. Conwenna had a dull green and pink shot silk dress, and Tandi chose one of brilliant blue, and looked more beautiful than ever.

'You can hardly call us un-enterprising,' said Lee boastfully, when they had all returned. 'We've just pulled off the most daring escape of the century!' What he said was true.

'Don't get too puffed up,' added Raynor gravely. 'We've either been extraordinarily lucky or unbelievably well cared for in some way, so we'd best preserve our humility lest things should take a turn for the worse.'

'Why are you so serious, Raynor?' asked Conwenna.

'When Stellamar told me I had to lead the group something happened to me. She gave me a level of courage which just wasn't there before. There was an almost magical quality about her as she stood with us in the moons' light. Even her name, which means Star of the Sea, was so fitting, and her personality radiated an almost shining quality of hope and courage.'

Raynor told us in more detail how he had used the key to kill the Specials and what a miracle it had been that we had reached the island at all. Then we all understood how serious things were. He said he felt sure that this house was the beginning of our journey, not the end.

'I agree with you,' I said when he had finished his gruesome tale, 'but let's enjoy ourselves while we're here. I've got something to show you.'

We walked further along the corridor outside our rooms and saw some lovely scenes. On the ceiling were stars, moons, comets and so on. We looked in speechless wonder at them, moving and revolving as if the dance of the heavens had been speeded up. All these celestial bodies looked so real; it was like walking through whole universes. On the walls were strange geometrical designs and we could feel them affecting the various inner centres of our souls: we felt a coolness in some part of our bodies, or perhaps like Derwin when Stellamar healed him, a heat followed by a coolness. We could have gone on exploring forever except we all felt very hungry.

We were more than happy when we returned to our living room and found Ma Ganoozal waiting with a delicious meal, and lots of it. As we sat down, the others realised how exhausted they were. It was even an effort to eat and one by one they went to their rooms and fell into a long, relaxed and dreamless sleep. I did not sleep straight away. Strangely, I did not feel tired and wondered if it had anything to do with the fact that I had been wearing the jewelled key most of the time we had been escaping from Teletsia.

In the morning we woke up to find the sunlight streaming in through the long windows of our rooms, which were on the ground floor. We went out onto the veranda where there was a wrought-iron table with chairs around it, laid for breakfast. Lee and I were the first to go out, and were met by a large peacock that strutted up and down and kept a beady eye on us. When it first saw us it fanned its tail and let out a few mournful screeches. This must have been a sign because shortly afterwards a smiling, round faced man arrived with trays of hot drinks, fruit and pancakes. We called the others and soon were all sitting down to yet another mouth-watering meal.

In front of us gardens stretched away: wide lawns, shrubberies and in the distance a line of trees. We wondered what had happened to Nog and the horses, and just as Raynor and Ahren decided to go and have a look for them, Nog came panting up to us. Tail and body aquiver, he collapsed at Raynor's feet.

'It's not that bad, old boy,' he laughed, 'you've only been away for the night!' Raynor and Ahren went off in the direction that Nog had come from, assuming that dogs and horses were to be found near to one another. Sure enough after walking along an avenue of flowering bushes bordering a paved path, they found themselves at the entrance to a group of buildings arranged around a courtyard. From the different animal noises they could hear it was the right place. The way into the yard was through an archway and as they went under it a tall man with a grey beard and short hair, dressed in breeches, a smock and a cap, came towards them.

'Can I help you?' he asked pleasantly.

'Yes, we're looking for the horses and ponies we came on last night,' said Ahren.

'We have them here. I must have a word with you about them. Good thing you came round. My name is Ganoozal, Pa Ganoozal. You met my wife last night I believe?'

'Yes, and pleased to meet you, sir,' replied Raynor.

'I'm the head keeper of the animals here. Would you please come into my office for a minute?' The healthy, weather-beaten man was not angry, but his manner was firm. He led them into a cosy office with pictures of all sorts of animals on the walls: camels, elephants, donkeys et cetera, and some pictures of odd creatures like prehistoric monsters. Ahren decided he would spend a lot of time with Pa Ganoozal if he could.

'Do please sit down,' Pa Ganoozal said. By the state of his office he was more at home with his animals than his paperwork. 'Sorry about the mess, but all the animals have different diets and I have to write them out so the keepers can feed them correctly. I won't keep you boys long and I'll come straight to the point. Your dog and ponies are fine, but some of those horses, wherever did you get them from?'

Raynor and Ahren looked at each other somewhat sheepishly. 'We - um - well - um sort of acquired them on our journey here,' Raynor muttered. He fidgeted and they both avoided Pa Ganoozal's eyes.

'We stole them!' said Ahren gaily. Raynor looked at him in horror. Pa Ganoozal appeared not to hear, or if he did, not to take in this remark.

'You see there's something wrong with them. I think you'd better tell me the whole story.' The saga of the stealing of the horses came tumbling out. Pa Ganoozal had a very low opinion of the Specials and banged his hand on the desk, and said things like, 'Good for you, boys!' at the appropriate places. When Raynor had finished his tale, Pa Ganoozal looked earnestly at them.

'Ah, that explains it,' he continued. 'This is a very unusual island and I couldn't understand how those Specials' horses had managed to land here at all. I suspected from the bad feeling they emitted that was what they were. Anyone or anything that sets foot on this island has to be in tune with nature as a whole. The guard last night knew you were our friends the moment you set foot on the beach, even before.

'If your motives had been wrong, Father Sea would have swept you away before you landed and if you had somehow been able to negotiate the causeway, you would have found the beach like lacerating glass chips. The Specials have never managed to set foot on this island and never will, because if they did, the lighthouse that called you so warmly would send out rays which would cook them where they stood. What you find here depends on you.'

'The Sorcerers never mention this place,' Raynor was puzzled.

'No, probably not. My master is very displeased with them. They think they can dominate others by manipulating powers and forces which are not theirs to handle. They refuse to accept that Mother Earth herself has intelligence and will eventually react.'

'Stellamar, who sent us here, mentioned something,' interrupted Ahren. Like Raynor, he was wondering just how much this bluff-seeming Pa Ganoozal knew about us. He evidently knew a lot more about life than how to feed animals, and the two boys warmed to him by the minute.

'Lady Stellamar is very wise. It was your trust in her, combined with your innocence that enabled you to cross the causeway so easily. Sometimes it is better not to know too much.'

'What are you going to do with the Specials' horses?' inquired Raynor. 'We did steal them, so if you could possibly arrange it maybe they'd better go back.'

'That's not difficult, but if we do return them and they're found wandering along the beaches the Specials will know where you've gone.'

'Couldn't we consider them as spoils of war?' suggested Ahren. 'After all, it would be unkind to send them back to their horrible masters when they've helped to save our lives. Isn't that enough to give them the right to stay here?'

'Very well then, they can stay on and we'll find a use for them. If they're away from their sinister masters they'll come right in no time. That answers my questions.'

'You're saying that on this island all judgments are made depending on how things harmonise with the whole pattern of creation?' asked Raynor.

'Obviously. What else can you use as a basis for making decisions?'

'Well, most people use their intellects or their emotions or sort of feel the answers to things. Some just go by what they've been told and don't have any ideas of their own at all.'

'That's the whole problem, isn't it? Living your life by judgments made on wobbly, ever changing foundations, like quicksand.' Pa Ganoozal gave Raynor a searching look.

'So what's the solution?'

'Isn't that what your journey is all about? Finding it?' Neither of the boys said anything; that hadn't occurred to them. 'Don't worry, you'll find your answers. You've hardly started yet. This is the Island of Creations - a great place for starting out anew and leaving the past behind.'

CHAPTER 9

THE ISLAND OF CREATIONS

Pa Ganoozal took the boys to see our horses and ponies. Ahren's old pony looked much happier and less decrepit; the ones we had stolen from the Specials seemed calmer and our own from Teletos gave the boys a welcoming whinny. The stables were clean, light and airy, and smelled of fresh hay and straw. Grooms ran around busily, greeting Pa Ganoozal with friendly respect.

'I'm going round the fields and pens. I've got a lot of animals to check up on this morning. Do you boys want to come with me?' he asked, after the tour of the yards, where they saw some strange animals that looked like primitive horses, cattle and so on.

'Yes, please,' Ahren cried enthusiastically.

'Thank you, yes,' said Raynor, more cautiously.

'Let's go then.'

The world of Pa Ganoozal was something like a game park or zoo, except the animals did not pace around their pens looking as if they wished the people would stop staring at them. All the successful types of life on the planet were represented somewhere on the island. Raynor and Ahren were enthralled.

Some species that had not been successful and had not fitted in with the flow of life in their environment, if they had been too large or too aggressive, had been written out completely. Also, animals that didn't survive because they were not aggressive enough obviously did not exist any more. They asked Pa Ganoozal what kept the different animals from wandering around all over the place, because they kept to well defined areas. Mr. Ganoozal explained that they were limited in their movements by powerful force fields.

We rested for most of that first day and on the next went to explore the gardens. They were divided into sections and each section grew all the plants from a particular area or climate. Like the animals' part of the garden, some plants were from far off countries and others were extinct except in this garden. We met a gardener who explained more or less what Pa Ganoozal had said, that these were botanical gardens, living records of different times and places for scientific purposes. We walked around and noticed that even the climates changed; some were hot and dry, where rattling thorn bushes and fleshy cacti grew, and over the next hillock it was fresh and cool and tundra poppies bloomed.

The gardener warned of some areas where the plants were dangerous and had poisonous feelers that might lash out and fatally sting the unwary. He said that someone had once written a book about such plants and the way of creation is that every idea in people's minds also exists on the physical level somewhere. In fact they were pathetic little things and were always getting eaten by snails. He went on to say that the changes in temperature and humidity were limited by forces that kept the plants within their boundaries and stopped them from spilling out all over the island, as if they were in invisible greenhouses.

We were so absorbed we forgot the time. The sun was well past midday when a bank of clouds covered the sky and rain was imminent, so we fled from the approaching downpour and made our way back to the house, then sat in our living room and stared at the rain, which looked as if it had set in for the afternoon. Ma Ganoozal came in and I could see Derwin was going to ask for something to eat. As I was about to stop him a meal appeared, brought in by the same plump, jolly man who served all our food.

Life was a holiday then and we felt relaxed, in good hands and safe, but I was beginning to wonder how long it would last. Since we had visited the Temple of Support, something strange had happened to us. We had an inner urge to move on, to seek northwards. I suppose this is how migrating birds feel when it is time to fly north, or south, or wherever it is they have to go. Something was pulling us northwards and that something began in earnest at the temple, that morning when we had to make our quick getaway from the Specials. To begin with I thought it was just me, with my insatiable desire for seeking truth and the goal of our quest, or that I wanted to be as far away from the dreaded Specials as possible, but as time went on the feeling became stronger and stronger in all of us. Raynor said we were being drawn by the same force of attraction that was written about in the prophecy.

After eating and exchanging a few stories we had a rest, then in the evening, when it was still pouring with rain, we decided to have a further look at the house. It was cool, so we girls all wore the red shawls we'd been given. We walked down the corridors, looking at the stars and other heavenly objects floating on the ceilings, and noticed that one of the many doors was slightly open. Ahren could not resist having a look inside and the rest of us followed.

As we crossed the threshold it was as if we had walked into a different world. We looked behind us and the door was not to be seen, but there was a design in rocks in the shape of a six-petalled flower to mark the place on the ground where, presumably, we could step back into our own world. As we walked through the door, we walked into a different place and time, or so it seemed. Ahren checked by going back through the doorway and as he did so, the scene was gone. We all wanted to look some more, so he came back inside again to join the rest of us, saying, 'It's only some sort of illusion, so we must be safe.'

In here it was much cooler and a damp wind blew. We were standing on a beach of pinkish coloured sand over which crawled purple crablike creatures. Further inland were forests of what looked like giant sized seaweed waving in the wind. Growing out of the nearby lake were huge flowers similar to lotuses, coloured pale mauve. The sky was overcast and pale grey and through the haze I could see a vast crimson sun. On the distant horizon volcanoes belched out fire and the ground shuddered underfoot every few seconds. Derwin picked up one of the small crablike creatures by the body, so it could not pinch him, and started chasing Conwenna with it.

Fortunately for Conwenna, who was not enjoying this at all, the air smelled very sour and within a minute or so everyone was gasping for breath. We all stumbled back into the corridor over the six-pointed flower design on the floor in the doorway. As we looked back into the world we had just left, we could only see the plain walls and floor of an unfurnished room.

'This is the strangest house I've ever been in!' exclaimed Derwin after we had all taken some deep breaths of breathable air and no longer felt half suffocated.

'Where's that crab?' said Conwenna dubiously, looking Derwin up and down and wondering if he had it hidden up his sleeve for future use.

'It just disappeared as I came through the door, but why couldn't we breathe properly?'

'The air smelled foul, perhaps that was it,' suggested Tandi.

'Did you see that gigantic red sun?' cried Ahren excitedly.

'We stepped into another world, yet it was all so real,' murmured Lee, trying to work it out.

'Let's try another door. We might find somewhere better for humans,' said Ahren.

'I don't think we should,' Conwenna cautioned, mindful of the crabs. 'We might get stuck in there or something.'

'Oh come on, don't be so pathetic,' insisted Ahren. He didn't have Conwenna's dislike of crabs or unnecessary adventure; she thought he was an idiot and neither of them understood each other at all at that point. Conwenna looked imploringly at Raynor.

'All right, you choose,' Raynor was hesitant, as these illusions were too realistic for his liking. Nothing daunted, Ahren chose a door three further along the corridor and this time we all stepped into a world of green. The air smelled of sulphur but it was breathable. The sky was cloudy, but between the fluffy rain clouds we could see a brilliant bluish sun. Around us were high tree ferns and the ground was covered with giant mosses almost up to Conwenna's waist. As we forced our way through them it was as if they fingered us inquisitively and when I broke off a stalk it oozed a sticky white substance. We could hear raucous cawing noises coming from a valley in the middle distance.

Just like the first room, once inside, the space was not confined and stretched away to the far horizon, but at our feet were the same big stones shaped like a six-petalled flower, to mark the doorway. We ploughed through the mosses leaving a clear path where the damp plants had been flattened by our feet and could see a swamp at the bottom of the valley. In it was a bright green monster with a tiny head, a long sinuous neck and a large body, browsing on weed in the water. The pond was chrome yellow and the whole scene was very jarring to the eyes.

'Let's go and have a look at that monster,' shouted Derwin eagerly. 'It's bigger than the trees!'

We crept through the undergrowth and down the hill towards the reptile, careful to remember the whereabouts of the marker stone. As we came nearer the placid animal it looked up and opened its jaws for a yawn. Its mouth was bright red, the same colour as our shawls.

Suddenly we heard a crashing and a splintering of tree ferns and another monster, as tall as the tree-ferns, lurched towards the swamp, plunging into the water with a resounding splash. This one, a flesh eater, had its mouth open to reveal rows of enormous teeth. It also had fearsome slashing claws the length of a man's arm. With all this noise and commotion a third giant, also with a flesh eater's large teeth, came to join in. The browsing reptile had no chance and though it tried desperately to bat the two flesh eaters with its tail, it was soon caught by the first monster. Its great jaws closed around the long thin neck and neatly beheaded the plant eater, while the third animal tore lumps of muscle and bone out of its tail.

Soon the two remaining monsters were fighting with each other. The third one had four or five long pointed horns as well as teeth and claws, and these horns gave it the final victory. The swamp was now a morass of blood and bodies and victor stood up on its hind legs and gave a deafening caw. Up to now we hadn't taken this seriously, and had treated it like an exciting storybook, but then the surviving monster appeared to spy the red of our shawls. It lumbered over the corpses in the swamp after this new prey: us. It was wounded and kept tripping over tree ferns.

'Take your shawls off. Run!' Raynor shouted desperately.

We turned and ran for our lives up the hill and back to the door, every moment sure the monster must be getting closer, and the mosses kept getting in our way. We were all gasping for breath from running so fast. Fortunately the noise of pursuit stopped, and just as we were too exhausted to go on, there was the star shaped design of rocks. We flung ourselves onto it and pulled each other through what became a door.

Once again, as we did so, and collapsed in a heap on the floor of the passage, the whole scene faded into thin air. We slowly regained our wits and recovered from the shock of our narrow escape. Soon our fear of monsters faded out, like last night's nightmare, and we picked ourselves up. Even Ahren's desire for adventure had been satisfied for the time being. We did not go into any more of these rooms but instead walked along the corridors looking at the magnificent display of stars on the ceilings. Once or twice I peeped into a room and caught glimpses of animals, plants, insects, birds and other unknown life forms. The whole house was a work of art, every nook and cranny carved and painted with the utmost love and care. Derwin was near a half open door and the aroma of a hot, well-cooked meal wafted into the passage.

'I'm hungry!' he whispered to Conwenna. 'Let's go in and see if we can find something to eat.'

'Me too, I've had enough of monsters and comets,' she added, and they crept around the corner of the door and away from the passage. The rest of us were absorbed, looking at a golden egg-like star cluster and I said it reminded me of my dream of the beginning of creation.

I noticed that Conwenna and Derwin were not with us and we all began to smell the food as well. We followed the smell into the room it came from and saw a table, spread with a white damask cloth and piled high with food and drink - soup in a silver tureen to start with, for the main bite of hunger in the middle there were all manner of hot and cold dishes of meat, fish and vegetables, and nuts, fruits and ice cream for spare corners at the end.

'What a spread!' I cried, unable to control my delight. By this time Conwenna and Derwin had already filled their plates with food.

'Yes, come and join us,' said Ma Ganoozal, standing in the corner, and we also noticed her husband at the side of the table.

Above the dining table on the wall, one each side of an open fire, were portraits of two figures. The man, on the right, had a look of great wisdom and the lady, at the left, was tall like her husband and very stately.

'Are those portraits of the master and mistress here?' asked Derwin.

'Yes indeed,' replied Ma Ganoozal. 'Lord Jarwhen and Lady Mercola, but they don't do their sitters justice. By the way, I presume you've been exploring the house?'

'Oh yes, and it's very exciting!' Ahren answered for all of us.

'We were chased by a monster!' added Derwin.

'There's no end to what you can see here, but perhaps you'd rather join us at supper?' continued Ma Ganoozal.

'That would be great,' said Ahren.

We went to the laden table and helped ourselves. Ma Ganoozal sat at one end and her husband at the other, as if it were a family gathering with the children down the sides. The Ganoozals showed us their off-duty side, very different from the workaday people of the previous meetings. Pa Ganoozal left his wife to look after our needs but was overjoyed when each new dish was a tasty surprise for us.

'A record is kept of all the work done here,' he explained. 'Some of the knowledge is recorded in the form of boxes that look like books. If we want to check up on something we take out a box and put it on a machine in one of the special rooms. The machine recreates the scene that is stored in the mathematical dials and symbols of the boxes in all its sense impressions: sight, sound, touch, taste and smell. You needn't have worried when the monster came for you. It was just coincidence that he changed course in your direction. He's been dead many a long age. It is like a painting, but it affected all your senses, didn't it?'

'Yes, very much so!' laughed Raynor, and we all smiled at having been taken in by the illusion. In one way we knew there had to be a trick in it somewhere, because we didn't really believe you could find monsters in someone's library.

'It's a very unusual way of recording knowledge, don't you agree?' asked Ma Ganoozal.

'And half!' went on Raynor. 'It's incredible.'

'What happens when the machine is turned off? Is it just a bare room?' Tandi sat up and took note.

Yes, that's it,' said Ma Ganoozal. 'I'll give you back your shawls tomorrow,' and Tandi looked surprised, because this was exactly what she had been thinking about.

Memo
To: Lord Jarwhen and Lady Mercola   *From: Jack Ganoozal*

The young Teletsians have arrived and are much more at ease now. They have had time to rest and look around. They are losing the fear and tension they brought with them from Teletsia, which shows that they are responding well to the good vibrations of our island. We even left some doors unlocked in the 'Scenarios of Past Times' wing, so they could have a glimpse of how life can be seen as a drama, and moreover a drama that doesn't always end in disaster!

You are so right to have gone to the mainland to help cover their tracks and fake their deaths. They are delightful young people and are definitely the ones we are expecting. I began to wonder if they would ever be coming. It's been such a long wait. The vibrations coming from one of the girls, Asha, and one of the boys, Raynor, indicate that they have already found and used one of the keys.

They have all the necessary qualities for the task ahead of them and any shortcomings they may have will work out in time. One can only hope so, because coming from Teletsia they are bound to be affected somehow or another by the deviant ways of the Sorcerers.

Excuse me for leaving this note, but I have to go over to Kracka Kamma to check on the sugar cane crop and it may take some days.

Pa Ganoozal's Diaries and Memos, Archives, Island of Creations

CHAPTER 10

THE KEYS OF WISDOM

Whenever I think of the Island of Creations I remember the mournful cry of the peacocks. They were our guides, our sentinels and our alarm clocks. That morning it was not long after dawn and our friendly peacock screeched on the veranda to attract our attention. We got up and had breakfast and then the bird was after us again, tugging at sleeves and skirts with its beak. We followed where it led, out into the garden along endless paths of white gravel, paving stones and grass. The sun shone on the wet gardens and as we moved the raindrops of the previous day shone like diamonds. We went through flower gardens, water gardens, gardens with formal flower beds and statues, gardens with pots and urns filled with shrubs and trees, wild shrubberies and gardens of bare earth waiting for their plants to fill them with life and colour.

Finally we lost the peacock altogether but followed in the direction of some trees where we had last seen it. Beyond the trees was a hollow and in it was a lawn with a small round summerhouse at one side. The grass, neat and smooth as a bowling green, led down to a large round pond that took up the whole of the rest of the hollow. Around the edge of the pond were water lilies: sky blue, pale pink, yellow, white and apricot. We sat down by the water's edge to watch some small yellow frogs hopping from one lily pad to another, and dragonflies swooping overhead. We noticed that the water was completely transparent and the bottom of the pond was made of some reflecting material. We saw Ma Ganoozal coming from the direction of the summerhouse, and the peacock was with her.

'Good morning, did you all sleep well?' said Ma Ganoozal in her friendly way.

'Yes, thank you,' I said.

'I have some advice to give you,' she led us into the summerhouse, where we sat down in its airy shade, on window seats. 'I know you want to leave us soon, but which direction do you want to go?'

'We only know that we have to go north,' answered Raynor. 'We want to find a kingdom in some far mountains in the northern continent. I've been reading a prophecy and it says it's only there that we could find a way to help our country and also ourselves.'

'You've studied well. Have you told your entire group what you've found out?'

'Yes, I've explained as much as we've had time for. We don't know who it applies to though.'

'That doesn't matter. What is important is that you want to find this northern kingdom, and you have a dire need to be as far away from Teletsia as possible, isn't that so?'

'Yes, it is.'

'We can help you. First of all, the name of the kingdom is Sasrar, which means the land of a thousand waterfalls. Do you know your way there?'

'Not really - in the old book we read that there are some keys or jewels which would help on the journey. Asha did, in a strange fashion, find a jewelled key at the Temple of Support which helped us to get away from Teletsia, but in the prophecy it definitely said that these travellers would need more than one. I don't know if that applies to us too, or whether these keys are symbolic. We don't understand that part.'

'No, not yet, but you found and made good use of the first key. The keys exist on many levels of creation and in many forms on each level. The Temple of Support itself is a key, in that it opened a way for you and awakened a new type of desire within your hearts. Your motives were pure, while those of the Specials were contaminated by greed. That's always the case with them, unfortunately. They're completely lost. The keys will always work against evil and in favour of good and will remove obstacles, but never hoard them as a miser does gold. It's written in the prophecy, isn't that so?'

'Yes.'

'Now,' Ma Ganoozal went on, 'listen carefully. In this house a record is kept of many things that have been created, as you saw. Sometimes the races of creatures do not turn out perfectly. They do not fit in well with the overall pattern of creation and disturb the harmony, so Mother Nature destroys them, like those monsters you saw last night. In the same way, the fate of humanity is very uncertain at this time. People must grow out of their pettiness and self-destructiveness or we will go the same way as those monsters. At least, some, like a lot of people in Teletsia, will.'

'But what are we supposed to do about it?' cried Ahren desperately. I'd never heard him say anything like this before and it made me realise there was much more to him than I had thought up to now.

'As my husband said, that's what your journey is all about. It depends on the use you make of the keys I'm going to give you a short time from now,' continued Ma Ganoozal. Suddenly we were all completely alert. This was it and we knew it. We all felt a mighty blast of coolness flowing over us, even

76

though there wasn't a single ripple on the pond.

'These keys correspond to the subtle centres within you and match your inner spiritual jewels. If you listen to your inner awareness, they will not let you go far wrong. The jewelled keys will help you to feel these inner jewels. Coolness will emanate from these jewels, these subtle centres within you if they are all right, but you'll feel heat and maybe even a dull pain if they aren't.

'I must give you one word of warning, because you come from a country where everything is out of balance with the whole, and few people appear to know right from wrong any more. You should not see the inner jewels, because this is not given to us as humans. If you actually see the jewels of people's souls within their bodies then it means you are sliding into those realms of creation and you may see, and get caught up by, other things that reside there too. Unfortunately some of these are dangerously destructive: ghosts, devils and demons.

'To be able to see whether another person is trustworthy by looking at their inner jewels may be very useful, I know, but this ability is altogether too close to the powers of the Sorcerers and the realms they delve into. They would like to suck you down, and there are many of their sort everywhere.

'I repeat, you must feel the inner Tree of Life of your soul, and the shining flower on your head, not see it. You must be within yourself, not look from the outside. The Tree of Life is one aspect of the greatest force of all. It is common throughout creation and you young people must learn to know it in a different way. It is the power of love.

'The sign for you that a person is in tune with that force is this: when you put your attention on them, you will feel coolness, like a gentle breeze, coming from them. You will also feel that their mind is calm and peaceful. If you feel pain or heat in any part of your body when your attention is on them, this is a sign of someone who has problems, and if the pain or heat is very intense that person may be quite evil. But beware; there are many tricksters about, who will seek to deceive you, so you must always use your common sense and these sensations of cool or warmth to make judgements.'

Lee, Raynor and I looked at each other. Everything made sense, although for me some of it came as quite a shock.

'Come, now for the best part, follow me,' she said enthusiastically, and led us across the lawn to a little jetty. She invited us to squeeze into a small boat moored there. From the outside it looked like a large golden water lily but inside was a seat around the inner edge covered with a soft red material like silk. In the centre of the boat was a large wooden box from which Ma Ganoozal took a stringed instrument, beautifully inlaid with ivory and coloured woods. We helped her paddle the boat out to the exact centre of the pond.

Ma Ganoozal tuned the instrument and began to play. She explained that it was a very special one, lent to her by the master and mistress of the island, and also that the pond had a unique quality. We did not understand what she meant but listened to her as she played. The instrument not only gave out beautiful music from its twenty-four strings but also a very powerful form of vibrations, and we could feel the subtle inner centres of our bodies, the jewels of our souls, starting to dance with delight as the music thrilled through us. The different centres within us were affected by the different notes and chords in the music. The calm surface of the water rose in an intricate pattern of waves that responded as the notes changed and soon the pond was alive with the vibrations, which translated into waves in the water element.

She played six different tunes, each one entrancing, and when the music stopped the waves died down. The pond was crystal clear again and the reflective bottom of the water showed the blue sky, the base of the boat and the trees overhanging the pool. As I looked over the edge of the boat she pointed down into the water.

'There are your keys!' she said, and lying in the deepest water were six golden keys shaped like flowers, each with a different number of petals and a different gemstone colouring the petals. Each key was attached to a golden chain. Six graceful swans with golden beaks came swimming out from the side of the lake and with their long necks picked up the keys from the bottom of the pool, then placed them carefully on the sides of the boat. We gasped as we looked at the flawless jewels close up.

'It's done!' exclaimed Ma Ganoozal. She explained that each of us was to take one to wear, except me, and that it was best to keep the keys hidden under our clothing. Ma Ganoozal put each key on a particular person and immediately they could feel their power. It made everyone more joyful, more confident, but at the same time more humble. It was very difficult to describe.

'Now you each have a copy of one of the Keys of Wisdom, or shall we say the Keys of Navi Septa,' she went on.

'What's Navi Septa?' asked Raynor.

'It's the true name of this planet, this Mother Earth that we live on. It means new seven and relates to the powers of the subtle centres. That's another thing you'll learn about later on.'

All of us noticed that although some time had elapsed between the keys being placed in the hot sunlight on the side of the boat and Ma Ganoozal's handing them round, they were cool to the touch like the water from which they had been made.

I couldn't help feeling left out, because I didn't get one, even though in a way I'd already had one. Then something made me put my attention on us as a group, not seven individuals and I felt great joy and confidence that here was the help we really needed, and this was the beginning of the fulfilment of the prophecy. Although the first key had already left us, I could feel its effects within me and all of us and I was sure that would be with us always.

'I hope you like the alchemy,' she said with a smile. Everyone was delighted with their keys and could already feel joy and confidence flowing into their souls. Ahren's had six petals, with a jewel in each one. No one could really grasp what had happened: how could gold and jewels appear out of clear water? Everyone was quite certain that there was nothing on the bottom of the pond before Ma Ganoozal played the six tunes.

'The house is a reference library and the grounds the research department,' she went on. 'The water of this pool has a special power and today you have seen it in action. If one exposes the water to the right sort of sound sequence, the water will produce material objects of great benefit, such as the keys. Those melodies were each an encoded set of instructions.

'Oh yes, one last thing, Ahren, with the key you are now wearing, the servants will give you anything you ask for, provided it is sensible.'

We were silent. This was a new world for us – a world of positive magic, instead of the dark arts of the Sorcerers. We honestly didn't have any idea how to say 'thank you' for such gifts, but we did our best to show our gratitude. We helped row the boat back to the jetty and stepped out. Then we went off into the gardens, bemused by the day's events.

Raynor, Ahren and I were together later on.

'I hope you realise what an important task you've got, Ahren,' said Raynor. 'You're going to have to think about this very carefully.'

'You think too much,' replied Ahren. 'Living among those Sorcerers in Teletos has made you too much in your head, too overcautious. You've got to trust me, even if I'm very different from you.'

Some days later we decided to explore the shores of the island. We rode our horses and went out with Nog at our heels because the northern shore of the island was some distance away. The horses we had brought to the island were now looking sleek and happy and Nog was in the best of health. We rode slowly along the beach, watching the breakers crashing on the pink sand and looking at the empty sea to the north.

By this time we were discussing with each other how to continue our journey, because our desire to continue going north was becoming stronger all the time. Ahren suggested building a raft, but Lee wasn't very keen because he knew it would have to be very strong to withstand the sea swells. Raynor wished he had his prophecy to consult and Derwin wanted to ask someone for help. Tandi was quite content to stay on the island for the time being and both Conwenna and I had decided that something would soon happen if we kept our wits alert and our eyes open. Since we had left Teletsia she was opening up and trusted me much more now, so I didn't mind her sometimes excessive affection, and her new habit of grabbing my hand when she felt nervous and alone.

We asked the staff of the house and grounds for a boat and the possibility of exchanging our horses for something to cross the water on, not wanting to ask for anything too large by way of a gift, but they didn't seem to know what we were talking about because for them the world started and finished on the island. The people living here couldn't comprehend anyone's wanting to leave, but offered us any amount of food, drink, clothing, hunting and fishing equipment and all sorts of games to play.

Ahren felt confident enough to wear his key outside his clothing, on this safe-seeming island, but all the rest were hidden. His key was golden and was in the shape of a flower with six golden petals that had jewels in them. These jewels sometimes looked yellow and sometimes had a mauve tinge, like amethysts. This key, Ma Ganoozal had explained, related to the intrinsic nature of the island itself, which was creativity and pure knowledge.

During our ride, he was leading his horse in the shallows of the beach and bent over the water to look at some interesting shells. He leant down to pick one up and as he did so he caught the chain of the jewelled key in the horse's bridle and he took it off to unhook it. As he did so it fell into the water lapping around his feet.

'I wish that the power that made the keys could make us a boat so we could sail across the sea,' he called out hopefully as it lay on the sand, 'it's nice here, but we must try to get to the northern kingdom.' He stooped to pick it up and noticed something very strange.

'Look!' he shouted in surprise. 'It's floating, and getting bigger! Come and see, everyone!' By the time the other boys had reached the spot it had not only grown, but had also turned into a wooden raft, oval in shape with a tall mast growing out of the centre. At first it was like a perfect model toy, but it became bigger and bigger. We stepped back and it sort of blew up. It was quite extraordinary. Soon it was life-sized, with two cabins roofed with woven bamboo, a square yellow sail with a flower painted on it. We gaped in astonishment. I touched it to make sure it wasn't a hallucination; all this was far removed from my experience of life.

'There must be something unique about the water just here,' said Lee when he had found his tongue, as he was highly suspicious about the reality of the raft. 'Are we sure it isn't just an illusion, like the monster, that will suddenly disappear?'

'No, we're not in a room, with a machine, or anything like that,' Ahren replied, a trifle sadly because he had lost his key so quickly. In his heart he knew his prayer was being answered, because as Ma Ganoozal had said, provided his requests were sensible, his desires would work out. He gave it a push and it rocked in the waves.

'Look,' said Raynor, who had glanced behind him, 'do you see that stream which comes into the sea from the woods over there, between the hills? That is in the direction of the round pond. Perhaps that has something to do with the transformation.'

'Yes,' added Lee, 'and what's more it is flowing in a northerly direction.' We looked at the raft, which by now had become very large and was beginning to float out to sea.

'Stop it, everyone!' Ahren shouted. 'It's going to leave without us.'

'Why don't we make it fast with those ropes hanging off it and go back to the house for provisions and our clothes?' suggested Tandi. We girls had been watching the antics of the boys from further up the beach and now decided that some common sense was needed if we were going to start this voyage in the right way.

Ahren was all for jumping aboard and sailing out to sea there and then but after some discussion we all agreed with Tandi. We tied the raft securely to a tree trunk which had rolled down to the water's edge after falling in a storm, and took our horses back to the centre of the island to ask the staff if we could have some food and other helpful items.

They were wonderfully cooperative and Lee was in charge, because he knew about sailing and the sea. Thank goodness, at least one of us had some idea of what to do. I'm all for challenges but the Great Sea, or Sea of Illusion, as it was called on this island, had a dreadful reputation. Lee insisted on our taking tanks of water, fishing lines, fresh fruit and a selection of berries which even in their dried state helped prevent ghastly diseases like scurvy. He asked for, and was given, watertight trunks for spare clothes, spare ropes, spare sails, a spare anchor, tools for mending bits of the raft that might get damaged, et cetera, et cetera. Rather him than me.

The next day we returned to the raft, when Lee was finally satisfied. We piled whatever couldn't be carried by our horses or those of the servants onto the back of a cantankerous donkey called Heggo. The islanders were fascinated at Lee's tale of the raft and wanted to come and see it for themselves. Pa Ganoozal came to see us off.

'I'm through with that Heggo, you'd think he'd come from Teletsia. You can take him along too if you can get him on the raft. I'll send some food with him and he might be of use to you on the other side of the sea,' he said.

We returned to the beach and had just finished loading our bits and pieces onto the raft, and were wondering what to do about the donkey, when we saw Ma Ganoozal come walking onto the beach along the side of the stream where it left the woods.

'So, you're ready to continue your journey,' she said encouragingly. 'My husband is right about that donkey, I'm sure you'll find him useful as a pack animal when you have crossed the sea, because you have a long way to go even then. He doesn't eat much and the little cabin on the right of the mast is ideal for him.'

'Thank you,' said Ahren, as he was at that moment holding the foul tempered beast. The rest of us weren't prepared to risk its teeth or hooves, and even he was wondering if it was such a good idea to take it along.

'You've made good use of this key as well,' Ma Ganoozal observed, looking out to sea past the raft. 'The power of creation flows from the pool and out into the sea via this stream here. Ahren, you had a sensible desire, that is, how to cross the sea, and your wish was fulfilled. But beware! You're about to cross the Sea of Illusion. There are many pitfalls on your way: people or things that look genuine and aren't, or ways which seem very wise and are a false route to disaster, a short cut to something which turns out to be the opposite.

'There's a current in this part of the sea; a continuation of this stream and the river which came from the Temple of Support. This flows north right through the sea until you reach the other side. Because you are in the flow of creation, it will carry you across, and if you keep on that you will be safe, but if you leave it you may or may not meet trouble. The current is like the power which generates all creation, keep in tune with it and you are all right, but leave it for your own free will and anything can happen.

'In the centre of the sea you will find an island where the Emperor and Empress live who rule this realm. If you can get there you'll be doing well, but beware of all the other islands, they may not be as harmless as they seem. And now you must go, because the wind is filling your sail and the current is ready to take you. But remember, nothing can force you to complete your quest, only your own desire.'

We respectfully took leave of Ma and Pa Ganoozal and thanked them and the other kind people on the island for their help. The donkey, for all its habitual perversity, did not mind being hauled and winched onto the raft and was soon shut into its little cabin. It merely gave a few 'hee-haws' to announce its presence to everyone. Nog had been with his humans all the time: swimming in the sea, then shaking himself and wetting whoever was nearest, then gleefully repeating the process.

We seven travellers climbed onto the raft, pushed off through the waves and soon the sea was taking us northwards. Ma and Pa Ganoozal stood on the shore waving. For one moment I felt we had made a foolish decision, to leave the comfort and safety of the Island of Creations for the uncertainty of the Sea of Illusion.

The brightly painted sail billowed in the wind and soon we were out of sight of land. Within a few hours we were in the middle of a round blue sea with a round blue sky up above us in the shape of an upturned bowl, with a few birds and flying fish for company. The only sounds were the creaking of the raft's timbers, the slapping of the water against its sides and the flapping of the sail above.

Lee took the first turn at the rudder, and Ahren sat and talked to him. Lee was praying hard to Father Ocean that the rest of us would quickly adapt to a life on the high seas. Our combined experience of boats, apart from him, consisted of rowing around the canals of Teletos, the odd trip on a waterbus, or a boat trip down the estuary on sunny afternoons. Any sane adult would have said we were crazy, which is perhaps why we, and not more mature people, were the ones foolhardy enough to make the journey. Lee, Raynor and I had a short talk that evening.

'I'm still not sure about Ahren,' said Raynor. 'I feel it was just luck we somehow got this raft.'

'Yes, I know what you mean, he's too much sometimes,' I added. 'But whether you like it or not, he's got a lovely shining Tree of Life.'

'Let's face it, we all have our own style, and even if it was luck that his key turned into this raft, it was his luck and his key,' said Lee.

'Even though Ahren is a very rough diamond, he's still a diamond, and maybe we should rethink our sophisticated ideas about people,' I said.

'Point taken,' conceded Raynor.

The Third Key

Sustenance, Seeking, Right Values

Now we come to the third subtle centre. This has material well-being as one of its blessed qualities. It is surrounded by the Void, which permeates the material universe. This is also the area of our seeking, whether for food, money, power or the higher goal, our seeking for unity with our eternal self. Within us it is the abdominal area, on the planet this centre is found in the Emperor's Citadel, and the Void is our Great Sea or Sea of Illusion.

Theon, the Master Mariner. School Records Book 11

CHAPTER 11

CAPTAIN LEE

For some days we floated northwards on the current. The weather was usually hot, settled and sunny. I knew we were going almost due north because each night we could see the Twelve Starred Crown, the north polar constellation, rise a little higher in the sky directly ahead of us. The 'crew', if one could call us that, were adapting well to a life on the high seas. There wasn't much to do, except adjust the sail to catch the wind and keep the raft pointing north so it remained on the current. Life at sea affected all of us in a variety of ways, but at least none of us fell overboard. By some luck or blessing it was the season when storms were rare and the wind was usually soft and southerly.

Ahren was very bored, but looked after the donkey and took it for walks around the raft. It was gradually sinking in to all of us that we were out of Teletsia, and we would talk openly now about how we had handled the place. In Teletsia, those of us from the city had withdrawn into ourselves for protection, but Ahren told us he had a different method of keeping himself from losing his inner freedom. He would go into the countryside and just laugh, because he thought the Sorcerers were lunatics. It was typical Ahren, both admirable and foolish. It's a good thing we got him out of Teletsia when we did!

Derwin and Conwenna did a great deal of fishing. Conwenna had infinite patience and was prepared to watch the lines for hours at a time, but she needed Derwin when she caught something. She wasn't too keen on the slimy, slippery bodies of the fish which had to be dehooked and killed. They caught a curious selection of sea creatures, some of which Lee said were edible. He knew about the different types of fish, because he sometimes went out fishing on weekends with the retired fishermen who were friends of his father, and who ran his small boat building business with him. Lee showed Derwin how to gut a fish but he couldn't quite handle that, so Ahren often did it. We ate a lot of fish grilled on the little charcoal brazier in the cabin.

Derwin annoyed everyone by endlessly chasing Nog around the raft. He also spent quite a lot of time teasing Conwenna. He was good at that; the result of a combination of natural ability and dedicated practice. Mostly she put up with it. Her occasional outbursts of temper when Derwin annoyed her beyond reasonable tolerance were a welcome change – at last she was beginning to give vent to her emotions. There was more anguish in her than in the rest of us, and I was only just beginning to realise this.

Conwenna had a lot of time to think when watching those fishing hooks. To begin with the rest of us assumed she was quiet, balanced and determined to make the best of having to run away from home. But she surprised us when she opened up as we sat together watching the stars in the evenings. It turned out that she, like Tandi, had major family reasons for escaping. A couple of months previously she had begun to suspect that her father was spying for the Sorcerers – on us. She only became certain a few days before we left Teletos. She had overheard a discussion where one of the Specials was threatening her father to take her, Conwenna, away, if her father refused to continue to spy for them. Slowly she began to speak out more freely and her face began to lose its stiff, glasslike expression. Like all of us from the city, for her, the only safe place in Teletos had been within the quiet joy of the soul, and not to appear too alert or intelligent.

I was worried about Tandi. We were all a bit seasick to start with, and then got over it. She didn't. After some time she became dehydrated and lost a lot of weight. She looked awful, and was getting weaker every day. We decided that if we did see an island we would to have to stop for a day or two to give her time to recover.

But the real worry at that time, although I didn't know it, was me. Apparently Lee was watching me with concern right from the start. He noticed that something was seriously wrong when he saw me spending hours staring silently at the waves in an almost hypnotic trance. He asked me why I didn't even react when Derwin played hide-and-seek all around me with Nog. I will quote from Lee's own log book which he kept when 'captain' of the raft.

Our Journey, by Lee, Day 6

Asha and I, being first cousins, have known each other since we were both crawling. I have been watching her for some days now and that moodiness isn't at all like her. She may play a game of being withdrawn and stupid to deceive the Sorcerers, but she is usually able to stand back and observe the lunacy around her, inwardly alert, while she keeps smiling outside. Her relationship with Derwin is a key indicator. They are very close and she is like a little mother to him. When she virtually ceases to notice his existence, I know there's something very wrong. They may argue, like all brothers and sisters, but when Asha is oblivious of him, it's not natural.

Our Journey, by Lee, Day 9

I have persuaded Asha to tell me what is troubling her. I was watching the tiller last night, and asked her to keep me company. We worked round to the fact that she is going through considerable private turmoil because she does not want to lose her supra-normal vision, her capacity to know a person's inner state by looking at the colour of their inner jewels. As we well know, she sees these on the subtle golden thread, the loom of the soul, as she calls it, within everyone when she puts her attention on their inner nature.

She admitted to me that she doesn't want to be like the rest of us who only feel these inner centres of power. She treasures her unique ability because she is sure it could help us out of trouble, and maybe even save all our lives. She can't resist practising on us to make sure she can still see within people. Naturally, forcing her mind to go into this state of awareness, instead of letting it happen naturally, pushes her more and more into a permanent semi-trance. This is why she has been staring at the water for hours on end. Raynor has also noticed this tendency of Asha's to be only half with us, but said that she has always been dreamy, and left it at that. We will keep a watch on her in case she gets worse.

Nog had different problems and being chased by Derwin was only one of them. To begin with he was highly suspicious of this unsteady world, but soon began to enjoy himself when he discovered that he could catch the flying fish that periodically flopped onto the deck. So he joined Conwenna in the fishing department, except his method was to prowl slowly a round the boat waiting for a flying fish to fall at his feet. Sometimes he picked it up and delivered it to Raynor. Other times he ate it because there wasn't much else for him.

We had now been floating northwards for twenty days. Food and water had begun to run low: especially water. This was because one of the water barrels was tipped up when Derwin was chasing Nog around the deck. Regrettably the top had been off the barrel at the time and most of its water has been spilled. Although we travelled a great distance we had not so far seen any land, and apart from some rain, and one rather windy day, the weather was excellent. That afternoon Ahren espied an island over to the east, almost on the horizon.

'We're going to have to get some water very soon or we'll have to start squeezing liquid out of the fish,' said Lee after looking at the state of our water supply.

'Don't joke, I feel ill enough already,' groaned Tandi.

'It's not a joke,' said Lee sharply, 'that's how sailors survive when there's no fresh water.'

'In any case, unless an island presents itself in the current we must make for that one over there,' I insisted, temporarily coming out of my daydream.

'But we were warned not to leave the current,' said Conwenna anxiously.

'Maybe we'll soon get to the Emperor's Island,' added Raynor hopefully.

'We'd best decide soon,' Lee continued, at the rudder, 'or I won't be able to turn the raft.'

'Heggo can't live on fish juice,' muttered Ahren.

'What harm can we come to by just filling our water tanks?' I pleaded.

'Plenty,' Lee sighed, but no one took any notice of him.

We voted on it and it was four to three in favour of landing on the island or anyway having a look at it from close quarters. Raynor was more concerned about everybody's health than anything else; Ahren's boredom was making him especially restless and Tandi longed for dry land and something solid underfoot which didn't heave like her stomach and the sea. I had a strange attraction for the island, a kind of fear and curiosity at the same time.

Soon after we had changed course and were sailing towards the island a large school of dolphins came swimming up and tried to stop the raft from making headway. They butted the sides of the raft with their snouts, jumped in and out of the water in front of it and made progress very difficult. We were about to start beating them off with ropes and Ahren was considering shooting at them with his bow and arrow, although no one seriously wanted to harm these beautiful creatures, when we saw the sinister triangular shapes of sharks' fins approaching. This was worse, as the sharks, judging by the size of their fins and the long shadows of their bodies just under the surface of the water, were large and dangerous.

Conwenna and Tandi screamed and ran into the cabin but the rest of us stayed by the rudder and watched, too fascinated to move. The sharks were trying to force the dolphins away from the raft, which after a short scuffle they managed to do. The dolphins knew the moment to escape, and after they had gone the sharks disappeared too. The sun was burning and brilliant and the heat, the glare of the sea and the strangeness of the whole incident bemused all of us. Everyone felt uneasy but no one felt confident enough to abandon what appeared to be our only hope of fresh water and food.

As we came closer to the island we saw that it was covered with trees and rich vegetation, especially on the lower slopes. It consisted of rolling hills, with bays and beaches in between stretches of high cliffs around the coast. As we cautiously approached the surf, which indicated reefs surrounding the island, we all, not only Tandi, felt sick and had a cramp in the hollow of our stomachs. We put it down to nerves about the dangerous coral reefs around the island, which had to be carefully negotiated, even in this calm water.

Raynor and Ahren, who were at the front of the raft taking depth soundings, found a broad channel and with their help Lee successfully steered the raft through to the quieter water beyond. We anchored the raft in a horseshoe shaped bay almost surrounded by high cliffs and saw that the island was indeed beautiful, with wisps of cloud hovering over the highest hills in the distance. It was definitely a place where we would find water and most probably food as well, so we left the raft anchored in the natural harbour and took the dinghy that was stowed on the deck.

We began to row ashore, watching carefully for signs of life, but saw nothing and even persuaded Heggo to swim after us in the calm clear water. Having reached the beach we hid the boat well above the high tide marks, under some trees. The water barrels were left with it while we searched for a suitable stream. As we landed on the shore we again all felt a cramp in our stomachs. Despite our urgent need for water, Lee had a sudden desire to leave as a wave of revulsion towards the place overcame him, but even with all these subtle warnings we did not turn back. We did not yet understand that these inner messages were far more accurate than our rational minds, which could weave dangerous 'truths' within us.

Ahren tethered Heggo by some lush grass at the side of the stream and we followed it through the woods up a steep hill. We decided to see where the stream came from before filling our water barrels. There were plenty of birds calling in the trees up above but not much else in the way of animal life. It was a tropical climate, so while some trees had fruits, some had flowers and others were resting with bare branches. We recognised most of the fruits and nuts, and took turns to climb up the trees, shake the branches and make the produce fall off so we could collect it.

Tandi recognised some pumpkins growing on a vine in a tall tree. They were shaped like yellow wheels. She told us that they were well worth the climb, because they were good to eat and lasted a long time without going bad. Derwin was excellent at climbing but as he was to have to do some acrobatics to get them he took off his precious key: the one with the green jewels on its ten petals, and gave it to Lee to wear for safekeeping.

Further up the hill we found the source of the stream. The trees thinned out as we went higher, and from here we had a good view of the island. We sat down to have a rest and could see fold after fold of wooded hills interspersed with open grassland. In the valleys we thought we could see some cultivated patches, but it was difficult to be sure in the heat haze. Somehow all the warnings slipped our minds, and we assumed we were on a beautiful, but probably uninhabited island.

We went down by a slightly different route, but instead of finishing up at the bay we took a wrong turning and found ourselves in a narrow valley further inland. The valley bottom was clear of trees and we saw a small cottage with a thatched roof badly in need of repair. In front of the hovel was a garden filled with a few flowers, lots of weeds and some straggly rows of vegetables.

The others stopped while still in the trees, but something got into me and I walked straight out into the open. It was as if I was being drawn. As I looked at the cottage, for a moment I saw a smutty pall of smoke hanging over it. A part of me said: 'Danger! Avoid it'. But then a strange mesmerizing attraction took over. I felt a strong desire to walk towards it.

Apart from Lee, and Nog, who Lee was holding onto by his collar, the others followed me; they all trusted my judgement. Two scrawny women came across the meadow: one was elderly, skinny and looked like a witch while the younger had a pale, drawn face. At the same time, two enormous black cats and a wolf-like creature came bounding towards us and caught our attention with their hypnotic leers.

'Please don't go away!' cried the younger of the women in a pathetic voice. 'The animals won't hurt you.'

Nog and Lee were at the back of the party. Nog whimpered and he and Lee quickly and quietly withdrew into the foliage. Lee signalled to him to be quiet. Mercifully he was and they climbed the hill through the thick undergrowth to a spot from where Lee could see and not be seen, as something very odd was happening to the rest of us. When I had first caught sight of the two women, I had noticed for a split second that the inner jewels of their souls were a rotten brown colour.

'My name is Lamprey. Do come to our cottage,' whined the elder lady. 'We are cooking a meal of some lovely vegetables from our garden. Won't you come and join us?' Raynor felt hot on his hands and the whole left side of his body was burning even though he was still in the shade. All he could think was, 'Surely if there is anything wrong, Asha would have picked it up?' We were invited in, and soon the meal was served. The women explained to us that they lived simply because they had given nearly everything they had to the ruler of the island.

'He is called Sir Tootle Dumpattick,' whined the younger one. 'He's going to start a New World Order, beginning with this island.'

The food tasted stale, but as guests we did not complain. After we had finished we sat outside in the garden feeling nauseous. Nog and Lee were hiding in the trees and Lee was snacking off the delicious fruits and nuts we had collected earlier. When he saw the rest of us after our meal he was shocked at how pale and ill we looked. He was just about to come out of hiding and try to do something, when down the path behind the shack came a cavalcade of people riding asses, which had such stupid faces that even Heggo would have looked intelligent beside them. The procession came to a halt and the two women came out to meet them.

'Hello, I see you've got some recruits for our glorious New World State,' said the leader of the band, a weedy man with a long nose and very long ears. 'I have come to invite you two noble ladies, and your new friends too, to a meeting which Sir Tootle Dumpattick has called. We are going to witness the start of a great new experiment to help us rule the world.'

Lee realised they were raving mad. However he decided to stay in hiding for the time being and see if an opportunity should arise to rescue us. These people and their creepy animals had some sinister power, but for some reason Lee was immune to it.

Soon the whole group, including us, made off into the woods. Ahren had left his bow and arrows and a couple of fat birds he had shot outside the cottage, and when he left had forgotten them, for some strange reason. When the coast was clear Lee ran down to the empty cottage and picked up the bow and arrows, then crept after us at a safe distance as the path wound its way through the hills into the middle of the island. He now realised where he had gone wrong when we came down the hill and this time he put notches in the trees with his hunting knife, so he would not get lost again.

After some time the party came to a deep valley with sadly whispering pine trees growing on the sides. The bottom of the valley was open and he saw a palace, which reminded him of a plate of cream buns. The sides of the valley were steep and the pine trees grew close to the walls of the building, so Lee was able to hide out of sight once more. When the rest of us arrived at the gatehouse of the palace, we were all questioned. After a short argument we were let through the gate without being searched. There was not much mutual trust among the inmates of Dumpattick's headquarters.

Lee and Nog sat on a bed of damp pine needles on the hillside and Lee commanded Nog to "stay." He gave Lee a look of disgust, then put his nose on his tail and went to sleep. It was evening by now, the light was fading and Lee left him and crept closer. The meeting to which the six of us had been invited was in a large council chamber. Lee watched us going in, and after walking along the side of the valley he climbed up a suitable pine tree, from where he could see through one of the floor-to-ceiling windows at the side of the large room.

Inside were row upon row of animals. In front of them were people with sickly faces and vacant expressions. Some of the animals looked vaguely human and some of the humans had long ears and facial hair, which made them look very bestial. Dumpattick was seated on a rostrum in the centre of his followers. He had a beaky nose and small eyes and looked as if someone had dressed him up as the King of the Crows for a fancy dress party. We Teletsians had entered and were standing at the back of the room.

Something made Lee clasp at the key hanging around his neck. Not his own, but the ten petalled, green jewelled key that Derwin had given him for safekeeping. Instantly his fears vanished. The people looked pitiable, the animals grotesque and he chuckled to himself. He wondered how anyone could possibly fall to the tricks of the old fellow.

A lot of straw had been laid out all over the floor. On the gallery at one side, a number of Dumpattick's human followers were standing, perched precariously on the guardrail. They were all wearing artificial birds' wings. At a signal from him they all launched themselves off the gallery, frantically flapping their wings. This however did no good whatsoever and they fell in a heap into the piles of straw.

'Wonderful!' said the old crow. 'Tremendous progress!'

Lee found it extremely hard not to giggle and wondered just how much worse they could possibly have been to start with, if this pathetic performance was progress. The audience was clapping wildly.

'Madcaps,' Lee thought, clutching the emerald inlaid key. Dumpattick began to speak.

'We need certain magic powers to make us the greatest people alive! Then you will rule the world. To get them, we have to travel to the secret kingdom in the north. If we can learn to fly, we'll get there fast and easily. Soon we'll be able to fly to the mountain kingdom and I'll be the king!' The old crow's thoughts had run away with him, but he quickly recovered and went on, 'I mean, the kingdom will be yours, I'm merely the guide.' Lee, watching carefully, was astounded that not a single person in the room had reacted to the old crow's slip of the tongue.

Lee had seen enough and decided to leave matters until the saner light of morning. He climbed sadly down the tree and crept up to where he had left Nog, but the dog had had one of his lapses of obedience and had taken off somewhere. Lee dared not risk calling him and was near despair, because he had known all along that this island was cursed. He blamed himself that he had not stopped the rest of us from landing here. Nevertheless, he made his way down the valley. It was a long walk back to the bay and hopefully the raft. The night was pitch black; to begin with none of the moons were up and he could not find the notches he had cut in the trees. He stumbled on blindly until he was well out of sight of the Cream Bun Palace, then sat down on a rock and to drive away despondency took out his flute and started to play - the same tune that he and Raynor had sung at the Temple of Support. Slowly his courage and optimism returned.

After that he stopped playing, clasped the green jewel and immediately two things happened. Firstly, Nog came running up and by the smell of him he had been hunting for his supper. Secondly, the bright Moon of Good Fortune rose over the wooded hills and shed enough light for him to walk by. Nog took the end of Lee's overshirt in his mouth, tried to look comforting and led him back to the bay. There they found Heggo munching the grass in the moonlight, the boat still safely where we had left it and the raft at anchor out in the calm water of the bay.

Lee left Heggo near the stream and rowed himself and Nog out to the raft. It was warm and he lay down on the deck on his bedroll and tried to sleep, clutching the green and gold jewel as if they were his only hope, because somehow he knew green went with the water element. Nog howled at the moon until Lee shouted at him to stop it or take a quick swim. Finally, at the end of the worst evening he could ever remember, he went to sleep with Nog pacing uneasily round and round the raft. He kept going to Raynor's bedroll and sniffing it, ill at ease about his beloved master. Nog was friendly towards all of us, especially if we had titbits, but Raynor was the human that mattered most to him.

Lee awoke just before dawn to find the raft rocking a great deal. Nog was dancing around in an excited fashion, barking and wagging his tail. Lee crawled sleepily to the side of the raft, still clutching the emerald key, and saw the water churning with the backs of many dolphins, swimming around the raft and trying to push it out to sea.

'Oh, no, not again!' he grumbled out loud. At that moment a big dolphin popped its head over the parapet, and he was so surprised that he dropped the green jewelled key he had been holding and it fell onto the deck. In a trice the dolphin had it in his mouth, flopped back into the water and swam away out of sight, followed by its companions. What more could go wrong? Utterly dejected, Lee went into the cabin, hoping for oblivion, but it did not come. After tossing and turning and wondering what on earth to do next he gave up the hopeless task of sleeping and went out to have a look at the sunrise. Nog came and made a fuss of his human.

Somehow, regardless of how awful the events of the night had been, when the sun cast a golden path over the water to herald the arrival of a new day, Lee felt slightly better. At this moment he remembered what Stellamar had taught them and wondered if it could cure emotional pain as well as it had Derwin's physical problem. He put his left hand towards the rising sun and his right hand on his forehead. Immediately his depression lifted.

The first thing he needed was some breakfast, so he made himself some from the stores on the raft. After eating he raised the anchor and sailed it over to the other side of the bay and hid it in a cleft of the rocks at the base of the cliffs that towered above the further side of the cove. He told Nog to stay aboard and guard it. He didn't quite know how the morning would develop, but to be on the safe side, he took his own hunting knife, catapult, Ahren's bow and arrows and Raynor's catapult with him, then rowed back to find Heggo. He also made certain that the dinghy was well hidden. If he did manage to rescue us the boat and raft were essential for our escape.

He moved Heggo's tether, then walked up the hill where we had been the day before, so as to have a good look at the island. He was careful to keep himself hidden and this time climbed to the very top of the hill. He had a look around him and then, feeling tired because he had not had much sleep, lay down on his back in the long grass to have a rest. At once he was in his own small world where all he could see were the tops of the grasses and flowers in a circle above him and in the centre the dark blue sky with a few clouds floating overhead. He gazed up into the infinite blueness and soon dozed off.

It must have been mid-morning when his attention was caught by what looked like an enormous bird flying in the sky, wheeling down in large circles in his direction. At first he thought it might be just coincidence, but the closer this thing came, the stranger it was. It was too big for a bird and was more of an oval shape - a flying bird's nest? A boat? He thought that he too was being affected by this mad island and was hallucinating. He lay very still. His heart sank and he wished he had stayed under the shelter of the trees, but the last thing he expected was to have to face danger from the skies- he assumed that in the long grass he would be safe. As it came nearer he hid behind a little bush. By now he was sure it had seen him. Soon he heard a whoosh and a strange humming noise like distant bees, and felt the only too real hallucination's shadow as it blotted out the sunlight. He cringed in suspense, fearing the worst.

CHAPTER 12

HELP FROM THE KEY

There was a heavy thud as 'it' came to earth. The humming stopped and then he heard footsteps coming in his direction. Lee curled up under his bush, not daring to look and wishing, for the first and only time in his life, that he could be a grasshopper, just for a short while. Then a hand placed in front of his face a green and gold jewelled key which either was, or was identical to the one he had recently lost to the dolphin.

'Is this by any chance yours?' someone inquired. Lee looked up, relieved. He saw a strongly built young man with black hair, a dark skin, full smiling lips and simple clothes: a rough cloak, plain tunic and leather sea boots up to his knees.

'Yes, more or less,' Lee replied, almost speechless with delight to see someone who was neither corpselike nor mad.

'At least one of you is all right then. Were you wearing this jewel?'

'Yes, but...'

'Well take it and put it on. No ramblings, no long explanations, be brief and to the point. Keep your attention centred, between over-confidence and fear, and maybe we can salvage the situation.' The stranger was firm but seemed apprehensive of what state Lee was in, as if he did not want to get too closely involved, but at the same time wanted to help. 'The dolphins indicated that you were not alone to start with and that you have a boat of some kind. Is that so?' he continued.

'Yes,' Lee mumbled, trying his utmost best to be brief, as the stranger demanded. The young man saw the joke and smiled; the ice was broken.

'Where are the rest of your group?'

'The last time I saw them they were in the palace of that old crow creature,' Lee started to get his wits back. The young stranger smiled again, and compassion and friendliness came over his face.

'That crow creature, as you so aptly call him, is a very dangerous black magician. His empires are the souls of people seeking truth, but who think they can find it for themselves without humbly respecting the power of greater beings than we humans are. With luck we'll be in time to save your friends.' He turned to the strange contraption nestling on the ground behind him. 'This flies by a combination of a powerful mind on the part of the driver and a mixture of mercury and sulphur on the part of the machinery. It'll take us to the crow's headquarters. Oh, by the way, my name is Merien. What's yours?'

'Lee.'

'Pleased to meet you, Lee. Let's go. Get in. We don't have any time to waste. Bring your weapons with you because we may need them.'

The machine did look slightly like a bird. It had retractable wings for landing, and perhaps steering, and also large moveable hooks, one on each side, rather like a vast eagle's talons. It had more attachments that could be used as weapons, and it would have been a formidable adversary in a battle. There were two seats, one behind the other, and a control panel which had a wheel and some scientific instruments in front of the forward seat, so it was like sitting inside half a very large egg. The young man pressed some buttons and the humming started. Lee, sitting in the back, was nervous, but this was no time to admit it. They slowly floated up into the air, Lee had absolutely no idea how, and the young man had his attention fully on the dials and knobs. He wondered if Merien's degree of concentration was what kept the machine up. It didn't bear thinking about. What if he sneezed? Or had an uncontrollable itch?

They began to fly slowly towards the centre of the island where they espied the palace, looking more than ever like a plate of cream buns as it nestled in its valley below. Lee began to enjoy the ride, as Merien was skilful and confident, and held the craft steady.

'My master keeps this flying machine at his island,' he called out. 'It's on loan from the Emperor in case of emergencies like this.' They floated down in some pine trees at the top of the valley where the palace was built. 'Now, we'll fight black magic with white magic! Come on, we're going to rescue your friends. My master has told me more or less how to deal with these horrendous types and we'll improvise if needs be.'

Lee assumed that if Merien had some contact with the Emperor he was fairly powerful. Lee hoped so, because he knew that people like the Sorcerers and Dumpattick could be terrible if they were threatened in any way. Merien might laugh, but the joke could come to a sorry end, and very soon, at that.

They walked through the woods and sat down on the ground near where Lee had left Nog the night before. They could see the courtyard and the whole place was deserted even though it was midday. Merien and Lee crept down nearer the palace to a window where they could hear voices behind drawn curtains, hid in some evergreen bushes close to the walls and Lee recognised the voice of the old crow.

'My dear Lampray, you've excelled yourself,' he began. 'Those children have fallen into our trap, thanks to the drugs you put in your cooking. The rulers of Teletsia warned us of them by carrier seagull. Do you know they could ruin all our plans?'

'I felt there was something hostile about them,' replied Lampray.

'They too are seeking the northern country. If they get there before we do it will be the end for us and the Teletsian High Priests. When I return these children to the Teletsians I'll be rewarded with weapons and money, which we need to conquer the northern country when we get there.'

Merien and Lee had heard enough and went back up the hill. Once they were sitting safely hidden again, Merien looked gravely at Lee.

'Your friends *must* be rescued, and fast,' he looked worried. 'I understand now why he so wants to catch you.' Lee nodded. A light wind set the pines lamenting, reflecting his mood.

'Why don't they set guards?'

'Although they're more than half mad their powers of mesmerism are formidable, so they assume they don't need them. As long as you've got that green jewel they can't control your mind.'

'What if I just walk in and ask to see my friends?'

'Yes, why not?' Merien was impressed by Lee's courage. 'Go to the doorkeeper and ask to see them. But don't look directly into the eyes of either man or beast and on no account eat or drink anything. When you find your friends, your most difficult task will be to persuade them that they need rescuing. They may think you're the one in trouble. You must show them the jewelled key, and take these six extra keys to this realm, and put them around the necks of your friends.' Merien gave Lee six keys similar to the one he had borrowed from Derwin. 'If that has no effect, throw some of this water over them.' At this Merien took out of his bag a small bottle of carved crystal with a golden stopper. 'This water, like the key, transmits the power of this area.

It's ordinary water but the Emperor and Empress who rule this part of Mother Earth have supercharged it with concentrated force. They took it from a well on their island, which expresses the spiritual power of this part of the world. Then they asked the all-pervading power to imbue it with even more potency, and the result is a very special type of water. If that fails too you'll just have to do the best you can, but don't waste time arguing. That'll just get you caught in the web of lies and mesmerism as well.

'While you're inside, I'll take the flying machine and do a few things to help us. I'll meet you back here, hopefully with all your friends. My master is the deadly enemy of Dumpattick.'

'Why are you taking all this trouble over us?'

'I'm a pupil of Master Theon, the renowned sailor and teacher of wisdom, who tries to guide sincere travellers across the Sea of Illusion. Anyone seeking to cross it in a northerly direction is best to keep straight on the central current. You and your friends, like so many others, had to leave it. But the green jewelled key you have holds the power and freedom of this realm. It and the water will create invisible bonds of love and protection around you and your friends. The dolphins recognised your key and tried to stop you from coming here, because they are the sentries of the sea.'

'Why doesn't the Emperor destroy the old crow?'

'That's the problem. The Emperor could wipe out all these creatures in the twinkling of an eye, but he is righteous and moral. Unfortunately in times gone by Dumpattick did certain deeds to please the Emperor and was offered a reward, because His Imperial Highness is very bountiful. This crafty devil asked to have just one little island, the first in the sea, and now he catches travellers as they venture across it. I ask you, that's some way to show your gratitude!'

While Merien was talking he dug a little hole in the ground by his side. He poured a few drops of water from the crystal bottle into the hole and said a few words that Lee did not understand. Within a minute or so, to Lee's utter amazement, a spring of water began to flow out from it down the hillside into the valley where the palace stood.

'The power of the Emperor will be strong in this stream,' said Merien. 'How many are you?'

'Six and me.'

'Seven is a good number. Go now, and try to come back seven.' Merien gave Lee the bottle of water and he hid it and the extra keys under his jerkin. 'You'd better leave me that bow and arrows, because they'll not let you take them in. We might need them later.' Lee gave them to Merien but kept his small catapult and a knife, just in case, and hid them inside his jerkin. Then he walked out of the woods towards the gatehouse of the Cream Bun Palace. His heart glowed in the hope that with the help of Merien, his magical water and the keys he might be able to save his friends.

Lee's knees felt weak with apprehension as he stood before the gatehouse wondering what to do next, and he tried to remember how brave Raynor had been when he had faced the Specials and the quicksand. If ever there was a time to call on extra powers it was now, and he allowed his attention to go to the top of his head, the place of the many petalled flower at the top of the Tree of Life. As he did so his awareness settled down and he began to feel calmness and courage, as the subtle, all pervading power flowed through him. He clutched the green key around his neck, felt more confident, smiled, and simultaneously the sun appeared from behind a cloud. He banged manfully on the great wooden door with its snarling knocker. There was a total silence except for the echo of the knocker in the hollow hall of the gatehouse.

Lee banged on the knocker again, the one screw that had been holding it into the door fell out and the whole thing came away in his hands. He was left holding the grimacing copper face, green with age and neglect, and felt somewhat bewildered. What next? He placed the knocker on the ground and tried the equally decrepit bell pull at the side of the door. He gave it a tug, half expecting that it too would come away in his hand. It didn't, but it didn't work either.

He stepped backwards, cupped his hands around his mouth and yelled to the window above, 'Oi! Anyone around? I'd like to come in!' Again there was silence but after a minute or two a woman's head appeared at the window, hair in rags for curlers, looking like a scarecrow.

'Wait, I'm coming down,' she called out and Lee soon heard the noise of shuffling feet. The door creaked and an anaemic woman, wearing a dressing gown fit for the dustbin and slippers that were mostly holes, peered around the crack of the door with bleary eyes.

'What d'you want so early in the morning?' she asked sleepily.

'I am part of a group of people who arrived here yesterday to seek an audience with your leader. I got lost and would like to rejoin my friends. It's lonely out here by myself,' Lee recited his rehearsed speech.

'Oh, all right then, you'd better come in. We have to stay quietly in our rooms today while our great master does rituals to ensure the success of our avowed mission to become a New World State.' He was amazed that this bemused ragtag of a woman could come out with such high flown words, and realised that her speech was part of the mind-numbing jargon of her fanatic calling. 'You're supposed to be searched for anything metal before you enter,' she went on moodily, 'but I want to go back to bed and have another snooze, so I'll let you off. We have to be up all night, you see, because our master is stronger then.'

She yawned, indicated for Lee to follow her, and led him through the gatehouse and out into the sunlit courtyard. He wondered what 'metal objects' she was supposed to search for and then returned to his state of inner thoughtless peace. It was safer than musing about what went on in this place. The woman pointed to a building separate from the main palace.

'That's the guesthouse, they're probably in there,' she drawled and shuffled off. He noticed that the toes which peeped out of the holes in her slippers were remarkably claw-like, but thought it was because she never got around to cutting her toenails.

The door of the guesthouse was standing partly open and Lee sidled in unobtrusively. He heard snoring coming from the downstairs room leading off the hallway, peeped cautiously round the door and then drew back with a start. He saw, to his horror, two wolf-like creatures and a whole clutch of black cats curled up and sleeping together, emitting very human snores and murmuring in their sleep in human voices. He assumed he must have misheard. He left them sleeping and went stealthily up the stairs at the end of the hallway. As Lee did so his heart jumped for joy because he could hear Raynor and Tandi talking to one another in the upstairs room. He entered the room and saw they were alone, but both looked very out of touch with reality.

'Hello, am I glad to find you!' Lee cried, delighted to see them more or less all right.

'You got left behind,' murmured Tandi, her brows puckered as if she were trying to remember something.

'I've come to rescue all of you,' Lee went on enthusiastically.

'Why? We're fine here,' Raynor slurred.

'Here we go,' thought Lee, 'just as Merien warned.'

'There's something odd about this place, but it's not too bad,' continued Tandi. 'Why don't we stay here for a while and see if we like it?' Lee forgot for a moment that he was not supposed to try and reason with them.

'These people are out of their minds and they want to make us crazy too,' he exploded. 'Plus they're going to send us back to the Sorcerers,' then he stopped as he remembered what Merien had said about their being under hypnosis.

'But they might have a quick way to the mountain kingdom,' drawled Raynor. 'They seem to be trying to get there too.'

'This lot,' Lee interrupted, 'are in cloud cuckoo land. Come on, you two! Snap out of it! Put these keys around your necks and let's go and find the others.' He took two of the keys Merien had given him, and before either of them could protest he placed one around each of their necks.

At that moment he heard the hiss of some black cats and the bark of a wolf as they came bounding up the stairs to see what was going on. He took out the bottle of supercharged water and ran out into the passage hoping to stop them. They were coming up the last flight of stairs and he threw some water at them. Two or three drops landed on each creature.

They yelled in agony as if they had been burnt with boiling oil, writhed in pain and fell backwards down the stairs onto the landing in a semi-conscious heap. He was still holding the rest of the jewelled keys on chains, and the bottle. Lee was surprised at how easily the nightmarish beasts had been stopped, but realised it was only temporary. He darted down the stairs after them, drew his hunting knife and sunk it into each of them before they could come to their senses. As the life drained out of their bodies and they died, a horrible thing happened. The cattishness and the wolf skins fell away from them, and there, lying on the landing, were four small human corpses.

Lee jumped to his feet and bolted up the stairs once more, sick with shock, but more determined than ever to get us out of this place. Raynor and Tandi had lost their vacant stares and now looked plain frightened.

'Wherever are we?' asked Raynor, bemused. 'I've had the most demonic dream.'

'So have I,' wailed Tandi.

'We're in big trouble,' Lee said. 'You must show me where the others are, like now!'

'Let's see,' Tandi was still vague and distracted and not at all her usual self. 'Yes, it comes back now. They're over there, through the door in the corner. You don't have to go out into the passage again.' She stood up and led Lee into the next room where the rest of us were sitting on the floor in a complete trance.

'Why are they like this?' Lee cried in dismay. 'You two were bad enough but they're a thousand times worse.'

'They felt sick this morning and some woman came and gave them a special inhaling treatment; they were told it would make them better. She had them inhale some sweet smelling smoke and now look at them!' said Raynor. 'Tandi and I went into the other room because we thought it smelled ghastly.'

In this second room Ahren was murmuring something about the birds on the ceiling, which were in fact part of the wallpaper, coming off and flying around the room. Conwenna was smiling vacantly and following these imaginary birds with her fingers. Derwin was walking around on all fours and growling, and I was sitting in the corner by myself. Lee knew it was a waste of time saying anything so just took out the bottle of water, undid the golden stopper and sprinkled the water round the room and over us, his bemused friends.

Immediately the muzziness in Lee's head and the singing in his ears disappeared. The muzziness either came from the residue of the smoke or from the fact that he shared the inner sensations of the rest of us, but whatever, he felt better. He went over to the windows, which were tightly closed with the shutters pulled across them, and flung open both the shutters and the windows to let the sun in. He stared in surprise at what he saw outside.

The whole area outside had turned into a large pond and more water was pouring in by the minute through the archway of the gatehouse and between the different buildings. The people, cats and wolves were afraid to enter even the shallowest water, and those who did went into contortions and screamed as if the water had been vitriolic acid. Lee looked at the sky and saw that the great-grandfather of all storms was brewing down in the valley and approaching rapidly.

He turned around to see what was happening to the others: Ahren and Conwenna seemed much better, Derwin had stopped growling and was standing up, but I still sat on the ground and looked confused. Lee took the rest of the green keys and put one around each of our necks. The others looked around as if someone had just removed blindfolds from their eyes.

'Oh please don't put the nasty thing on; can't you see I'm bird watching?' I pleaded. 'That's why I'm so still. That water made the birds go away. They fly so easily, I wish I could do the same.'

'Put this key around your neck, or we are going to have to leave without you,' Lee threatened, in no mood for imaginary birds.

'I don't mind if you do. Who are you anyway?' I gazed at him as if I had never seen him before. Derwin, improving by the minute as the key and the water took their effect, snatched the key from Lee.

'Asha, it's me, you idiot!' he shouted. Something woke up in me and I smiled. Raynor took me firmly by the arms. Derwin took the key and put its chain around my neck.

'Ow, it hurts! What are you doing to me? It stings, the chain!' I shook my head and woke up. 'Where am I? What's going on? Was I asleep?' Raynor let go and Derwin hugged me, utterly relieved that I was all right.

'It's a crazy nightmare island,' Lee cried. 'Come quickly, or we'll never get away.'

'Look, we're in luck - a back window,' called Ahren, 'there are ladders and scaffolding outside – probably builders.' Even semi-drugged, he had been looking for a way out. He climbed out onto a ledge and moved one of the ladders so it was against the window, and another that could lead us down to the ground that was now disappearing under a rising flood. He helped Tandi out first. I had to be carried by Raynor, but somehow all of us except Lee managed to climb down the ladders into the water. The ground sloped upwards at the back of the building so the water was not so deep here. Lee was still up above in the room, and shouted to us below to make our way up the hillside.

'There's a chap up there who'll help you. Tell him I'm coming in a moment,' he yelled as we waded through the flood.

Before leaving, Lee bolted the doors from the inside, and as he did so he heard the sounds of people and animals coming up the stairs. By the anger in their voices he realised that they had found the bodies he had killed. It was definitely time to go. He jumped out of the window and slid down the ladders. No time to climb down. As he splashed into the water below he smashed at the scaffolding with the lower ladder and the whole rickety structure collapsed into the deepening flood. He heard the noise of someone breaking down the door he had bolted and saw the woman from the gatehouse staring furiously at him as he stood in the swirling waters up to his waist.

This was not the moment for the niceties of chivalry, so Lee took out the catapult he carried with him, loaded it with a stone from his pocket, and aimed at her yellow catlike face. She withdrew to avoid being hit and a wolf appeared at the window. Lee loosed the stone and caught the beast right between the eyes. It toppled out of the window, hit the water and disappeared screeching under the surface. A black cat appeared and he reloaded his weapon - the cat looked as if it was about to jump down on top of him. He shot again but this time missed, then turned and waded as fast as he could through the floodwaters. The water was now deep enough to swim and the cat lost its nerve and went back into the room. Only later did Lee discover that this supercharged water burnt like fire those who opposed the power of the Emperor, the spiritual guardian of the sea.

We waited anxiously for Lee under the cover of the trees. He joined us and we ran on, and collapsed at the feet of Merien. None of us was adversely affected by the water. On the contrary, it had further woken us out of our trance. Merien smiled calmly, sitting as he was by his now gushing torrent that poured out from the ground where he had made a tiny spring shortly before.

'All present?' he enquired.

'Yes, thanks,' Lee croaked, completely out of breath. 'This is Merien, folks.'

'Glad you're all in one piece. Looks like the Emperor has had enough of this lot!' Merien pointed at the cascading water, then asked Lee, 'You all right? Was it easy to rescue them?'

'Not too bad, thanks to your keys.'

'We're not safe yet. Let's get out of here,' Merien stood up. 'You boys, take your weapons.' We made off as fast as we could, scrambling up the tree-covered hillside. We could hear the din of people shouting and screaming inside the palace, but there were also noises of pursuit.

Fortunately we had a good start and soon came to the place where the valley began to narrow into a ravine between two hills. Here the storm which had been brewing broke over us with a great crash of thunder and rain began to come down in earnest. We battled against the downpour until we reached the narrowest point in the valley.

'Don't worry about the weather,' shouted Merien, 'I've been taught how to deal with this!' He laughed and raised his hand and the rain died down to a shower for a short time so he could speak without making himself hoarse.

'Give me back the extra keys I lent you, Lee. I'll put them on the paths, and those creatures will be scared to come near them.' Merien lowered his hand and the shower turned back into a cataclysmic tempest. He took the spare keys and disappeared into the wall of water. Our lungs hurt from all the running, and Tandi and I sunk to the ground in exhaustion.

As he went away and we were alone in the storm, we heard the screeching of cats, the barking of wolves and the shouts of men and women. The cold rain had brought us well back to our senses.

'Quick, up the sides of the ravine!' Raynor said, and we all scurried up to a deep dry ledge half way up, with overhanging rocks above it. The sounds of pursuit became louder. Lee took out his catapult again. Raynor also had a catapult and Ahren a bow and arrows. He took the waterproof cover off the bow, strung it and took out an arrow.

The cats and wolves came around the corner of the ravine. A blinding flash of lightning split the sky in two and we girls levered out rocks and dropped them on the heads of the vicious beasts, aiming as best we could. The animals hesitated; they were frightened of something. When the next flash of lightning came I saw it was one of the green and gold keys that Merien had placed just below us on the path. Although some of the animals were now wounded and all had halted, they didn't give up and started climbing the sides of the ravine to try and get at us from above.

At this point some men also appeared around the corner, and Ahren, deadly accurate with his bow and arrow, managed to seriously wound two of them. We jumped down onto the path again and began to run for it. At that moment, out of the skies came some large rocks. They crushed two of our pursuers and temporarily scared off the rest. Up above in the clouds was Merien in his flying machine, with more rocks in its 'talons', which he dropped on the remaining

men and beasts.

We ran for our lives, not knowing when or where we might meet more of Sir Tootle's lynch mob. After a while we stopped again for breath and heard a roar almost like another earthquake. We looked back and saw Merien in his flying machine aiming more rocks at strategic points on the sides of the ravine. Part of the hillside fell down and made a dam across the valley below the Cream Bun Palace. We saw the tiny figure of Merien high in the sky waving with both hands as if all was going as he intended. We heard another roar and felt the ground shudder as more of the hillside collapsed into the valley floor, and the flying machine disappeared into the cloud cover, this time permanently.

All sounds of battle and turmoil had ceased, the torrential rain quietened to a steady downpour and seven very wet young people later reached the bay where we found a bedraggled Heggo sheltering under a tree. We untied him, launched the dinghy, filled the water casks and loaded them onto the small boat, then rowed out to the raft where Nog had a mild fit of ecstasy at seeing Raynor again. Heggo, swimming steadily at the end of his rope, found all this emotion most unnecessary but allowed himself to be winched onto the raft with the little crane put there for that purpose. We crawled onto the deck and pulled the dinghy up too, then saw that the dolphins were waiting nearby. They took some ropes hanging off the end of the raft, and holding them in their mouths, began to tow us. Soon they were in the open sea, pulling us fast in a north-easterly direction.

We huddled together in the cabin, very cold and wet. Initially no one felt like saying anything and we sat in silence listening to the rain beating down on the raft. We were all in a state of shock except Derwin, who was depressingly jolly and did not appear to understand what we had just been through.

'We always finish our adventures soaking wet, don't we?' he said brightly.

'Tell me something new,' said Tandi moodily.

'This time we're even wetter than before, aren't we?' continued Derwin, not easily squashed.

'Oh dry up, Derwin,' grumbled Ahren, not realising he had made a dreadful pun.

'Very funny,' said Tandi acidly. She was exhausted, both physically and emotionally.

'And this time we don't have a nice hot bath to jump into,' added Conwenna, teeth chattering like a woodpecker.

'We could change our clothes,' suggested Raynor.

By the time we had found spare clothing and changed, sure enough the hot sun had come out once more, because the storm was localised in the area of Tootle Dumpattick's island. After warming ourselves up on the deck we all went into the cabin and had a sleep, but Lee awoke some hours later to hear the most exquisite singing accompanied by clear music.

He crept out onto the deck, where, by the light of two moons, was a sight which made the day a mere shadowy memory. Sitting on the edge of the raft, as the dolphins pulled it steadily through the black and silver night sea, was a party of mermen and mermaids, singing serene and gentle songs to the music of glass pipes. They were devotional songs, praising the Emperor and Empress, the beauty of the sea, its surface moods and the secrets of its depths, and thanking their form of god for guiding lost sailors who went astray on their voyage through the sea of life. Lee sat in the doorway of the cabin watching them, and the events of the recent past faded from his mind. He would have loved to have talked to them, but did not go any closer in case they should slip away.

Lee had been the only one to escape unscathed. He was sure that if he hadn't been wearing the key he too would have been caught in the sinister web of madness and mesmerism, and now the music and the starry sky exhilarated him. He was a seeker of truth and he had found his reason for living. How different he felt now from the deadening hopelessness of Teletsia! Rescuing his friends *had* been scary, and he suspected that many more tests lay ahead, but he felt courageous and joyful.

Lee hoped the soothing music was washing the nightmarish experience out of the rest of us as we slept, but I constantly moaned in my sleep. I struggled to ward off imaginary blows and twitched spasmodically. The only thing I remember about that time is darkness and fear.

Chapter 13

Return to Sanity

The next morning we all slept late, and the dolphins continued to take turns in towing us through the sea. Eventually everyone except me woke up and had a late breakfast. In the afternoon we reached a coral atoll. The dolphins towed us to the inner side of the atoll and left the raft fairly near the shore of the central island. On the seaward side was an arc of small, flattish islands which marked the outer edge of the atoll and on these islands were coconut palms, tall and graceful, bending their heads humbly towards the sea. In the centre was a larger island made up of a number of volcanoes, some extinct and some apparently still active. This island was clothed in forest right up to the lip of the volcanic cones.

In the cabin, I was still moaning in a fitful sleep, and tossing and turning in a disturbing fashion. I occasionally put my hands up to ward off unseen blows, as on the previous evening. Unfortunately all efforts to wake me failed but I did calm down whenever Lee or whoever was sitting with me at that moment directed the power in the elements, the sea or the sun, towards me, as Stellamar had taught us. At these times the bad dream which engulfed me temporarily passed away, but as soon as they stopped giving me this healing, I slipped back into insanity.

Derwin and Conwenna dangled their feet in the warm water over the side of the raft and saw a brilliantly coloured underwater garden beneath them in the clear lagoon. Derwin drew everyone's attention to the shoals of tiny, colourful fish. Then they heard voices over the water, and looked up to see two rowing boats coming towards them. One of the rowers was Merien.

'Hello, did you have a good journey with the dolphins?' he said to Lee.

'Yes, it was great.' Lee answered, as he was the only one who had spent much time watching what had gone on the night before. They all noticed the other man in the second boat.

'This is Uncle Mazdan, one of the sons of Master Theon. Master Theon is the master of all things worth knowing, but he is away on the other side of the world at the moment.'

'Good evening!' said Mazdan with a voice like a foghorn. 'Pleased to meet you. I'll take those of you who can't fit into Merien's boat.' Mazdan was stout and strong. His dark hair was tied back in a ponytail, sailor fashion, and he had a thick beard. In one ear was a gold earring and he wore a long loose shirt with leather breeches and high boots. He had a compelling expression on his face and might have been taken for a pirate as there was certainly a fierceness about him, but as Lee looked into his dark eyes he could see he was a person of profound wisdom, patience and love.

'Bring whatever you need and also the animals,' said Merien. 'You will probably be staying for a few days.' Merien helped the others get ready. Mazdan was not the sort of person who involved himself in the untidy details of everyday life and watched this decamping operation with an innocent amusement from the further end of the second rowing boat. He only raised his eyebrows slightly when Nog floundered into his boat to give him a right royal welcome.

'Um, sorry about the dog,' apologised Raynor, and tried to call Nog to heel, without any noticeable success.

'He's an excellent dog, no need to worry about *him*,' Mazdan patted Nog. By the way he said this, they felt he meant there was someone among us they should be worrying about. They all thought of me, still sleeping fitfully. Ahren and Lee were in the girls' part of the cabin with me.

'Let's carry her to the boat. She's bound to come around sooner or later,' suggested Ahren.

'But she's still groaning and throwing her hands around,' Lee added, extremely concerned.

'Perhaps Uncle Mazdan can help us with her,' Conwenna looked at me in horror from the door.

'All right, you ask him,' said Ahren, not too sure about this stern looking Mazdan. Conwenna walked along the deck near to where he was waiting in his boat.

'Excuse me uncle uh...captain. Could you help?' Conwenna didn't know what to expect from this imposing man who was to be our host, but she was game to come to my help when I needed it.

'Of course, little one, what is it?' replied Mazdan gently.

'One of the girls, Asha, she's older than me, keeps tossing and turning and moaning as if she's scared. Could you, could you possibly have a look at her?'

'Yes, that's why Merien had you come here. Show her to me at once!' Mazdan hauled himself onto the raft and Conwenna led him into the cabin. When he saw my pale and strained face he immediately knelt down, took me in his strong arms and soothed me like a baby. I vaguely remember this, among the nightmares. He was too shocked at my condition to say anything, but he picked me up, cradled me in his arms and laid me in his rowing boat. My fit had passed once again, and Mazdan started rowing me to the shore, leaving the rest to go with Merien.

They collected themselves and their belongings and all squeezed into Merien's boat. The atmosphere was less strained there.

'Your donkey's a good swimmer, isn't he?' laughed Merien.

'He's getting better with practice,' commented Ahren.

'Uncle Mazdan's wife will put your clothes to rights,' went on Merien, looking at the sodden and grubby piles in the boat with them. We had been at sea for some time and none of us were very domesticated, with the exception of Tandi, so this was good news. Lee looked up at the largest of the volcanic cones rising high above them on the island ahead. It was smoking considerably.

'Does it ever erupt?' Lee asked Merien anxiously.

'Oh yes, and half! Especially when Master Theon is angry! This island reacts to his moods, but the volcanoes never do us any harm. When rocks and molten lava are spewed out they always go down to the sea on the other side of the island from where we live, and when the lava reaches the sea and cools off in a cloud of steam, then Master Theon becomes calm again, because the water element has absorbed the anger.'

'Isn't it scary living with someone so powerful?'

'Theon's anger is always righteous anger. If you're more or less in tune with the laws of nature you've got nothing to fear,' replied Merien.

'Has he been angry lately?'

'Yes, we had quite a noisy and fiery eruption this morning. The dolphins have a system of sending messages through the sea and word was sent to Master Theon about Dumpattick having tried to capture you.'

'You mean the island responds to Master Theon even when he's not on it?' asked Raynor.

'Naturally,' responded Merien. 'He's furious with that devil for hypnotising you with his horrible cats and wolves. Those creatures were once people, but with his sorcery Dumpattick changed their bodies and personalities almost completely into animals.'

'Then it wasn't my imagination,' Lee groaned. 'I killed some of them when we were trying to escape. They turned back into human corpses when they died, but I assumed it was all a part of the whole mad nightmare.' Lee felt suddenly afraid. 'Was it murder?' He said anxiously, almost to himself.

'Was it wrong? Is that what you're trying to ask me?' interrupted Merien casually, and continued to row the boat as if they had been discussing the weather.

'Yes, was it wrong to have killed them?' asked Raynor, somewhat more detached than Lee.

'Hardly,' continued Merien, 'you were in a battle and you happened to kill a few of the enemy. If you hadn't escaped, your fate would have been much worse than physical death, I assure you. Forget it, you did the right thing.'

Heggo began to walk on the sandy bottom and Merien rowed more slowly.

'What did you do when we were running away?' Tandi asked Merien.

'Oh, nothing much. The flying machine did a good job with those landslides.

The whole valley will be under water by now, Cream Bun Palace and all. The water will burn Dumpattick's creatures like acid. I put the extra keys on all the tracks around the valley to stop his followers from escaping the flood. Because the followers are themselves negative, they see the keys as dazzling wheels of fire that blind and terrify them. The keys and the supercharged water will help you, but work in reverse if a person emits a negative, rather than positive feeling.'

'Will Dumpattick's creatures be killed?' enquired Ahren eagerly, not exactly sympathetic towards the cats and wolves.

'Some of them, but old Tootle is a tricky one. Uncle Mazdan does have a weapon which would fix him for the time being, provided Master Theon lets him use it. Uncle Mazdan has control over an enormous whirlpool which moves about all over the Sea of Illusion, keeping it clean and pure. When it reaches a severely negatively charged island it turns into a bottomless pit and sucks down everything in its path. Dumpattick and everyone on his island will simply cease to exist on this level of creation. When Uncle Mazdan sets it going it takes all matter in its path and deposits it in another space-time continuum. The problem is that all matter has to be dumped somewhere in one of the universes: heavens or hells as you call them, and none of them want Dumpattick and his crowd. Fortunately that's Uncle Mazdan's headache, not ours.'

'How can he kill whole groups of people? I mean, I felt awful just killing one or two,' said Lee.

'He's totally uninvolved. He just destroys the evil, then forgets he's done it,' added Merien, avoiding a small piece of coral sticking out of the water.

Merien stopped talking and concentrated on bringing the boat to the shore, through a channel between the sharp lumps of coral that littered the shallows. The others jumped out of the boat after Merien and splashed through the warm water to the beach, then pulled the boat up onto the pink sand.

'Here we are!' shouted Merien, and a group of girls and boys of about Lee's to Raynor's ages came running out of the trees to greet us.

'Hello!'

'My name's Zarko, what's yours?'

'Hey look, they've got a donkey!'

'Are you Lee? Merien told me you're amazingly brave.'

'Good you made it here!'

'Nice to meet you,' and so on.

The boys and girls on the island were students at Master Theon's Academy, where young people from all over the world came to study wisdom and the art of good government. Most, though not all, were the sons and daughters of the rulers of their respective lands. The theory of Master Theon's Academy was that you could only govern others if you could govern yourself. They learnt all the usual school subjects plus such things as law, politics, navigation, and for the boys the arts of war, but the real reason for all the classes was so the students could learn to 'know themselves.' Merien watched them all run off together up the beach to a building half hidden in the trees, the school where they lived. They pulled the unwilling Heggo with them on the end of a long rope. Raynor stayed behind with Merien.

'What about Asha?' he enquired gravely.

'Uncle Mazdan has taken her to his house and he and his wife will look after her. For some reason she has been much more deeply affected than the rest of you, but he'll put her right if anyone can.'

'It's interesting, what you say,' mused Raynor.

'Why?'

'Because of all of us she is the most intuitive, and the one with the psychic gifts.'

'Like what?'

'Well, she sees lights, or blackness, in people's hearts and heads - things that are difficult to explain.' Raynor could feel a healthy coolness coming from Merien when he put his attention on his inner centres, but did not know what Merien consciously knew about this side of life.

'You must tell this to Uncle Mazdan. It might make his task easier and quicker. Come on, he'll be up at his house by now. We'll take the short cut up the mountainside: this way.'

Merien set off at a smart pace across the beach followed by Raynor, and soon they reached the edge of the trees. Their path climbed the mountainside for some distance, then led inland for a short while to a small valley between two hills. There was an open space where the forest had been cleared and a neat garden planted. Raynor could see, among the fruit trees and vines heavy with their harvest, a small square house with a veranda all around it, built out of pink coral rock from the lagoon, and the roof was tiled with large scallop shells. Nog, who had tagged along behind Raynor, growled then wagged his tail as Mazdan's large watchdog came out to meet them. The boys went into the house and the dogs surveyed each other coolly, then made their peace.

Mazdan was in the kitchen with his wife. There were clouds of steam coming from a bronze cauldron. It smelled strong and spicy, permeated the entire house and no doubt contained an asphyxiating concoction of something very powerful. Mazdan was bending over his mixture.

'Hello,' he said without stopping. He was hurriedly putting measures of various liquids and substances into the pan. It was bubbling and hissing as if it had been part of the volcano. 'My wife will look after you,' he seemed to be saying, in a polite way, 'Can't you see I'm busy and don't want to be disturbed?'

'Raynor has something to tell you which will help, about the girl,' persisted Merien, not taking the hint to go away.

'Yes, young man, what is it? Tell me quickly, because she's going down fast,' Mazdan turned to Raynor.

'Asha sees things, things inside people. That is to say...' Raynor was put right off balance by Mazdan's disturbing words about me.

'You can speak plainly to me,' said Mazdan, putting Raynor at his ease,

'about the inner Tree of Life and its subtle centres, or jewels of the soul, or whatever you call them. So Asha used to see them as lights inside people and so on? Did she see the dark side, ghosts, and all that?'

'Yes. The wise lady on the Island of Creations warned us that it was dangerous and she'd have to let go of this ability.'

Mazdan stopped stirring the brew. 'Go on.'

'The lady said that seeing these things is taking Asha close to the realms of consciousness from where evil people like the Teletsian Sorcerers get their power.'

'Exactly.' Mazdan continued to stare into Raynor's eyes in the most unnerving fashion. 'With what my father has taught me we can cure her, but we can't stop her from sinking back unless she changes her attitude, because neither I nor anyone else can cross the boundary of her freedom. If Asha prefers to look at psychic jewels rather than make the journey to the northern kingdom, where much greater powers can be hers, then we cannot stop her. She'll eventually sink into one of the other levels of creation via the vortex: the whirlpool that perhaps Merien told you about. It will entrap her as she crosses the Sea of Illusion, and if you have her on your raft then it will take you down too. Although she doesn't realise it, she desires powers like those of Dumpattick at the moment, because his henchmen have hypnotised her badly.'

'But why her?' groaned Raynor in despair. I was like a younger sister to him. 'Why not me or any of the others?'

'Because she wanted that sort of experience. Very dangerous. Come on, enough talk; let's get her out of this.'

Mazdan ladled out a dishful of the strong-smelling brew from the cauldron on the hob, put a spoon and some bread on a tray with the bowl and then led them into another room.

I was dozing on a bed, with sunlight flickering over me through the open window. Outside the trees moved in the slight breeze and the boom of the surf against the outer coral reef could be heard in the distance. Mazdan's wife soothed me when the fits came over me. I felt as if some unseen thing was trying to attack me, and I would moan in pain and cringe to avoid it.

'Why was she all right yesterday, when we were running away? Why has she got worse again?' cried Raynor.

'If there's a weakness the negative forces will try to return,' said Mazdan. His wife took a spoonful of the broth he had made and tried to make me drink it. I spluttered and grimaced after swallowing one gulp, then looked wildly round for a means of escape.

'Get the lemons and chillies,' Mazdan calmly instructed his wife. She returned with seven green chillies and seven pale yellow lemons. Meanwhile Mazdan explained to Raynor what was going on.

'This is the part of the world where the water element is the strongest power, so I've tried healing Asha with a few drops of the supercharged water mixed with coconut milk and some healing herbs. Unfortunately the fell spirits that have taken control of her stopped her from drinking much, so now we'll try something different. The lemons and chillies will draw out the negativity from the subtle centres of her soul.'

My face was contorted in expressions which were patently not my own as the spirits fought for possession of my mind. Mazdan laid out the lemons and chillies, said some words in the classic language and moved his hands over them. He opened a small leather bag with a drawstring at the neck.

'Merien,' ordered Mazdan, 'hold her firmly. Raynor, take her hand and stand where she can see you. She needs someone she knows to give her courage and help her regain her will to reject evil.' Mazdan took up a lemon and started chanting, and they could see there was a battle going on. The more he chanted, the more agitated the something inside me became. Suddenly Mazdan made a gesture as if he was picking something out of my stomach and threw the unseen entity into the lemon in his other hand. As he did so the lemon shrivelled and became a dark brownish yellow, whereas I looked much better.

Then Mazdan picked up a chilli and repeated the process. When he put the unseen entity into it, it became dry and blistered. He threw the spoiled lemons and chillies into the bag and I improved dramatically. Each time he chanted a different group of words and moved his hands above a different centre of my inner Tree of Life. After he had used all of them in this way, I looked fresher than Raynor had ever seen me.

'Merien, go and put these in the sea, and the whirlpool will find them and suck them down,' said Mazdan. Merien disappeared with the bag and the atmosphere in the room improved dramatically. Mazdan spoke sternly to me, but his words were tempered with compassion. 'I've taken the evil spirits out of you. They were trying to plague you and came from Dumpattick, but unless you stop wanting to live in this world of visions and psychic lights, you leave open the door in your soul for the demons to get to you again. If you want to continue your journey across the Sea of Illusion, you must snap out of all this. It's just your ego that makes you want to see more than your friends. I warn you, your magic raft won't carry you any more if your soul harbours these negative entities. If you love your friends and want to stay with them, stop desiring to see more than them.'

'I thought that with this power I might save us from getting caught by evil people,' I burst into tears.

'No, far from it. You must understand that it's the all-pervading power of divine love that looks after you, and if you try to bend the rules of what is, and is not, permissible to humans, you court disaster. Forget it now – it's over.' Mazdan and Raynor went out of the room and I was left with Mazdan's wife, who was as sweet and gentle as her husband was firm. She was kind and motherly and soon had me helping her cook the evening meal.

'She'll be fine,' said Mazdan to Raynor. 'I had to be severe to make her see sense.' He smiled and looked very pirate-like. 'I'd better go and see what my father's pupils are getting up to. When the cats are both away then the mice are sure to play!'

As they walked down to join the others Raynor was pensive. He knew a bit about what mesmerism could do, but never at such close quarters, and on someone he knew well. Although helping Mazdan had been a shocking experience, it hadn't frightened him, because he was certain Mazdan was in control. Just as Lee was beginning to see himself as a warrior, Raynor was starting to gain a rock-like inner confidence, and an ability to lead and make decisions; it emanated from that inner sense of peace and stillness radiating out from his heart.

CHAPTER 14

TRAVELLERS' TALES

While Raynor was up the hill, Lee and the others were meeting the students and exchanging stories over a tasty meal. The school consisted of a number of low buildings built around a paved yard a little way back from the beach. As was the case with Mazdan's house, there were fruit trees growing round about, some bearing fruit and some blossom. Exotic flowers and creepers grew in the gardens and the buildings were of the same pink coral rock as Mazdan's house. They had high-pitched roofs and were thatched with palm leaves, so they were beautiful, even though they housed a strict school. The students were sitting outside under the trees, cooled by a pleasant breeze, drinking coconut milk out of green coconuts and eating a kind of pancake with pickles and grilled fish, off plates made from palm leaves. Various different conversations were going on and each of the new arrivals had a small group of pupils around him or her.

Lee was sitting with four boys of about his age. They wore white tunics over drawstring trousers of some rough cotton material and either plain sandals or no shoes at all. At first glance they looked like peasants' children in their holiday best, poor but clean. Two of the boys had bluish black skin and hair, one was fair skinned with blonde hair and the fourth had a lightly tanned skin with a rusty tint. Lee told them his story, leaving out any bits he felt were better kept secret. He was a Teletsian and used to being cautious.

'What about you?' he asked. 'Where do you come from and why are you here?' The two tall, ebony skinned boys, brothers named Zarko and Varko, began talking together. Varko stopped and let his brother continue while he went to fetch more coconuts for all of them.

'Our father rules a group of islands far to the east of your land,' said Zarko. 'We stopped off at Teletos on our way here. Horrible place: all those Sorcerers. No wonder you left. I took a tour of your "Teletsian Academy for Advanced Spiritual Study." As different from this academy as night from day.'

'The whole country is pretty grim, but one day it's going to be beautiful. Tell me about this school. What do you learn here?'

'All sorts of things that will make us better able to rule our people,' Zarko went on enthusiastically. 'I mean more worthy, not more high handed or violent like your Sorcerers. Today we were learning about humility and how the ideal ruler never thinks of his own comforts until those of his subjects are satisfied, especially in times of war and famine. We're going on field courses soon, to overcome the need for comforts and learn how to be extremely hardy if necessary, as an example. The king must inspire his people, not be a tyrant or despot,' said the young prince. Lee felt he was quoting from a lesson, but the boy with blond hair was not going to let Zarko off lightly.

'That's a good one, coming from you!' he laughed.

'You're right,' replied Zarko, 'you'd better tell Lee the story,' and his friend related the story of Zarko's first day at school.

'When Zarko arrived here he was, how shall I put it? Very different. I had ridden for a week through my father's poor, barren territories and then worked my passage here on a merchant ship, but for Zarko it was not at all like that. He arrived on a great sailing ship with a carved and painted figurehead, a bodyguard and a band of buglers, and the sails of the ship and the uniform of the crew were purple and gold. He left his galleon and came ashore on a barge with cloth of gold awnings, and he was carried across the beach to the schoolhouse in a litter. Varko came the following year in the same boat.'

'I'd never served my own food and had hardly ever seen a kitchen,' Zarko put in, 'let alone worked in one as we all do here. At home my spacious bed chamber had every luxury imaginable, even servants to fan me to sleep when the nights were hot.'

'All right, point taken,' interrupted his friend. 'Somehow Zarko managed to get through supper that first evening and nobody minded when he persuaded one of the others to get his food, but the trouble was sleeping. There are two large halls here. In the day they are classrooms and in the night we sleep in them, boys in one, girls in the other. We each have a rush mat to go underneath us and one blanket each. No privacy, no extra blankets when the nights are chilly and certainly no servants to fan us into dreamland. Zarko was still very much His Serene Highness Crown Prince Zarko of the Melitsian Isles (crown princes, by the way, are two a coconut here). He stormed up to Master Theon and demanded a room to himself and a bed, still wearing his rich clothes and chains of gold and pearls.'

Zarko, whose plain white tunic was tied at the waist with string and whose feet were calloused from walking without sandals, put his head on his hands and laughed bashfully.

'Master Theon told him gently that there weren't any beds,' his friend continued. 'Zarko became even angrier and said how could he, a king's son, sleep on the floor with so many commoners. He didn't know that some of the simply clad boys and girls were heirs to far greater thrones than his father's.

At this Master Theon was very apologetic and said he was sorry about the lack of beds, but if Zarko wanted to be away from the other boys he could sleep in the courtyard. Zarko was given a bedroll and out he went.

'We all knew what was bound to happen but none of us wanted to spoil the fun. Now Master Theon has some tame snakes living in the foundations of the buildings to keep the rats down. They never harm us; they never harm anyone, but Zarko didn't know that. On that particular night, Zarko lay in the courtyard, fiendishly uncomfortable, for some time and then one of the moons came up. He'd heard the occasional slither on the flagstones in the darkness, but thought it was leaves blowing in the night breeze. In the moonlight he saw the snakes wriggling towards where he was lying, near the fountain in the centre there.'

Zarko's friend pointed to it then went back to his tale. 'They'd only come to drink, but Zarko was up and away like a deer chased by a lion. He vaulted through the nearest open window into the boys' hall and lay down as quietly as he could. You never saw a crown prince so eager to share his bedroom with twenty other boys, whom he assumed were mere commoners, in your life. I know he vaulted through the window because he nearly landed on me when he did so. Nothing more was said on the subject of beds and bedrooms to Zarko, but that was lesson one for him at the school. It's like that here; sooner or later we all learn to laugh at ourselves.'

Ahren was in another corner of the yard; he was sitting by a boy with a fair skin and mid brown hair, whose father was the overlord of a number of tribes famed for their herds of cattle, donkeys and horses. He was called Persheray, and Ahren asked him how to deal with difficult donkeys, then the conversation turned to Persheray's journey to the island, which had been quite as eventful as Ahren's own. Persheray's father had chartered a boat to bring his son and three relations from his land to the school.

Once out of sight of land it became clear that the sailors intended to do some exploring and trading on the way. Although the whereabouts of Theon's island was well known, much of the sea was uncharted because most of the ships kept to the lands around the edge. Many a well-built ship had disappeared without trace and Persheray's father had been forced to pay an exorbitant sum to persuade the sailors to take his son, nephews and niece at all.

'So what went wrong?' asked Ahren.

'The first delay was because the sailors had heard a rumour that there was an island nearby where there were so many gold nuggets on the beach that you could fill a trunk with them in half an hour. After a few weeks' sailing we stopped at an island for some water, and lo and behold! There were the nuggets washed by the tide and shining in the sun. The captain and his crew went almost mad with greed, loaded up the boat and headed for the nearest port back on one of the larger islands. The men had stored the gold nuggets in boxes, each to his own hoard. The port we went to was some distance up a river and back from the sea wind and salt water.

'The captain found a gold dealer who was dubious and asked if it was real gold. At this our captain became very angry and the first casket of nuggets was brought in and placed on the floor. The box was opened; the great moment had arrived. The captain and his men were about to become millionaires and we were extremely unlikely to be brought here.

'The box was opened and there weren't any nuggets. At the bottom of the box was a lot of grey dust and black grit but no gold. The captain ordered another box to be brought in. All the boxes which had been filled with shining gold nuggets had nothing in them but grey dust and black grit.

'Meanwhile the gold dealer, a peevish man with a hunched back, bald head and spectacles, said nothing but noisily drummed his fingers on the weighing table as if bored. Finally the captain bellowed at him, "Well, my man, what have you to say to all this?"

"Oh noble sir," replied the miser, "I have seen this so-called gold many times. As soon as it is away from the sea air, it decomposes into this strange dust and grit. You had best tip it onto the floor - my boys will clear it up for you - and betake yourselves and your boxes back to your ship. Good day, I have business to attend to." So off we went, leaving the dust and grit behind. The joke was, that was worth a fortune, and that's why the old miser had us tip it onto the floor.'

'What's it used for?'

'Uncle Mazdan told me they cook it up with silver and a few other things and it turns back into a golden alloy that's hard, doesn't rust and has a hundred uses. Not only that, the dust can be used as fuel. It's incredibly concentrated and goes many times as far as the same weight in coal.'

'Did the sailors bring you here after that?'

'Oh, no such luck! No, the next adventure was even worse. We were blown south by a terrible gale and reached an island about as big as this one. It was covered with a thick hazy cloud and the captain landed on the beach with his two mates, and one other crewman. They said they'd be back in the evening.

'We waited for three or four days and then two of the younger seamen, strapping lads not much older than me, decided to go and have a look for the captain and his men. They took the second dinghy and also disappeared into the fog. By now there were only three crew members left aboard with us four and we waited for another three days.

The second dinghy reappeared out of the swirling mists surrounding the island on the third afternoon but in it were six strangers. There were five men and a woman clad in tattered garments made out of animal skins. They had grey hair and deeply lined faces, but after talking to them we discovered they were friendly and asked them to come on board. Two of them looked vaguely familiar and said they had been wandering around the island for years in search of the captain of their ship, and it was not an island but an enormous deserted continent where they had completely lost sight of the seashore.

'Although they never found any trace of their captain, they did come across the four other people now with them, who said they'd also been lost there for years. The six of them had unexpectedly come across the seashore and found a dinghy pulled up on the beach. They decided that whatever the dangers involved, they'd try and sail away in it. At this point the two who seemed familiar, and we on the ship realised that they'd been involved in some sort of time and space warp. The two old men were our two young sailors. In three days they'd aged a good thirty years, which was how long they said they had been on the island, seeking a way out.'

'Wh...what did you do next?' stammered Ahren, mortally glad we had merely fallen foul of Sir Tootle.

'Oh, then we finally did come here. I'm afraid we left the other lost sailors to their fate. The survivors had by this time had enough of the Sea of Illusion and came to the conclusion that their only hope was to fulfil their contract in an honourable fashion.'

'But there is a happy ending,' interrupted the girl who resembled Persheray. She was his cousin and had come with him.

'Tell me.'

'When we arrived here with our geriatrics,' continued Persheray, 'and Master Theon heard their tale, he took them to his house. The next day six people in their late twenties, joyful and healthy, came down to see us at the school. Master Theon said the ageing which had occurred on the island was from a different reality and he transferred it into the realm of dreams. The six of them had suffered some shocking nightmares during the previous night but when they woke up in the morning their old age had fallen off them like cobwebs, and gone into the land of dreams.'

At this moment Mazdan and Merien arrived to tell everyone the good news that I was going to be fine, but that we should stay for a few days to make sure I was completely recovered.

Some days later we were talking to Mazdan in the kitchen of his house where we had all been invited for supper. His wife was showing us girls how to make various sweets from coconuts and other exotic fruits and nuts and Raynor was asking Mazdan which of the islands to watch out for in the sea.

'Nearly all of them,' laughed Mazdan, 'For example there's one island near here where a fierce old hermit lives. I once sent a pupil there on an errand and the boy said something to him he thought was disrespectful towards my father. So he threw the pupil in a pit and left him there for a few days and told him he was not fit to be the great Master Theon's disciple.

'I intuited some problem and sailed over to see what was going on. Even so I had to beg the hermit to haul the poor boy out or he'd be there to this day, maybe! Sometimes the young people land there assuming it to be Master Theon's island and the hermit can be very dangerous. He only takes on a few pupils, and those solely after rigorous tests where they have to prove themselves dedicated to discovering their true inner selves. We on the other hand will take anyone who succeeds in crossing the Sea of Illusion and reaching our island.

'Then there are the islands with time warps, as Persheray told you about. Also there are islands that are mirages. Ships sail towards them for days but instead of coming closer the islands recede into the distance and finally disappear over the horizon. There are others inhabited by wild beasts that enjoy making meals of unwary mariners. It's a very tricky sea, but people tend to get caught by the particular island that exploits whatever weakness they themselves have.'

'Don't the weird qualities of the islands affect you?' asked Raynor.

'No, illusion and delusion don't affect me. When you've travelled to the northern kingdom, you'll also learn how to recognise and guard against this side of things.'

'Do you and Merien rescue lots of people like us, who get into trouble on the different islands?' I ventured.

'That depends, firstly on what they're seeking, and secondly on whether they want to be rescued. Some people are happy being turned into black cats, while others appear to want to spend their lives looking for fools' gold. If the deeper desire of the person is to be put back on the right track, then yes, we always try to pull them out of whatever disaster they've got themselves into.'

'How do you know people are in trouble?'

'Easy - sometimes intuition, mostly dolphins. They're a very effective communication system.'

'Are all the islands in the sea best avoided?' asked Lee.

'Perhaps, perhaps not. The sea is too wide to cross without stopping somewhere to take on more food and water. On some islands the dangers are too great for anyone to negotiate, while on others one can expect to get off fairly lightly, having merely become a little wiser from the experience.'

'So we're not the only ones to have come to grief?' asked Raynor with a grin.

'No, far from it!' laughed Merien, who had just come in behind them.

'Why did we fall for that one?' I wondered.

'You tell me. Didn't you come from a land thick with psychic mind-bending?' said Mazdan. 'That's your weakness.'

'True enough,' observed Raynor.

'I'm going to leave you the log book I wrote on the raft,' said Lee. 'It might be of use if other people come from Teletsia.'

'Thank you,' said Mazdan. 'There's one island in the sea which is different, and that is the home of the Emperor and Empress. They are the rulers of this sea and many other lands, as you already know. Their island is surrounded by another stretch of water, in the centre of the Sea of Illusion. We call it the Milk Sea, because the water there looks like milk. There's a strong current, rotating sometimes in one direction and sometimes the other, making it hard to navigate. The dolphins guard the area, so pirates and other shady characters never get near the Emperor's Citadel.'

'Will we get to see it?' begged Ahren.

'Indeed, you've been invited there by Merien's parents, but I was waiting to make sure that Asha was all right. Merien will go with you.'

'Can you sail through the swirling current?' asked Raynor cautiously.

'Yes, I've done it many times. I lived on the island as a child and go back often to see my folks,' Merien reassured us.

'Merien is a distant cousin of the Emperor and the son of his Prime Minister,' explained Mazdan. 'He's also one of my father's most dedicated pupils, and these two factors are why he was able to borrow the flying machine to rescue you.'

A couple of days later, the seven of us were sitting under some palm trees near the beach. The students of the academy were not with us.

'Are you better now?' Raynor asked me.

'Yes, I think so, but it's been quite a shock. Here was I, thinking that when I saw inside people I was somehow getting there, and it turns out I wasn't. Merien is the sort of person we should be. He's so - normal,' I still felt hurt, ashamed and even slightly lost to discover that my second sight was not so great after all.

'We were so in awe of you and I always thought, "Oh, Asha's the special one – she sees things. We only feel,"' added Conwenna.

'I'm really sorry I got you all into that mess.'

'Don't be,' said Lee. 'I should have been stronger with you. I mean, you did make me the captain of the raft, but we've learnt from the experience, and we've come through it in one piece. I'm going to trust these cool and hot feelings much more in the future.'

'Me too,' said Raynor. 'All my book study can backfire. Relying on my so-called rational thoughts can be a disaster. We've got to go deeper or we may not be so lucky next time.'

'Yeah, but we might not have got this far if you hadn't studied those old books, so don't put yourself down too much,' insisted Ahren. He was beginning to admire Raynor's seemingly endless book learning and was starting to see that his own rather frantic and headlong approach to life could lead him into problems. Also, although he liked to think of himself as the practical country lad, he realized now that Lee was just as capable in his own way. 'You lot think too much, but maybe I need to think a bit more,' Ahren went on. 'It's all going to work out, you'll see. Just be positive.' But instead of avoiding making friends with us by pretending to have to look after Heggo, he became much closer to Lee and they discovered they complemented each other perfectly. The change came after Lee pulled us all out of trouble.

While we were doing a debrief of the journey to date, Derwin said nothing and drew designs in the sand with his fingers. He had been badly frightened, and didn't want to think about what might have happened to me, and the rest of us, if Merien hadn't turned up. Tandi also said nothing, for different reasons.

She felt sick after about half an hour on the raft, and had been dead scared, not only by our experience, but also by the stories she had heard from the other students. She stared pessimistically at Derwin drawing in the sand. She felt so alone. She didn't realise that Raynor, in his quiet and shy way, was becoming very fond of her, and we all appreciated her caring motherly qualities. What she lacked was the burning sense of adventure and destiny that the rest of us had, so she felt hopelessly out of it.

The best thing about spending time at this school was that we met young people who in some ways were like us, but because they came from saner countries, in other ways were very different. Where we tended to be closed and suspicious, they were much more open and trusting.

Merien joined us, full of plans for the next part of the journey, and any doubts disappeared like cobwebs before a feather duster. His breezy enthusiasm was infectious and after half an hour we were again living in the moment, but we had all changed. We were aware that we couldn't just leave our problems behind in Teletsia, and apart from Tandi we were more confident that having got so far, maybe our luck would continue to hold.

CHAPTER 15

A TASTE OF PARADISE

The next morning the raft was ready and well stocked with provisions. Nog climbed aboard at the first opportunity, not wanting to be left behind, and Heggo was also winched up after he had carried some water barrels down to the raft from a spring on the mountainside. We thanked Mazdan and his wife for their hospitality, said goodbye to the students and boarded the raft, accompanied by Merien. Soon we were sailing past the outer ring of islands, beyond the treacherous coral reefs and out into the sea once more.

We made our way northwest with a good strong breeze behind us and continued in this direction for a few days beneath the same bright blue sky and hot sun. We were surrounded by endlessly churning sea, wave after wave after wave. Occasionally we saw islands, sometimes in groups and sometimes single ones that were volcanic, but Merien, guiding us, avoided all of them and kept to the open sea.

I felt better than I'd ever done. An inner joy and confidence radiated out from my heart but I saw no more inner jewels and didn't feel tempted to try, either. What touched me was that everyone was so nice: not judgmental or patronising, but just nice. I was one of the gang, not some strange creature who had nearly gone crazy. Conwenna and I sat together and talked quite a lot.

'Do you miss Teletsia?' I asked her one day.

'You must be joking! What's there to miss? My mum's dead, my dad's a spy and my life's in danger there,' she replied vehemently.

'Don't be too hard on your dad, because after all, he was spying to save you.'

'Yes, you're right. It's just it was all such a blow, and I'm not over it yet.' I didn't know what to say to that. We looked at the sea in silence for a few moments.

'I don't miss Teletsia either, but I worry about my family.'

'There's not much you can do about them, is there? Maybe Stellamar managed to sort something out. I hope so, but it's almost too much to expect of her.'

'I keep having dreams that tell me we're being looked after and if we can just keep going and keep together, we'll be all right.'

'I don't have dreams, but I do have this feeling that what we're doing is so right. I feel this bubbling joy when I wake up in the morning and we're further north - kind of strange if you think about it. We don't have a clue where we're going, or what lies ahead.'

'It makes a lot of sense if we are the young people in the prophecy. Then it would be natural to want to go north.' My second sight may have gone, but my deep and revealing dreams hadn't. In them it became clear that we were the ones prophesied in the old book.

'You have to be right. Otherwise why is it that we don't feel scared and lost? Compared to those boys and girls on Master Theon's island we've had dreadful lives, and yet we've survived.'

'I agree. But let's keep this to ourselves – for the moment.'

Only Tandi still felt nauseous and kept saying she wasn't cut out for adventures like this. Raynor spoke to her, and although she was animated when talking to him she did not have the same enthusiasm as the rest of us.

One morning Derwin awoke first and went to talk to Merien, who was taking his turn at the rudder of the raft.

'When will we get to the Milk Sea?' he asked.

'Soon. See, the current is already beginning to swirl.' Merien had to keep changing course to compensate for the swift current which was lapping against the sides of the raft, first in one direction and then in the other. The swirling became ever stronger and soon we all had to take turns in holding the rudder steady. When it became really powerful we had to paddle with oars as well.

Later on that morning I was the first to see something glinting on the horizon. The sea had become the colour of cream and the current was gentler; the sun shone silvery out of a gold haze and a school of dolphins swam up to us and barred our way. Merien spoke to them in the squarks and whistles of dolphin language. However they still would not allow the raft to pass and Merien explained to us that rumours had reached them of plans for an attack on the Emperor's Citadel. Consequently they had to be extra careful as to who to allow through the Milk Sea.

At this Derwin took out his green and gold ten petalled key and showed it to the dolphins - he had only lent it to Lee on Sir Tootle's island. Immediately they parted and the raft was allowed to continue. They even swam alongside the raft for some time to escort us and we felt very honoured.

The gleam I had seen was the Island Citadel and as we approached we sailed into the harbour we saw a town with many of the buildings covered with mosaics and semi-precious stones. Behind the sumptuous warehouses of the port stood the palace of the Emperor, covering the whole of the hilltop with its shimmering magnificence. Behind the buildings were extensive pleasure gardens.

The harbour master and his attendants were so richly dressed that at first we thought they were the Emperor and his retinue, because their clothing was encrusted with gold and jewels. Even the dockworkers' clothes were made from the finest silks and velvets. Their hearts seemed full of joy and they radiated love as beautifully as the world around them shone and glowed, as if it reflected the contented mood of all the people living there.

Tandi, who had come from the countryside, was especially dazzled by all this material luxury. She was in a complete daze and just stared and stared almost as if she had been drugged. She began to go on about the place in such a way that we found it a bit too much; in turn she could not understand why we didn't share her feelings.

Those of us who had come from the city of Teletos had all seen jewels and finery on the rich men and women of our capital many times. We even had to suppress the odd thought of suspicion. Nearly all the great wealth of Teletsia came from very dubious sources and initially it was hard for us Teletsians, conditioned as we were, to believe that there could be a place where such wealth could exist without a great deal of suffering and corruption as well. Nevertheless, we soon entered into the general mood of feasting and fun and our doubts disappeared.

We were graciously received by the harbourmaster, his assistants and their families. The harbourmaster welcomed us with low bows and flourishes of the hand, after which we were all taken to a well-appointed guest house, where we bathed and changed into some luxurious clothes which we had been given. These were apparently normal daytime garments for the young people here. The harbour master then offered us a meal that for most people would have been a feast but for him was an ordinary lunch.

Afterwards our host had some business to attend to so he left Merien to look after us, and we all went for a walk in the nearby gardens. The most striking thing about all the flowers, bushes and trees on this island was that at first sight they looked as if they had been formed out of gems and precious metals of all colours, but when one felt the leaves and petals, they were soft and growing like normal plants. Many trees and bushes were blossoming and a number had shining fruits hanging from their branches. The scents of the different blooms were overpowering and bees hummed tipsily from one flower to the next, gorged with gold and silver nectar. Birds of many shapes and sizes sang choruses of songs, now and again flying from one tree to another on wings of brilliant colours. Tandi was again quite overcome by this treasure-house of a garden.

'Is it always the same? All these jewels and blossoms of precious metals?' she asked Merien. 'Or is it just the time of year for these things?'

'No, it's always like this. But there's more to these trees than their exotic appearance.' He pointed to a small bush with golden flowers and fruits like rubies, already cut so as to have many facets. 'For instance, if you have one of these flowers or fruits and keep it carefully in your home, there will always be love and harmony between the members of the household. Should you be fortunate enough to be given one of these small flowers by the Empress, whose garden this is,' he pointed to another bush, laden with mother-of-pearl blooms, shaped like lilies, 'you have only to smell the delicious perfume and any diseases you might have will go away. The flowers will never die, provided you look after them properly.

'There, to the left, is a tree whose fruits shed a skin of pure gold every morning, so anyone with one of those fruits will never be short of money. The jewels that cover the clothes, the houses, and everything else here all come from these gardens in an unending harvest of wealth - but only for the people who live here. They are not for sale. The saps of all these plants are fragrant oils, and all of them that are not hard and gemlike are very good to eat.' Tandi looked longingly at the living jewels, and noticed that even the earth and the pebbles underfoot were shining and glittering in the sun.

'Do they all belong to the Emperor and Empress?' continued Tandi. The rest just stared in wonder.

'Yes, but if you please them they will usually give you whatever you ask for.'

'How do you do that?'

'You avoid going to excesses in your life and obey all the traditional guidelines for right living, which shouldn't, in theory, be that difficult. But as you know when you study history, we somehow manage to make a complete madness of things, time and again. Then your inner subtle centres go out of balance, problems start and compound each other, and you probably won't be offered any jewels.'

'But no one's perfect, so how on earth does anyone ever get given any?'

'You don't have to be absolutely perfect. Who is? And virtue is much easier when there's no shortage of anything.'

'I don't know about that,' said Raynor thoughtfully, 'Teletsia has been extraordinarily blessed by Mother Nature, and should be very rich, but most of us struggle in every way and our country is a disaster.'

'We humans make a complete mess of things and manage to go wrong worse than any other living creature I can think of,' said Lee wistfully.

'That's what Master Theon's Academy is all about,' went on Merien, 'learning to live in a sane and harmonious way. Sadly, when the young princes and princesses go back to their own countries they often get lost in the Sea of Illusion on the way home and their hard won knowledge comes out all snarled up and scrambled around in their heads. When they reach their lands again, too many of them remember what suits them and forget the rest. The difficulty is that we have free will. That's the sticking point and that's what makes us human. Anyway, it's not something to brood over here. Let's walk on again.'

Merien had a marvellously detached way of looking at things, which made me realise that he had grown up in a completely different environment from us. His was a world where problems were there, but could always be resolved, and the good guys always came out on top. It was refreshing, but I realised the yawning gulf between us and wondered how he would deal with Specials and Sorcerers on a daily basis.

We pondered Merien's words as he led us through endless gardens, which reminded us of descriptions of paradise. As we were returning to the guesthouse an attendant in a sumptuous green and gold livery came up to us, and like the harbour master bowed low with a flourish of his hand. Maybe everyone bowed low to each other here, or maybe it was because Merien was quite an important person. In any case, he informed us that we had been commanded to attend an audience with the Prime Minister, Merien's father, in the Throne Room of the Emperor's Palace.

We followed the attendant through the town, past the palatial residences of the courtiers and approached the palace over a drawbridge held up by silver chains. The drawbridge spanned a moat where clumps of glimmering water lilies hid brilliantly coloured fishes which nevertheless were ferocious and had jaws like sharks. They prevented unwanted intruders from swimming it. There were no sentries anywhere but Merien explained that the whole place was protected in this way by unseen guards of various types.

The Emperor's palace was even more gorgeous than the rest of the island. The floors were of inlaid precious stones; the walls were lined with slabs of emerald, lapis and crystal; the ceilings were gilt; swags of gemlike flowers tumbled out of jewel-encrusted vases and we walked through courtyards surrounded by filigree marble cloisters. In the centre of the courtyards were ponds into which fell coloured waters from fountains carved from rocks of various colours set with pearls and corals. Everywhere the strains of hidden musicians could be heard: soothing melodies in dulcet tones. It would be easy to lose touch with reality here.

This was the formal, administrative part of the palace, where we were to meet the Prime Minister. The imperial throne, in the centre of the meeting room, had the appearance of a round flower, decorated in green and gold. Behind it was a canopy in the shape of a many headed sea serpent, made of pale gold and diamonds. The Prime Minister and his wife were seated on a cushioned divan at its side and we bowed low, first to the throne and then to the Emperor's representative. We were by now both overwhelmed and dazzled by all the splendour.

We were warmly greeted by the couple and invited to make ourselves comfortable on large cushions. These were offered by attendants who unobtrusively lined the walls. We sat down and looked at our noble hosts, a complete contrast to the workaday Merien, their son. The Prime Minister was clad in yellow and green and his wife in red and green, both wearing the richest jewels we had ever seen. The finery was so dazzling that we needed some time for our eyes to become accustomed to the intensity of the light.

Merien's mother, the Prime Minister's wife, called Raynor over. She had a sweet and welcoming manner and a face, which though beautiful, was reassuring rather than haughty. She put Raynor at his ease by asking him to tell her and her husband the story of our journey. As he related our adventures she smiled softly, showed great interest and now and again stopped him for details, or asked one of the others to expand on their part in the tale. He finally finished speaking and she smiled but did not reply. We sat in silence and listened to the fountains in the nearest courtyard. The musicians strummed their lutes and the birds sang in the pleasure gardens. After the musicians had finished the piece they were playing she spoke to me.

'You undoubtedly deserve something better than the country you've come from. Do you like this island?'

'Yes, indeed, Madam,' I replied, 'it's incredible. I never even dreamed a place like this could exist,' and the others agreed.

'If you like,' said the Prime Minister, 'you can stay here. You will have health, wealth and happiness for more or less as long as you want.'

We found this hard to take in and couldn't believe what we were being offered. For some time none of us spoke, partly because we were overcome by the opulence, music and the whole saturating onslaught of sensory pleasure, and partly because some of us were turning over the invitation in our minds. After all, we had come from a terrible country and had been through some harrowing experiences to get this far. But what of our vow? What of our journey? What of the prophecy? Even the most doubtful of us were by now beginning to suspect it referred to us, although we felt inadequate to fulfil it. Nevertheless there was a deep and powerful desire within most of us to try to reach the northern country, and this was the most important thing in our lives.

'Would that really be possible?' the words were out of Tandi's mouth almost without her realising it, 'I'd love to stay here for a while.' None of the rest of us wanted to, and we certainly didn't want to lose Tandi, but we knew this was not the moment to have a collective discussion even though it was vitally important to do just this, so we were silent.

'Why don't you go outside and talk about our offer over some refreshments?' suggested Merien's mother. Except for Tandi we all went into the courtyard, where we found another feast laid out, with attendants waiting to serve us and a cloth of gold awning shading us from the hot sun. Tandi stayed inside with the Prime Minister and his wife. It was obvious a change had come over her recently but we tried to make ourselves believe it was because she had been so seasick again on the voyage from Master Theon's island. Merien stayed in the throne room with his father and mother and later told us what transpired.

'Have you made up your mind to stay here?' enquired the Prime Minister.

'Yes, at least for the time being. I didn't have any idea our visit to the Temple of Support would lead to this.' Tandi couldn't face any more sailing, any more dangers or any more anything, and now she had been completely dazzled by this beautiful island.

'All right, my dear, if that is your decision, so be it. You can be a companion to one of the princesses,' said Merien's mother.

Immediately an attendant came forward to escort Tandi to the apartments of the princess in question. At first Tandi thought to go outside and say goodbye to us, but as she reached the doorway and saw us tucking into our feast: talking, arguing, teasing and joking together in our usual fashion, and did not dare. She no longer felt a part of our group, so turned and left without even bidding us goodbye.

After some time the rest of us had eaten our fill and decided what we wanted to do. There wasn't much discussion because we five from Teletos city had committed ourselves long ago to seeking the northern kingdom or dying in the attempt, and the heady lure of luxury was already beginning to wear thin. Ahren certainly did not have much time for a world of gold, jewels and music and was the least attracted to the island of any of us. We wondered why Tandi had not come out to join us, but were too much in awe of the Prime Minister and his wife to try and reason with her in front of them. We were called back to the audience chamber.

'Where's Tandi?' burst out Ahren. Raynor gave him a look which was supposed to mean, 'Can't you have some manners, you country bumpkin, some sense of protocol?' Ahren got the gist and was silent.

'Don't worry about your friend,' replied the Prime Minister. 'She's a kind and loving girl and will have everything she wants. Now what about the rest of you?'

'Please,' began Conwenna in her small but definite voice, 'we all want to continue our journey. We find your home so lovely that we can hardly believe it's real, but whenever we stay anywhere longer than a few days, we find ourselves sitting on a beach looking north, wondering how to get on with our quest.' I was surprised, but also delighted, that Conwenna had been the one to speak. She really was beginning to open up.

'Is that the case with all of you?' asked the Prime Minister's wife, scrutinising each one of our faces.

'Yes, there's no turning back now,' I said, I hoped for everyone.

'We can't leave our adventure half finished,' added Ahren.

'It's vital to the future of our country to try to go on,' Raynor tried to sound mature and leader-like. He felt a pang of loss and realised Tandi meant a great deal to him. He wondered why she had gone off without bidding us farewell. Did she not, in the end, care about us? Did we mean so little to her compared to all this material luxury? He hoped against hope that there was some other explanation and tried to put his attention on the Prime Minister.

'I agree with Ahren and Raynor, and want to go on,' put in Lee.

'We made a vow,' I said.

'I'm missing my parents, but I wouldn't see them even if I did stay back,' said Derwin.

'That's true,' this was Merien's mother. 'If you went back to Teletsia now you'd be in deep trouble.'

'If you can all get to Sasrar, then at some time in the future return to Teletsia and try to win back your country, you could get back together with your family,' said the Prime Minister.

'I understand that, and most of all I don't want to be left behind without Asha. She's my sister.' Life without me was simply not an option and anyway, Derwin thought all the jewels and luxury on this island weird.

We hoped we hadn't said completely the wrong thing, but then the two noble and unavoidably imposing people in front of us broke into warm smiles.

'You've made a good choice,' said the Prime Minister. 'Here you can have a fine, long and gloriously happy life, and whatever the material world has to offer. But when you reach Sasrar you can have something more, a joy that comes from within, that you can always turn inwards to find, and is a thousand times deeper than the happiness which comes from anything outside you.

'The joy you'll find in Sasrar comes from within your deepest self, radiates from you and makes you one with the entire creation. It does not wear out or become trivial, meaningless or boring and does not depend on what is going on around you. You will share this with everyone who lives there and will not only be able to destroy evil with the power of your love but will also be able to offer this gift to others. You will radiate joy like a beacon light in a storm. But I'm telling you too much! Even on this island, every day has a dusk and every created thing must have an end. To go beyond that you must go to the northern kingdom.'

It was like reading the prophecy. We could only believe him and hope this was really possible for young people like us, with a lifetime of conditioning of a very different sort. We thanked Merien's parents, and by now were somewhat less in awe of them, and took our leave. Conwenna hung back. I hoped she would not say anything out of place because so far we had managed not to reveal too much of our lack of sophistication in the presence of these regal people.

'What is it, my child?' asked Merien's mother.

'I didn't know that this island would be almost completely made of jewels, but when we were on Master Theon's island, I made the Empress a necklace from red jewel coral and shells that we found on the beach.' Conwenna took the necklace she had made from her pocket, 'Do you think she would like it?' She wasn't going to give up. I wasn't sure about this present, as it wasn't grand enough in all this luxury, but there was nothing to be done. I looked imploringly at Merien's mother. She gave me a quick smile and a slight gesture of her hand showed me she was also a mother and understood the innocent charm of the gift. She smiled at Conwenna.

'A necklace that is so prettily made with such love and care is far better than diamonds and emeralds! I'm sure Her Imperial Majesty will love it. I'll see she gets it.'

I breathed a sigh of relief. She took it, and it was very attractive, made of pink and red coral and many coloured cowrie shells, and put it on the throne, from where the light in the room seemed to originate. After being on the throne the shells and coral sparkled as if they had been stars plucked from the night sky, and the light in the room was even more intense. It was a minor miracle, and we all watched and understood without anything being said. Now we were sure that the true splendour of the island came from the power of the Emperor and Empress themselves to transform the whole surroundings. One thing I had learnt recently was that what went on at a subtle level within people had an enormous effect on what went on outside and around them.

'Before you go, here are some souvenirs for all of you to remember our island home by,' Merien's mother took a perfectly matched string of pearls for me and a similar one for Conwenna from a basket of woven gold. The boys were each given a large white pearl set on the end of a golden pin for a tie, turban or cravat. 'Keep them safe and you will never again want for anything material. These pearls always attract good fortune.' We thanked her as best we could, but it sounded puny in comparison with the gifts, and took our leave.

Later on, in the evening, Raynor went walking in the gardens with Nog but his thoughts were not those of a contented young man taking his dog for a run. The unity of the group had been broken. He was well aware that we had not yet reached the part of the world where Tandi's key would help us over difficulties and he was worried as to how we would manage without it.

We talked far into the night about what lay ahead. What about the keys we hadn't yet used? What about all that the wise men and women we had met had said to us? Having been pulled out of trouble a few times by the keys we had total faith that whatever we were supposed to achieve was going to work out. I decided it was time to tell the others that I was sure we were the young people mentioned in the prophecy. As I cautiously started speaking about this we felt a strong coolness flowing from the tops of our heads, our hands and all around us. It was like a strong wind, even though we were in a room with closed windows. This told us, and by now we were prepared to believe the sign, that the keys and the journey we were on were going to take us to the end of our quest, if anything would.

PART 2

THE LIGHT OF SASRAR

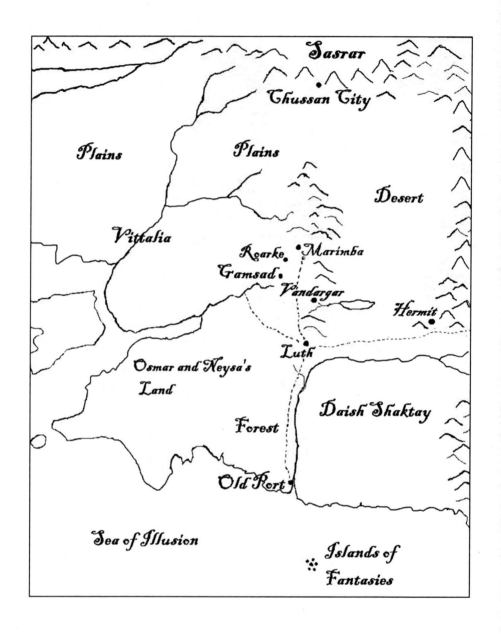

The countries to the north of the Sea of Illusion

Chapter 1

Fantastic Dragons

The Emperor's Island was a non-stop party. I was so full of food I just wanted to go for a very long walk and then have a very long sleep. I'd seen enough dancers, heard enough music and watched enough other sorts of entertainment to last me a very long time, and longed for the peace of the open sea as we sailed north on our raft with the current.

Perhaps I was somewhat fanatic, but Ahren was the same, 'If we're going to Sasrar, then let's leave as soon as we can,' he said, but the others rather enjoyed taking life easy. Raynor was moody at times, and appeared to be looking for something, or someone as it turned out, while Tandi had completely disappeared into the luxurious life that attracted her so much. Conwenna had a way of blotting out reality by getting very involved in whatever was going on at that particular moment, and Derwin got totally involved as well, without even thinking about whether he was blotting out reality or not. Lee found the whole place fascinating and strange, and was intrigued by one thing or another from morning until night.

However, the desire to go north to Sasrar was so strong that it wasn't long before the six of us were down at the docks loading up the raft. Nog was sniffing around the pleasure gardens, and Heggo the donkey was at the quayside, doing some work as a pack animal. No one took the slightest notice of his noisy efforts to try and attract attention to himself by braying and complaining about having to carry not very heavy loads to the raft. These consisted of food, water and so on, and also some stores for a small clan, relations of Merien's who lived on an island some days' journey to the north. Merien asked Raynor to deliver these things and save him a trip. He was giving some last minute advice to Raynor.

'The island where the stores have to be dropped is one of a group of six. It's easy to find because it's the first land you see after leaving here if you're going north on the current. My relations live on the largest one.' He took out a rough map he had drawn and pointed to it, 'See, they live up this creek. Leave the raft in this straight, then take your dinghy.' He was about to speak further when Lee came up.

'What about when we hit the northern coastline?' he interrupted.

'Well,' replied Merien, putting down the map, 'as far as I know, the end of the current is at the mouth of a large river, and you can sail up some way before you get to some tricky rapids. You won't get past them on your raft. Before that there's a half ruined tower, part of a port that's been more or less swallowed up by the jungle. There's an old road through the jungle which starts there and leads north. It's kept useable by the folk who live round about. You'll see the tower if you sail up the river.'

At this moment the harbour master arrived on the quayside with a troupe of musicians, dancers and acrobats to give us a farewell show. After yet another feast we were given a great send off, with a magnificently dressed crowd cheering us on our way.

One of the port pilots stowed a boat on the raft and came with us as far as the edge of the Milk Sea which surrounded the Emperor's Citadel, to help us through the churning current around its edge. Although he regularly piloted ships and other craft through it, like the servants on the Island of Creations he had absolutely no interest in what lay beyond. Once he had set us back on the northerly current he reckoned he had done his job. He wished us a safe journey, launched his boat and went bobbing back through the choppy Milk Sea for his next assignment.

After we were out of sight of the island we all agreed that if it hadn't been for our gifts of pearls, it would have been hard to believe that such riches and luxury could exist in reality. In Raynor's heart the greatest jewel we had left behind was Tandi, and he was concerned that the unity of our group had been broken. To the rest of us she was a dear friend, but one who had decided on another path.

Eight days and two minor squalls later, Raynor pointed to some islands near the north-eastern horizon, and everyone agreed that this must be where we had to leave the stores. Lee changed course and sailed towards the islands. Soon he had anchored the raft between two islands in the straight that Merien had pointed out on his chart. In a short time Raynor was ready with the dinghy, packed full of gifts and stores for Merien's relations. Lee felt that as navigator he should be going too, but there was no room.

'Don't get any funny ideas in your heads or do anything half witted,' Raynor called to us as he started rowing. 'Let's see if we can manage *not* to have an adventure!'

'Look who's talking!' returned Lee. He sometimes stated things a bit too strongly. It was the fact he had the key which stopped him being caught on Tootle's Island, not any superiority on his part. Raynor left, and it was a lazy sort of afternoon with little sound except for the breeze in the nearby woods that covered the low islands. Ahren, getting restless, struck up a conversation.

'What do you think are the dangers on these islands?' he began provocatively. 'After all, we were warned that every island's got something to watch out for.'

'Let's not think about that stuff,' I answered sharply.

'Why wouldn't Raynor let any of us go with him?' Ahren went on, not easily discouraged.

'Because there wasn't any room. Couldn't you see that the dinghy was about to sink?' said Lee, hanging over the side of the raft to look at something in the clear water.

'I wonder what Tandi is up to,' I mused. 'I wish she hadn't left us.'

'We all miss her, don't we?' said Conwenna, who enjoyed Tandi's motherliness and practical good sense.

'She was much closer to us, much more a part of us than we realize. There's quite a hole without her,' Lee was still looking over the side of the raft. 'It was nice to have someone to look after us a little. You know Asha, you're a girl too.'

'So?' I replied.

'I mean, maybe you could have a go at washing and mending my things. Girls are better at all that.'

'I'm the cook. You're a sailor, and sailors always look after their own kit.'

'Asha can make a good meal out of any old odds and ends,' Conwenna came to my defence.

'What are you staring at?' Ahren asked. Lee was looking at something in the clear water.

'Look at these,' Lee beckoned to us. Ahren, Conwenna and I went over to where Lee was lying on his stomach looking at a shoal of small creatures, as long as a hand, which looked like lizards with long legs and wings. Every now and again one would break out of the water and fly through the air for a short distance, and when they surfaced Lee threw scraps of food at them, which they guzzled voraciously.

'If they had smoke coming out of their mouths they'd look like baby dragons, reckon?' laughed Ahren.

'They'd be really scary if they were big,' observed Lee.

'Which they're not,' I said.

'Let's catch some and put them in the hencoop,' suggested Ahren. The hens had refused to lay so we'd eaten them some time before.

'Wouldn't it be better to leave them where they are?' pleaded Conwenna, but Lee and Ahren quickly caught two and imprisoned them. They did not approve at all, and with their sharp little teeth tried to bite through the wire mesh and escape. I gave them some bits of dried meat. After a short while everyone forgot about them in the hot afternoon sun. Derwin lay snoring in the shade of Heggo's cabin, at the other end of the raft.

Ahren and Lee began talking about whether there really were dragons and whether something alive could breathe fire. Lee was sure it was just someone's lurid imagination. I said that even if they did exist, I sincerely hoped I never came across one. We became more interested in discussing mythical dragons than the little lizards left in the cage. After a time I remembered them, and went to see how they were getting on.

'I'm sure they've grown,' I said when I returned.

'Oh, come on,' joked Ahren, 'we only fed them just now, they can't grow that fast!' I was uneasy but not certain enough to argue with them. Then Derwin, still looking woolly from his snooze, came up.

'What on earth are those enormous crocodile things doing squashed into the hencoop? It's hardly big enough for them.'

'Tell us another!' teased Ahren, and to me said, 'Do you remember the story of the dragon that would only eat young maidens, and the prince who had to come and rescue his princess?'

'Yes,' I answered, 'and then the prince arrives on his white charger, with a long lance, so he can get at the dragon without being grilled by its breath.'

Suddenly there was a crash and a splintering of wood, followed by a braying from Heggo and a yowling from Nog. They both jumped headlong into the calm water between the wooded islands, and swam desperately towards the nearby beach.

'What's going on?' shouted Lee, leaping to his feet. Two small dragons, each as large as Heggo and growing by the minute, lurched towards him with jaws open and smoke and flames pouring from their mouths.

'Help!' I screamed. 'In the cabin!' We scrambled in and shut the door tightly behind us. We could feel the raft rocking as the dragons nosed around and stamped their feet.

'What now?' cried Derwin in anguish.

'Haven't a clue,' I groaned, terrified, lacking ideas and squeezed into a corner, 'Lee and Ahren were so keen to catch the wretched things, and now they've gone and turned themselves into dragons.'

'Unless some dragons have just landed on us from out of the sky,' suggested Ahren hopefully, as if this was a safer alternative.

'I wish Raynor would come back,' howled Conwenna, also scared stiff. Ahren bravely opened the door to see what was going on outside.

'Oh, no!' he cried fearfully. 'They've grown even bigger, at least twice as large, and...'

'And what?' demanded Lee, shaking Ahren by the shoulders.

'Their breath is setting the raft alight,' I said dryly, hiding my fear. I'd been looking through a crack in the side of the cabin.

'Quick, buckets!' shouted Lee. 'There, in the corner of the cabin. You girls fill them from the sea and throw the water at the fires, and we boys will try to beat off the dragons with, um, with our catapults and, er, bows and arrows.'

Lee didn't sound too hopeful. The mighty dragons were now practically tipping up the raft, but it looked as if we would either be roasted or eaten or both if we didn't do something fast. We all took deep breaths, and went out to meet the foe before the already smouldering raft should burn up completely.

'Us boys first,' cried Ahren gallantly, 'then run out behind us and fill the buckets.' We tripped over each other and as soon as we were all out on the deck the angry beasts, now nearly as long as the raft itself, turned and saw us. They took no notice of the arrows, which glanced harmlessly off their scaly hides, and came menacingly towards the boys, who were endeavouring hopelessly to shield us girls. Ahren went bravely forward, only to receive a nasty burn on the arm from one dragon's flaming breath, and Lee was cut on the leg by the other one's spiked tail as it swung around to chase him.

'It's no use,' yelled Lee, 'back to the cabin!' We all managed to get back inside the cabin except Derwin. He was trapped behind a pile of ropes at the end of the raft. The rest of us didn't realise he wasn't with us until it was too late, and then Lee opened the cabin door, only to see both the dragons bearing down on him.

'Jump overboard!' shouted Ahren. 'Swim to shore, Heggo's done it!'

Then Lee remembered. He pushed Ahren and me out of the doorway. He could see the backs of the dragons and flames coming up from the pile of ropes where Derwin was hiding.

'The key, Derwin, use your key!' he shouted above the roar of the dragons. 'Swing it, throw it! Anything! Have faith in the key!' Lee screamed at the top of his voice and hoped Derwin had heard him in the chaos of dragons, flames and the violently lurching raft.

139

Derwin was barely aware of Lee. He had much bigger things to attend to. Two fiery dragons with rows of fangs like giant alligators were bearing down on him. Smoke was everywhere, dazing and confusing him even more. Whether he heard Lee, or whether it was his own inner urge, in a last desperate gesture he took the key from around his neck and threw it at the nearest dragon.

Suddenly the flaming breath and roaring noise stopped. Derwin crouched behind the smouldering ropes, shut his eyes and awaited the crunch of vast jaws. He wondered if the silence was because he was already dead, but kept his eyes shut and didn't move, just in case. There was no sound except water and wind and the occasional bird or monkey in the distant woods.

'Derwin, where are you? Are you all right?' I called out.

He opened his eyes and looked about him. Through the smoke he could see me peering fearfully out of the cabin door. He waved at me, but didn't say anything; he was trying to see what had happened to the dragons. There was a crackle as the deck started to burn, but no dragons anywhere. Derwin peeped further round the pile of ropes. He was so stunned that he wasn't aware of the fire starting in front of him. He noticed two dead lizards, but the jewelled key had completely disappeared. He had no time to wonder where it had gone, because the deck started to burn much more fiercely.

'The dragons are gone but the raft is on fire! Hurry! Buckets of water!' he cried.

The rest of us stumbled out onto the deck, retrieved the buckets from where we had abandoned them, filled them with water and soon put out the fire. It wasn't very bad, as we had caught it in time, but there were nasty black marks all over the deck from the dragons' scorching breath.

The battle having been won, I dressed Ahren's burn and Lee's cut, neither of which were serious, only painful. We were all lying on the deck recovering from our dreadful experience when Raynor rowed peacefully round the point of the island, humming a tune to himself. He climbed onto the deck in a leisurely fashion, but his expression changed when he saw the boys' bandages, our distraught faces and the black marks all over the raft.

'Whatever happened?' he asked in dismay.

'We were attacked by dragons,' replied Ahren, as if this was an everyday occurrence.

'What?' Raynor's brow furrowed as he wondered if Ahren had finally completely lost it.

'Well, not quite, they were lizards really.' Raynor's mouth dropped open and he looked at each of us to see whether we had *all* gone mad, or just Ahren.

'We're all safe,' put in Derwin, who nearly wasn't, 'but my key has disappeared with the dragons.' We had looked for it everywhere, but there was no trace of it.

'Lee, you'd better tell me,' Raynor was totally bewildered.

'We caught some lizards that looked like dragons and they grew and grew and started to attack us and set the raft afire. We tried to beat them back and couldn't and then Derwin threw the green key at them and they shrank back into lizards again and died and finally we put the fire out.'

'I suppose you were fantasising about dragons and knights in armour doing gallant deeds and so on?'

'Um - well - yes. How did you guess?' I asked.

'Easy, the people on the island warned me. These are the Islands of Fantasies. If you weave a story in your head, or have fantasies about something, it comes true almost at once. Thank goodness you had the key; that's complete reality.'

'Perhaps it would be better,' I suggested, 'if in future we try to keep our attention on what is actually happening rather than telling fairy tales, because there's quite enough danger around without fabricating any more.'

'Yeah, well, I don't know with you lot sometimes,' said Raynor solemnly.

But we all burst out laughing; it had been so utterly bizarre. We put the raft back in order, coaxed our animals back on board and were finally ready to leave. Before we did so we took a last look at the ferocious little lizards swimming and jumping in and out of the water. I gave Derwin a big hug and was very proud of my young brother, because even if they were fantasy dragons, they had been very real and frightening at the time. We sailed out into the open sea once more and the wounds the boys had got while fighting the dragons and the burn marks on the deck disappeared entirely. It was very strange but nobody was complaining - after all, this was the Sea of Illusion.

Five days later the current carried us within sight of a coastline that stretched right across the horizon and we knew we were nearing the great northern continent. Somewhere, far, far beyond the endless line of dark green forest we could see on the shore, beyond who knew what lands and peoples, lay our goal: the land of Sasrar. As I looked at the wall of green, slowly getting nearer and nearer, I couldn't but wonder if we would ever really get there.

The Fourth Key

The Heart. The Seat of the Spirit

'The qualities of the heart centre are many and subtle. Not only is it the seat of the eternal spirit, but also reflects the loving protection of our family and is the source of courage and security. On our world the seat is Daish Shaktay and its influence also extends over Prince Osmar's lands and the monkeys' realm of Vandargar.'

From 'Luth's Wisdom', by Ahren Dairyman

CHAPTER 2

IN THE JUNGLE

The next morning we saw the estuary of the river almost ahead of us. The current had died down, and we hoisted the sail. The wind was behind us, so we didn't have any problem sailing upriver, as it was broad and flowed slowly. The jungle-clad banks were so wide apart one could hardly see from one side to the other. No one said anything but we all prayed the road Merien had told us about really did exist or we were in for a very hard time in the near future.

By the following day the banks were closer together, and in the afternoon the tide was behind us pushing us on. This was a good thing because the wind had dropped and the fresh water was now flowing down towards us with more force than before. The sun was just setting when Derwin thought he could see something that might be a ruined tower poking up through the jungle, and then as we rounded a shallow bend we all saw it: a dark silhouette against the apricot sky of dusk. We decided to drop anchor and sleep on the raft, because we could see what we were doing better in the daylight. Also, the ruins looked spooky.

In the morning the tower looked less foreboding, and we could see a lot of other ruined buildings too, half overgrown with creepers. The roots and branches of many forest trees were doing their level best to engulf what little masonry survived. We all helped to punt the raft up to a half-vanished jetty, avoiding the fallen blocks just under the surface of the water and trying not to get our poles tangled up in the water weed. Ahren nearly got himself left on the top of a pole which got stuck in a mud bank, because he didn't have the sense to let go when it wouldn't come out.

It did not occur to us, in the morning sunlight with the birds singing and monkeys calling in nearby trees, to go and scout about to see if it was safe to land. Once we had landed we could see the forest was quite open, without much undergrowth, so we started taking off the stores we wanted. Some of us made up backpacks, while Ahren loaded up the donkey. For him the long holiday was over.

Derwin walked off a little way down the shore, jumping from one boulder to another and keeping his eyes to the ground in case of snakes. He had his fishing rod with him and soon found a good place to try for a late breakfast, out of sight in a small creek. There was a tasty fish in these shallows that Derwin could see darting around in the water and soon he had four or five plump ones lying in a row beside him on the bank. He heard some footsteps behind him and assumed it was one of us come to see how he was getting on. He could not have been more wrong.

'Hello, what have we here?' said the deep, rich voice of a man.

'A little fish, just waiting to be caught!' said another with a laugh. Derwin dropped his rod, but it was too late to run for the cover of the forest. The two men came and stood menacingly over him. They looked like pirates or at the least people on the wrong side of the law, any law. They were bristling with weapons and one of them reminded Derwin of someone that he had met recently. In his panic he couldn't think who.

Derwin had to stand still, and because of this he had a moment to collect his attention. He wondered what I would have done in this situation and then it came to him: feel their inner natures. Despite their aggressive appearance, their inner feelings were very cool. Derwin fervently hoped that if they were in tune with the universal flow of life they would never murder or kidnap.

'You'd better come along with us, young one. This is not the place to question you,' growled the first man.

'Come on, hurry up. Keep quiet and don't make a fuss,' threatened the other.

Derwin had no choice but to do as ordered. His heart was thumping and his knees were like jelly. This was as bad as dragons. He didn't want to give away that there were more of us, so did as they asked.

'Right, stand still. It's blindfold time. We're going to the Pirates' Lair,'

One put a coloured handkerchief over Derwin's eyes, but not very efficiently because he could still see where he was going through a crack at the bottom, by his nose. The first man had such a kindly smile it was almost as if it was a game, but nevertheless Derwin felt scared. The second man brought along the fishing rod and the fish. Now the others would have no clue at all as to what had happened to him, Derwin thought gloomily.

Once inside the jungle, where he was being pushed and pulled along a well-worn path, the first pirate held Derwin's hand firmly and guided him round roots and rocks in the path, then later took off his blindfold. After a few more minutes he heard the sound of many more voices and smelled a fire with fish frying. He recognised some of the voices as being those of the rest of us and his heart sank even further. He wondered why we didn't sound remotely desperate, rather the opposite.

'Look, there's Derwin!' cried Conwenna, between mouthfuls of food.

Derwin saw he was in a stronghold that had been put together out of one of the ruins. The walls consisted of bits and pieces of columns and other parts of different buildings: a carved portal here and a large square block there all put together in a hotchpotch fashion.

'Come and sit down,' said the girl who had been doing the cooking. She led Derwin to a spot near the fire and gave him something to eat. We had already been let into the secret, but didn't think to put Derwin out of his confusion. The breakfast was too tasty and we forgot. The man who had blindfolded him came and sat next to him, on a block of decorated marble which served as a seat.

'Sorry to have had to take you by surprise,' he began, 'but there were some shifty characters watching you from the other bank. I didn't trust them, and didn't like the way they were eyeing you through their telescope. So we captured you ourselves.' Derwin wasn't sure about all this. 'We're supposed to be slavers among our other trades, none of them legal, of course!' he laughed heartily. 'By the way, how's my cousin Mazdan?' Derwin realized who he looked like.

'Mazdan's fine,' mumbled Derwin, totally confused. 'Look, sorry to be rude and all that, but just what is going on?' He wanted to say, 'You people have a good cool feeling coming from you so you should be all right', but he didn't know how to put it to strangers.

'My name is Zafan, and we work with Master Theon in guarding the sea, the islands and some of the lands around the edge. At the moment we're posing as a gang of pirates or whatever. We can find out more about our enemies that way. The Emperor knows all about us; pays our salaries in fact. Your friends told me you've been with Mazdan and Merien and the rest. What beats me is why Merien didn't tell you to look out for us.'

'We haven't been here that long,' said another pirate. 'He might think we're still up the other end.'

'Merien may not have told you about us,' Zafan went on, 'but we've been getting messages about you. At least I think they were about you. Whoever was after you before is still after you. Was it that Dumpattick fellow?'

'It's more complicated than that,' interrupted Raynor, coming to sit on a nearby rock. 'It goes back to the Sorcerers of Teletsia.'

'Nasty one, but don't worry, you should have quite a head start on them. It's very difficult for their ships to sail straight across the sea. They have to go round the edges and that takes time. If the Sorcerers' ships do try to sail across, they meet with hurricanes or their compasses turn in circles, that sort of thing.' Zafan stared into the fire, and the cook came up.

'Here, we've nice coconut milk,' and she served everyone with green coconuts that had had their tops chopped off so we could drink the milk.

'Meet my sister Zafeena, one of our most accomplished spies,' but she was too busy feeding everyone to stop and talk. I looked more carefully at the cook, and underneath her untidy hair was a brave and proud expression, with dark, piercing eyes. We felt great joy and courage when we put our attention on her inner being. 'We had messages about a group of seven, but you are six. How so?'

'One of the girls stayed back at the Emperor's Citadel,' said Raynor glumly, then quickly changed the subject. 'We saw some mountains this morning, in the far distance, and over towards the east. Are those by any chance the mountains of the northern kingdom of Sasrar that we're making for?'

'No, those aren't mountains; they're the hills of Daish Shaktay, a very troubled country at present. You must travel up the centre of the continent, and it's a long way yet. The centre is easier to travel, but there are a lot of dangers: lawlessness, petty wars and worse.'

We talked for some time, letting our breakfast sink down. Later on Zafeena took us into the jungle and showed us which plants and fruits we could eat, and which would be helpful as healing herbs. She also gave us a small box of tinctures and dried herbs that she had previously picked and prepared. Since my father's business was medicinal herbs, this was very interesting for me. At about midday we went back to the hideout, where Zafan was mending fishing nets. We sat and watched him, and chatted, and after some time one of his mates came in. He had been taking his turn watching at the port, from a hidden vantage point in one of the ruins.

'Funny thing happened just now sir,' he said to Zafan.

'Mn?' Zafan had a piece of twine in his mouth, and was more interested in his net than anything else.

'I was up in the peephole in the tower, looking round as usual, and noticed the raft those young 'uns came in on. Seemed normal. Then I looked again, and I could have sworn it was smaller. The third time I looked – I don't know – it looked like it was melting. I thought I'd had a late night or something, but the more I looked, the more it appeared to shrink and melt.' The mate looked anxious, waiting for Zafan to make some strong comment, probably on the state of his eyesight. Zafan looked up and took the string out of his mouth.

'Then?' he wasn't overly surprised. If he was Mazdan's cousin he wasn't going to be fazed by this sort of thing. The mate went on, eyeing us nervously. Maybe he thought we were going to melt too.

'So then I think to myself, "Dan, this is mad. Go and have a closer look". Now sir, I don't expect you to believe what I say, but......'

'Go on,' Zafan went on mending.

'By the time I'd walked down the stairs of the tower, and you know they are very old, and spiral, and you've got to look sharp or you can fall.'

'And?'

'I walked over to the quayside, and all I could see of the raft were a few ropes and shreds of sail floating in the harbour. And then the strangest thing of all: I looked into the water, very clear there, and just where she'd been moored, on a rock was a beautiful jewel, like a flower. It had six petals, and each petal had a jewel in it. How it got there I don't know.' We smiled at each other. 'It was a treasure, no doubt, and I picked it up. As I held it in my hand it dissolved into dust and water right there in front of my eyes. Before it did though, I felt a strange coolness flowing through my body. You must think I've gone mad.'

'Possibly not. Let these young folk tell us their story.'

We told them about our magic raft which had carried us so well over the Sea of Illusion, and telling our tale gave us confidence for the unknown that lay ahead. Talking about miracles makes one believe them and also makes one realise how amazing they are. We'd become like fish in water that don't realise what good stuff it is. As we talked, I saw that we had been beginning to take all the extraordinary things that had happened to us for granted, as if they were our right. In my heart I thanked the Mother Earth, or whatever it was that was looking after us so well.

The next morning, for the benefit of anyone who might be spying on Zafan or us, we 'escaped' our captors. Zafan did not want to blow his very useful cover as a pirate, so we made a drama of sneaking out of the camp while Zafan's crew feigned sleep. We all had backpacks; Heggo was heavily laden, and only Nog continued to treat the whole journey as the most wonderful and longest dog outing in history.

The road led through thick forest but was relatively clear. It was made of large worn paving stones and had seen a lot of use over many years; the overhanging branches had been cut back many times, and not much moss grew on the stones. We trudged on, very unfit. Lee was starting to get blisters and Derwin moaned that his backpack was too much for him. I didn't do the big sister thing and take some of his stuff, because my own pack was so heavy. No one spoke much. It was quiet and still, then Ahren broke the silence.

'Do you think there are dangerous beasts in this jungle?'

'Bound to be,' I muttered, feeling hot and tired.

'You don't have to remind us,' said Lee moodily. He was trying to tell himself that his blisters weren't as painful as they felt, so wasn't at his best.

We walked on through the patchy sunlight. Lee and Ahren kept their bows and arrows ready, and Raynor had his catapult, with which he could be lethal. Give them their due, they were at least trying to make us feel safe. We didn't see any forest animals but heard scuttlings in the trees now and again. Once we heard a noise that sounded like a hunt, as if different sorts of animals were chasing each other.

Twice we met mule trains laden with goods, bound for the old port, because Zafan had told us that a few boats still came in there. The muleteers were armed and warned us of trouble further on but didn't say what. Later in the afternoon, after stopping to eat and rest in the heat of the day, we saw a group of hermits, sitting under a tree and chanting to their god, oblivious of anyone else, looking skinny and the worse for wear. I hoped Zafeena would give them a decent meal if they wandered in her direction. So the journey went on for some days. We got less stiff, less blistered, and used to trudging rather than watching the sea go by.

Then one day we had decided it was time to stop for our midday rest and food. Conwenna had noticed a stream by the road, a short way into the forest, and insisted that we should all paddle our hot feet in it, which we did. Ahren had shot a brace of birds which he plucked while I made a fire. Zafan had given us some of the black dust - the 'fool's gold' that Persheray had told us about. A few grains of it burnt for quite a time, long enough to get even damp wood going, for cooking on.

In the absence of Tandi, I was the cook. I'm good with herbs, being as we grew them professionally back home, and Zafeena had shown me some tasty ones growing hereabouts. I stewed the birds in our iron cooking pot, with some roots we had found, and it turned out rather well. We had some hard cakes which Zafeena had given us to mop up the gravy. Everyone was happy and I felt mellow. It's nice to know your cooking is going down well.

We were all sleepy, except Lee. He had that tidy mind of a sailor, and liked to wash up after a meal before he could relax. No one was going to get in his way, and as was his habit he collected up our plates, cooking pot, and communal knife and scooped up some ash from the fire to use instead of soap. Then he went down the stream to a shady pool to 'do the dishes' jungle style.

We lay around and ate some bluish fruits, a cross between a plum and a mango, which we had found. They were messy and squishy but tasted quite good, and after that we were sinking into drowsiness when Lee came running back from the pool, hanging on to the cooking pot and plates, in a great hurry. We sat up and shook off the cobwebs of sleep, as Lee looked very alarmed.

'Quick, up those trees!' he cried. 'I've just seen two large tigers, sniffing around and looking for something. Don't bother about the animals; they'll have to look after themselves. Hurry! Any tree will do – that one – it's got creepers.'

We'd never seen Lee so frenzied, and within seconds we pushed and pulled one another up a large tree directly above us. We climbed as high as we could, not knowing if tigers were good climbers too, and hoping they weren't. Unfortunately Heggo didn't like being left out and came and stood under our tree, braying loudly, and Nog did his bit to attract any creature within earshot by barking frantically as well.

'Oh shut up Nog!' shouted Conwenna, 'Ahren, get your donkey to stop that racket!' But Raynor and Ahren were far too busy trying not to fall out of the tree to worry about their animals.

'Oh no! Look along the road!' whispered Lee below the noise of the animals, who showed no sign of letting up. Lee could see through a gap in the foliage that below us, walking majestically along the road, were not just two tigers, but a whole group of them sniffing the air and peering in every direction. They were looking for something and we hoped it wasn't us or our animals. I was on the lowest branch and had the best view of the road.

'I often see those tigers in my dreams!' I cried. 'They'll help us!'

'Shh, Asha. Are you mad?' said Raynor, trying to be calming and sensible. 'Do you want them to come over here?'

'Asha, you're on a wild trip again,' said Lee patronizingly. 'You've got to snap out of this nonsense. You know what Mazdan said.'

'Maybe you're still in your dream. With luck we all are,' added Ahren.

I was confused; my confidence shaken for a moment. I fell quiet. The tigers padded on towards us. They stopped at the foot of the tree, and showed absolutely no interest in either Heggo, who had taken off into the jungle by now, or Nog, who had also run away to a safe distance. As I looked down they were horribly close to me, perched on the lowest branch. I could see something even more extraordinary; they had gold collars around their necks. No one said anything for a few minutes, and the tigers sat down and waited. We were all wondering how long we were going to be stuck up this tree, and then something came over me and my courage returned.

'Please believe me, I've had dreams of these tigers every night since we came into this forest,' I repeated. 'They even have gold collars on in my dreams, and they always reassure me that they're guarding us, but can only help us if we trust them. We've got to actually ask for their help.' No one said anything, because we were all numb with fear. One of the tigers was trying to climb the tree, but not managing to. So far.

'Fine then,' muttered Ahren, 'you go first then.' Then he wished he hadn't, because at that moment there was a resounding crack and the branch I was on slowly collapsed and deposited me in the middle of the tigers. Derwin wailed in horror, and Ahren started clambering down to try to help me. The others were silent from shock.

The tigers bounded towards me and everyone above assumed it was all over. They couldn't see me because I was lost in the greenery, and as the great beasts came for me, time slowed down and the dream I had had the night before came back to me in a flash.

'We tigers guard this realm,' one had said, 'and we've been trying to guard you, because one of you has the key. We've been fighting off creatures that have been trying to kill you for days now. It would make things much easier if you could ride on us, but you've got to be brave enough to trust us. All you have to do is ask for our help.' At this point I had woken up from the dream because even more mosquitoes than usual had bitten me.

The tigers were standing over me and I could even feel their breath on my face. I looked at them through the leaves and they looked back. I wished I could faint from fear but it didn't happen. Nothing happened. No one made a sound. Then all of a sudden my fear went away, and as it did, the tigers lay down and put their heads on their paws, all except one, that made its way carefully through the leaves and put its right forepaw gently on my hand. Then it picked its paw up and stood with its head bowed. I don't know what happened next, but somehow it seemed perfectly normal to climb on the broad striped back of the tiger and clutch onto the golden collar around its neck.

The others still insist I must have been stunned from my fall, but I know my mind was quite clear. I remember the tiger taking me for a short walk, and when we got back to the tree something equally dire was happening. Conwenna and Derwin had already tumbled out of the tree and were cringing at its foot, almost underneath the rest of the tigers, who were roaring and pouncing in a terrifying fashion. Lee, Raynor and Ahren were still up the tree, fighting off an unseen foe. As my tiger came up to the tree it knelt down and gently tipped me off, then went to join the fight.

I saw what the boys and tigers were fighting - very large birds, with few feathers and vicious beaks. They had black leathery wings, but their appearance was not what horrified me so much as the fact that they were trying to attack all the others. The tigers were doing their best to defend Conwenna and Derwin, who were lying on the ground. The birds kept swooping down and trying to claw at the children's eyes, while the tigers snarled and roared and pounced. Many birds, some as large as Derwin, lay dead on the ground nearby but more and more kept coming. The air was whirring with their wings and one by one the three older boys half fell, half jumped out of the tree as the onslaught of the birds became too much. As long as they cringed under the tigers they were all right, and after a few more minutes the birds flew up into the tree to have a breather. We now noticed that the whole tree was full of large nests and we had disturbed the birds at home. My tiger came up to me and nuzzled me to get on to it again, then made the same gesture to the others, to get onto the other tigers.

'I know you lot think I'm mad, but these tigers have just saved us, and it looks like it's either tigers or birds. I'd rather go along with the tigers at this point,' I said, and clambered on mine. Then I had an inspiration, and got off again. I went up to Derwin, sitting in a shaken heap on the ground, picked him up and put him on the nearest tiger before he could do anything about it. The tiger didn't mind at all. Then I did the same with Conwenna.

At this moment we heard the ominous cawing of the birds, which started to attack again in greater numbers, and the three boys got the message. We grabbed our backpacks and other belongings, climbed on the closest tiger and hung on to their gold collars. We found tiger riding a very slippery business, much harder than keeping on the back of a horse. They bounded up the road and away from the colony of birds, who were not interested in us now we were not threatening their nests. Nog appeared out of the undergrowth, and somehow we managed to find Heggo. Ahren held onto him with a long rope, and did fall off more than once when Heggo, always difficult, stopped in his tracks, but strangely, our animals were not afraid of the tigers.

They ran on for some time until we came to the top of a rise from where we could see the jungle below us like a green sea. Here the tigers stopped and we slid off them, shocked, exhausted and not knowing what to think of this latest turn of events.

Lee and Ahren came up and apologized to me. I said not to worry, it wasn't surprising they had thought I was crazy. Ahren was already making a friend of the tiger that had carried him, but Conwenna was still very afraid of hers. I tried to calm her down but she was shaking with fear. She had been in jungles with her father on his prospecting trips, and had a very fixed idea about what tigers did to people. Finally I persuaded her that these were different and had just saved our lives, and honestly didn't look as if they were about to eat us. Even if they were, there wasn't much we could do about it, but I didn't say that aloud.

Raynor looked ahead over the country to the north. Trees, trees and more trees to the horizon. He was cautiously stroking his tiger, and thinking that yet again we had been saved in the most extraordinary way by what could only have been at the least benign fate, and at best something very near magic. The tigers made it very clear that they did not intend to leave us yet, and soon we mounted them again and lolloped up the road.

Chapter 3

The Monkey at the Crossroads

For three more days we travelled along the old road through the jungle, which thinned out as we went north. With our swift steeds we went much faster. Raynor fell off once; he turned his head to look at something and lost his balance, and Conwenna still shook with fear when she had to get on her tiger, even though she was better once we got going. Although she was good with domestic animals, she never felt happy with the tigers. Lee was in seventh heaven as his blisters from walking had never cleared up; he just bravely stopped grumbling about them.

At one or two places the tigers left the road and made a detour through the trees to avoid villages; they understood that they would terrify any watching villagers if they loped through with humans on their backs. Through breaks in the trees we could sometimes see groups of mud walled huts thatched with leaves, always surrounded by stockades. On one occasion we were sitting by the side of the road eating a meal, and the tigers had gone off into the undergrowth. A mule train came past, and the muleteer had a nasty face and eyed us suspiciously. We pretended not to notice and greeted him politely.

On the afternoon of the third day the heat had passed and a breeze came up. We left the jungle for a more barren upland where the grass was dry and bushes and cactuses grew in clumps. The tigers slowed down and we could see a crossroads, but because of the lie of the land we couldn't work out which road led north. The tigers stopped and stood panting as we slid off them. Above us was a large column, engraved with aged and worn writing in three different scripts. Above the inscriptions was a design of a wheel with twelve spokes, also very weathered. Raynor got all scholarly about one of the scripts and started deciphering it. He exercised his brain and we sat on the side of the road in the shade of the column to rest.

As was their habit the tigers slunk off into the thicket where no passer-by would see them. Derwin opened his water bottle, a leather covered gourd with thongs attached to the neck, which had come all the way from Teletsia. He passed it round and we all had a swig. Then Lee brought us some cactus fruits he had found, with little hairy thorns, but very tasty. We were endeavouring to eat the fruits and not prick our fingers, and didn't notice a wizened old figure coming towards us out of the long grass.

At first we thought he was an old man with long arms, short legs and a long cotton garment, but as he came closer he began to look more like a monkey or primeval man. He walked up to us and Derwin stood up politely and offered him some water. He didn't say anything, but accepted the water, sat down beside us and started to scratch his nose in a rather monkeyish fashion. We tried not to stare, but kept glancing at him and then away, and there was a silence between us. We were all wondering the same thing: could he tell us the way to go?

Nog solved the problem. Now and again he really proved his worth even though most of the time he was mainly interested in food, love and attention. He had found a long straight stick, came trotting up out of nowhere with it in his mouth and presented it to the old man, laying it carefully at his feet and demanding a pat in recognition of services rendered.

'Thanks dog, I was looking for that,' said the old man.

'He does sometimes make himself useful,' Raynor began.

'Yes, he's a good chap,' said the old man kindly, giving Nog his well-earned pat.

'Please sir, could you tell us which of these roads leads north?' went on Raynor.

'That one,' said the old man, pointing at the track which went west, 'but you'd be unwise to go along it right now. There's trouble ahead that you should avoid if you can.'

'But we have to go north,' broke in Lee. In answer, the old man started drawing something in the dust. Lee watched with interest as he traced out the design of a twelve petalled flower with a stalk. Lee clutched at the key hidden around his neck, which had twelve petals. We simultaneously felt the old man's inner nature: coolness, peace and great power. Also, we all felt a strong sense of love and confidence, but we said nothing. The old monkey-man shook his head despondently. Again he traced the shape of the flower in the dust. Ahren, with what seemed to us to be his usual tactlessness, was the one to speak out.

'Look Lee! He's drawing a flower like the one on top of the key you wear!' Everyone glared at him and the old man went on gazing at the dust. Ahren couldn't work out why the rest of us couldn't grasp that the old man was saying, 'I'm here to help you.' After a few more moments of strained silence, he levered himself to his feet with the help of his stick, and started to hobble off down the road. We all looked at each other.

'Lee, show him your key!' cried Conwenna. Lee felt for the golden key studded with rubies under his tunic. The old man turned round and came back to us.

'Very difficult to make you humans see sense. You do make your lives unnecessarily complicated sometimes.' He spoke in perfect Teletsian, a somewhat harsh dialect of the common speech. He sat down and we did too. 'Now listen, all of you. I haven't got time to hang around while you decide whether to trust me. You'd better look to your dog in future. There are enemies ahead and there's soon likely to be a war in these parts. Although this land is ruled by a good man, there's an evil king to the east of here who's trying to find an excuse to invade us, and his spies and soldiers are all over the place.

'I saw from my hiding place that you arrived here riding tigers. Not many people do that, even round here. You must have one of the keys to be able to ride them but perhaps you don't understand that it helps you to work with the tigers. Let me show you how.'

Lee's key was now outside his clothing. Without so much as a 'May I?' the old man whipped it off Lee's neck. As he held it I noticed for the first time that its stem was hollow.

'When you want to call the tigers, do this,' he said, held it to his mouth, sideways, and played it like a very small flute. He blew a high-pitched note and within seconds the tigers were standing obediently in a row before us. The old man said something to them and they again slunk off into the long grass. He returned the key to a stunned Lee.

'Only those like you, whose desires and hearts are pure and clean can use the keys in that way. If someone with bad intentions tries to – well, I'd rather not risk the fury of those creatures.'

The sun was sinking low and the shadow of the column stretched across the plain, and we still did not know where to go next. Raynor was about to ask the old man when he said, 'I have a hermitage near here, and you'd better come and spend the night. I'm going to stay up here as I have to watch for someone, but you go ahead. The tigers know the way. Humans don't trust those not of their own kind. Tend to think they're the only ones with sense on this earth.' I had just been wondering how someone who looked like an evolved monkey could be so wise. Guilt overwhelmed me, because I was sure he had read my thoughts.

As dusk crept up around us we were on our way. After two or three bends in the road, the darkness deepened and the tigers slowed down as they came to a hollow. They froze, snarled and looked carefully from side to side. We tried not to be frightened, and in the stillness heard the sound of some animal making off into the trees. I was last and as we were about to round the next bend I turned and thought I saw a solitary figure on a mule, standing on the road behind us. I said nothing, because it could have been my imagination.

The Moon of Good Fortune was in the sky and the tigers left the road and wound their way along a narrow track. The plain stretched out endlessly in the moonlight, but suddenly a deep valley presented itself in front of us. We took a steep path between two boulders, and the tops of the trees below were almost level with the plain we had come from. We dismounted and scrambled down the side of the valley, holding the tigers' collars for support.

In the valley we could see lights and a dog barked, perhaps it had caught a whiff of tiger. Once on the valley bottom, the tigers made for a group of simple hut-like houses by a stream. Then they disappeared and left us standing with Nog and Heggo. The dog inside continued to yammer and soon a young man came and opened the wooden gate in the stockade surrounding the compound. He held a lantern, and from his noble bearing, strong body and commanding voice looked more like a warrior than a hermit.

'Who are you? Good gracious. Children! Well, mostly. Did Luth send you?' he began.

'Yes,' Raynor replied, 'if that is the old man we met at the crossroads.'

'That's Luth all right. Come in. Young people like you shouldn't be outside at this time of night.'

CHAPTER 4

PEACE AND CONFLICT

Another moon now rose, and what with their light, and the light of the lantern, we could see that the man who had let us in had a wonderful smile, one of those radiant expressions which warms your heart and lightens up everything around. He was of medium height, with thick dark hair and had that casual confidence of someone who is used to being in charge, but also had a modesty about him, as if we were important to him. He wore a pair of simple cotton trousers and a tunic and on his feet were wooden sandals. Once inside the compound we could see the buildings were made of mud bricks and thatched with reeds, all very neat and tidy. A number of young men, presumably monks from their shaven heads, were scurrying around on their evening business.

'My name is Osmar,' our welcomer began, and noticing Conwenna and me, he said, 'Come and meet my wife, then we'll take it from there. Oh, and give that donkey to one of the monks.' Then he called one of them, who dutifully took Heggo away, after Ahren had showed him how to get the better of Heggo's stubborn nature.

Osmar led us through the compound to where we could see a small cottage with a garden in front, a little away from the other buildings. In the open doorway was a beautiful lady. Like Osmar, she was early in the prime of life and despite her simple garments she too had a regal bearing. She greeted us and asked us to come in.

'This is my wife Neysa,' he said. 'Tonight we have visitors from afar, my dear. Can we give them a good meal?'

'Naturally, it's a pleasure. You must be very tired,' and she beckoned us. We left our shoes outside and went into the spotlessly clean cottage, decked with flowers. We noticed weapons hung on the wall: a large bow and arrows, a sword and a simple gun; Osmar was no pacifist monk. Neysa took us into one of the rooms, and we were soon enjoying the luxury of warm water to wash with. She insisted on lending us some of her clean clothes, which were too big for Conwenna, but she didn't refuse the offer. The boys went to a bathhouse across the yard and were given similar treatment by a young monk who came to help.

Raynor went outside with Osmar to see about Nog. Osmar explained that Luth was from a race of beings different from humans - another strand of evolution - who were highly intelligent, could speak perfectly, create fine art and appreciate beauty in all its forms, but unlike humans they were not so troubled by ego, that tendency to think of 'I' all the time, and to be dominating and violent. He also told Raynor more about the hermitage and how many young humans and some of Luth's folk came for a longer or shorter time to get away from the world and look within themselves. Raynor wondered what Osmar and Neysa were doing there but it didn't seem polite to ask.

We sat on the floor of the veranda, and Luth came and joined us. 'Good,' he said, 'I knew Osmar and Neysa would look after you.' Neysa served us with a delicious meal; she offered the food to Luth first and treated him with great respect. We were given plates made of large leaves stitched together with twigs, and on these were placed many delicacies made from nuts, roots, milk and fruits. There was also a stew that might have been deer. After we had finished, the plates were fed to the cows: a very sensible way of not having to wash up. To drink we were offered a cordial made of large red flowers that grew nearby and flavoured with forest honey.

'I did some eavesdropping after you left, up at the crossroads,' Luth explained. 'The ogre king who's trying to invade this country has been sent word about you by one Dumb Pet Tick, or some such name. There's a large reward out for you, but fortunately they're looking for a group of seven, not six. Maybe they made a mistake, good thing for you if they did. This king has spies all over the place. Unfortunately one saw you twice today - he was disguised as a muleteer.' Raynor told him why there were only six of us, and Luth continued, 'Where are you making for?'

'We are looking for a kingdom called Sasrar, and we need to travel northwards.'

'There's so much trouble around here at present, it would be hard for you to get through.'

'What can we do?' asked Lee.

'The situation on the northern road is so bad that you might be best taking the almost impossible route through the desert and over the mountains. I don't know if young humans could survive that journey though.' Luth spoke these words as if he was referring to puppies of a rather delicate breed.

'There's a hermit in the mountains not too far to the east of here who could advise you,' put in Osmar. 'If you could get there quickly, you could visit him to see what he said.'

'They've been lent the tigers,' said Luth.

'In that case you'll be fine,' said Osmar. 'At the moment, those tigers guard this hermitage, and when they disappeared last week I knew to expect something. They've been here for some months, guarding us, but they came to find you because they respond to the subtle power radiated by that key you're wearing.' He looked at Lee.

Conwenna and I slept in the main room, and the boys put their bedrolls on the veranda. I missed not having the stars above me, but it was good to know that if it rained I wasn't going to wake up wet, which had happened twice recently.

The next morning we went out to the bathhouse in the garden to freshen up and saw Luth sitting under a tree in the corner of the yard, saying prayers to the rising sun. We sat respectfully by him and joined in. After he had finished, he greeted us and asked us how we had slept. We wanted to ask him about our hosts and he understood that before we asked.

'So, you want to know why Osmar and Neysa are living here?'

'Yes, please,' said Ahren.

'I'll give you the short version, otherwise we'll have a cold breakfast.' Luth was not remotely bothered about cold breakfasts, but Neysa and one of the young monks were preparing food for us, and he was very particular about politeness, especially towards our hosts.

'Some years ago,' began Luth, 'a horrible race of creatures invaded the lands to the east of here. They started off as humans, but they became more and more evil, and more and more terrible looking. The king of these ogres enslaved many people and took over many lands. He wants to occupy the country around here and was looking for a reason.

'When Prince Osmar came to find a wife, he met Princess Neysa and knew she was right for him, but unfortunately the ogre king also had his eye on her. Neysa's father decided to have a competition to win her hand, so there was a shooting contest, and Osmar won against many others, including the ogre king himself. The king didn't accept the outcome of the contest, and threatened to steal Neysa away by force.

'Osmar and Neysa decided to take matters into their own hands. Osmar announced he wanted to get away for some time to keep the peace, and intended to go on a long journey with his new bride Neysa. They've been living in hiding here until everything settles down. We're still in the land ruled by Osmar's father. That hasn't really solved the problem of the ogre king, who's planning to invade the country anyway. I reckon the business with Neysa was just an excuse to make trouble. In the absence of Osmar there's no one to lead the armies and defend the country, so it looks as if he's going to have to go back to his father's palace. That's why I have royalty living in my humble abode, and that's why the tigers look after us. The tigers serve the spiritual guardians of this realm, and those like Osmar who have one of the twelve petalled keys.

'Let's have breakfast. We mustn't keep our princess waiting. She's an excellent cook.'

Breakfast was as tasty as supper had been, and afterwards the boys prepared to leave for the mountains, to seek the advice of the wise hermit. Luth wanted us girls and Derwin to wait at the hermitage, and then if it was possible to travel to Sasrar through the eastern mountains, the older boys could come back and get us in a few days time. Since the incident with the dragons Derwin had started to grow up; he was becoming more independent and spent more time with Lee and Ahren than with me, so wasn't too pleased at being left with us and the animals, but Luth was adamant.

Lee whistled through his key and sure enough the tigers were soon waiting outside the stockade behind the cottage. When they realized only three of them would be needed the others melted back into the trees. Osmar opened a back gate and they came into the garden, saw Neysa and came and lay respectfully at her feet, purring happily. She patted them one by one.

'You must never be afraid of these tigers,' she said. 'As long as you have courage, and the key, they'll always obey you. They only kill for food and are not unnaturally aggressive. They'll protect you, and attack anyone who tries to harm you, especially if your attackers are out of tune with the balance of creation. They feel your inner selves and act on those feelings.'

'Do you ever ride a tiger?' Raynor asked Luth

'I have, on occasions. We're old friends, and I've known these from when they were cubs, and their fathers and grandfathers too,' said Luth. He walked to the top of the ravine with the boys, and once on the plain said something to the tigers in the classic language, which is used internationally by learned people everywhere. 'I've told them where to take you. As long as you go with the flow and don't let those human egos of yours spoil everything, they'll get you there.'

The tigers bounded eastwards, knowing the boys didn't want to waste any time. These tigers were as big as a small horse and all that day, and the next, they ran on and on through rolling plains, making wide detours to avoid villages, and at about midday of the third day were going along a part of the road that was little more than a dusty track. They had again been skirting villages and avoiding roadside farms, but now, with the boys' legs aching from gripping to stay on their backs, they stopped and knelt down. This was their 'please get off' signal. The tigers left the boys on the road and disappeared into the bushes. Lee noticed that round the corner was a village, and they walked on until they came to a well in the centre of the group of houses.

As they reached it, very thirsty, a woman was just leaving. She wore a long, brightly coloured dress, gold earrings and silver bangles, and was carrying three large brass water pots on her head, one on top of the other. With her was a young child who was chasing a hen and its chickens. Some village dogs managed a few half-hearted growls and a lazy bark, but it was too hot to get serious about frightening off strangers and they soon went back to sleep. As soon as she saw the boys, the woman put down her pots, went back to the well and let down the bucket to get them water. First they drank and then she poured the extra water over their dusty hands and feet, which was very cooling.

The boys insisted on carrying her pots for her, and when they reached her home she invited them to share her simple meal of pumpkin and boiled grains. She told them her name was Kanta, and about her life: hard work, often monotonous, but nevertheless, until recently, secure and peaceful. Her husband came in, a comfortable farmer who was content with his lot in life. He told them things had not been too good of late, and some hideous, ogrous creatures had been seen that very morning, riding large mules. Both he and his wife were nervous of letting the boys go on, but they were determined. They realized that maybe the tigers had been avoiding their enemies as well as villages, but said nothing.

They waited until they were well out of the village before Lee called the tigers with his key, but they must have been followed by at least one inquisitive urchin. As the boys were mounting, they heard a great hue and cry in the village, and heard people shouting 'Tigers! Tigers!' They made a quick getaway, and laughed that they had left the good villagers something to gossip about for a long time afterwards.

By the close of the day they were well into the foothills of the mountains. They were exhausted, and as they were about to lie down and sleep they heard a rustling in the undergrowth. Lee called the tigers with his key, and they soon came up. The rustling had stopped as soon as he had whistled, but the tigers were not happy about something, and swung their tails and sniffed about before slinking off again. By this time the boys were completely worn out and practically collapsed where they stood. Lee forgot to hide his key, and went to sleep with it hanging loosely around his neck. It twinkled in the moons' light and the rubies glowed dark red.

Later on, when the boys were sound asleep, a gruesome figure padded up to them. It was a vile specimen of a horrible race of beings. They had originally been humans, but they worshipped a terrible crocodile faced creature, and as the years passed, and their inner selves became more and more evil they slowly turned into these ghastly creatures. This one had horns, a pointed nose and ears, and its body was covered in scales. Its feet had claws instead of toes. Over its back were a bow and some arrows. It espied the golden key and bent over it, gloating to itself, and rubbing its clawlike hands together in glee.

It stealthily took some powder out of a pouch slung around its neck. He put a pinch under Lee's nose. Lee sneezed, and soon slid into a deeper state of unconsciousness as the anaesthetic in the powder took its effect. The ogre looked around to check that the other boys were sleeping and carefully removed the key from Lee's neck, holding it gingerly as if it were burning him. It crept back into the shadows to await morning, gloating over its prize. This was a little extra bonus to the much bigger reward he intended to pick up as well.

The three boys woke up early in the cold dawn light, before the sun was up. Lee had a throbbing headache, and only realized his key was gone when he wanted to call the tigers. Then he recalled a horrendous dream he had had, in which some ogrous monster had tried to strangle him. Lee searched for the key where he had been lying, and the creature of the previous evening stepped out of the trees in the gloomy dell. Its long teeth were showing out of the corners of its mouth, and it tried to speak the classic language of diplomacy, but it came out all snarled up and sounded like a cross between a screech and a groan. It had an arrow on its bow, aimed at Lee's heart. He was barely two arms' length away from Lee so there was no question of making a run for cover. He could just about understand what it was saying.

'I've got your key, and if you want it back you must do as I say,' it snarled. 'My master will soon be the king of all the lands around here. He's very friendly with a certain Dumb Pet Tick who lives on an island in the Great Sea. Mr Tick is very interested in you boys, preferably alive, otherwise dead will do.

'He knows you have great powers, but my master will spare your lives if you work for him. Then he won't need this Tick chap, and won't pass you on to him. I want you to tell me where Princess Neysa has gone, because my master is going to win her for himself sooner or later. If I help him find her he'll make me very rich. I'm sure you know where she is, because they say you kids can know anything.'

Between the ogre's difficulty speaking the language, his own difficulty understanding it, the ogre's odd shifts of logic and his own rising fear, Lee was very confused. Raynor, who had been standing behind, explained to the ogre that Lee didn't know the classic language, and gave a quick whispered translation. Lee saw a glimmer of hope for escape. He went into his inner fortress of thoughtless awareness and a calm stillness came over him. Panic receded and courage returned. He asked Raynor to translate for him.

'All right, we do know where the princess is and we'll take you to her,' Lee admitted, 'but it's a long way from here and she won't be there long. We can't walk back, because it would take ages, so we'll have to go on our mounts. They're entirely obedient to whoever has the key, so if you have it, they'll obey you. All you have to do is blow through the stalk of the flower, and they're at your service. They can easily carry all of us.'

The ogre muttered and replaced its bow and arrow with a cruel looking machete, which it wielded with one hand.

'Could it be persuaded to whistle through the key?' Lee thought, and prayed it would be stupid enough to use it. He remembered what Luth had said about what would happen if anyone with dark intentions called the tigers. Ahren and Raynor realized what was going on and also prayed hard. It was a tense moment. The ogre put the key to its mouth and whistled, but instead of a clear, silvery sound coming out, as it did when Lee used it, the key emitted a wavering wail, which echoed spookily through the nearby rocks and trees.

The boys heard a snarl and the tigers rushed towards them through the undergrowth. They pounced on the ogre, jaws open, fangs exposed and lacerating claws outstretched. Lee staggered back, out of the way of their fury. It was like another earthquake and he realized they had only been playing with the birds in the jungle, compared to this all-out attack on their sworn enemy. The three boys heard the ripping of flesh and saw blood spurting out onto the ground as the tigers reduced the ogre to a pulp of flesh, blood, bones and torn clothing. Even Ahren, the butcher's nephew, was horrified.

Soon it was all over and there was silence again except for the gurgle of a nearby stream and the birds singing their dawn chorus. Lee's tiger, with bloodstained mouth and paws, came and knelt at his feet and gave him back the golden key which had saved them all.

The boys picked up their backpacks and left the gory mess on the ground. They led the tigers to the stream and helped them wash themselves off; the tigers understood this was done in gratitude, so let the boys clean them up with damp grass. Concentrating on washing off the beasts helped dispel the shock of the whole incident. The boys were in a dilemma as to whether they should go on or not, but Lee insisted that everything the ogre had said was idle threats. Ahren felt that having got so far, it would be mad to turn back, so they set off again, and the tigers knew exactly where to take them. Raynor said nothing, for although he was getting braver by the day, and was fast coming out of his shell of scholarliness, he still wasn't too good at violence and the sight of blood.

CHAPTER 5

THE HERMIT IN THE MOUNTAINS

All the time the land was rising and the tigers pressed on. They hardly even allowed the boys to stop for a drink of water at a mountain stream and by evening were well into the high land, running up a valley that had a flat bottom, steep sides and a torrent of greenish water, flecked with white where it fell noisily over the many rocks and rapids. Ahead the snowy peaks of the mountains shone yellow and pink as the setting sun caught their tips, and they could already feel the cold, especially after the fiery heat of the plains.

They stopped under some pine trees where the fallen needles would make a soft bed, and this time the boys found a concealed spot to spend the night. They had a quick supper round a small fire, then lay down to sleep but were not afraid because they had the tigers to watch over them. Some time later Lee woke up again as he felt some warm furry creature snuggle up close to him. By the Moon of Compassion he recognized the face of his tiger. He was safe and secure, having it so close, but that was the problem, it snored so loudly and had very ticklish whiskers, which played across his face as it breathed rhythmically. Eventually exhaustion overcame Lee and he went back to sleep.

In the morning they were up at dawn and soon on again. The tigers skilfully jumped over rocks, and easily found the paths made by wild sheep and deer. The valley led to the highest peak in the area; it twisted and turned so much that the boys wondered if it was ever going to end, and then, suddenly and without warning, the tigers turned off the main valley into a little corrie at the side, hidden from the valley below, and to their surprise this part was much warmer. The boys thought it was because it caught more sun and less wind. Flowers bloomed, and birds sang in the trees which grew here, even though the rest of the area was above the tree line and there were only stunted bushes and heathers.

The boys slid off the tigers, who disappeared, and they had a feeling that they had arrived, whatever that meant. They sat resting in the meadow among the wind-tossed flowers and heard voices coming towards them, so ran and hid behind some nearby boulders. From behind some pale green larch trees they could soon hear the thumping of many feet as well as voices, and round the bend above them came a very odd group of beings, of all shapes and sizes. Some were giants, some dwarfs, some had dark gnarled skins from being in the hot sun and others had pale podgy faces as if they spent their lives mostly underground. Some had one eye, or an unusual number of fingers or toes. They all looked vaguely human, but with their hunched backs and knobbly knees the boys had to look twice to make sure.

Raynor and Lee had the sense to feel their inner natures and realized they were good and gentle, but Ahren was caught up by their odd outer appearance. Along with these strange humanoids, there were some animals: two lions, an old dog, a small elephant and a large snake. They were all singing and dancing in various odd ways and generally having a good time. The boys stepped out of their hiding place but Ahren, overcome by this ridiculous sight, started giggling uncontrollably. The others tried desperately to hush him but by now the strangers had seen the boys and came ambling over to them. Ahren was doubled up with laughter, and the other two were acutely embarrassed by his behaviour.

'Who are you?' enquired a one-toothed caricature of a man in a polite and cautious tone. He saw Ahren was completely out of control, and asked gently, 'Are you all right, lad?'

'It's just that it's all so funny,' Ahren said between cackles of laughter.

'What is, young one?' asked the man in a puzzled way.

'Everything - you - I mean -' the man looked suddenly hurt at having caused Ahren discomfort, but unfortunately he didn't notice. The monstrous creature in front of him may have looked strange and ugly, but he wanted to be friendly. Ahren didn't get this at all and went on in a tactless vein, 'Who on earth is the leader of this weird lot? Is he – ' but he never finished what he was saying, because out from behind the large boulder where they were standing slithered and hissed the large snake, and it darted towards Ahren. Everyone, including Ahren, went instantly quiet, and stood still as stones, but the long serpent went straight up to Ahren and bit him on the little finger of his left hand.

The entire band, which had been singing, dancing and generally enjoying life, became silent. They formed a circle around Ahren, who sank to the ground, gasping for breath and pale with pain and shock. Raynor felt utter anguish for not making Ahren shut up before it was too late. Lee was about to bend over Ahren to cut off his finger in an attempt to save his life, when a young girl, who could not have been more than ten or eleven, came running up. She wore a simple white shift, no shoes and her long black hair was loose, and wet from bathing. They could see she was the gentlest soul imaginable, and felt a great tenderness coming from her heart when she saw Ahren. She looked round for an explanation.

'He was about to say something very disrespectful about your great uncle,' said one, who had a kind smile.

'How dare he, a mere child?' complained an apish being.

'The snake bit him before we could stop it,' added a third.

'Poor lad, he didn't know what he was saying,' continued the one who had first spoken.

Meanwhile the young girl knelt down beside Ahren, who was on the edge of a coma, and gently held his hand, which was already swelling on account of the venom.

'I felt there was something wrong,' she began, 'that's why I came running up.' She stood up and said firmly, to folk twice her age and size, 'Please, all of you, forgive him, he's only young. We must take him to my great uncle while there's still time. Quick, make a stretcher – there isn't a moment to lose.'

The creatures helped Raynor and Lee lift him onto a makeshift stretcher, and three or four unearthly beings picked him up and made off with him, disappearing round the corner from where they'd come. Raynor, Lee and the young girl followed, wading through the field of flowers. As they stumbled on they heard the sound of rushing waters. The meadow came to an end and the valley turned into a stony gully, with a stream rushing through it from the base of a cliff. In the cliff were a number of caves, and from the top of it fell a thundering waterfall, pouring down cloud after cloud of bubbling water, some rising again in rainbow tinted spray.

On a flat rock at the side of the waterfall was a man, sitting cross-legged, completely relaxed and oblivious to the water pouring down nearby. His greying hair was long and tied up in a knot on his head, and he was wearing a simple woollen robe. The band of followers stood round him, and Ahren was laid out in front of him on the rock. Raynor and Lee stood at the back trying to see what was going on, but not wanting to push themselves forward. Their eyes met the seated man's, and they felt pure compassion coming from him.

'Young ones,' he began, looking at Lee and Raynor, 'what did your friend do to anger my followers, all of whom have so much respect for me?' They were silent, not knowing what to say. 'You must understand that many of them, because of their trust in me, have been saved from even worse states than your friend is now in, so they will hear nothing against me. Forgive them and he will be forgiven.' Lee and Raynor had not at any time felt anything against the strange band, but had been acutely ashamed of Ahren's behaviour.

The hermit now took Ahren's hand, and it was so swollen that his fingers were like fat carrots. Then the young girl arrived, and gave him a small sharp knife, and he made an incision in a vein of the arm, and began to suck out the poison. As he took out the poison, he took out many of Ahren's other problems as well.

The swelling immediately began to subside, and then the hermit began moving his hands over Ahren's body, as if he were raising some energy up his back and down towards his heart. They had seen others who had helped them use similar gestures when healing the rest of us. Ahren woke up, but froze in terror almost at once. He was now lying on his back, and we did not notice that the very snake who had bitten him had innocently come to have a look at the proceedings. It was quite docile now, and also respected the hermit, and no one was frightened of it. But the first thing Ahren saw when he opened his eyes was the snake peering at him, its beady eyes looking down on him from above. He flopped backwards.

'Oh no, not again!' He said weakly. Everyone laughed and the tension was broken. The unfortunate snake slithered off to the back of the group, somehow aware that it had done the wrong thing.

'He'll be all right now,' said the hermit. 'He may be rude and uncouth, but he's brave and courageous. He has a pure heart, and a strong faith in the loving power of the creator. If he didn't have that faith, he wouldn't have recovered. My great niece and I are merely instruments of that power.' A gust of wind blew a cloud of spray from the waterfall over us and he went on. 'Your friend must learn humility and respect. He may not be so lucky next time.' Then he turned to Raynor and Lee, 'Did you come looking for me?'

'We've come to ask your advice, sir,' Raynor answered, as politely as he could. 'We're looking for a safe way to the land of Sasrar. We were told to come and ask for your guidance by Prince Osmar, his wife Princess Neysa, and Luth. The tigers brought us here.'

'Hmn, yes. Osmar, Neysa, Luth, and tigers. Yes, you're in the flow. I knew that, of course, the moment I saw you. But some rough edges...' he looked at Ahren. 'Still, the heart is in the right place and you're getting a lot of help. Yes, I know about Sasrar. No, you'll have to go up the centre of the continent. The route through the desert north of here, and the mountains, is too difficult and dangerous. It's a good thing you came to see me, because this one,' he pointed at Ahren, 'would never have got into Sasrar with all that brash arrogance, and that means none of you would get there, because you have to go together.'

The hermit was silent and only the roar of the waterfall remained. Ahren was taken away and made comfortable in one of the nearby caves while the other two stayed sitting quietly by the master, who sat in meditation with his eyes closed and with most of his followers gathered around. The Teletsians felt peace and serenity creep over them and had the strange experience that this was reality, and everything else: Teletsia, their journey, even the tigers, were somehow shadows, a great illusion. At some point they heard the hermit say, 'Enjoy the bliss, my children.'

Raynor and Lee did not know how long they were there, but later they looked up and saw Ahren was again with them. His face looked healthy, and there was a gravity in it, a wisdom which had replaced the former look of impish mischief. Time passed and peace blew over them, a cloud of cool spray. The hermit opened his eyes and looked deeply at each of the boys. At least for that moment, anything which should not have been there was washed away by the spray of the waterfall.

'You are all good, very good,' he said deliberately, 'and now you must leave, because time runs differently here, and your companions will be wondering where you have got to.' Then he looked at Lee, and said, 'The snake and the lions that guard the pathway may not be so forgiving if I am not around, so show them your jewelled key, then you will be able to pass.' Lee wondered how he knew it was there, hidden under his tunic. Something prompted Lee to take it off and give it to the hermit to hold. He held it up and the sun flashed through the rubies.

'Gold and jewels are not for me,' he commented. 'The only gold I value is the joy in your hearts.' He gave the key back to Lee as if it had been a child's toy, and closed his eyes in meditation. All three boys felt a rush of power, peace and joy, radiating out from deep within their beings. Then they silently left.

Sure enough, on their way back to the flowery valley, there was the snake and the two lions barring the way, but when Lee held up the key they backed away respectfully. Once back in the valley, they all felt incredibly sleepy, and lay down for a nap. It seemed such a very good idea to lie down under the warm sky among the sweet scented flowers for half an hour or so.

When they woke up everything had changed. The tigers were lying by the boys' sides, muzzles on paws. Neither the warm valley, nor the flower filled meadow were anywhere to be seen. The boys were lying on a barren slope where only spiky grass and scrubby bushes grew. It was early morning.

'Did I have a dream about a flowery meadow, and a strange band of creatures?' said Raynor.

'No, not unless I had the same one,' replied Lee. 'Look at the jewels of my key, how rich and shiny they are!'

'Oh, come on, you philosophers!' laughed Ahren. 'My arm still aches like a hundred wasp stings, and I have little tooth marks on my finger.' He held it up for the others to see.

'This journey gets stranger and stranger,' added Lee.

'I think it makes more and more sense,' said Ahren, unexpectedly.

'How so?' asked Raynor.

'Asha got there ages ago, but she didn't think we would take her seriously. I overheard her talking to Conwenna,' continued Ahren. 'When she used to go off into her visions and things, she used to see the colours of the different centres inside people's subtle beings, and that they had different numbers of parts, like petals. She said they match the keys exactly. Like, the first one, at the base of the spine, is reddish, and the first key had four red jewels. Now we are at the fourth key, and the fourth subtle centre is at the level of the heart, she said. But she can't remember the colours any more, that knowledge has left her.'

Raynor shivered and pulled his cloak around him to ward off the chill wind blowing down from the snowfields above them in the mountains. He was eager to be off, but he couldn't resist asking this new Ahren one last question. 'So what about these people and animals we keep meeting, who help us so much?'

'Oh, that's easy. I mean, Luth spoke of that. They are the spiritual helpers, guardians, of the different countries, which are the different subtle centres of the earth. Mother Earth has subtle centres, like us. That's why we keep meeting them, because the keys draw us to them and them to us.' Ahren came out of his new profound mode and looked at the sky. 'If we don't move fast we're going to be caught in a blizzard.'

Above them piles of towering clouds were pouring over the peaks. The boys picked up their packs, climbed onto the tigers, and without even waiting for a word of command they bounded down the mountains, in a hurry to return to the warmer plains.

CHAPTER 6

THE TRIALS OF WAR

To begin with the tigers were their usual undauntable selves, and masters of whichever route they chose to take, but as they approached the villages, farms, towns and even forts of the plains country once more, they avoided the road even more than on the outward journey, and clung to the shadows and half hidden paths. When darkness came they ran on while the moons rose and night drew on. When they did stop for their riders to dismount, they more or less forced the boys to hide themselves in a dense thicket and one or other of the animals kept watch all the time. After a couple of hours they nudged the boys to wake them, and were off again before dawn. They eventually neared the village where they had been given food and the boys tugged at the gold straps around the tigers' necks to indicate that they wanted the animals to take them into it.

The tigers didn't want to obey their riders' instructions, but eventually did as they were asked, and deposited them in the same place, just outside the village, where they had picked them up before. Dawn was beginning to lighten the eastern sky. Raynor, always aware of dogs' behaviour, wondered why none barked as they entered the village. As they neared the first cottage they could see something was drastically wrong. The morning light was growing brighter by the minute to reveal house after house which had been burnt and abandoned, and all that remained were cracked walls and rafters.

The three of them paused, not knowing what to do, but decided to go and have a look at the house they were seeking to see if they could find any clue as to what had happened. They went along the side of a maize field and around a tree covered hillock. It was a winding path and difficult to find, especially as they had only been there once before. Some moments after the sun had shown itself above the horizon, they saw smoke rising from where they knew the farmhouse to be. They stopped in their tracks, lest whoever had burnt the rest of the village was at work here too. But as they cautiously came nearer, they saw that the smoke was coming out of the chimney. At least this house had been spared.

The door was locked and when they knocked nothing happened. Then Lee saw Kanta peeping from a window. Finally the door opened a crack, and she beckoned them to come in. She barred the door behind them and took them straight through to the kitchen at the back. She looked at them oddly.

'Praise the gods that you are safe!' she began. 'Sit down, and let me bring you some warm milk and honey.'

'That would be great,' said Lee.

'Um, what about eh, your tigers?' she added nervously.

'They won't trouble anyone. They look after themselves.'

'You lads were the talk of the district - great warriors who have tigers as steeds,' she laughed, but there was a brittle edge to her laughter.

'What happened? The fires, I mean?' said Raynor.

'It was awful, but somehow they missed our house. At least no one was killed, and the others from the village have gone away to stay with friends and relations elsewhere.'

'Who are 'they'?' asked Raynor, but in his heart he knew.

'A group of those terrible creatures, that look more like reptiles than men, came to the village. They were looking for you, and said they were going to take over the whole country soon. They were also looking for a princess. When they didn't find what they wanted, they started burning the cottages. Everyone fled, and ours was the only house they didn't find. Luckily you can't see it from the village.'

'How dreadful,' Lee apologised, 'to think we were the cause of this.'

'Don't feel so bad, we discovered they'd burnt many villages round here, even before you came our way.' She gave them each a plate of a kind of porridge, and went on, 'The following week an old man who looked like a monkey visited our village and found my house, even though I'd hardly been out since the fire. I get my water from the stream now. Somehow he knew where to come. He told me his name was Luth.'

'Luth!' cried Ahren. 'How did he know we stopped here?'

'Said the birds told him,' she said, and went on stirring the porridge. They looked surprised. 'I don't know why that bothers you. Young men who chase around on tigers shouldn't have a problem with monkey-men who talk to birds.' The boys felt she was a little afraid of them, and was caught up in something too dangerous for her quiet village existence.

'Luth is rather special,' Lee explained, and was about to continue when she took a letter from off the shelf above her.

'He left this in case you came back this way,' she gave it to Raynor, who opened it. This is what it said:

If this should by a miracle reach you, follow these instructions as soon as you can. Do not return to the crossroads where we met. The fiends are waiting there for you. They are also watching the hermitage. Your companions will be safe, but you must make a detour through a very dry land to the north of you, in order to avoid the trouble that is fast turning into a war.

Travel due north of the village, and move at night. Take water with you. After about two nights you will see an extinct volcano rising out of the desert, and there is a large salt lake there too. Follow the shoreline westwards and you will reach the river that feeds the lake, and then follow the river up its course. After another night of travelling you will come to a place where a large tributary feeds the river. Say the word 'Vandargar', loudly, a few times, blow through the key, and wait for a monkey-man like me to come and meet you.

I hope to see you again soon,

Luth

Raynor read this out, said they would like to leave at once and thanked Kanta for her kindness. She sensibly pointed out that if this wise monkey-man had told them to travel at night they should hide up in the barn until nightfall and then leave. They argued about this, and meanwhile, without being asked, Kanta set about making up some packs of food for them, and took off the wall two water bottles which were hanging from nails by straps. She refused to take anything in return, and they eventually had to leave Lee's handy fold-up, multi-blade knife lying around where she would not immediately find it, as a parting gift.

Then she went out for water, and told them to wait in the house, and she was a long time. They began to worry but finally she reappeared. She said she had been to the well in the village and had seen two ogres far off on the further hill, going in the other direction.

'So please,' she pleaded, 'take my advice and rest in the barn until nightfall. As long as my child and I are here alone they won't suspect me, even if they did find me.'

'Where's you husband?' asked Raynor.

'Didn't I tell you? He's gone to fight in the war.'

'You mean it's started?' asked Ahren.

'Yes, I thought you realized that. The king of the ogres, his ogres, and his ordinary human soldiers, have invaded the country west of here, and they say he is trying to capture Princess Neysa, who is married to the crown prince. So an army is being raised to drive them out. Or try to.'

'When did all this happen?' said Raynor, assuming a great deal must have been going on in the last few days.

'Now let me get it right,' Kanta counted on her fingers. 'Yes, that's it. The band of ogres came two weeks ago, and burnt the village. Then the old man came about ten days back, and....'

'Two weeks!' cried Ahren.

'And how long after us did the ogres come to the village?' asked Raynor, sure there must have been a mistake somewhere.

'About three days. Why?' Kanta wondered what was going on.

'So you're saying we left the others three weeks ago?' said Ahren in near despair.

'Well yes. Did you lose track of time or something?'

'But we've only been away three days!' put in Lee. Raynor put his finger to his mouth to indicate they should talk about this later, when alone.

'We are all incredibly tired,' said Raynor. 'We haven't slept much recently. Can you show us the barn, and wake us up this evening?'

Kanta did so and they hid under a pile of dried straw. They went to sleep at once, woken periodically by the itchiness of the stalks, and the scurrying of rats that ran around all over the place once the barn was quiet. It was not evening, but afternoon when they heard her voice.

'Wake up! I've had a message that those ogres are coming this way, and they've been searching farmhouses all over the district. Blessedly they are not burning houses any more. Your best chance is to escape on your tigers now, if you can.'

Lee was up in a moment and whistled softly through the key. Within minutes the tigers were in the farmyard, and he forgot that this was likely to cause pandemonium amongst the farm animals, which it did, attracting anything within earshot. The three of them hastily picked up their belongings, and made a quick getaway, galloping north through a maize field. The plants were at least twice as high as a man, and the boys were fully occupied in trying to hang on as the tigers wound their way through the vegetation. They could not see the two ogres waiting at the end of the field, where it gave onto the road.

The ogres did not expect the boys and their tigers to come speeding out of the field like bullets from a gun, so the ambush was not a complete success, but it was not a complete failure either. One ogre managed to fit an arrow into his bow, and shot it at Lee, who was last. It was at long range and although the arrow missed Lee it glanced off his tiger's back leg, and left a deep wound. The brave animal winced and stumbled, and Lee nearly fell off, but then it righted itself and ran on. It was lame and bleeding, but would not stop, so they escaped; past the farmlands, past the grazing lands and into the dry bush land beyond. Lee's tiger kept on running but began to drop further and further back. The others slowed down to let it catch up.

They went on into hotter, drier and lower country, until even the thorn bushes were becoming few and far between, and the only plants were cacti and spiky aloes. Lee's tiger was labouring more and more but still would not rest. Finally when darkness came Lee forced his tiger to stop by tugging on its gold collar, and he could see by the moons' light that the wound was still oozing blood.

The other two were some way ahead, and stopped at the edge of the dried up river valley. The boys dismounted and the tigers came back to see their friend. The sick tiger groaned in pain, and Lee wished they had brought some of the herbs and tinctures Zafeena had given them, but he at least tried to wash the wound with some of their precious water. As he did this, the tiger gave a mighty groan, breathed its last, and flopped back onto the sand. Ahren and Raynor came up and realised how brave it had been. The tendon was almost completely severed and it had given its life helping them escape.

As is the way with animals, once their comrade was dead they took no further interest in the body, but the boys covered the corpse with stones so as to give it a makeshift burial. They had lost a great friend. In the darkness they could not see each other's tears, which were a good thing, as men were not expected to show emotion in Teletsia. Mindful of Luth's letter, they knew they had to go on, as it was night. They were wondering what to do, when Raynor's tiger came up to Lee and Ahren and began nudging them both in turn.

'I think it wants us both to get on it,' said Ahren.

'It'll soon let us know if it doesn't,' added Lee.

So Lee, short and stocky, and Ahren, tall but lanky, both rode what had been Raynor's tiger, and Raynor rode Ahren's, which was smaller. They passed through desert country all that night, and found a shallow cave to sleep in during the heat of the day. They went slower now, with only two tigers, and at one point thought they might have missed the salt lake, but then saw the extinct volcano rising out of the plain, exactly as Luth had described it. By this time they had no water left and both tigers and humans were thirsty. The moons shone, the saltpan around the lake shone, even the top of the mountain shone, and it was very eerie. And it was awful to see all that water, but not be able to drink it, because it was salty.

They turned westwards and went up the side of the lake, keeping back from the scrunchy salt crystals rimming the waterline. Raynor tried squeezing some water out of a number of barrel shaped cactuses, and they all drank some of the bitter liquid. The tigers drank first, so the boys presumed it wouldn't be poisonous. It was horrible, but eased their parched throats.

The next day they couldn't find anywhere very shady, and spent the day moving round a group of high rocks to keep in what little shade they could as the sun moved too. Then in the night they went on again, and when their throats were beginning to swell with thirst, and the tigers were gasping, they finally reached the end of the lake, found the river that flowed into it, and drank and drank of the sweet water.

This gave the tigers energy, and they followed the river up its course to higher land. By dawn they had reached a hilly, forested district, with high trees and little undergrowth and soon after found the place where the tributary reached the river. The water of the larger stream was clear, and the other brownish and murky. They got off the tigers and Raynor said 'Vandargar' loudly, a few times. Nothing happened, and then Lee remembered he was supposed to blow through his key. Still nothing happened.

'Now what?' said Lee.

'Let's wait, it's early yet and not everyone has been up all night like us,' suggested Ahren. They sat down and soon nodded off to sleep. A large white monkey swung down from one of the higher trees in a leisurely fashion, and walked around the forest floor.

'Now where on earth have they got to?' it said to itself. 'I heard *something* crashing around. Must have been humans. They are so noisy.' The boys snored on, and then it called again, louder this time, 'Where are you, young ones?' They all woke up with a jerk. 'Ah! There you are. What's the password?'

Raynor and the others looked blank, then said, 'Vandargar'.

'Yes, well that's all right, but what about the other thing? I mean, you could have guessed that. They told me to be very careful.'

The three boys looked blank again, because they were very sleepy. Lee didn't know whether he should get out the key in front of this stranger. Then one of the tigers sauntered up and Raynor stroked it without thinking, and the monkey, instead of being afraid, looked relieved.

'All right, Luth did say you'd be on the tigers. That's good enough for me.'

'Are you the monkey he told us to look for?' asked Raynor.

'Yes, of course. Wherever did you get to? I've been waiting up that tree for nearly two weeks for you.' Raynor didn't know how one apologized to a monkey that had been waiting up a tree for two weeks. Two hours yes, but two weeks? He tried to explain that they had been unavoidably delayed. 'Well you're here now,' added the monkey, 'that's the main thing. Don't be put out. I like sitting up trees. My ancestors have been doing it for hundreds of lifetimes, but seriously, we must get a move on. Those ogres are still after you, even though they haven't come this way yet.'

'Is this still Prince Osmar's land?'

'Yes, but there's a war on. Maybe if you came out of the desert you didn't know that.'

'We did know. That's why we came through the desert,' explained Lee.

'I'll come with you to Vandargar, our capital, to show you the way, so let's go,' then he said something to the tigers, who seemed to know him. The boys climbed on their backs, and were soon off once again. The river bent northwards and the path with it, and soon they left the river altogether, and went through some open grassland. The monkey lolloped beside the tigers, and they made a fair speed. Then they went down into another valley, this time filled with trees with enormously wide trunks. The track was narrow and winding and not easy to follow, and the monkey led the way. They came to an open part in the wood, and there was an old moss-covered statue of a monkey. Raynor noticed that around the neck of the stone monkey was a key, part of the statue itself.

Behind the statue was one of the enormous trees, at least the trunks were enormous. There was a rift in the trunk of this one, and the white monkey told them that they had to go inside the trunk, which was hollow and the beginning of a tunnel. They dismounted from the tigers, which disappeared into the woodland. The boys and monkey went inside the tree trunk, and there ahead was a long tunnel, dimly lit from chinks in the roof where the daylight filtered through. Eventually the tunnel opened out into a cave, which had been carved to resemble a courtyard or large room flanked by pillars. Here there were ferocious looking monkey guards, who barred their way. But when they saw the white monkey they were allowed to pass.

The walls of this cave had been flattened and smoothed and were covered with paintings: animals, people, flowers and many scenes telling stories. The boys stopped to look but the white monkey hurried them on.

He led them out into the brilliant sunlight. They were in a hollow surrounded by cliffs, and many caves: dwellings, temples and administrative halls had been carved out of the rock. It was a whole rock-cut city. The monkey led them round the edge of the open space in the centre of the hollow, which was filled with gardens and trees, and a stream running through the middle. There were monkeys everywhere, scurrying about their daily business and no one was interested in the newcomers.

The boys were taken to a side section of the cliffs, into one of the smaller caves honeycombing the rock face. They were greeted by another monkey, given water to wash, food, and even clean clothes. Then they slept, feeling safe and comfortable for the first time in many days. Some time later the white monkey came by.

'You are invited to an audience with the king: our monkey king,' he said. 'Please follow me.'

They were led to the largest and most ornate cave, which had a façade of pillars, statues of monkey heroes and many designs carved into the stone. At the door two monkey guards again barred their way, and this time the white monkey said, 'Show them your key'. Lee did not know how the monkey knew about the key, but didn't argue, and again the guards parted to let them through. Inside, the halls were lit by hanging chandeliers of cut stones in pastel shades. They were self-luminous and gave out a soft and soothing glow.

They went into a large audience hall, and the three boys could see the king on a raised throne at the further end. There were many monkeys sitting quietly in rows, and the newcomers settled down at the back of the large cave. Seated next to the monkey king was Prince Osmar, and their heads were bowed in serious discussion. Then came the big surprise: they heard someone come and stand beside them. They turned to see me, Asha, beckoning them to come outside for a moment.

'You made it!' I, Asha, cried and gave them all a hug. As I did so I felt the most extraordinary exploding joy in my heart for all three of them, and knew we just had to be together. 'They said you'd arrived, but when I came to find you earlier you were all asleep. You've taken ages to get here. What happened?'

'Somehow we went out of time when we were with the hermit,' said Raynor.

'What's going on here?' asked Lee.

'Listen, and you'll get the gist,' I nodded towards the council chamber.

'What about Conwenna and Derwin?'

'They're fine. Probably with Nog and Heggo.'

'How did you get here?' asked Raynor.

'Oh, we dressed up as a party of monks and nuns on a pilgrimage, along with some of Luth's novices, and came here in disguise a couple of weeks ago. The ogres were about to search Luth's hermitage and he had us make a quick getaway. Don't worry about what you hear; it's all part of the drama being played out.' The boys crept back to their place in the shadows at the back of the hall. The king was about to speak. There was a shuffling and a rustling and then all the monkeys became quiet.

'As you all know,' he began, 'we are going to war to help Prince Osmar and his father to rid this land of these ogres and their king, who says he has come to this land to take Princess Neysa away. He insists he won her in a contest for her hand. This is not true, and he really wants to take our lands for himself, and make us his slaves, like he has the countries to the east of us.' The king paused. 'The problem is, he has already captured Princess Neysa. Some of the seven children from the south, who they also wanted to capture, have disappeared as well. We're not sure what's happened to them. We do know that the ogres attacked and ransacked Luth's hermitage and the princess and children were last seen there.

'None of you is being forced to come with me to rescue the princess, which is the first step towards ridding this land of the king, who is called King Blagart, and his men and ogres, but I'm asking for your help, and to defend our land is in our own interests.' Here there was a murmur of approval. 'Tonight the conjunction of all three moons is very favourable, and we will be able to attack the place where the princess is being held, just before dawn, when our enemies are at their weakest. It is not far from here, but we must leave at once.'

The white monkey now beckoned to the boys to follow him to a small passage in the rock, behind them in the corner of the hall, and they went along it and up some stairs. The monkey's city was full of such things. The passage led them to a cave, which gave onto the outer side of the line of cliffs, and they could see on its further side an opening, like a large window, which opened onto a view of the forests and hills beyond. Somewhere in those hills Princess Neysa was being held, so most people thought. They immediately recognized the voices of Conwenna and Derwin, sitting on the carpeted floor and playing some sort of a game with a third figure. Before the boys had time to say anything Nog recognized his master's footsteps and came bounding towards Raynor, scattering the game and nearly knocking Raynor over as he greeted him.

'We thought you were lost,' cried Derwin, rushing towards the other boys.

'Or maybe you'd gone to Sasrar without us,' said Conwenna. The third figure had quietly gone into the other room, and after returning the welcome, we asked who it was. 'Big secret, you'll soon see.'

Just then the white monkey, who had been standing at the back, began to speak. 'Young wanderers, it would be best if you leave as soon as you can, before the night falls. The ogres will be fully occupied with our force of monkey people, and will not be interested in you. If you leave on your tigers, you can be far away by the morning, and back on the northern road. It comes to a point where there is a ferry that can take you across a large river. To call the ferry you must blow through your key, Lee. That river is the border of our lands, and the tigers do not usually go beyond that point, but they can take you a bit further, to get you out of this war zone.'

The three boys forgot to ask about the veiled figure who had been with the two children. We loaded Heggo up, and packed backpacks for the next stage of the journey. The monkeys were very helpful, and gave us packs of nuts and dried fruit to take with us as food. In the late afternoon we all left Vandargar by the same tunnel as we had come in by. We moved everyone round, so that Derwin and Conwenna shared a tiger - they had a few words as to who was to go in the front, but eventually sorted themselves out.

The white monkey came with us as far as the old road, much more overgrown here and in very bad repair, but the tigers still managed to make their way along it, now and again having to jump or climb over fallen trees and bushes that had grown up between the paving stones. Some time after night fell, the faint Moon of Compassion was in the sky, and we saw the black, oily water of the river with the road running up its side. Then later we heard a muffled roar, and saw ahead a fairly large waterfall. We climbed around the side, where the road zigzagged up a steep incline, and above the falls the road came abruptly to a stop at the river's edge.

'Now what?' asked Raynor.

'I don't see any ferry,' said Lee gloomily.

'Key, Lee, key,' I reminded him.

'Oh yes, I forgot.'

I could see that Lee was very tired from so much travelling, He blew through the key, and although it didn't seem loud enough for anyone to hear over the noise of the waterfall, after some time we saw a ferry, or rather a raft, come sliding across the river from the other bank. It came up to where we were standing, and we could see that the boatman was actually a boat monkey.

'Hello, I've been waiting days for you,' he grumbled.

'Sorry,' Raynor was constantly apologising to monkeys recently.

'There're an awful lot of you. Do you want all those animals to come too?'

'Please, if it isn't too much trouble.'

'I suppose I can just about fit you all on, but you'll have to help me punt.'

'Couldn't we go further up?' asked Conwenna.

'No, not unless you want to cross where there are lots of crocodiles.' Conwenna looked afraid. 'We'll be all right. That's why we have the ferry here. The raft is attached to a chain that's tied to both the banks, so we can't be swept over the waterfall. No one suspects it's here because of the crocodiles, so it's the monkeys' secret crossing place, between the crocodiles and the waterfall.'

Always a catch, I thought to myself. I looked at some large logs floating further up the river, then looked again. They were crocodiles.

'Right, let's get to it, and trust me, we'll be fine,' said the monkey, and we were. Once across, the monkey ceased to be scratchy and invited us to stay the rest of the night in the old stone boathouse that was his home. He was a canny fellow, and there were no secrets from him. 'So, you've got Princess Neysa hidden at Vandargar, have you?'

'But that's supposed to be a secret,' I said.

'Not from me, young lady. I've known Luth since I was a very small monkey indeed.'

'What's Luth got to do with it? I thought Princess Neysa had been captured,' asked Lee.

'Luth has the power to take on the appearance of anyone he likes, but only for a few days,' explained the monkey. 'He has impersonated Princess Neysa, and she escaped to Vandargar disguised as a shaven headed nun.'

'The veiled figure playing with Derwin and Conwenna,' I said.

'Ah, I get it now,' said Raynor.

'What happens when Luth starts to look like Luth and not Princess Neysa?' asked Ahren.

'By that time there should be a battle on between the monkeys, Prince Osmar's men and the ogre forces. At a time like that, who's going to be bothered about one old monkey hermit slipping out of a side door?' I said.

'No one, let's hope,' said the monkey. 'No one has caught Luth yet, and he's been playing games with humans and other monkeys for a very long time now.'

The next morning we slept late, and when we were eventually ready and about to leave, a bird arrived, flying in and cooing as it did, carrying a letter tied on its leg for the boat monkey. He opened it, and read it to us.

'The expedition was a success in that Luth escaped. The war is not over, but the ogre army is in flight and Prince Osmar is pursuing them. Without us monkeys he could not have done it – we are the most valiant of his followers, he says. Long live the monkeys of Vandargar!

Jo, the white monkey.

The Fifth Key

Collectivity, diplomacy and the brotherhood of humanity

'This fifth subtle centre is at the level of the throat. Its qualities are collectivity, diplomacy and seeing everything and everyone as parts of an integrated whole. It also governs our five senses, which enable us to interact with the world around us. Between the eyebrows, the top of this centre's sphere of influence, is the point of discrimination. On the earth, this fifth centre is Vittalia, the land of Prince Roarke, and also the realm of King Gamsad.'

From 'Memoirs of the Professor', by Raynor Antiquarian

CHAPTER 7

LOST AND CAPTURED

On the northern side of the river the monkey showed us where to pick up the road again. There had been a ferry crossing place further upriver for many a long year, as we could see from some ruins at the side of the river where the road started off again. It continued in a more or less northerly direction, but became increasingly overgrown until it virtually ceased to exist. We followed it but had to climb over a lot of branches and around trees that had begun to reclaim it. The weather became cooler, and we did not know whether it was because we were on higher ground, or because we had left the tropics. Our way passed through hills and valleys, and there were always rivers in the valleys. Originally there had been bridges over the rivers, but now we had to do some wading and even swimming. The bridges had either already collapsed, or looked as if they would at any moment.

On the afternoon of the fifth or sixth day we were well out of the thick woodland and into a part of the country where there were a lot of open spaces between the clumps of trees. We stopped to rest at the edge of one of these clearings, and the tigers yawned and lay on their backs to rest. Then we heard carefree, chattering voices in the distance, beyond some trees. We also heard the ringing of bells, and soon, from behind the trees, came a herd of cows wearing cowbells, being driven by a group of boys and girls.

The cows became aware of the tigers and were very frightened. They halted, blew noisily through their nostrils, and began to lumber heavily back through the trees, tails in the air and bells ringing. Some of the girls and boys tried in vain to calm the cows, shouting at them and waving sticks, others looked for a suitable tree to climb to get away from the tigers, while still others stood dumbfounded at the sight of six young people lounging around on the grass, in the company of five tigers with gold collars around their necks.

Out of the melee of cows and strangers we saw two figures emerge and walk confidently towards us. One was a tall, handsome girl of about my age, and the other a shorter, plumper girl with a snub nose and a smiling face. The taller girl had long hair, she walked fast towards us and carried herself with grace and dignity, as if she were a chieftain's daughter at the very least. Her face was shining and she was laughing with her friend, who hid behind her nervously. She came straight up to us, not in the least perturbed by the tigers, which by now had slunk off out of sight.

'Welcome to our land of Vittalia!' she said. 'You won't need your tigers here. If you must ride them you'll have to take another route. We're cowherds here and our animals are terrified of them.' This young lady was sussed, sophisticated and firm, but she had a lovely smile. I felt her inner self and there was peace and joy.

'I'm sorry if they disturbed your cows,' said Raynor, rather awed by her presence. 'We didn't mean to make problems.'

'Don't worry, I can see that,' she went on confidently. 'Maybe it's time the tigers went back to their owners. We can guide you, if you don't mind walking.'

'Let me talk to the others.' Raynor turned to us so she could not hear him. 'What do you reckon?'

'I feel coolness coming from her,' I said, and the others agreed.

'I'm going to call the tigers,' said Lee, and blew through his key.

The tigers came up to us, and the largest one did something very strange. Lee was still holding the key in his hand, having taken it from his neck to blow through it, and the largest tiger came up to him and neatly put it in its mouth, then tugged so Lee had to let it go. All the tigers drew back, bowed to us and sped away to the south, keeping close to the clumps of trees and that was it. We looked at each other and said nothing for a good minute.

'Well,' said Ahren, 'that solves that one.'

Lee was silent. His beautiful key had gone, just like that. He looked wistfully after the tigers, a streak of brown and yellow in the distant meadow.

'Hey, snap out of it,' I put my arm around his shoulder. 'We've all lost our keys somehow. They're not for keeping anyway.'

'I know, but it was so great to be able to whistle and have a whole lot of tigers come running at my command.' Lee smiled uncertainly and I smiled back. He's a good sort, always has been, and let's face it, we all get a bit egotistical now and again.

'So, now we must accept our new friend's offer of help,' said Raynor calmly. We went back to where the two girls and a lot of other young people were waiting in the meadow.

'My name is Marimba,' said the tall girl, 'and this is Brindan,' she indicated to her plump friend. 'The rest of them can introduce themselves.' We gave our names, and Marimba led us back across the grassy meadow. Raynor and I walked with her, and the others fell in with the rest of the group.

'Where are you heading for?' she asked, and we gave our usual reply. 'In that case, you must go and see my brother. He lives in the city and is bound to be able to help you.'

'What does he do there?' asked Raynor, expecting her to say something like, 'He's studying,' or 'He's in business.'

'He helps run the place,' she went on casually.

'You mean he's in the civil service or something?'

'No, he helps run the place,' she repeated, and changed the subject. 'By the way, we're having a festival tonight. It's quite a way to our village and you can stay with us. You'd never make it to the city today, plus you look as if you could do with a bath and some good food.'

Marimba was determined to mother us, which was fine by me. The boys were even happier, and only Conwenna was a little in awe of her very open and confident nature. All of the members of her group were curious to know where we had come from, and when we said Teletsia, they said they'd never heard of the place, apart from Marimba.

'Yes, I've heard of it,' she said with a sigh. 'Far away from here, but bad news travels, and if I put my attention on it I feel ill. Don't worry though, my brother and I will help you all we can.' She helped Conwenna and Derwin to ride on two of the cows, insisting they must be tired. Ahren struck up a conversation with one of the boys.

'It'll be great to come to your village,' he began.

'No problem,' replied the boy. 'It's nice to have visitors from afar. Are you part of a travelling circus or something? I mean, those tigers.'

'Not really,' Ahren didn't know what to say, and concentrated on leading Heggo.

Conwenna was riding a cow and talking to Marimba's friend Brindan, who was leading it.

'Tell me more about Marimba; she's so beautiful - and more like a city girl than someone who's always lived in a village,' said Conwenna.

'Yes, you're right,' replied Brindan. 'She and her brother Roarke spent a lot of time here as children. In our country, young people who live in the towns are sent to the country during their vacations to get a feel of country life. Roarke and Marimba enjoyed it so much that Marimba still comes here a lot even though they're both grown up now. The difference with Roarke and Marimba is that their parents are very important.'

'What do you mean?'

'They rule the country.'

'Like, is Roarke's father the king?'

'Yes, but in this country, it's both parents. Also, Prince Roarke, as we call him nowadays, showed such a talent for getting everyone to be friends, and to work together in harmony, that his parents decided he should help them, so he's a sort of unofficial co-ruler nowadays.'

'You serious?'

'Yes, why not? Prince Roarke's very special.'

'What about the festival this evening?'

'Oh, we'll dance in praise of the woodland gods and goddesses, under the moons. I hope you won't be too tired to join in.'

'No, I'm sure we'll be fine,' but Conwenna rather wondered if she would be.

'There's always good food after we've danced.' Conwenna suspected that food played a large part in Brindan's life. Ours hadn't exactly been home cooking for much of the last months, and a good meal was always more than welcome.

In the evening, having been introduced to the chieftain and his wife, who were Marimba's honorary aunt and uncle, the six of us joined in the dances. The people of this country had a perfect grasp of rhythm and melody, and sang and danced many different dances. Some were accompanied by various musical instruments, so Lee joined in with his flute. Other dances consisted of everyone dancing in a circle, with each person holding short wooden sticks that were cracked together in time to the music. The food, as promised, was great.

The next morning we were up at dawn with the rest of the village. Cows had to be milked early, and then taken to the pastures to graze. Marimba took us to see her uncle again. He told us that they made cheeses in the village, and had some large ones, the size of cartwheels, for delivery to the place where Marimba's brother Roarke was presently staying. We would save someone a trip into town if we could deliver them, and could also borrow the bullock cart they were going in. We could leave it in town and someone would pick it up, as people were always going there from the village. So by mid morning we were again on the move, this time wending our way through country lanes, meadows and woods. It was a pleasant morning, and even Heggo was happy, as most of his load had been put on the bullock cart and Ahren was riding him.

We had been warned that it was quite a long way, and so when the town was nowhere in sight after two days, we didn't worry. Lee was confident that we were going the right way, but a network of winding country roads crisscrossed the whole area. We had been given a map, but the roads were so confusing and we hoped that by going more or less in the right direction we would eventually get there. We did ask a few people but they were all rather vague. They reckoned that as long as they told us something to keep us happy, that was good enough.

'I'm sure we won't come to any harm in this country, at any rate,' said Lee, as dusk was beginning to fall. 'We have the jewelled key, and it's such a friendly sort of a place, isn't it?'

'You can never be too sure,' I cautioned him. I had had a disturbing dream the night before, but was still loath to talk about my dreams, so didn't say any more.

'Dusk is traditionally a time when things go wrong,' warned Ahren.

'You're so serious these days,' teased Lee. 'What's happened to the not-a-care-in-the-world Ahren?'

'I've got a feeling we may have taken the wrong road. I've got a very good sense of direction, but maybe all the roads lead to the capital so it won't matter in the end.'

Raynor was driving the pair of bullocks, thinking about something that had been lurking in his mind ever since their conversations with Luth, and the hermit in the mountains. If it was necessary for every member of their group to get to Sasrar together, and if they were right in assuming that each key helped us through a particular country, then how were we going to manage without Tandi? Also, he couldn't forget her: that radiant smile and infectious laugh. He wondered what she was doing at that moment, and then a much more pressing thought came to him. Who had the key of the country they were now in?

After a short time, Raynor's musings were cut short. We heard the sound of many hooves galloping in the distance. Darkness was fast approaching and we were looking for a place to spend the night. Ahren and I had already found a place in a wood with a stream, a little way from the road. We had taken Heggo there to give him a drink, and Nog was with us. Lee, Derwin and Raynor were still on the road waiting for us to return and tell them if it was a good place to stop or not. When they heard the galloping hooves coming closer, Raynor was for hiding themselves and the bullock cart, but Lee disagreed.

'What are we doing wrong? Why shouldn't we be on this road? We can ask them for directions,' Lee objected.

Then it was too late to move, because round the corner came a troop of armed soldiers, led by a man who from his dress and attitude was definitely their leader. They were going very fast, and only just had time to pull up and not run down the bullocks and boys. There was utter confusion as they slithered to a stop, the riders behind buffeting those in front, with much strong language and abuse.

Lee's jauntiness drained out of him, and he wished he could have disappeared into the wood as Ahren and I had done. The more they saw of the horsemen, the worse they looked and it occurred that maybe they were bandits, not soldiers. Ahren and I kept out of sight, and Ahren put his hand over Heggo's nose to stop him braying. I crept closer but kept well hidden.

'Halt, in the name of King Gamsad, through whose territory you are now passing,' shouted one man. 'Who are you and what are you doing here?'

'We're looking for Prince Roarke, who we were told is staying nearby,' said Raynor, trying to sound more assured than he felt.

'You're on the wrong road. This isn't his land. It's King Gamsad's,' went on the man who had spoken before.

'Isn't this the road for Prince Roarke's town?' cried Lee in dismay. The last shreds of his puffed up confidence were disappearing with the daylight, and leaving behind a scared boy, because these people had the most awful feeling coming from them: hot and discordant and a sense of cruelty.

'You'd better come and have a word with our general,' the man pushed Lee and Derwin, who were standing on the ground, in the direction of the leader. Raynor was also surrounded and could only do as asked. The general demanded light, and a torch was lit, and whether there had been light or not, the boys realized this man was seriously bad. Raynor felt his hands burning as he looked at the general. Derwin clutched his throat as his body painfully registered his evil nature on his subtle centre in the throat area. The general's eyebrows met in the middle of his face, and his curled moustache framed his sneering mouth.

'So,' he said menacingly, peering at the three boys by the light of the torch, as by now it was quite dark, 'boys from the south, by the look of you. Why are you going to see Prince Roarke, so late at night?' The boys' hearts were pounding, and they were much too uneasy to say anything, even if they had wanted to, which they didn't. After some moments of silence the general smirked, as if an idea had entered his perverted brain. 'Yes, if you want to see Prince Roarke, I think that can be arranged. Not in the way you had planned, of course. Your skins lead me to suspect that you are Teletsians. You might be spies from the Sorcerers. We know about them from when we've traded with them. We don't trust their magical ways at all. You may be innocent, or worthless, but maybe I can ransom you back to your overlords. It's worth a try. I've got a living to make too, you know.' Ruffians with swords surrounded the three boys, and they couldn't even move, much less escape.

'Yes!' he roared with a cruel laugh. 'Even if I can't sell you to the Sorcerers, you'll make pretty slave boys when you've been cleaned up! This little one,' he pinched Derwin, 'will do as my new pageboy. The last one died when I beat him for being lazy.' The general now turned to a particularly nasty looking henchman, 'Right, bind 'em up, and put 'em on those spare horses. Leave the cart tied to that tree so the bullocks don't wander off, and we'll stop at that inn down yonder and have someone collect it later. Now look sharp, we've a long way to go tonight.'

'Yes sir,' said the henchman, and set about doing as asked.

'The joke is,' added the general to anyone listening, which happened to be me among others, 'that another two hills further on, if you'd taken the left turning, and continued on for another day's journey, you'd have been at the town where Prince Roarke is at the moment. But don't worry, you'll meet him in due course.'

It was over in a minute. They got on their horses and off they went as the Moon of Wisdom rose above the trees. The shouts and pounding hooves faded into the distance and were replaced by the sound of the crickets. Ahren and I crept cautiously out of hiding, holding Heggo and Nog. He had somehow managed to keep both of them quiet, and I could have hugged him for doing so. Ahren had some brilliant qualities, and the less good ones had disappeared recently, thank goodness.

'It all happened so quickly!' he moaned. 'At least the animals didn't give us away too,' he went on, trying to look on the bright side of a very gloomy picture.

'You're amazing. How did you manage it?' I asked, patting Nog.

'With great difficulty.'

I burst into tears. Nog looked ashamed and put his tail between his legs, he felt something had gone very wrong for his humans, and Ahren looked pained and tried to cheer me up.

'Where's Conwenna?' I was frantic, as I always felt responsible for her, the youngest of us.

'I thought she was with you.'

'No, don't you remember?'

'Did those men take her?'

'Don't think so. I only heard them talking to the boys, but I'm not absolutely sure.'

'Conwenna, where are you?' we both shouted, but there was no reply, only 'Conwenna, Conwenna' echoing down the valley, getting fainter and fainter as it bounced off the hills into the distance. Then one of the bullocks, tied to the tree a little way up the road, stamped its foot, and we went to untie it. There, burrowing her way out from under the packs, was Conwenna.

'Why on earth didn't you answer us?' I cried anxiously. 'Things are bad enough. There're just us left now.'

'Are you all right?' asked Ahren.

'Yes, of course I am. I hid so those men wouldn't see me. I'm not that stupid. When you called I thought it might be a trap, so I peeped carefully to make sure you were alone.' Then I hugged Conwenna too, and we both burst into tears together.

'We've got to get to this Prince Roarke, and soon,' Ahren tried to sound optimistic, as if somehow Prince Roarke would wave a magic wand and everything would be all right again. He wasn't feeling that way at all. We had lost Raynor, our leader, and Lee who often had such good ideas, and Derwin, but there was more to it than that, because the bond between us all was so deep that we three could actually feel the terror and fear of the others, leaving us further and further behind with every moment that passed.

'Listen, we've got to leave here as soon as we can, because someone might come back for the bullock cart,' I said.

'That's all very fine, but which way?' said Ahren.

'Easy, that way, turn left on the top of the hill, and it's a day's journey.'

'It's night,' Ahren pointed out the obvious.

'Well, a night's journey then, if the bullocks can make it.' So, afraid and lost, the three of us took turns to persuade the already tired bullocks to trudge on, which they nobly did, hour after dark hour.

The three boys also had a long journey ahead of them. The band of ruffians rode on through the night in the other direction, and after some time they stopped at an inn. The boys were roughly pulled off their horses, carried into the front parlour and dumped in the corner of the room on the floor.

'Do you know it's my birthday today?' said Derwin when they were alone.

'Derwin, this is totally my fault, and I haven't the first clue how we can get out of it,' said Lee, 'and you've got me to blame. Here was I, thinking I was a bit better than the rest of you because I didn't get mesmerised on Tootle's Island, and with my stupid ego I've got us into just as bad trouble now.'

'Don't be too hard on yourself, Lee. Maybe Derwin's next birthday will be better,' sighed Raynor.

'It could hardly be worse,' confessed Lee, feeling terrible that he had got his friends into this hideous state of affairs.

'True enough,' said Derwin. For the first time in many weeks he wished with all his heart that he was at home, having fun at his annual party and being a normal child. He was enjoying our journey enormously now, as long as everything went right. Adventures were all very well when they meant missing school, but it was another story when they went so wrong.

Soon the soldiers were busy ordering food and drink, and the innkeeper and his family were run off their feet. The boys could not move because their hands and legs were tied, but kept their eyes and ears open. Their guard, a gouty faced man in middle age, had a very free tongue after the first beer or two, and between burps and belches revealed to the farmer sitting next to him that the leader of the group, General Khangish, was the Prime Minister of the country where they now were. The rest of them were his bodyguards and they had just come from a visit to Prince Roarke. King Gamsad, the king here, had ordered General Khangish to invite Prince Roarke to visit him at his summer palace. King Gamsad had the idea that maybe a marriage could be arranged between Prince Roarke and his daughter.

But, and this was where the guard's big mouth came in handy, the whole thing was much more devious, because General Khangish, the leader of the band, wanted to make an alliance with Prince Roarke and oust the rather unintelligent King Gamsad. Prince Roarke was quite enthusiastic about coming to visit King Gamsad, and appeared not to understand the darker side of the plot. General Khangish assumed he was just a foolish young man who would fit into his plans. The three boys now understood how they were going to meet Prince Roarke, as slaves of his hosts.

'If only I hadn't been so sure of myself we'd all still be free,' moaned Lee. Raynor and Derwin agreed, in their hearts, but kept quiet as it wasn't the moment to criticise their friend. The meal was bought to their captors and eaten, and their guard offered the boys some crusts of bread. None of them felt hungry. The general struck up a lively conversation with the innkeeper and his wife. Some form of payment was now due for the twenty or so servings of chicken and duck, and the quantities of beer. The general was trying to get out of it, saying that the innkeeper should feel honoured to have entertained him, the Prime Minister, and shouldn't want to be paid.

The innkeeper didn't see it that way at all, and presented the bill. His four strapping sons were called in, and things looked as if they might turn ugly. The general didn't have any money on him. He had spent it all on having a good time the previous week, and none of his followers were any better off. Then some of the other regulars: farmers, villagers and the like, came in on the side of the innkeeper. The situation was getting worse and worse, voices were rising and then the general had an idea.

'I know,' he began. 'We'll have a dicing match! If the landlord wins, we'll give him our fine new slave boys, recently bought at the auction, and originally spoils of war. If we win, we get a free meal. How's that, my man?' The landlord realized his position was hopeless, so he could only agree.

'We'd have more chance of escaping from here than from those soldiers, so we'd better hope he loses us,' Lee whispered.

One of the soldiers played for the general, and watching carefully from their position on the floor, the boys could see he was an accomplished cheat. He kept changing in dice he had hidden up his sleeve and his dice were weighted in his favour. Raynor prayed that somehow they would get out of this dire predicament; Lee was furious with himself for the mess he had got the others into and Derwin was in tears, and as his hands were tied he couldn't even wipe them away.

The innkeeper kept losing and was becoming suspicious of the dice. He asked that they play cards, and the general knew his man could also cheat at this game, so agreed on the change. A grimy pack was produced from a box in the corner of the parlour. The cards pictured devils, angels, scorpions, dogs, and so on, but the best one in the pack was the twelve starred crown: the northern constellation in the night sky and considered to bring good luck. There was no luck in store for the innkeeper, as another soldier crept behind him and told the cheat, by means of sign language, all the cards he was holding at any one time. The innkeeper lost a number of rounds and the general lost interest in the game.

'Old man, you had better admit defeat,' he said. 'But for the sake of good relations, if you go back along the road some way, you'll find a bullock cart tied to a tree, near a stream. You can take it. The owners don't need it any more.' The landlord mumbled thanks. What else could he do? Then they all left.

Lee and Derwin were tied onto a great lumbering horse, and Raynor was made to ride a smaller one. The soldiers led them and they jogged on hour after hour.

'At least we're going to be slaves in a palace, not in a country inn plucking ducks and chickens for the rest of our life,' Lee said.

'You may be right, but let's keep hoping,' replied Derwin. 'Maybe the others will do something to help. It's a blessing some of us are still free. Whatever happens, I'm not going to forget this birthday in a hurry.'

CHAPTER 8

PRINCE ROARKE

The bullock cart crept onwards; the night was old and the town was nowhere in sight. All three of us began to feel despondent. I was worried sick about Derwin, and when I put my attention on him I felt despair from him. We took turns to urge on the bullocks, but finally they stopped to rest and no one was alert enough to whip them on. Within seconds we were asleep. Some time later we woke up together.

'I wonder where we are,' I yawned.

'I don't know, I'm exhausted,' said Conwenna, also yawning.

'Let's stop at the first house and ask,' I forgot this might turn out to be another disaster.

'No way,' Ahren, the most awake, objected. 'I don't trust folks around here. Plus it's still dark, although dawn will be here soon.' The sky was beginning to lighten in the east.

'I wish we could find Prince Roarke,' moaned Conwenna.

'I'm going to try to get the bullocks moving again,' went on Ahren.

'I think we may be nearing civilization,' I said, peering over the edge of the cart. The road was quite well surfaced. We managed to get the bullocks to shuffle on, and as the light came, we heard a whirring and rattling of wheels behind us. We turned round, afraid, and saw an extraordinary sight coming towards us. Round the corner came a man on a three wheeled contraption, sitting astride the front wheel, pushing something at the sides of the wheel up and down with his feet, which made the wheels go round. We stared open mouthed and he sped past, singing to himself.

'Whatever's that?' asked Ahren.

'Stop him!' I urged. 'He feels all right, and he'll know where we are.'

'Hey mister!' shouted Ahren.

'Please sir!' cried Conwenna.

'Help, please stop!' I cried. The man looked behind him, stopped his contraption, and came walking back to us. He was a good-natured fellow, and the feeling coming from him was cool. We asked him if we were on the right road for the frontier town where we had been told Prince Roarke was visiting.

'Why, yes. I'm heading there myself,' he replied cheerfully. 'I'm going to see my son in town. Come to think of it, I've got a friend who works in the stables where the prince is staying. You might be able to meet Prince Roarke there. He's a friendly sort, they say. Let's be off then. If you like, one of you can ride with me.'

He offered to take me in the back of his contraption, which also had some vegetables and fruit in it. After asking in my heart, 'Is it all right?' and feeling coolness flow on my hands, I accepted. He went slowly, but had a very good effect on the bullocks, who woke up and went a little faster. The sun soon broke over a landscape of gentle hills, woods and fields, and we could see the outskirts of the town we were making for, and felt less depressed. When we reached the town he led us through a lot of narrow streets, still empty at this early hour.

Our destination was a large estate on the edge of town. As we entered the main gate we could see a grand looking house on rising ground in the distance. We soon turned off the main drive towards a jumble of houses and outhouses, and eventually reached a large yard, with stables for horses and stalls for bullocks.

Soon our guide found his friend and introduced us. When we said the bullock cart was on loan from Prince Roarke's sister, we became important guests, and someone offered to take it from us. We unloaded our belongings and Nog, who had been sleeping in the cart, and we all sat down on a pile of straw and fell asleep. Nog did his guarding bit and sat by our sides. Heggo stared vacantly into the distance, head lowered, and didn't move; he was very tired as he had been trotting along beside the bullock cart all night long.

'Hello!' said the well-educated voice of a youngish man, almost a boy. The only reply was a series of snores. 'Hey, are you all right?'

'Yes, more or less,' replied Ahren, waking up. 'We didn't get much sleep.'

'That figures,' went on the younger boy. 'Are you the people from Marimba's village?' he peered at us one by one.

'Well, sort of,' mumbled Conwenna, half asleep. 'But that's the problem, some of us got caught by these bandits or soldiers or whatever they were.' She was too tired to fully explain the ghastliness of it, but her expression said everything.

'Hmm, we thought something must have gone wrong. That sounds dire,' the young man was concerned. 'Tell you what, Prince Roarke's expecting you, and as there's this crisis, you'd better get yourselves out of that straw and come and meet him. Right now.'

He held out a hand and pulled us up. We brushed off most of the stalks and followed both of them across the yard, accompanied by Nog. We weren't looking exactly princeworthy, I thought, as we shuffled after them. Soon we were walking through gardens and courtyards, and then into the house, almost a palace, that belonged to the parents of these two.

'Prince Roarke is our cousin,' explained the younger boy. 'He always stays here when he comes to this part of the country. Don't worry, he's not a scary prince.'

We were taken into a pleasant room that had large windows open to the countryside. Prince Roarke was gazing peacefully at the view of the rolling hills, having just finished his breakfast. As we came in the room I felt a blast of coolness coming from him and a sense of dancing joy radiating from his heart. He was tall, slimly built, with light skin and shoulder length dark hair. He looked about the same age as Raynor, and his smile radiated joy and fun.

'Come, sit. You must be from my sister's village? We had a message via carrier pigeon,' he began. We said we were, and sat respectfully on the floor. 'I thought there were more of you. You're rather young to have come so far alone.' I waited for Ahren to speak, but he didn't, so decided I'd better say something.

'Your Highness, a dreadful thing happened to us last night. My little brother, my cousin, and the oldest of our group, Raynor, were kidnapped by about twenty soldiers led by a man they called General. We three were hiding and managed not to get caught.' It was all too much. I wiped away a tear, couldn't find a handkerchief and started sobbing hopelessly.

'Cheer up,' he smiled kindly. 'Look, I'll do what I can, and you've come to the best place.'

'They said something about a King Gamsad,' said Ahren.

Conwenna also burst into tears, and we both excused ourselves and went out of the room for a few moments to try and control ourselves. An older lady, presumably a relation of the cousins we had met before, appeared and began to mother us. Ahren stayed with the prince and talked.

'As long as they're taken as slaves in a palace, they won't come to any harm in the short term, and we may be able to work something out,' explained Prince Roarke.

'But how are we going to get back together again? I mean, we can't just leave them to their fate,' said Ahren, agitated.

'I have a meeting set up with this King Gamsad in a few days time. That's why I'm here. I'm waiting for some presents from my parents for him, and a retinue which will impress the old boy.' He looked out of the window for a moment, then went on: 'Now, I think the way to deal with your problem is this: you come with me when I go to meet Gamsad and his general, who everybody knows is evil. Gamsad is a bumbling fool with no discrimination so he's always getting taken advantage of by someone or other. It amazes me that he hasn't lost his kingdom altogether by now, but the neighbouring rulers do try to help. As far as this visit is concerned, if you don't mind you'll have to pretend to be my slaves or attendants, then at least you'll be able to get close to your friends or find out if they are there.'

Conwenna and I returned and sat down again. Prince Roarke radiated bubbling confidence, and I had a strong feeling that somehow we were going to get back with the others. It was almost as if the whole drama was just that: a drama. Then this faded, and there we were, the three of us, in yet another hospitable stranger's house. We'd lost Tandi, and were already missing, and desperately worried about, Lee, Derwin and Raynor. Were we mad to have come this far? We had passed up so many chances of stopping somewhere safe and now we were in a complete mess. At that moment, Prince Roarke looked searchingly at us.

'Have faith. I'll do my very best to help you,' he said quietly, and my hope and optimism returned.

Soon we were shown to comfortable rooms where we could wash and change. We were given a delicious breakfast, then went to sleep. I kept waking up and worrying about the boys, especially Derwin. I still tended to think of him as a helpless child, and hadn't noticed that he had grown up a lot recently.

Two days later the retinue of people, and the awaited presents, arrived from Prince Roarke's parents. We set off together with an elephant, a number of horses and the three of us got up as slaves. Nog and Heggo were part of the procession. The animals had harness of gilded and coloured leather and everyone, including us, was in elegant, brightly coloured clothes. Two days after this we were nearing King Gamsad's palace. As we approached we were met by an advance party of young lords who had been sent out to welcome the prince.

Ahren was posing as the aide of Prince Roarke and was doing his best to look polished and sophisticated. He stuck close to him and said as little as possible, so no one would realise he was raw to court life. It worked, because the advance party assumed his quiet way was because he was haughty, noble and dignified. After some time one of the young lords, a lively man with a twinkle in his eye, sidled up to Ahren and gave him a letter, telling him to give it to Prince Roarke in a private moment.

Prince Roarke noticed this, and as soon as we had been shown into our luxurious temporary quarters - large tents on the lawns of the summer palace, he asked Ahren to give him the letter. He scanned it briefly, asked everyone except the three of us to leave and then said, 'It looks as if my visit will have been in vain. In another way it will be a complete success, as you will see.'

He explained that a number of people from King Gamsad's court had come to see him in secret for some months prior to his arranging to come here, complaining about General Khangish. He had been looking for a reason to come and see what was going on. His mother and father were right behind him and had given him various ideas for solving the problem. He read out the letter he had been given, so we could get a better idea of what was going on. It was from Princess Clemata, the daughter of King Gamsad.

'Respected Prince Roarke,

As a royal prince of a neighbouring country, and one whose reputation for upholding right and just action is second to none, I pray for your help at this difficult time. I have heard of your bravery, your compassion, and your ability to resolve tricky situations.

Please help me! I know I can count on you as a prince and a brother. My heart is already given to Lord Jared, the bearer of this letter, but for diplomatic reasons, my father would like me to marry you. Not only that, the wicked General Khangish is about to overthrow my father, and may even kill him, and then he intends to force me to marry his own despicable son. I am considering running away to the jungles in the south or something even more drastic. My fate, and that of our kingdom, is in your hands.

I am at your mercy,

Clemata.'

'What do you all make of that?' asked Prince Roarke.

'Must be ghastly being a princess,' said Conwenna.

'Is that why we've come, for you to get married?' asked Ahren.

'No. My parents and I felt I should let old Gamsad think I was interested in his daughter. Hence all the gifts and retinue.'

'Do you think this general is the one who captured our friends?' went on Ahren.

'Pretty sure of it.'

'He sounds horrendous,' I said. 'Do you think there's any chance of rescuing the others?'

'We'll give it a try. See, this old rhino, the general, is so greedy for power that he'll think I'm after Clemata to enlarge our country. Round here, she'd be expected to bring some of her father's lands as a dowry. In return our family is supposed to be an ally in times of trouble. We'll see if we can use that somehow. Keep your eyes open and try to find your friends, and don't get lost or captured, for a change!' We laughed, as we had filled him in on our travels to date.

Prince Roarke went to the palace to meet King Gamsad after this, but we stayed in the luxurious tents in the garden. He returned later, but did not say much to any of us. It was after nightfall when the visit really began to resemble a pantomime. Soon after the first stars winked out over the gaily-coloured tents a messenger arrived. He was nervous and jittery, and the whites of his eyes flashed. His speech was stumbling and it turned out he had been sent, much against his will, by General Khangish. He was, without a doubt, a complete failure as a conspirator and wanted to get the meeting over as soon as possible. He asked to see the prince alone, and Prince Roarke told us to hide where we could hear what was being said.

'Why do you want to see me alone?' began Prince Roarke, sounding inexperienced at politics and diplomacy.

'Your Highness, I bring an extremely important message from General Khangish.'

'Oh, fine, but why all the secrecy?' Prince Roarke pretended to be surprised.

'The general wants you to meet him tomorrow evening, at nightfall, in the garden-house by the lake near here. He knows you want to enlarge your parents' kingdom, even if you have to marry Clemata, who has a very shrewish nature. He has a proposition to put to you so you won't have to be tied to her for life, and which could help you get what you want in a much simpler way.' The messenger was silent. He had learnt his speech by heart and now it was done. He fidgeted some more.

'I'll think it over. Tell your general I'll definitely meet him tomorrow evening, on one condition.' Prince Roarke gave him a piercing stare, and he felt incredibly uncomfortable. He wished he had gone on being a village tailor, and had never been lured into the service of the wretched general.

'The condition is that I'll consider whatever the general has in mind as long as he brings me those new slaves he has, as a gesture of his goodwill and serious intentions. They have honey brown skins. I heard he has three and I want them all, or the deal is off.'

'Yes, my lord, I'll see what I can do.' The messenger wondered how this visiting prince knew about those new slave boys.

'All three of them.'

'Yes, I'll tell him you want them brought along,' said the man as he groped his way out of the dark tent.

'Right, they're here!' Prince Roarke called us out of hiding when the messenger had gone. 'Now to rescue them!'

I got the feeling he was enjoying all this. He invited us to sit down and we talked over the day's events. He suggested we should sleep in his quarters in case the general should try any further kidnapping. With the help of some attendants we moved our bedding into a side part of his pavilion, and were thinking about going to sleep, but as we did so heard more visitors approaching. One of Prince Roarke's guards came in.

'Sir, there's a man and a woman with a slave girl outside and they say it can't wait until morning. They say you know them, and can they come in?'

'Not more secret visitors?' Prince Roarke yawned.

''Fraid so, sir. Shall I send them away?' The guard disapproved of these intruders even more than the last one.

'No, better sort it out now, I suppose. Any more details about them?'

'They said they're friends of yours working as slave traders. They look like gangsters to me. With respect sir, I can't see you'd ever have any friends who were slave traders.'

'Send them in,' said Prince Roarke blandly.

'Would you like some extra guards, sir?'

'No, just come in with them yourself.'

In came three cloaked figures, and behind them the guard, arms at the ready, looking disgusted at these despicable traders in human flesh. We all felt a sense of familiarity towards them, but in the dim lamplight none of us could see each other clearly. One of the women was handcuffed and stayed in the shadows with her head hung down in either exhaustion or despair. The other two bowed respectfully to Prince Roarke after removing their cloaks. We were all standing at the back of the pavilion, but could see the woman in the front was dressed in gaudy and ostentatious clothing and wore a lot of tasteless jewellery, as if she had recently risen from poverty to affluence and didn't know what to do with her newfound wealth. The man looked tough, strong and equally newly rich. Then he began to speak, in a voice that we immediately recognised.

'We heard that you were interested in Teletsian slaves, Your Highness, and being as General Khangish has also recently begun a collection, we thought you might like to see this female before he does.' We knew the voice of Zafan the part-time pirate anywhere. And yes! The woman was Zafeena, almost unrecognisable under all those baubles and bad taste in clothes. Neither of them noticed us standing at the back of the tent. Prince Roarke's face was as passive as a theatrical mask. He told the guard that he wanted to be alone and sent him on some errand.

Once the guard had gone, a broad smile crossed Prince Roarke's face and he embraced Zafan, the slave trader, as if he was an old friend. Then the sad looking figure in handcuffs looked up, and to our utter delight we saw that it was Tandi. She looked tired, wan and extremely confused, and I remembered Derwin's similar confusion when he had been 'captured' by the 'pirates'. Since then we had learnt to check people's inner feelings, and our pirate friends, as always, radiated coolness, tender hearts, and enthusiasm for everything life threw at them. Tandi had not seen us yet, and stood alone looking imploringly at Prince Roarke.

'Who is this?' he asked.

'The young lady had better speak for herself,' began Zafan. 'It was necessary for my sister and me to play the role of slave traders in order to rescue her. We were going to bring her to you, but then we heard you were coming here, and that there were some other Teletsian slaves here, so we thought we'd better come here instead.' Zafeena meanwhile removed Tandi's handcuffs.

The three of us ran over to her, hugged her, and we all, including Ahren, burst into tears of joy. Looking back, I realised how much we had changed recently. In Teletsia we would never have been so open with our emotions, especially Conwenna and me, who had been brought up to keep our feelings strictly to ourselves. It was like a great gushing waterfall as we tried to explain what had happened and joyfully told Prince Roarke that this was the lost seventh member of our group. At this point none of us thought to ask Tandi how she had finished up as a slave; we were so delighted to have her back.

We gathered that Prince Roarke had met Zafan and Zafeena on Theon's island, because like many young princes he had been at school there. Before we went to bed we asked Tandi what had happened to her paradise island life. It turned out that after some time she had begun to miss us terribly, and had finally found herself on a ship going northwards, with a chance to catch up with us. Events didn't work out quite as planned, because she was captured by slavers - our common fate at that time - and then sold to this rich looking couple who turned out to be her salvation. When Zafan and Zafeena learnt from the rest of us that Tandi had been left behind, they immediately suspected that she would soon try to rejoin us, and sent out spies to watch the ports in case she appeared. There were now various groups of evil people trying to catch the seven Teletsian rebels with magical powers, so they reckoned the best way to protect Tandi was to capture her themselves.

Ahren had another thought. Did Tandi still have her key? As if in answer, Prince Roarke did something to show he was completely in tune with the flow of events.

'Zafan, this young lady must have cost you dear. I don't have that much spare gold on me, but I do have a very special jewel that I could give you, by way of recompense,' and before Zafan could say anything, Prince Roarke took from round his neck a sixteen petalled key, identical to the one Tandi originally had.

'Roarke, that isn't necessary. We have an allowance from the Emperor for such expenses, and I know as well as you that certain jewels are not to be bought or sold,' replied Zafan.

'True enough,' Prince Roarke turned unexpectedly to us and went on, 'I feel somehow that there's another key like this nearby. Do any of you by chance have one similar?' We were silent for a moment. Did Tandi still have it after all her adventures? Unlikely. We looked at her. To my relief, after hesitating for a moment, because she did not know quite what was going on, she stepped forward.

'I do. I hid it when I thought I might be searched,' she said.

'Excellent! These keys emit a very powerful force, and I felt it when you came in. Now, I'm going to show you something. This key has a power of bringing people together in harmony, but it also has another use. It can be a weapon against those who try to split and destroy. Give it to me for a minute.'

Tandi gave her key to Prince Roarke. It had been hidden around her neck under her clothes.

'I'm going to show you how to transform your key into a deadly weapon. It seeks whatever target is trying to destroy your group, and never misses once you direct it. Whoever is your leader is to take it. Put your right index finger in the little indentation behind the flower. It will unhook itself from the chain, then you must direct it and let it fly through the air. Remain detached and go into your state of quiet inner peace, but only use it when I say to do so, or if I'm not there, only use it if death faces you.'

He demonstrated, and we saw the innocuous jewelled key transform into a fearsome weapon, revolving around Prince Roarke's finger. Tandi was amazed and a little afraid. Prince Roarke gave it back to her and it reverted to its former appearance.

'One more thing,' said Prince Roarke, 'tomorrow, at the reception, there is a good chance that you'll meet the rest of your group. If you do, Ahren, you should tell the oldest one how to use the key as a weapon in an emergency. It might be important to do so.'

Ahren said he would do his best. Everyone was yawning, and Conwenna had given up trying to stay awake and was snoring, head in my lap. Soon we all followed her example, as the next day was going to be busy, to say the least. Tandi had her first night free of nightmares for weeks.

CHAPTER 9

THE SIXTEEN PETALLED KEY

The next morning we rose early and spent a long time making ourselves look elegant. That is everyone except Tandi, who wasn't that well and spent the day resting. Prince Roarke had his physician to give her some tonics and left some guards watching over her in case anyone should try to capture her again. Later in the morning the reception started: endless speeches, each more boring than the last, and official exchanges of gifts.

King Gamsad arrived with his daughter Clemata. He was a florid, overweight man who managed to appear disorganised and untidy even at this official do. He didn't appear to be in control of what was going on at all. Princess Clemata didn't look shrewish, although you couldn't be sure, but instead of keeping her eyes modestly down as would have been expected, she looked imploringly at Prince Roarke, and he gave a slight nod, as if to say, 'Don't worry, I got the letter'.

General Khangish was much in evidence, as were his new Teletsian slaves, wearing pink silk which set off their skin very fetchingly, so he was not slow to mention. Prince Roarke's 'slaves' and those of the general tried not to betray their feelings when they saw each other, especially when Ahren whispered to Raynor that Tandi had reappeared. He also managed to explain about the key and how it could be used if it was necessary.

I couldn't resist saying, very quietly, to my brother, while he was handing round plates of food, that Prince Roarke was going to try to rescue them. Derwin nearly spoilt the whole thing by reacting as if he knew me. My heart was thumping as I pretended not to recognise him. Somehow we made it through the morning. When looking at the pink silk gear of the boys I was reminded of a family of parrots who'd had their wings clipped to stop them escaping.

Ahren had another very important message to deliver. He located Lord Jared, Princess Clemata's beloved, among the throngs of prominent citizens and rich people who were important enough to be at the reception. Ahren explained to Jared that he and some trusted man friends should go to the garden house at dusk, fully armed. The general was not to know they were there. I also had a mission - to give a message from Prince Roarke to Clemata: 'All will be well, just trust in the power of righteousness.'

Prince Roarke was distantly diplomatic towards King Gamsad when the general was around, and friendly towards the general when the king was elsewhere. The general was bloated with pride, as his three new boy slaves could see with every move he made. He thought his long planned coup might soon become reality. Raynor overheard him say this to one of his stooges, his mind already racing ahead to when he would double cross Prince Roarke, once he no longer needed the young, and as he thought, naive prince. After the reception was over Prince Roarke said he wanted to rest for a few hours before the evening's entertainments. King Gamsad disliked these receptions and was only too happy to grant his guest's request.

When we returned to our tent hotel, Roarke asked Tandi if he could borrow her key once more, for the afternoon. She gave it to him and then we all had a siesta. He gave it back to her when we all woke up some time later.

Shortly before dusk, Prince Roarke, the four of us Teletsians: Conwenna, Ahren, myself and Tandi, along with a servant who brought along Nog and Heggo, set off on a walk around the grounds which took us to the garden house by the lake, in the large pleasure gardens, past flowering bushes, flowerbeds and groups of statuary. As we neared the garden house, we espied Jared and his friends lurking in a stand of bamboo. The garden house was made of wood, and would have been a perfect picnic spot, but not this evening. As the pavilion came into view, Prince Roarke stopped.

'Tandi, when we go into the pavilion, I'll try to arrange for you to stand close the oldest boy who's been captured. What is his name?'

'Raynor, Your Highness,' replied Tandi.

'Have Raynor hold your key in his hand, out of sight,' ordered Prince Roarke. He smiled as the setting sun threw a few last beams over the lake. Tandi followed the prince into the large room of the garden house, with Ahren at his other side, holding a large fan to cool him while he walked. I followed with Conwenna, keeping close to the door as Prince Roarke had requested. General Khangish was already there, waiting inside with the three boy slaves and a handful of henchmen.

'Ah, hello general,' began Prince Roarke. 'Glad to see you've brought those slave boys with you. I must say, I'd go a long way to get such a fine collection together.'

'Yes, unusual shade of skin, wouldn't you say?' said the general, making polite conversation.

'Quite so. Now, let's not waste valuable time. We've got more important matters to discuss than slaves. Have them stand over there by mine. Let me just have a look at this tall one.' Prince Roarke took Raynor gently by the ear and had him stand close by Tandi. Raynor had a very hard time not greeting Tandi, who stared at the floor to hide her emotion. The prince lost interest in all of us, and turned to the general, saying: 'We all have to attend the reception in the palace tonight, don't we? That would be a good moment. Now what do you want to discuss?'

'Prince Roarke,' began the general, 'like all rulers, you would like to enlarge your family's territory. I'm sure that is why you want to marry Princess Clemata. She does not have many other attractions, being somewhat plain and with a reputation for having a sharp tongue.'

'You've said it,' said Prince Roarke enigmatically.

'So if I were to offer you all the land west of the River Pingle, in exchange for helping me to persuade the old king to abdicate and offer me the crown, you would have a large slice of fertile land, without the entanglements of a difficult marriage alliance.'

'It is correct that marrying the princess would not solve my present problems, and I would much rather remain on good terms with you after the old king is no longer ruling.'

'Fine, leave the details of the coup to me. I knew I could count on your support. I'll arrange for the removal of the king and no one will blame you in any way. Later I'll dispose of him more permanently and it will look like an accident: perhaps a poisonous snake in a bowl of fruit, or something similar?' The general had understood Prince Roarke's remark in his own way.

'Can I have a word with your son Chang?'

'Why, yes, of course. He's been keeping an eye on your slaves, our noble gift of good faith to you.' Chang came over and Prince Roarke glanced outside. Jared could no doubt hear every word that was being said in the quiet dusk. Tandi handed Raynor the key once no one was bothered about them any more.

'Chang, how can you help in all this?'

'I'll do whatever my father says, because he's much stronger and more capable than Gamsad, who's allowing the country to go to wrack and ruin. This land needs an iron hand. He could get things moving very fast, not like that old duffer in charge now. My dad's going to kill him off once he's in power, he's told me so masses of times.' Chang blundered on, encouraged by nods from Prince Roarke, who sauntered over to his new slaves. It was getting dark, and Prince Roarke whispered to Raynor.

'Get ready to use the key as I showed you.' He turned to Chang, who had by now run out of words, and said, 'Yes, quite so, very interesting. You've stated your position very accurately. Now take the consequences.'

Prince Roarke turned to Raynor, who put the key on his finger. As Roarke finished speaking to Chang, the flowered key had grown into a shining plate-sized weapon, whirling around Raynor's upheld finger. Even though Raynor had been told what to expect from it, what happened next left him staring open mouthed.

'Now! Aim at the general!' whispered Prince Roarke, and the discus flew off Raynor's finger and sped first to the general then to his son, beheading both of them. Prince Roarke called for Jared, and he and his friends ran in, weapons ready, and began fighting.

'Unfair! We've had no warning of a fight!' one of the general's men cried out.

'What warning did the young Teletsians have when you captured them? Take what's coming. This is what happens to people who kidnap innocent boys, and try to overthrow a just king!' shouted Prince Roarke.

We all ran outside, and in the dusk I couldn't see what was going on. There was a clash of swords, groans and screams of pain, as Jared and his armed friends finished off the remaining traitors. It was over so quickly, and the key settled back to its former size and shape, losing its blinding shine. A torch was kindled and it was found on the floor below Prince Roarke's feet.

'Did you hear what was said?' demanded Prince Roarke of Jared and his men.

'Yes, we'd suspected him for ages,' replied Jared.

'Fine, then you're witnesses. Tell everyone what happens to people who meddle with King Gamsad or his allies. We couldn't have overcome the general's guards without you, but I think one man escaped. I saw him run off when the fighting started. No matter, the problem is solved. Lord Jared, the princess is yours. She loves you and you've earned her.'

'Prince Roarke, I never thought you of all people would help me win my bride!'

'How could I marry a young lady who loved someone else?' I'll come to the wedding, but as a guest, not as the bridegroom.'

'I'd resigned myself to seeing Clemata as your wife, and kept telling myself that princesses marry princes, not mere lords.'

'Accidents of birth aren't signs of nobility. You've been brave and true, that's the important thing. Tell King Gamsad he must outlaw slave trading at once, and must free all the slaves in this country. Otherwise I won't come and sort out his problems for him any more. Oh, and warn him to have some discretion when choosing ministers and generals in future. His daughter has a fair amount of sense in that direction.' Jared embraced Prince Roarke like a brother. Roarke smiled, and having disentangled himself from the emotional young man, said, 'Now let's get out of here. We're going to burn this place down, and these traitors with it.'

Prince Roarke took the sixteen petalled key, which winked softly, its smoky-blue lozenge shaped jewels adorning each of the many petals. Once outside he said some words in the classic language, blew on it, and set it round Raynor's index finger once again. It grew and glowed gold and fiery, and he told Raynor to throw it towards the wooden garden house, which had the corpses of the general, his son and his men inside. As it left his hand, it seared round the house, which burst into flames where it hit. It then fell to the ground and Raynor ran to pick it up before the wooden walls began to burn too fiercely. He gave it back to Tandi, who looked at it with a mixture of fear and curiosity to think that this was the harmless jewel she had been wearing for many days, as a memento of her lost friends. The courage and confidence with which Raynor had followed Prince Roarke's instructions when using the discus amazed her. This was a new Raynor, and she had a feeling in her heart for him she couldn't quite understand. Was it pride at knowing a young hero? Was it admiration? Or something more personal? Raynor also felt confused at the way she stared at him a bit too long when he handed her back the jewel. But there was still a part of the shy, bookish young scholar of the days in Teletos, and there was a way to go before he admitted to himself what he felt for her.

The wooden garden house crackled and the flames leapt up into the darkness, against the backdrop of trees and the night sky. The scene was reflected in the lake, and the man who had escaped was followed and caught. He was brought before Prince Roarke and Jared. He turned out to be the former village tailor, and the herald when the boys had first been captured. He begged for mercy and thanked Jared for delivering them all from the general. The prince told him to go back to his village and forget the whole incident.

'Please explain to the king what has happened,' Prince Roarke asked Jared. 'Tell my retinue, and my friends Zafan and Zafeena to make their way home. I have to get these Teletsians away from here, because much worse people than Khangish are after them.'

Without further ado, Prince Roarke had us follow him up a path through the wood, away from the palace and pleasure grounds. We turned round and had one last look at the flickering embers of the garden house, waved Jared and his friends good-bye, and disappeared into the woods, lit by the light of one of the moons.

'Enough of being a prince; let's go and pay my sister a visit,' said Prince Roarke. I wondered how we were going to do this in the course of one evening, but said nothing. Raynor was lost in thought, trying to analyse in his mind what happy accident of fate had made Tandi turn up again, and just at the very moment we needed her key, which was somehow connected with Prince Roarke.

Ahren and Lee were talking about the key too, but were more interested in how it had transformed itself into a fiery weapon, than its connection with any people. Conwenna loathed the dark and hung onto me, not wanting to admit she was afraid, but her clammy hand in mine said it all. Derwin asked Prince Roarke if there was any chance of his getting out of his uncomfortable clothes, because he was still wearing the pink silk getup he had been dressed in for the morning reception. The prince smiled, said yes, took his hand, and I knew we were going to be all right for the time being anyway.

Soon we came to the end of the wood, and beyond us we could see fold upon fold of forest and meadow covering the rolling hills, all black and silver in the soft night light. Ahead of us was a sight I'd never forget. Lit by a translucence coming from within was a large rounded craft, like an upturned bowl or circular boat, but with no sails or keel and made of some semi transparent material. It was covered with outlandish designs and bits sticking out, and the whole machine was humming and vibrating and hovering a little bit off the ground. We all gaped in surprise, and Prince Roarke laughed to reassure us. A man was standing by it, someone from Prince Roarke's retinue, and with him were Heggo and Nog. Nog ran towards us, full of his usual tail wags and greetings. Heggo cropped the grass.

'This is my flying ship,' said Prince Roarke. 'Very handy for getting people out of trouble fast.'

'Incredible!' Ahren agreed. He had been longing to have a chance to fly ever since Lee had told him about flying with Merien on Dumpattick's island.

Derwin stopped worrying about his uncomfortable clothing, and his face lit up at the thought of flying in this magical bubble. He could hardly believe that a week that had had such a dreadful beginning could end so well.

'Right, we all get in here, except that donkey. He goes in there,' Prince Roarke pointed to two doors, and Ahren took Heggo and, as always, managed to get him to do what was wanted, and put him in a stall round the other side of the craft. Prince Roarke pointed to a number of metal tongues protruding from the bottom of the craft like petals. 'These bits sticking out revolve when we take off and make the ship rise and fly. Well, there's more to it than that. It's like the key. There's a lot of subtle power locked up in it. Anyway let's go, we mustn't waste time.'

We climbed in and Nog became agitated about something in the woods behind us. Raynor called him to heel, and we were soon inside with the door closed. Prince Roarke told us to sit down on the benches and cushions. He was in a great hurry and went over to the bank of controls at one side, turned on some switches, immediately the craft began to hum and vibrate more, and slowly took off and rose up above the trees. We saw a number of soldiers and one or two figures that looked like ogres came out from the trees and wave angrily at us.

'Just in time!' said Prince Roarke. He asked for Tandi's key again, and fitted it into a slot on the control panel. Then he set the dials, directed the craft in a certain direction, and came and sat down with us. Derwin stayed watching the controls, absolutely fascinated. Prince Roarke warned him not to touch any of them; he promised he wouldn't, but was rooted to the spot watching as lights winked on and off and the ship somehow knew what to do on its own. The rest of us were more concerned about our pursuers.

'Who are they? They're not too pleased that we've given them the slip,' asked Raynor.

'I don't know, but a worse lot than you've met here,' said Prince Roarke. 'Zafan warned me. Khangish wanted your bodies, but the masters of those people chasing you also want your souls.'

'What do you mean?' Raynor went on.

'The Sorcerers of Teletsia don't give up easily. They're in league with Dumpattick and the ogres. Ultimately they all want to be on top, and will fight each other, but they'll team up to catch you. Zafan had a feeling they'd look for you hereabouts. By keeping you boys out of sight until today, General Khangish might have saved your lives.

'Also the fact that you were split up helped, as the word is out that there are seven of you. One of the qualities of Tandi's key is bringing people together in harmony, and if necessary destroying disharmony. Lucky for you, Tandi, that you had that one, or you might never have got back together with your friends. I'm not even sure who those characters down below are working for, but believe me, you need to be away from them as soon as possible.'

Raynor listened carefully to this. We all did, apart from Derwin, who was still at the control panel of the flying ship. We were silent and watched the moonlit landscape passing below us. I felt from the rest of us something close to fear. Would we ever really get away from our pursuers? After some minutes Derwin came to join us.

'How did you get this machine here?' he asked.

'I called it with my key,' replied Prince Roarke. 'When you were all resting this afternoon, I did some preparations. I walked down to the wood here, called it, and then I knew it would be waiting for us now. It only arrived an hour or so ago. That was one good reason for agreeing to meet Khangish in the evening – to give my flyer time to get here. Not many people know about our flying machine. It's a well guarded secret and we only use it on special occasions. I borrowed Tandi's key this afternoon to check it would work if we need to use it.'

'I've always dreamed of things like this! How does it fly?' We were happy that Derwin was changing the subject.

'That depends. Either it has to be driven by me or one of my family, or it has to be fitted with a sixteen petalled Key of Wisdom. This is one of the magic carpets of your fairy tales, but it only works in our lands, plus or minus a short distance. To drive it without the key your mind has to be crystal clear. You must be able to hold unwavering attention and operate from a level of awareness that is totally free from random thoughts. In theory anyone should be able to learn to do it, but so far only people in my family manage it. Even for me, it's much easier with the key. I just program it and it flies on its own.'

'Does that mean we could drive it? Or at least Tandi?' Derwin was doubtful.

'We'll see, tomorrow morning.'

We talked for some time, and then had some snacks. After this we looked out of the window at the night landscape floating past below us. Some time later, Prince Roarke interrupted our conversation with him.

'Don't talk to me for a minute or so, as we're nearly there and it's difficult to land in this woodland, especially in the dark.'

'Where are we?' I asked.

'Marimba's village, the best place to hide you,' said Prince Roarke as we floated slowly downwards. We looked out of the clear sides of the flying dome, and below we could make out the village where we had stayed before. We landed a little way away, behind some trees, left the craft and Prince Roarke led us through a grassy clearing and towards the village. The plants under our feet were dew-damp, and smelled delicious as we trod on them. The trees above were heavy with blossom.

Near the village, Prince Roarke stopped, sat on a log and started to play a small stringed instrument he had brought with him. Soon we heard the noise of voices as the young boys and girls of the village also heard it and came running to find him. Marimba was there, and there were greetings all round, and the next thing I remember we were all dancing to the sound of not only his music, but also that of many others: panpipes, drums, and bells. Faster and faster we danced, and the more we danced the more energy we had. Well - up to a point. After what seemed like forever we Teletsians collapsed in a heap under a tree, puffing and laughing. The ghastliness of the last few days had dissolved in the music and the dance.

Later there was food, and sleep, and in the morning Marimba and her friend Brindan came and gave us all thick greeny brown cloaks to keep out dampness and cold. Marimba explained we were going north, and might need them and that the soft colours would hide us from prying eyes.

Prince Roarke, as good as his word, let us try to control the craft. None of us managed it. There would be a humming sound, but as soon as our minds lost their pure concentration, it would sputter and stop again. I couldn't even get it to start, and Lee was a bit put out: he could only get it to fly a hand's height. The same went for Conwenna. Ahren wouldn't trust himself to try, and although Raynor got it to hover for perhaps half a minute, after that he lost confidence in himself and it sank down again. Tandi just laughed and said piloting flying ships was not for her. Derwin, strangely enough, was the most successful, but Raynor looked pleadingly at Prince Roarke, as if to say, 'Please, don't entrust our lives to an eleven year old boy', and the wise prince got the message.

'Right, plan B,' he said, with good-natured resignation. 'I'm going to fit your key into the flying ship, and instruct it where to go. It will take you to the northern border of our land of Vittalia, and will come down to earth for a short while to let you out. Then it will take off by itself and return to me, but the key must remain in the controls.'

We were all, even Tandi, quite happy with this arrangement. Anything to put some distance between ourselves and our pursuers. We told Tandi that all the keys left us when we had finished with them, and from her side she no longer hankered after jewels and finery. Her friends and our mission were far more important to her now.

'The ship will leave you on an open plain,' Roarke continued. 'There are no roads there, and it's to the west of the direction you need to go in, so no one would ever think you'd go that way. You'll have to walk, and be careful to fill your waterskins and bottles whenever you can. There are some rivers on the plain, but they aren't very full at this time of the year. I'm going back to my town now, and I'll put the word around that you're still with me, to give you some breathing space.

'In the next country you must be very careful indeed, because it's ruled by two evil men and the whole country is suffering as a result, but to get to Sasrar you have to go through the capital city, then on up the pass to the mountain kingdom.'

'Have you been there?' asked Raynor.

'No, but I know the way.'

At that moment Marimba came up, with new waterskins, packs of food, and everything she felt we would need. She and Brindan embraced us and bid us a good journey, and told us to look them up when we returned. They lived in a completely different world to us, where people did turn up unexpectedly for the evening, with no worries to creep into their quiet moments, or Sorcerers chasing them and wanting their souls.

Prince Roarke took us to the flying ship, put Tandi's key in the specials slot, and reprogrammed it. Then he bid us farewell, the flying craft took off and soon we were watching the hills and valleys, which gradually became less wooded, passing below us. How beautiful it all looked from up above! To begin with none of us spoke, but after some time Raynor and Tandi, sitting next to each other, broke the silence.

'I just can't tell you what a blessing it is that you're back with us,' he began.

'I missed you all so,' said Tandi, glowing again, now the shock of being a slave had worn off.

'A lot of strange things have happened to us since you left, and some of them have made us a bit wiser.'

I sat with Conwenna and Derwin, and we stared at the view below. Raynor and Tandi were talking; he told the story of the dragons, and how we learnt not to fantasise after that. He explained how we met the tigers, and the lesson there was that as long as we had enough courage not to be terrified of them, they were the best possible guards and steeds. The longer they talked the more relaxed Tandi became, and by the end of the flight she was completely her old self again.

After some hours we were flying over an open plain, and the craft put us down on the northern side of a wide, sluggish river. We took our animals and belongings out and while Nog ran around the plain barking with glee we prepared ourselves for a very long walk. Heggo was heavily loaded, and all of us had backpacks. When we were ready the flying machine silently took off and floated away to the south, like a giant jellyfish in the afternoon sun.

The Sixth Key - Forgiveness and Resurrection

The qualities of this subtle centre, found in the forehead, are forgiveness and resurrection. When the divine power flows through this centre, the person becomes peaceful, forgiving, and free from ego and damaging conditionings. This land of Chussan is the area of our world where this power manifests most strongly, and the summer home of the astrologers is its seat.'

Robin Markand's Manual of Instruction

Chapter 10

Across the Plains

We filled our water skins from the river and somewhat reluctantly began to walk in a north-easterly direction. This was a world of earth colours, and with our new greeny brown cloaks we blended into the landscape well. The grass was dry, brown and whispering, and the wind moaned above us. The sun shone out of a cloudless sky and there was not a tree, animal or building in sight.

Raynor was distracted and not as attentive as usual. There was a dreaminess about him, but no one thought anything of it. In the afternoon he was walking alone with Nog, some way away from the rest of us. He suddenly fell down and cried out, and we all rushed over to him.

'Oh no, I've twisted my ankle! I didn't see that hole,' he grimaced at the pain.

'Have we got any bandages?' asked Tandi.

'Yes, but we must go on walking, and that's going to be a problem.'

'Let's try to heal you, like we were taught,' I suggested. We all put our left hands to the sun, our right hands towards Raynor and prayed in our hearts that the pain and beginning of a swelling would go. After some minutes, to our relief, it did improve somewhat.

'Tandi, if you can put a support bandage around my ankle, I'll try and walk,' Raynor suggested. We rested for the remainder of the day, and the next morning he could indeed walk, even though he had a limp for some time. After that he avoided Tandi, and she noticed this. She didn't say anything, but when I felt her inner self, there was a sense of guilt. I assumed it was something to do with having left us, and then having returned.

Raynor had been overwhelmed by his emotions when talking to her on the flying ship. He had tried to downplay them, both to himself and her, but he could not get that wonderful smile out of his mind, and his utter delight at having her back. That was where his attention had been, and as the sharp pain of his fall came over him, he knew he could not live in dreamland for one moment if we were all to get to Sasrar in one piece. He over-reacted in the other direction by being very cool towards Tandi. A couple of days later she spoke to me when Lee and Ahren were off shooting rabbits for our supper. Like Nog, we ate a lot of rabbits at that time in our lives.

'Have I said something to annoy Raynor?' she asked uncertainly.

'No,' I replied. 'I think he's worried he might slow us down with his weak ankle. He knows it will take some days to heal properly, and we don't have any time to waste if we're to keep ahead of those people who were after us. You have to understand Raynor. He takes things on himself and chews them over in his mind. It will pass, you see.'

'I'll just keep a low profile for the time being. I was confused.'

We left it at that, but Raynor's attitude did not change.

We walked through the grasslands for days and sometimes crossed rivers which wound unhurriedly through the plain. They were low at this season, their rocky beds exposed. We refilled our waterskins when we could, but there was never enough water, except one afternoon when there was a flash storm and we all got soaked, but the sun and wind soon dried us out, the mud turned back to dust and we walked on. And on. Occasionally we saw herds of deer and wild cattle, or rather we assumed they were wild, and once we thought we heard the roar of a lion in the distance. We began to feel lonely and a little uneasy in all this emptiness and one afternoon I asked Tandi to tell us her story in detail, to take our minds off our sore feet and aching legs.

'You've all been so sensible, and brave,' she began. 'I feel such a fool telling you my story.'

'Maybe we've just kept quiet about the bad bits,' said Ahren. 'We've mostly done at least one fairly moronic thing, believe me.'

'Come on, tell us how you met up with us again,' said Lee.

'The only one who does always get it right is Nog,' said Derwin, watching him as he ran off after yet another rabbit.

'If you insist, I'll tell you what I can remember,' began Tandi. 'After you all left the Emperor's Island I was always busy with my duties as companion to the princess. She was pleasant, but had lived a totally sheltered life and liked me to tell her stories. I was learning to play a stringed instrument to entertain her, although I didn't have time to get good enough. It was a life of total leisure, like an agreeable dream, or eating a sweet dessert all the time.

There were other companions like myself, but they were all very sophisticated and cultured. They considered me to be a bit of a curiosity, but were very polite, for all that. They could sing like birds, dance like flowers in the wind, paint quite exquisitely and so on. They could also make intricate tapestries out of the jewels in the gardens, stitched from the silk of many coloured silkworms. I could go on for ever about the luxury and finery of that place.'

'So what went wrong?' I asked, thinking how strained I would have been, having to be on my best behaviour at all times. Tandi had been brought up on a farm, albeit an affluent and comfortable one. When we first met she had a hankering after the fine things of life, whereas we from the city had numerous empty headed acquaintances who went in for this sort of thing. Because we had seen a lot of fine clothes, jewellery and luxurious living, the island didn't have the same fascination for us.

'It's strange,' went on Tandi, 'how things happen sometimes. You make a silly mistake, and it puts you on a course where you start to put whatever is wrong deep inside you right. That's what happened to me. One day I was walking in those enormous gardens, up and down the paths lined with shrubs and trees weighed down with jewels and with leaves of gold and silver or covered with sparkling flowers. Suddenly it all began to sicken me and I longed for one of our meadows back home. Oh for a field of grass, weeds and a few cowpats, where I could sit and make daisy chains for my little cousins, and where Ahren and my brothers might be catching wild chickens for the pot in the nearby woods!

'I forgot to tell you. In the mornings we usually went picking fruits and flowers from the gardens with the older ladies. They knew which plants were for food, medicines, jewels or more magical purposes. One day I decided to make a dress for my princess and cover it with jewels, as a surprise for her - I'd seen people doing this sort of thing before. The tailor would sew the fabric together, and I'd embroider it with gold and silver cord made from a plant in the garden. Then I'd sew the fruits from the garden into the design, and within a day or two they would harden like ordinary jewels.

'One morning, when the sun was rising over the milky sea, and the leaves and sparkling flower-jewels were rustling in the dawn breeze, I wandered into a part of the gardens I'd never walked in before. I saw a bush covered in jewels like many coloured opals, and I picked some and put them in my silken apron. A few days later the dress for the princess had been sewn up, and I put these jewels into a design which decorated the top. I carefully stitched and cut and worked them in, but all the time I did it I felt increasingly gloomy about being away from all of you. I tried talking to the other companions about my home, our adventures and so on, but to them nothing was as good as the beauty and luxury of the island.'

'Anyway, the moment came to present the dress to my princess. We were sitting in a marble courtyard, listening to musicians, with the fountain in the middle playing. I expected her to be at least a little bit pleased, but to my despair she was horrified. When I had unpacked the dress from its coloured paper, all the people round about had frozen and the musicians stopped playing. It turned out that the jewels I had picked were taboo. The princess explained that only the Empress could pick and use them. Anyone else who did would have to leave the island. As you can imagine, I was in a turmoil, because deep down inside me I wanted to leave, but not like this. None of the jewels could be sold to people away from the Emperor's Citadel, but these were even more restricted in their use.

'She took me to see Merien's mother and father. As you know his father is the Prime Minister. We walked into the Council Chamber and he was with a delegation of merchants and sea-faring men whose rough leather boots and travelling clothes shook me, because I had become so accustomed to the wealth, colour and richness of the court. They had unkempt beards and weather-beaten faces, and were having a serious conversation. They related that there was much trouble in the outside world. Teletsia had problems with a rebellion of young people, who the Sorcerers blamed for a series of earthquakes. The leaders of this rebellion had escaped, and the Sorcerers were offering a large reward for their capture. The rebels had been caught on Dumpattick's Island, but had again got away, causing chaos there. The merchants wanted to know whose side they should be on, and how they should act if they found them.

'The Prime Minister was adamant. They shouldn't get involved with the Sorcerers or anyone else in league with them. He warned of another ally of the Sorcerers: a king who had in his service many ogrous, semi-human beings, with whose help he had overrun many countries to the northeast of the sea. The merchants went away, and it was my turn. I tried not to be afraid, because was not I one of the rebels?

'The Prime Minister's wife spoke to me. She was not angry, but explained that the beautiful jewels I'd picked shone with a lustre that reflected the best part of the inner nature of whoever picked them. As far as that person was concerned, their deepest desires would dominate him or her until he or she did something about them. That was the nature of the curse. It occurred to me that since I'd picked the jewels, I'd wanted nothing so much as to continue my journey north and find you all again. So I was to be sent with the merchants, and they had instructions to deliver me to Prince Roarke, who was known to the Prime Minister, as his territory was on the route north.'

'But how did you get caught by the slave traders?' asked Derwin. He liked a good gory tale, in common with most boys of his age.

'It was like this. There was a member of the crew on the merchant's ship who was rotten to the core, even though the captain didn't realise this. We sailed west to an island on the rim of the sea. It was a trading post and all the crew went ashore, but left me behind as it was not a good town for a young girl. The bent crewman stayed on board, ostensibly to guard me, but no sooner had the others gone than some shifty types, evidently friends of his, came on board and began talking to him in private.

'I would have gone to find the captain in the town, but it was dusk and I could see that the docks were bristling with rough characters, plus I hadn't a clue where the others were. I heard the bent crewman bargaining with his friends, but didn't understand they were bargaining over me, or I'd have run for it, swum for it, or something - anything rather than sit like a lamb being got ready for the slaughter. When he called for me I naively went into his cabin, and he took a long dagger from his boot, grabbed me and pointed it at me. I was dead scared and my heart was pounding, but he told me I'd come to no harm if I kept quiet.

'Then he and the slavers took me to another boat, by way of a dinghy. It was a grimy ship and dilapidated, and I was left with my new owners. I remembered the key around my neck, and whether it was that or something else, no one touched me and they treated me fairly well. We immediately sailed away, I presume before the merchants returned and found me missing.

'The next day the captain asked to meet me. He was a nobleman gone rotten. He took me into his private cabin and gave me a good meal, and was entirely different from his employees. For one thing he didn't smell and wasn't crawling with lice. He apologised for the crudeness of his sailors, but said times were bad and he had to make a living. Then he explained in detail, as if trying to make it all right, that he would have to sell me, which was a pity, as he didn't really approve of trafficking in humans. He gave orders for me to have the best treatment, and a nice cabin to myself, but when we went up on the deck my heart sank, because we were out of sight of land and I was at his mercy.

'Some days later I realised that he was also a pirate, because he captured a merchant ship, and after taking its booty and some of the sailors as slaves, he ordered it sunk. It was horrifying to see the ship burning in the middle of the sea and the other sailors drowning, without hope of escape. Our captain may have been courteous to me, but he was a cruel brute otherwise.

'When we got to the famous slave market at King Gamsad's port I was given some drug to stop me telling anyone I was supposed to be under the protection of the Emperor. After I had been forced to take the drug, before it took effect, I put my hand on the key and prayed. I don't know who or what I prayed to, but somehow the key was my last link with anything good and sane, so I prayed. That was the evening before the auction, which I was absolutely dreading, as you can imagine. About an hour later, when I was already feeling very odd from the drug, there were some visitors to our ship. I thought they were more pirates. It was Zafan and Zafeena, and they'd somehow found out that I was to be sold. They threatened to expose the pirate to the Emperor's troops if he didn't accept a modest price for me.

'I only really came round a day or two later, by which time we were well away from the port. Zafan and Zafeena told me what was going on, and that I had to pretend to be a slave. We eventually reached King Gamsad's palace and met up with you. So that was it.'

We trudged on, usually in silence. For Tandi it was a pleasure to be back with us and she put up with everything without complaining, which was more than the rest of us did. She found herself feeling a lot of admiration for Raynor, some of it misplaced. He had lost that scholarly stoop and now stood straight and tall. She saw him as brave, and much more confidant, which he definitely was nowadays. She also looked up to him as a natural leader, which he wasn't, often wishing someone else would make the decisions, and as being kind and considerate, which he had always been. She assumed his slight coldness towards her was because she had left us for some time.

Raynor also felt a lot for Tandi. He told himself his delight at having her back was to do with the success of our journey as a whole, and still tried to deny his personal feelings for her. She was beautiful, but most young country girls of her age were. She was sweet and gentle, but again, weren't most girls from good homes? He tried to put these thoughts out of his mind and looked carefully at where he was walking. The rest of us suspected nothing.

The real problem, or rather blessing, was the nature of our Teletsian society. Those stark plains were not the place to be starry eyed and out of touch with reality. Even though a lot of the traditional customs of Teletsia had been destroyed by the Sorcerers, one remained. In the majority of families, the young did not have girlfriends and boyfriends, but when they reached marriageable age, and our people often married young, the parents of both would consult together, frequently with the suggestions of their sons and daughters in mind, and relationships were arranged that way. To find one's own partner was considered forward, and often doomed to failure in the long run, and the young tended to trust their elders before losing their hearts to each other. So Raynor was in a fix because there were no elders to talk to. As a result he let matters be, and concentrated on the far more pressing problem of keeping us alive, together and out of trouble.

In order not to have to push our way through the long grass and occasional thorn bushes of the plain, and to have to be always looking at where we were treading, we walked up a shallow rocky canyon, a riverbed in the rainy season. We came to a pool of oily water in the rocks and had a quick paddle to cool our hot, sore feet. We took our backpacks and cloaks off and were lounging around feeling lazy.

Nog was chasing rabbits, and we could hear him barking as he found some. Then we heard a rumbling like distant thunder, and the ground began to shake. We thought it must be another earthquake, and ran into the open where there were no overhanging rocks, but no sooner had we done this, when round the corner came a herd of cattle, galloping full tilt, straight at us. They were panic stricken and stampeding in a mad mass. Their nostrils were flared, their horns flashing and they filled the entire canyon bottom. The walls of the canyon were no higher than a tree but there was no time to scale them now, so we ran behind a large boulder and pressed ourselves to the side away from the oncoming tide of galloping hooves.

Heggo careered off with the rest of the animals, gradually shedding his baggage as the cattle ran away from what they presumed to be a pack of howling wolves, in fact Nog. Conwenna hid herself in her cloak and lay flat against the rock, and as long as we pressed close to the boulder the cattle ran past and left us unharmed. Soon they had gone and peace descended again.

We were in trouble. We had lost our food, waterskins, almost everything. Most of our spare clothes and other things had been ground to shreds. We could probably catch Heggo again, but he too had lost his load. Nog came back, wagging his tail innocently. We sat around the pool wondering what to do next. Soon we would have to leave this riverbed if we were to go north, and then what? No food, no water. Raynor suggested we draw lots as to who would try to catch Heggo, to take our minds off the dire situation we were now in.

Suddenly everything changed. Over the lip of the canyon above us came three nomads riding ponies. They had light brown skins and mid brown hair, wore brightly coloured clothes and were short and stocky. They were not happy about something and saw us at the same moment as we saw them so there was no question of hiding. The nomads noticed their cattle, some way down the canyon and now grazing peacefully. They became less agitated, dismounted and scrambled down the side of the gully to where we were.

We automatically checked their inner feeling. They were not evil people, even if they were somewhat angry with us about their cattle. Not great and powerful spiritual personalities, but good sane folk going about their life's work. They wanted us to go with them to meet their headman.

They led us up onto the plain and we could see the whole tribe: flocks, wagons and so on. As we were led past family groups, curious faces of both people and beasts stared at us. After some time we reached a large covered wagon. We entered by some steps at the back, and inside it was cosy and friendly, a real home. The headman was sitting with his wife on some rugs and bolsters. Everything was patterned or brightly painted: rugs, walls, wooden carved shelves and cupboards. Raynor, who was wearing the key with the two petals, immediately noticed that the overriding motif of the rugs and painted designs was similar to his key. We were invited to sit on the colourful rugs.

The headman was a heavily built man. He was strong from a life on the plains and had a kindly face, perhaps from constantly looking after animals and all the families that made up his people; his wife had a round smiling face and twinkling eyes and both were deeply wrinkled from a life in the dry, hot air of the plains. The man spoke a standard form of the common language and we could understand him easily.

'So, southerners, I see,' he began. 'Your hound scared our cattle. Lucky they didn't run you down. You should look after him better in future.'

'I'm sorry sir,' began Raynor. 'We thought we were alone on the plain.'

'Of course you did,' interrupted his wife. 'How could you have known we were up on the top?'

We introduced ourselves, while Rhea, the wife, brought us an amber coloured drink flavoured with honey and spices. Lamech, the headman, went outside for a moment and then returned to say that one of his men had our donkey safely tethered nearby. He also said he would give us new waterskins and supplies. We may have fallen in with nomads, but they wanted for nothing and lived well. The meeting did not end there.

'We are wanderers,' continued Lamech, 'and spend our lives on the open plains. To the north are the foothills of the great northern mountains. The foothills are wooded and there are many farms, villages and some towns. The capital city is there too. The country should be ruled by a young man, but at present he's in hiding in the mountains, and his two uncles have seized power. His mother took him away when he was a small child, because these two wanted to kill him.

'We know he's still up there and one of these days he's going to come back. The two we've got lording it over us now have recently teamed up with some so called High Priests from down south who've come with 'advisors' to help us. Or so they say.'

'Did they just invite these people?' said Raynor, his heart sinking fast as he recognised the cursed Teletsian Sorcerers yet again.

'Not quite. One of the brothers who rules the country is very aggressive and outspoken and thinks he can do no wrong, and the other is such a wimp that he's afraid of his own shadow. Since these High Priests arrived the two brothers have become puppets of these characters. These magicians get the aggressive one to do what they want by appealing to his egotistical nature, and threaten the other one with spells if he doesn't toe the line.'

'Have they given you trouble?'

'Not much. The brothers did try to tax us, but we told them that we keep a watch on the southern borders of the land, and we made it clear that if they did tax us, we would of course want to be paid for our services. Otherwise we would take our flocks elsewhere, because these plains stretch through more than one country. So they've left us alone so far. Dreadful types if you ask me.

'The sooner our king comes back the better. Some officials came round a few days ago and poked around, saying they were looking to see the size of our flocks and how many people we had in the tribe. I never believe a word they say though.'

'These High Priests sound like the ones we are fleeing from.' Now we had committed ourselves, but I was sure Raynor had checked on his hands whether it was sensible to say this: cool would be all right, but a warm sensation when thinking about whether to say this, then not so wise.

The weather-beaten man looked piercingly at each of us. He nodded silently. Raynor had been kneeling forwards to catch Lamech's words above the moan of the wind outside, and as he did his two petalled key fell out from under his shirt, where he usually kept it concealed. Raynor didn't notice but Lamech did. I was sitting where I could see everything, but could say nothing.

'And you, strangers,' commented Lamech 'are most probably something to do with our latest crop of troubles. Young man, I suggest you put away your jewelled key before anyone sees it. There are spies even in my tribe, and you are wearing the emblem of the exiled king, the rightful ruler of this land. I noticed you saw the same symbol woven into our carpets, and we've had a few problems ourselves explaining it away. Don't show that except to a few trusted agents of the young king, or you'll be for it. It will condemn you or save you, depending on who sees it. Where on earth did you get it, anyway?'

'A long story, sir.'

'Well, no matter. Rhea, go outside and make sure no one is listening, will you?'

Rhea posted herself at the doorway and Lamech went on talking, but a herdsman who had been listening had already heard enough, and by the time Rhea had walked to the back of the caravan, he had slunk away. He got on his pony and rode towards Chussan City, the capital of the land, for all he was worth. He was going to be well paid for the information he carried.

'My informers tell me the real reason these southerners are here is to prevent a dangerous group of superhuman traitors against their country from reaching a hidden mountain kingdom which lies to the north of our country of Chussan. The story goes that if these traitors do reach this kingdom, then these High Priests will lose their power and be overthrown. They think that the people in the mountains have some fearsome weapons or something. It's said these traitors have the power to change their form, but are usually seen as seven young people who look innocent and lost. They also have a variety of weapons and magic at their disposal, and some ferocious animals as well.' There was a silence and then Lamech chuckled - a rich, fruity chuckle that said it all. 'You're not superhuman are you?'

'No way, but we're the ones. You can give us up or help us. It's your choice.' This new Raynor was careful, calculating, and courageous, and used the power of the warm and cool inner feelings to check out everything he said.

'Don't worry, I'll help you all I can. It's no accident your dog scared the cattle. Fate has a way of intervening. I suspected you the moment I saw you, but wanted it to come from you, just in case, because these southerners have some cleverly disguised spies.

'You'll have to go through Chussan City to get to the pass into the mountains. It won't take you to the mountain kingdom, but it's in the right direction. If you're very lucky, which you seem to be, you might meet people who can help you. Go with my wife now, because the first thing you need is a disguise. You're so obviously from the hot south, you won't have a hope of getting through the city as you are.'

'How can you help?'

'You'll see. Rhea has a few tricks she can use. Then come back here and we'll give you a good meal. Stay the night in the camp before you leave.'

Off we went to be transformed by Rhea. First we all had our hair bleached and dyed the soft brown of her people. Gone were our blue-black locks, at least for the time being. She said the dye was permanent but would grow out in time. Then, stranger still, she put some ointment on our skins. It made our faces very wrinkly but much lighter. This, she said wouldn't last more than a few days, and she gave us some pots of the ointment to touch up our skins when we started going darker again. We Teletsians have a warm, rich hue to our skins that is much admired in many countries, but is very distinctive and gives us away hopelessly. Right now we didn't look like Teletsians, but not like the herdsmen either, because most of us have rather long, thin noses and high foreheads, and these plains people had round faces, small noses and foreheads, and flared nostrils. That we couldn't do much about.

Then we were kitted out in the dress of the tribe: very colourful, with lots of embroidery, and I felt we were taking too much. Rhea said not to worry, they had plenty to spare and it was fine to give us one set each. We wore our own clothes underneath and the top layer was just for show or disguise. By then it was evening, and it was back to Lamech's wagon for a meal of roast lamb and wild vegetables from the plains. Lamech talked as we ate.

'I'm going to give you a letter of introduction to a friend of mine who lives in Chussan City. He deals in animals. We'll lend you some ponies, and when you reach his place you can leave them there. I need to send them to him in any case. He sells our surplus stock, and he always needs ponies at this time of year. I'll give you a map so you can find his yard. Don't want you opening your mouths more than you have to and giving yourselves away like that! The son of the family is the one you must contact, he's called Robin. My friend's a good enough chap, but Robin's your man. Hope he's in town when you get there.'

The next morning a family of nomads left for the city. They were riding ponies and the eldest girl had a baby, actually a doll, strapped to her back. They also had a dog and a pack donkey. As long as one didn't look too closely, or listen to their strangely accented speech, they more or less blended in with the locals. Walking has never been my thing, so I was unbelievably happy not to be collecting yet another set of blisters, and felt quite at home on my trusty grey pony as we trotted towards civilization with mid brown hair and wrinkled fair-skinned faces.

CHAPTER 11

NOMADS IN THE CITY

Naturally the ponies helped us cross the wave after wave of grass-covered hillocks much more quickly. Five days later we came to farmed countryside, and then further on to paved roads, villages and small towns. The fenced fields, and houses with gardens and orchards, reminded us of our homeland, although this was a much colder land than ours. We noticed that some of the people we saw had the same expression and attitude of many in Teletsia: 'We don't want to know you, mind your own business and let us mind ours'. Not a very good sign. Few said 'hello' as we passed. We also noticed that despite the neatness of the region and the apparently fertile land, the country folk looked surprisingly poor.

In every small town and even village was a building that looked like a place of worship. They were large and lavishly decorated. Derwin said, 'Yuk, that thing is so ugly,' at the first one. We saw people coming out of these buildings, and presumed they were priests and priestesses. They wore smart, costly clothes, in contrast to the worn and patched rags of almost everyone else. These people looked well fed and swaggered as if they were very important. We came to the conclusion they were, here.

'Perhaps there's a prize for the one that looks the most stupid,' said Ahren.

'Why do they look so rich, and yet they don't do any work?' Derwin wondered as we passed a group of 'priests' looking snooty in their fur-lined cloaks, with gold embroidery and red silk showing underneath.

'And the people in the fields work like dogs, yet they're thin and poor,' added Conwenna.

'It's fairly obvious, isn't it?' said Tandi. 'The folk in the fields do the work and the priests finish up getting rich. We've seen that before. Goodness knows how my parents keep going, with the amount of tax they have to pay to the Sorcerers on what we grow at home. We hide a lot of our crops at the end of the year when we do our returns. I wouldn't tell you that if we were in Teletsia. Ahren knows the scene; I'm sure his family do the same.'

'Oh yes,' laughed Ahren. 'We could teach this lot a thing or two about surviving hard times.'

'Trouble is,' this was Raynor, 'these people may have been conned into believing that it's good for them to give all they have to these priest types.'

'They can't be that simple,' objected Ahren.

'You'd be amazed what you can get people to do if you play on their beliefs and fears. What do you think they taught us at the Sorcerers' Academy? This place reminds me of Teletsia.'

'With luck we won't be here long,' said Lee. 'I got talking to Lamech and he told me a bit about this religion. The prophet of the god they worship was a perfect example of humility and simplicity. When he was on the earth he lived as a poor potter, showing men you don't have to be rich to be saintly. He gave people the example of humility, and told them they had to forgive each other and not hold grudges. When he made his pots, he said that moulding the soul, or higher part of a person, was similar to allowing the divine power to mould you like soft clay. He said you had to let the events of your life to teach you to become a better person, and not feel you'd failed if you weren't rich or powerful, because that wasn't going to get you to heaven in any case.

'After he left the earth, some of his followers set themselves up as priests and started giving nearly everyone else a hard time. They'd say, "You mustn't complain if times are tough, it's all extremely good for your soul", if the poor people were suffering. Very neat and rather nasty.'

Another thing we noticed was that when people weren't toiling, their only form of relaxation was to visit the many drink shops. We could smell that they were drinking some strong alcoholic drink. In Teletsia people were experts at using all sorts of stuff to blot out reality; some things were smoked, some drunk, and so on, but alcohol was not much used, because it gave you such a splitting headache the next day. Here it looked as if it was the main national occupation. I asked Lee if Lamech had said anything about that.

'Yes, that's also part of the way the religion has been twisted around,' he went on once we were in the countryside again and could not be overheard. 'He warned us to watch out for people who'd been drinking a lot, as sometimes they get violent. There's a berry which grows easily here, and its juice can be made into alcoholic drinks of various strengths.

'The priests are very rich, and have been for hundreds of years. They own vast areas of good farmland, and they use this to make their money. When their prophet was on earth, he forbade people from drinking alcohol, even though it had been quite popular before. He said it dulled people's awareness, and wasn't good for the health. After he went and the religion became the most widespread in the land, many of the priests realised this was a good way to make money, because you could easily get people addicted to it, and most of them didn't want to give it up anyway. The priests managed to get hold of all the copies of the book about what the prophet had said, and changed his message. When the 'holy' book reappeared, it said the prophet had done lots of miracles with alcohol to show how matter can be changed from one form to another if you had spiritual power, and that it was good to be dull and drowsy, because then you forgot your sorrows, which, Lamech pointed out, were many if you spent all your money on drink. The priests got the monopoly on growing and making it, and that's how they've run things ever since.'

'There's got to be more to it than that,' I said.

'Seeing is believing,' said Ahren as we passed through a village on the outskirts of Chussan City, with yet another vulgar temple, and yet more people sitting in the sun half drunk. The conversation finished then, because Raynor had the map, and we had to try to follow it to find the stables and yard of Mr. Markand, Lamech's friend and business colleague. We took some time, but in the end got there. The map enabled us to avoid the main road into the city, which had a checkpoint on it, so Lamech had warned.

We entered the yard and were met with a babble of animal noises. Several grooms ran up and took the ponies and Heggo from us, and we were left standing in the yard surrounded by a few stray chickens, with Raynor hanging on to Nog in case he misbehaved. A tall, grey haired man came striding towards us and we knew from what Lamech told us that this had to be Mr Markand. Raynor gave him the letter of introduction. He read it and invited us up some stairs to a large apartment above the stables and other animal sheds. Apart from the racket made by some of the animals, this was a quiet district of the city.

We met his wife, were shown where we could wash, and later sat down to eat in the home of yet another kind family. I noticed the design of the two petalled key on some of their belongings; not too obvious, but there if you looked carefully. Before starting to eat they dedicated a token portion of the food to 'our king in the mountains'.

After our meal, strongly flavoured with herbs from these same mountains, Mr Markand took us up to their roof terrace. There were flowers growing in pots and tubs on walls and ledges, and all around we could see red roofs. There were a lot of other roof gardens, and in the distance was an enormous dome. Behind, beyond the town, which was in a valley, were the fingers of mountains stretching down on each side of the built-up area.

'What's that?' asked Lee, pointing at the gilt dome.

'Oh that,' yawned Mr Markand, for this was where he had his forty winks in an ancient, creaking basket work chair, before going back to work. 'That's the Great Temple. You can go and see it if you want. My boy Robin will take you when he's finished feeding the animals.

'I never go to the place, especially since those weird characters from the south came to pester our lives. Call themselves priests, but they're as worldly as the critters we have in this country. Only yesterday I received a demand for extra taxation: "This levy is for their holy lordships who have come to help protect us from dangerous invaders". The only invaders are those unholy lordships themselves.' Mr Markand gave a hearty laugh, and stuck his legs out in front of him to relax. He took out Lamech's letter and read it again, this time more slowly.

'Right then,' he said when he had finished it, 'I'm to arrange for your onward transport too. You'll have to have a different set of clothes. You've got to go up the mountains, and you can to deliver the ponies I'm lending you. It can be very cold, so Robin will fix you up with some mountain shepherds' clothing.' He looked at us curiously. We did look odd, with our dyed hair and wrinkly faces, but he didn't comment further. 'That order is very overdue - good thing you turned up when you did. Robin will fill you in with the details. He looks after the out-of-town business. If you stay on the roof, I'll send him up to you.'

Soon we heard the footsteps of Robin coming up to the roof terrace. Our hearts danced with joy as he appeared, and we felt a gust of coolness which did not come from the slight breeze on that warm afternoon. We introduced ourselves and somehow had the idea that we had known him for ages. He was a year or so older than Raynor, had a smile that made you want to smile too, was tall and strongly built, with mid brown hair and a light skin.

'If you want to see some of the city, let's go, before its evening feeding time down below,' he said.

'Do you think it would be safe?' asked Tandi.

'It might be better if you don't all come,' he agreed, so we girls stayed with Mrs. Markand, and later went shopping in the market with her, while the boys went out with Robin.

The city was one of great contrasts. Some streets were paved with marble and lined with colonnades of this expensive white stone too, while a short distance away, out of sight behind the splendour, were filthy overcrowded slums where people were having a dreadful time trying to keep body and soul together in a respectable fashion.

'The trouble is,' explained Robin, 'we're all taxed so heavily to pay for the luxurious bits that show, and for the priests to have an easy life, that there's not much money over for the rest of us to build decent houses. There's such a shortage of housing. It's a good thing we live above the stables and cowsheds; otherwise we'd have some bureaucrat or priest billeted on us. Luckily they don't like the smell or the noise.'

The boys noticed an enormous number of drinking shops, where advertisements told you the way to heaven was through booze. A lot of the people in these places were just sitting staring into space like they did at the drug-smoke shops in Teletsia. There were also quite a few people who got angry and quarrelsome after drinking their drug, and a lot of people lying slumped in corners of the streets and under the colonnades. 'Drown your sorrows and support the state' was one slogan Lee noticed, the writing here being very similar to ours back home.

Soon Robin led them into an enormous open space in front of the Great Temple. It was oval in shape, and was used as a gathering place for some of the great religious festivals. There were a number of visitors today, milling around, and some brightly dressed guards slouching on stone benches outside the temple. They looked drunk and Robin said they usually were, and were only for show, despite their swords. There were also a number of priests flitting about in their gorgeous silken gowns. At the further end of the oval the boys noticed some sort of disturbance. There was a large metal cage and a lot of people standing round it, jeering and laughing.

'We'll keep away from that,' advised Robin. 'You don't go near trouble in this town, because sometimes the police pick you up just for being in the place where there's something going on.' Robin hurried the boys out of the square the way they had come in. He took them back towards his home along another street, and here they passed a large amphitheatre, recently put up by the two rulers.

Robin told the boys that on the day of the week when their peaceful god was worshipped, these two had taken to arranging bloodthirsty shows to amuse the people in the afternoon, after they had spent the morning in the temples. The shows consisted either of condemned criminals fighting each other until one was killed, or fights between different animals, or animals and people. Robin said they were very popular.

'I go up to the mountains on holidays. That's where my heart is,' he said. 'I see enough animals in my work, and spend my time trying to keep them calm and *stop* them from fighting each other.'

We all met up back at the Markand's place. We girls were in the kitchen helping make supper when they came in. Mrs. Markand gave us a hot drink made in a silver kettle with a fire underneath it, but I had some bad news and wanted to talk to the boys in private. I asked them to come with me, took them into one of the bedrooms and closed the door.

'We've got major problems,' I warned. 'The Sorcerers suspect we're in the city. I don't think they know for sure, but we're going to have to be extremely careful, and very lucky to get out of this place in one piece.'

'Whatever do you mean?' asked Raynor.

'I overheard some people talking in the market. There are definitely some Sorcerers here from Teletsia, to catch some dangerous rebels who have magical powers. If these rebels get through the mountains they're going to let off a weapon that will destroy the whole world. It will cause a very severe winter so even in the tropics everything will be frozen for years, or maybe there'll be floods, or earthquakes. No one knows for sure.'

'Us again, and the stories get more amazing as the countries change!' said Lee dryly.

'After we left Teletsia there were some earthquakes,' I went on, 'which damaged the Sorcerers' property much more than anyone else's. Sounds strange to me, but that's the gossip. The Sorcerers have a lot of people here spying for them. One woman in the market was looking at us in a very odd way, and kept following us. There's one spy everyone is talking about. He came up from Teletsia with the Sorcerers, and knows what the rebels look like, but yesterday he suddenly refused to spy for them. He's threatened to denounce the Sorcerers in public. They say that he's the brother of the oldest rebel.'

'It must be Mardhang!' cried Raynor.

'That's the problem, if it really is Mardhang. The Sorcerers have decided to make an example of him. He's been put in a cage with some lions, well fed and lightly tied up, but in a day or two, when they get hungry anything could happen. The cage is in the open space near the big temple. I'm surprised you didn't see it if you went that way.'

'What are we going to do? I can't just let him be eaten by lions.' We tried to sympathise with Raynor, but we all felt the same about his despicable brother, who had done his best to betray us. Raynor paced around the room. 'We'll have to try and rescue him. He may be a spy but he's still my brother. What if he's really truly sorry? I know, I'll use the jewelled key. Somehow it'll help. The keys always get us out of trouble.' The rest of us watched as he ranted and raged. I realised I'd made a major mistake mentioning what I'd heard.

'Look, we don't even know if it is Mardhang,' said Lee.

'Of course it is! Who else would recognise us, be a spy for the Sorcerers, and have a brother who's a rebel?' insisted Raynor. 'I'm going to try and save him. You all go on without me. How could I go seeking the mountain kingdom knowing my own brother was being eaten alive? Get real!'

'It's idiotic to go and get yourself caught by the Sorcerers now, having come so far. Plus you might finish up getting us all caught. Then we've all had it, not just Mardhang,' went on Lee

'You just don't get it, do you? He's my brother, not some stranger.'

'He's such a rat; look how he tried to betray us. I reckon finishing up lions' dinner is exactly what he deserves,' Ahren's words were callous but realistic. He said what we were all thinking, except Raynor.

At this moment there was a knock on the door and we all stopped talking. Robin opened it and asked politely, especially considering we were in his room: 'May I come in, or do I disturb you?' He smelled strongly of animals and had straw on his clothes, but his presence cleared the air. 'I need to get some tidy clothes. One of our wealthier clients has just turned up and dad wants me there to talk business. I'll change in the bathroom. Don't mind me.' He rummaged in a chest and took out a smart lace shirt and a pair of green velvet trousers, then went out again, with a towel and his washing things.

After that it was less of a tempest, and Raynor calmed down, but the more we tried to figure out a way of rescuing Mardhang, the more foggy the future became. After about half an hour, by which time we had got no further but had all given ourselves headaches thinking about the problem, Robin came back again. He crossed the room and sat down on the window seat. This was an old building, with thick walls, and the seat was set into the wall under the window.

Outside, through the leaded pains, we could see the town and the mountains behind. Robin glanced out of the window, then turned and looked at each of us in turn, assessing both us and the situation.

'My father and the client are still bargaining,' he began, 'but before they got going in earnest, they talked about the gossip of the day. Word is getting round that the superhuman rebels from Teletsia are in the city. The police, and the Sorcerers' spies, are looking for seven darkish skinned young people from the south. As soon as I saw you I knew who you were. Dad thinks you're something to do with Lamech and Rhea, and we've got to help you disappear into the mountains. Lamech is quite a rebel himself, so dad wasn't surprised at the hidden instructions in that letter. It was a stroke of good luck that you fell in with them, otherwise you'd have been caught already.

'By the way, I've picked up the mountain shepherds' clothes you're going to have to wear. They won't fit very well, but they'll have to do because you've got to get out of here tonight.'

'How did you know who we are?' asked Raynor.

'There are seven of you, and your disguise doesn't fool me! But there's more than that.' As Robin spoke he took out from under his shirt a key, identical to the one Raynor was wearing, gold with two petals, and inlaid with crystals or diamonds. 'I work for the king in exile in the mountains. He's called Lord Albion and soon he'll return to rule here. When he does, he'll set off a lot of changes, and they may be quite violent. So he's waiting, in case he can find a way to let it all happen more easily.

'Lamech didn't send you here for nothing. We all work together. I may look after the cows and horses and deliver goats to the butcher as a job, but your true intentions are as clear to me as the morning sun. I also feel the warm and cool sensations on my hands, and the centres of the soul, and can go into that state of joy beyond thoughts. Lord Albion has taught me all that and more.

Welcome! It's great to see you, the first of what we hope will be many groups. We'd almost given up hope that you were ever coming. We've been waiting so long.'

Robin stood up and gave each of us a hug. At this moment Tandi and Conwenna came in, having finished whatever they were doing in the kitchen. None of us who had heard it knew quite what to make of the last remark of Robin's, but we suddenly felt at ease, and our headaches had gone.

'I overheard some of what you said, and it is your brother Mardhang,' he affirmed.

'I can't just abandon him to the lions, even if he did try to betray us back home,' insisted Raynor.

'You know by now that you've got to make your own decisions, Raynor. Certainly, you'll never make it through the mountain pass unless you've forgiven him for whatever he tried to do to you in Teletsia. Forgiveness is one of the qualities you must have for this subtle centre to be all right. No amount of jewelled keys or helpers will get you to Sasrar unless you've got these qualities. You've also got to have humility, and to a certain extent lose any aggression and egotistical tendencies. You know all about the qualities of the subtle centres, don't you?' He stopped speaking and looked at our faces, a mixture of dawning revelation and slight incomprehension. 'Oh well, not to worry. You'll learn all that when you get to Sasrar. You've done all right so far. Now, this brother of yours. It might be possible to rescue him, but very difficult, and I don't only mean getting him out of the lions' cage. We'll have to leave the more long term liberation, the salvage of his soul, in the hands of fate.'

Raynor went into another frenzy and I felt embarrassed. Here was Robin, who was so deep, so normal, who lived in a country only marginally better than ours and here were we, behaving like idiots. We weren't a very good example of the groups of travellers Robin had been waiting so long to help.

'I've got to try to rescue him, however dangerous it is! But I'll do it alone. I'm not going to drag you lot in.' Raynor then turned to Robin. 'You, more than anyone, mustn't get into all this. You live here.'

'No! It's got to be all or none of us. You haven't got a hope in a million without me, that's for sure.'

'So what are we going to do?' Raynor was delighted that at least someone was taking some interest in his obsession with Marching. Robin stared out of the window towards the vast dome of the Great Temple in the distance, weighing up various alternatives.

'Pretend nothing has happened, and I'll wake you all up in the early hours of the morning. You'll not need much luggage, but get ready quickly and quietly when I wake you.'

'What about our dog and donkey?' asked Ahren.

'The dog can come as long as he can keep quiet, and the donkey may have its uses. Leave the animals to me. That's my job here.'

CHAPTER 12

BROTHER MARDHANG

We went to bed as soon as it was polite to do so, and because I knew Robin was going to come and wake us at an unearthly hour, I could hardly get to sleep at all. He woke the older boys earlier, as he had got hold of some false beards, which he helped them stick on. He said mountain shepherds often had beards to stop them getting frostbitten in winter. Soon we were all dressed as mountain people.

We went down into the yard and he had the ponies ready saddled. Heggo was there, and Nog tagged along, and we rode off through the empty streets, bright in the moons' light. The ponies shied at every cat and shadow in the dirty back streets that Robin then led us through. We had a hard time not falling off until they calmed down.

Robin led us to the vast open space in front of the Great Temple. Even in the night I could see that it was covered in statues of drunken people, and the gaudy decor was just too much, especially considering this was a temple dedicated to a religion that had started off in praise of simplicity and humility. Robin brought us up to the open space by a small side street, and we stopped under one of the colonnades around the edge, well hidden in the deep shadows.

Then Robin and Raynor crept towards the metal cage in the middle of the oval space. The temple guards were not there, only two snoring figures sitting on a stone bench near the cage. Robin took off his jewelled key, and wound the chain around his wrist. The boys held pieces of metal piping, thick enough to do someone a lot of damage. As I watched them the ponies stamped their feet in boredom, and I held even tighter to Nog's muzzle in case he should bark. So far so good; the cage guards were still asleep. There were two moons in the sky: the soft Moon of Compassion, and just rising behind the temple was the Moon of Good Fortune, large, golden and traditionally very lucky.

Raynor and Robin crept closer to the cage. They went up behind the guards, slumped in a heap and stinking of drink. 'This national addiction is a blessing,' thought Raynor. At a signal from Robin they each brought their thick metal pipes down on the head of a guard. The guards both fell to the ground, but the young men propped them up so as to make it look as if they were still sleeping.

Tandi and I looked at each other. We both felt a certain disgust at this cold-blooded murder, which it probably was, as Raynor and Robin gave them both a tremendous crack.

'This is war, don't get squeamish,' Lee whispered. Robin was meanwhile readjusting the hats of the guards to hide their crushed skulls, although there was blood all over the place, visible even from where we were standing. He had just finished clearing up the mess as best he could, and they were both about to enter the lions' cage, when Tandi gave a bark, the danger signal. Raynor and Robin ducked behind a stone urn between the guards' seat and the cage.

We had seen what we least needed, a group of the night watch or police, coming towards us along the colonnade. They were staggering along, singing bawdy songs. Being a night watchman in Chussan clearly included a lot of visits to drink shops. We could not move both ourselves and the ponies in time, and they reeled up to us.

'What do you think you're doing here at this time of the night?' demanded the leader of the band of Lee, who said nothing, because he was afraid his speech might give him away. The watchman peered at us with the help of a lantern he was holding, burped and went on. 'Mountain shepherds, I see.' He burped again, his breath foul. 'I want an answer.'

'Yes sir,' Lee tried vainly to imitate the accent of these parts. 'We've just arrived in the city, from our tribe far away in the mountains, and wanted to have a look at the Great Temple. Forgive us, we are poor and simple.' Lee's beard was falling off and it was tickling wickedly, but there was nothing he could do. The watchmen didn't notice. Luckily they were too drunk.

'You certainly talk funny. Now off you go to your inn or wherever you're staying. Come back tomorrow and you'll see some good sport with the lions in the cage there. I want you lot gone when I come round again just before dawn, or there'll be trouble. Right?' He and his men staggered off into the night, whooping and laughing.

'Whew - that was close!' said Lee.

'You did fine,' I tried to be encouraging, but my heart was still thumping in fear. I felt Conwenna's clammy hand find mine. I squeezed it and gave her a confident smile, which was the opposite from the way I felt. She became *more* nervous as the adventures passed, not less. Tandi waited until the drunken gang were completely gone, then coolly gave two short barks, the all-clear signal.

Robin and Raynor stood up. Robin took the key he had wound around his wrist, held it up in front of him and the crystal clear jewels shone in the moons' light. The jewels looked larger and more luminous in the light of the moons. He gently opened the door of the cage, and cautiously approached the lions. He swung the key rhythmically, and began chanting to them. At first they snarled, but then slowly fell under the calming effect of his voice and the key.

Raynor entered behind Robin, and crept to the further end, where a fearful, huddled figure crouched on the ground, chained to the bars. It looked up and Raynor saw his brother's thin, devious face gazing pathetically in the moons' light. He looked at Raynor as if he was trying to decide whether his long lost brother was a bad dream or not. Raynor stared at him for a moment, confused feelings of pity, anger and uncertainty flooding his mind, but he said nothing. He took a small hacksaw out from under his cloak, and was about to start sawing through the chain that held Mardhang to the cage, when Mardhang, thinking it was a knife, raised his hand to protect himself.

'Don't kill me. I'm really sorry,' he whined.

'Just shut up, can't you?' said Raynor. 'If I wanted to kill you, do you think I'd use a hacksaw? I'm trying to set you free, idiot. Stop wriggling, I can't get at the chain.'

'Please take me with you. I've had it with the Sorcerers, honest.'

'Keep your mouth shut or no one's going anywhere.'

After this Mardhang was passive, but he couldn't look at the shining jewelled key visible round Raynor's neck. This was strange because Mardhang was usually besotted by jewels. He was completely inert, like a wounded bird that has given up struggling. Soon Raynor had Mardhang free, and amazingly, Robin managed to keep the lions quiet by swinging his key and chanting to them. They hustled Mardhang out of the cage, closed the gate, and sprinted across the moonlit space to the darkness of the colonnades.

Ahren and Tandi were ready with the ponies, and Raynor and Robin scrambled on theirs, but there was no way Mardhang's would carry him. It bucked and kicked and he tumbled to the ground, luckily unhurt. He complained that he had been given an unrideable pony, and they tried another, but the same thing happened. None of the ponies would carry him, for some strange reason. Robin stepped in.

'I knew it,' he laughed. 'Donkeys must ride donkeys. Put him on Heggo.' It was only then that we noticed Heggo had a riding saddle on his back. Robin was right, Heggo didn't mind carrying Mardhang. In fact they got on rather well together and off we all trotted through the dark streets.

Mardhang was wrapped in a grey cloak to make him look like a mountain shepherd. Robin rode close to him, holding Heggo's bridle to stop him trying any tricks. Lee and Ahren had extra ponies, as we had to deliver the whole order and there were more than we could ride. I was next to Robin on the other side and heard him say to Mardhang, 'I've got a sharp knife under my cloak, and if you make any trouble I'll use it. Got it? When we get to the checkpoint on the outskirts of the city, we're mountain shepherds, and you can't speak because you're ill. If you do, you're dead. Your life means nothing to me. Understand?' Mardhang nodded weakly and looked terrified.

Robin let him see the lethal knife, to show he was in earnest. Mountain shepherds carried these to defend themselves against wolves, bandits and anything or anyone else that gave them problems. Although outwardly

Mardhang was looking afraid and cowed, inwardly he was smirking. His own plan was going perfectly.

There was only one road up into the mountains out of the city, and it had a checkpoint on it that we had to get past. Robin did the talking. He knew the checkpoint guards because he was always coming and going on business. It was a couple of hours before dawn, and the guards came out and asked him where he was off to this time. He produced a bill of sale for the ponies, and explained that we were a group of shepherds who had been visiting the city, and we were helping him to deliver the animals. The bill of sale was in order, the excuse was convincing, and we were allowed through without delay. The fact that we were eight plus Robin, not seven, might have helped. A lot of other travellers were leaving at that time, and some were being questioned and searched.

I was impressed at the way in which Robin twisted the guards around his little finger. For us, once we were out of here we were through with this country, but for him? He had to live here and deal with these people all the time. I'd never met anyone so cool and calm, considering what a dangerous life he led.

Regrettably, when Robin was talking to the city guards, he had to leave Raynor to keep an eye, and a lethal knife, on Mardhang, and Raynor wasn't as alert as he should have been. No one noticed when Mardhang took a sealed letter out from under his clothing, and threw it into the unlit street in the direction of the guardhouse. On it was the symbol of the two brothers' rule: a closed two petalled flower, and the flower bud was tied with a band to stop it from ever opening.

We assumed we had made our getaway unobserved and went fast along the road that led to the higher lands. We followed a long, flat-bottomed valley with steep sides and mountains up above. The moons were lighting our way, and after some time the dawn began to grope its way into the eastern sky.

Daylight also started to creep into the nooks, crannies and cobwebbed corners of the city. Eventually one of the guards at the northern gate noticed a letter lying on the ground. It had the rulers' symbol on it, so he picked it up and took it to his superior. The chief guard put it on the table and didn't notice it for some time because he was having an argument with a peddler who was trying to get out of paying the usual tax on his wares. After a while the poor man gave in, paid, became even poorer, and went on his way, and the chief remembered the letter. He too noticed the rulers' symbol and knew it had to be important. He opened it and read the following message.

'To whom it may concern:

I, Mardhang, am an agent for the allies of Shytan and Kytan, the revered rulers of this state. I am an instrument in the plot to catch the dangerous rebels from our country who are known to be at large in Chussan. They are trying to reach the mountain kingdom of Sasrar. Officially we do not believe it exists, but if it does, they must on no account be allowed to reach it. Some of the rebels are children, but they have magical powers, and are dangerous. They look helpless, but be very careful of them. If this letter falls into your hands, please deliver it to one of the city guards.'

The chief guard knew exactly what to do next. He also knew no lion was going to eat Mardhang. Well, not unless we Teletsians failed to reveal ourselves, or the lions got very hungry. He had been put in the cage as a decoy to attract us, and we had fallen for it, or rather, Raynor had. For this one service Mardhang was going to make enough money to be able to retire before he had done a single honest day's work. Spies and others had spread the gossip that we had heard in the market.

The chief guard immediately reported the matter to the signaller, who had his post on the top of the nearby hill. He was to inform guards posted further up the mountains. These guards were to follow us, in the hope that we would show them the secret pass. They had various ideas as to where it might be, though they weren't sure. If and when we revealed it, we were to be caught and delivered to the Sorcerers' agents in Chussan, preferably alive.

By now we were far up the valley into the mountains. The sun had risen above the high peaks at each side when we came to a dark, deep lake, which filled the valley, between clifflike precipices. There was a ferry, but usually it did not go this early. Robin, however, knew the ferryman and his assistant, and persuaded them that they could make a bit extra if they took us across before they began the day's work proper. They were wretchedly underpaid, like most people round here, so were only too happy to oblige.

Soon they left us on the further side, thus giving us valuable time to get ahead of our pursuers, although we didn't know it then. The road became a rough track, and we had to pick our way along the base of the cliffs like flies on a window. The ponies were used to this kind of country, but Heggo found it hard not to stumble on the loose stones and rocks which had fallen off the cliffs high above us. We went on and on, and the track became more and more torturous. First we went through some pinewoods, then across rocky ground where only sparse bushes and meagre scraps of heather grew.

'I can't take you all the way to Sasrar,' said Robin, 'but I'll go with you as far as I can. These ponies have got to be delivered, and in any case the way to Sasrar is such that you'll have to go on foot. The place we're going is in the forbidden area, meaning it's forbidden to people like the Sorcerers or the followers of the two brothers.

'When we get near the top of the pass, we have to cross a bridge, and then we go down into a valley. For our enemies, whenever they do manage to find it, it's a bridge that leads onto a crag, with loose, slipping stones that give way when you walk on them, and the path usually leads nowhere. Sometimes it leads to snowfields. The guards can't understand where I go when I come up this way.'

'Where do you go?' asked Lee.

'That's just it. For me, or all of you, because you have the key and your subtle beings are better, the path is very nice after the bridge. I tell the guards I go to see a hermit who lives in a cave in the mountains, and that he can be very fierce with people if they don't know him, the sort of recluse who curses people if they annoy him. Although what he does with all the ponies and things I take never quite gets explained. The guards are wary and tend to keep away.'

At last, I thought fondly, our dangers are nearly over. That endless tension was about to lift. I trusted Robin, and liked these mountains which had a friendly feel, despite their height and wildness. Mardhang looked sick and afraid, and Heggo stumbled yet again, nearly tipping him off. Nog was running in front up the narrow path, enjoying every moment and now and again barking.

The path wound along the side of the mountain. It went on for ages and the way got steeper and more frightening as we climbed ever higher. On one side was the cliff, and on the other a steep drop into the valley far below, with only the lower bends of the path beneath. I could see and hear the icy waters of a green river plunging over rocks far below. Conwenna was petrified of the enormous drop, and didn't want to move. We stopped for a moment at a corner, where there was more room.

'Don't look down,' said Robin. 'You should all look through your pony's ears. Leave it to them to keep to the path, because they're used to this terrain.'

'Be brave, this is the last big test,' I said hopefully. I was also terrified but knew if I admitted it Conwenna would never have the courage to go on. I kept telling myself if I did fall over the edge it would be a quick, easy way to go. Derwin, in front of me on his pony, turned and gave me a glance which told me he wasn't bothered at all. Nevertheless he understood Conwenna's fear.

'Look,' he said to her, 'Asha will ride ahead and I'll give my pony to one of the boys. I'll walk by your side and hold your pony's head, and I'll be there right beside you. I know it's tough for you, but we must trust Robin.' She agreed to this and we went on for perhaps half an hour more.

Suddenly Raynor and the others who were ahead of us saw a group of about eight men coming up the path one hairpin bend below us. They were armed guards, riding large horses, and the men were pressing them as fast as they could go.

'Stay where you are!' yelled the leader above the roar of the torrent. 'Got you at last! Now we know this is the path to the secret country. Stop in the name of the two brothers!' They fitted arrows onto wicked looking bows and we had to halt. Then we heard a sound we knew of old: the hollow laugh of Mardhang.

'Idiots!' he began. 'You really fell for my tricks this time, Raynor! So near and so far! What are you going to get for all your travels? The torture chambers of the Sorcerers - poor dear brother! And you thought I'd changed. Oh! Oh help!'

At this moment a lot of things happened at once. Mardhang pulled Heggo to a standstill, and roughly turned him round on the narrow path, so he could get a good view of his final victory over his hated older brother, who he'd always been jealous of, but to his horror Heggo lost his footing and began to slip over the edge of the precipice. Mardhang was never very good at heights but now he was also drunk with his own importance. He had a violent attack of vertigo, and was swaying on the stumbling Heggo. Instead of jumping off, he clung on, and this made the donkey even more unstable.

He might still have been all right if it hadn't been for Nog. Mardhang had forgotten his arch-enemy of old, who from puppyhood had never missed a chance to protect his master Raynor and molest Mardhang. Nowadays Nog was large, fit and heavy, and he had climbed the side of the mountain so he was above his enemy. He took a scrambling run and hurled himself on Mardhang, jaws barred and yowling horribly. Rocks and stones fell with him as he made for Mardhang's throat, and only let go when the staggering Heggo and Mardhang began to tumble headlong down the mountainside. He grabbed at bushes and rocks as he fell, but this only dislodged more and more rocks and stones until there was a regular landslide which crashed, along with Mardhang and Heggo, onto the guards and their horses below. The last we saw and heard of Mardhang was a terrible screech as he plunged down the side of the mountain into the roaring torrent far, far beneath us. The waters were stained red for a few minutes.

Robin shouted at us to go on. Somehow the ponies made their way round the hole Mardhang had left in the path. As we scrambled on up, we glanced behind. The large horses below plunged in terror and the guards had to let go their bows to hang on. Some fell off their panicked horses and over the edge, and the others had their hands full trying to stop their horses bolting back down the path. One horse slipped over the edge with its rider still on it.

We hurried on and after some time reached the turn in the pass. There we saw the bridge, and what a bridge! It was made of rope and slats of wood, and swayed in the wind. It looked like a cobweb and I was scared stiff. Conwenna screamed when Robin told us we had to cross it. He told Raynor to put his jewelled key at the beginning of the bridge, then grabbed Conwenna, kicking and struggling, and held her firmly in his arms. We dismounted and led the ponies, who in some miraculous way didn't mind this horrendously fragile bridge, and crossed in single file. When we had all got to the other side, Lee saw one of the guards coming up some way behind, on foot.

Robin quickly took Lee and Ahren to the side of the path, where there was a big, loose boulder. The three of them managed to pitch it onto the bridge, which collapsed in a mass of planks and frayed rope into the torrent below with a vast splash. Then we ran on to get out of sight, and hid behind some rocks, because the guard who had made it up the path was standing on the other side of the river, glaring at us and getting an arrow into his bow. Robin also had a bow and arrow, which he took out of his saddlebag.

'Give that to me,' said Ahren. 'I'm a good shot.' This was true, because for months he had been bringing down birds, rabbits and so on for our supper. He grabbed it, crept back to where he could get an accurate line on the guard without being seen, aimed carefully and calmly and soon had him writhing in agony, as he shot more arrows to finish him off. Ahren could kill a horse in Teletsia, and now a more mature Ahren would do the same to his enemy. He had grown from a tearaway farm boy into a brave and fiery, but totally controlled, young man. Nevertheless I noticed he looked horrified, because killing people was not in his nature: he was a carefree and forgiving soul.

Robin had left Conwenna sitting on the ground, and I spent some time calming her down. She was in a state of complete shock and I realised this journey was becoming too much for her by the day. We got on the ponies, and rode for some time, over the top of the pass and into a valley with pine trees here and there. No one said anything; we were too stunned. I wondered why Robin had sacrificed Raynor's precious key on the bridge. Did it mean we didn't need its help any more?

We went downhill, and came to where the trees' leaves were red and golden and the bracken underfoot was brown and dry. Autumn came earlier up here. Robin called a halt and we lay on the ground recovering, and the ponies' sides heaved. It was then we realised that Nog was not with us.

'We've lost a good friend,' said Derwin sadly. 'I mean Nog.' No one for a moment assumed he meant Mardhang.

'Maybe not,' added Robin. 'I thought I saw him jump clear when Mardhang fell down the cliff into the torrent. He may have a problem getting across the river now the bridge has gone though.'

Raynor sat silently on a rock. Tandi went and sat with him and tried to comfort him, but he would have none of it. Recently his coldness towards her had been replaced by a friendliness and warmth, and he would often spend time enjoying her company, but not at this point in time. He was confused, traumatized and hurt.

'Why did you have Raynor put his key on the bridge?' asked Lee, echoing my thought.

'If I hadn't, we wouldn't have made it across,' explained Robin.

'Why not?'

'Because this time I think the soldiers had found it. Someone had cut the ropes nearly through, and if we'd walked on it, we'd have fallen into the torrent. But the key has the power to transform the outer world; it can knit up the threads of matter to protect us. Or a bridge, come to that, while we were on it, although once we were over it the key would not hold it together. It would only do so for people in the flow of creation. If the guards get to that point again, it'll deceive and confuse them. The key of this area is the power of the spirit over matter. On the level this key operates, nothing can be destroyed if it's in tune with Mother Nature, because the subtle, the spirit of a thing, is more powerful than matter. It can make the mountain pass even more difficult to find than it is now.'

'Any chance of rescuing Nog?' asked Derwin, not much into philosophy, even if our survival depended on it. Nog was much more real and important to him.

'Possibly, but let's get all of you to safety first,' went on Robin. Raynor came out of his dazed trance at the mention of Nog, and Robin went over to where he was sitting. 'I know you wanted to bring your brother with you, but it was doomed from the start, because if a person's heart isn't pure, they'll never get through these mountains. Some people would call it magic, or whatever, but these mountains accept or reject you. That's it. Always has been. You saw how the mountain ponies refused point blank to carry him?'

'Yes, I know, but I'd hoped that somewhere deep down there was good in him,' Raynor stared sadly at a purple toadstool which was growing out of the dead leaves in front of him.

'He was rotten to the core, ever since we knew you,' I asserted.

'Maybe, but he was my brother.'

'We're your brothers now,' said Robin gently, 'and Lee and Ahren and young Derwin. You've got to forget Teletsia. It's another world.'

'Pity about Heggo,' observed Ahren, who had eventually come to an understanding with our headstrong donkey.

'In our country a donkey is the symbol of pigheaded egotism. I reckon he had to go too. You've got to have a certain amount of patience and humility and not too much ego to get through this pass, and Heggo, perhaps, didn't make the grade. Sorry to sound heartless, but that's the way it is in these parts. Now let's get you to the astrologers' house. It's their summer observatory and these ponies are to help them and their belongings go lower down for the winter. When we get there I'll see if someone can go and look for Nog. There are other ways across that river.'

Robin wanted to get us away from the pass, and nothing Raynor could say about Nog made any difference. Robin insisted it was dangerous to go back, in case any of the guards were still there and might try to kill or capture us. So on we went.

CHAPTER 13

ALBION AND THE ASTROLOGERS

We rode on through a high valley. Above us were snowy mountains reaching into the dark blue sky, and I longed to see the snow up close, as I never had, growing up in a hot country. The sparkling whiteness fascinated me. Robin smiled when I told him this and promised me there was plenty of snow in this area - weeks of it every winter. Tandi rode next to Conwenna and laughed and joked with her, and pointed out interesting plants and small animals as we rode through the open woodland. Conwenna gradually began to smile and talk again. We all shed a private tear or two for Nog, as we seriously never thought we'd see him again.

Once the shock had worn off about Mardhang, Raynor began to see that he had been atrocious. Next Raynor began having moments of the old too-thoughtful scholar, asking himself why he didn't feel sad that his brother had come to such a terrible end. I knew that half frown on his face; it meant he was brooding. Lee solved that problem rather neatly. He said he was fed up of having to hold an extra pony while he rode, and he wasn't much good with animals anyway, so gave it to Raynor, and it needed constant attention. We knew each other well by now, and as our journey progressed we had learnt to put up with each other's shortcomings. We had helped each other out of numerous problems, our hearts had opened and we all felt a gentle tolerance and affection for each other. It was not a conscious thing, but rather a glow from within, which we felt when we were together. Of course we still had disagreements, but they never lasted very long.

In the evening we saw the lights of a large house with what was apparently an observatory at one end, which housed a telescope, and there were all sorts of strangely shaped buildings in the grounds. We could make these out by the light of the two moons then in the sky. Round the main house were barns, outhouses and some cottages. Robin explained that the observatory was used for scientific research; the air was thin at this height, and clear, so the stars and moons shone brighter and were easier to see.

As we rode into the stable yard dogs barked to greet us and a man came out to help with the ponies, who were exhausted after carrying us for half a night and a whole day. It was cold in the evening here and it had been a very long ride. We went into a big kitchen where we met a large lady who had her long grey hair plaited and wound around her head. She was wearing an apron and cooking supper.

'Hello Mrs Pea-Arge. Look who I've brought you tonight! Can you feed seven extra?' said Robin, with that blissful ignorance of a young man who has always had a mother, or some capable person to do the cooking for him.

'Ah, Robin. Nice to see you again. Yes, we can manage a few more,' she replied. 'It's stew and that'll always stretch. Now,' she turned to us, 'you sit down by the fire in the staff hall over there through that door. You can get warm, and I'll bring you some hot drinks. Supper will come a bit later.'

We went into a comfortable room with bookshelves round the walls, easy chairs on each side of a fireplace with a crackling fire burning, and a long wooden eating table in the middle. Mrs Pea-Arge brought a tray of hot drinks for us, and as we sipped them we all started to feel unbelievably tired. Conwenna and Derwin were soon sound asleep, and I wished I could do the same. After some time Mrs. Pea-Arge came and bundled us upstairs, where we were shown into bedrooms. Oh joy! Sheets again, feather-filled quilts, snowy white and smelling of lavender, and best of all hot baths.

Conwenna and Derwin skipped supper and were soon snoring in their beds, but the rest of us crawled downstairs some time later, cleaner and slightly refreshed. Mrs Pea-Arge brought us the promised stew, with crusty home-baked bread fresh from the oven, dripping with butter.

'Well my dears, I hope you like it,' she said, referring to the food. 'It's a wicked long ride from Chussan City in one day. Robin's gone to see His Lordship, and said he knows you'll understand.'

'Who is 'His Lordship', if it isn't rude to ask?' said Lee, his mouth full of bread and butter.

'Oh, Lord Albion. Didn't Robin tell you? They're right close, those two.'

'The exiled king?' went on Lee.

'That's it, but you'd never know from looking at him, any more than you'd know Robin is his most trusted follower.' I was sliding into sleep, and soon we went to bed, and slept and slept. We didn't tell Mrs. Pea-Arge we'd had a close brush with death and a capture which could have been even worse. Maybe Robin already told her. Maybe she didn't need to know. Her world was one of home cooking and clean linen.

The next day we lay around, and rested and explored. We wandered through the grounds and checked out the observatory, some bits had staircases leading nowhere and others were shaped like crescents and so on, for measuring stars and seasons. Conwenna spent her day with Mrs. Pea-Arge in the kitchen, helping her prepare the meals, or just listening to her non-stop stream of chatter. It didn't strike me as strange, and I didn't notice that Conwenna was avoiding us. Derwin made friends with some dogs, found the kitchen garden and the gardener was happy to let Derwin help himself while he harvested apples, pears and other late fruit.

In the evening, we were all in the large kitchen again. Mrs. Pea-Arge was deep in conversation with a man who brought her a churn of milk from the cowsheds in the yard. We picked up the words 'Robin' and 'His Lordship'. Mrs Pea-Arge told us to go into the staff hall for another delicious supper and we heard voices in the passage outside. Into the hall came three men dressed like mountain shepherds, with sheepskin jackets and thick boots. They were carrying something in a sling made of a shepherd's cloak.

'Put him down here, in front of the fire,' said one. 'Be careful!' He knelt down and we all felt coolness coming from him, and a sense of joy radiating from his heart. He was tall and had thick light brown hair. Raynor jumped up from the table, because he saw that the motionless bundle of fur was Nog, or Nog's body.

'Is he alive?' asked Raynor.

'He's in a coma,' said the shepherd. 'Hiran, Balou, you can go now, and thank Robin for finding him, will you?' The other men bowed respectfully and left. None of us noticed this as we were crowding round Nog.

'Where did they find him?'

'Robin and those two men were out all day looking for him, and doing a few other things up on the pass. He must have been trying to follow you. They found him on a ledge and pulled him up to the path. Robin has gone to fetch some supplies from the veterinary shed, because among other things he's hurt his leg.' All this time the shepherd was gently moving his hands over Nog's inert body. Soon Nog opened his eyes. He gazed up at Raynor in a lost fashion and was at first unable to focus properly. Then he wagged his tail feebly and licked Raynor and the shepherd who was helping him. When Raynor touched his wounded leg he flinched and growled, but let the shepherd touch him without complaining.

'Let him sleep now. I've brought him out of the coma. I'll deal with the leg when Robin comes.' Then he turned to us. 'Let's have supper. I'm starving; aren't you?'

The shepherd sat at the end of the table and we noticed that nine places had been laid. He put his hand over the waiting food as if to bless it, and as he did so we felt a gust of coolness coming up from the table. Raynor kept looking at the shepherd as if he wasn't quite sure of something, then we heard the tramp of feet, and in came Robin. He put the basket he was carrying on the table.

'There are the medical supplies, and here's the key you wanted me to find. It was on the bank of the torrent. There were no Chussan guards around any more. They won't come up this way again in a hurry looking for us, even if they can find the path.'

We looked at each other with the same thought in our minds. This 'shepherd' was the young king in exile, and we hadn't exactly greeted him with due respect. Raynor was up in a flash, and went up to him, apologizing for our ignorance and bad manners. At least with the previous rulers and important people we'd met, we'd usually been forewarned and had tried to behave as we thought we should.

'No problem!' laughed Lord Albion. 'We're all in disguise these days.' He looked at our clothing and faces. Our clothes were a strange mixture of nomadic plains dwellers and mountain shepherds, and the dye was beginning to wear off our faces. We looked mighty odd, one way and another. 'You've done a great job, Raynor, and all of you, in getting here,' he embraced Raynor warmly. I noticed the two petalled key. Was it the one Raynor had left on the bridge? In Lord Albion's hands the crystal clear jewels in the two golden petals shone brighter, and radiated all the colours of the rainbow. 'I am one of the guardians of this key, at the moment,' he said. 'You won't need it any more, but it might easily help others, so I'll keep it if you don't mind.'

He asked the rest of us our names, and about our journey, and knew we wanted to go to Sasrar. Although he had a nobility about him, he emitted a sense of friendliness, like an elder brother. The relationship between him and Robin was very special; Robin trusted Lord Albion completely, and he had tremendous respect for Robin. Soon the meal was finished and this time it was Robin who was going to sleep at the table. Lord Albion stood up and went over to Nog, who thumped his tail on the ground in greeting.

'It's not as serious as I thought,' he said when he again felt Nog's leg. 'It's just badly bruised, not broken. Raynor, put some of this green salve on it, and bandage it up, and he should be fine in a day or two.' Lord Albion mentioned something to Robin about meeting the astrologers later in the evening, and left. Robin moved to one of the easy chairs and was soon having a snooze. The rest of us lingered over dessert until Mrs Pea-Arge came in.

'Young gentlemen and ladies, your presence is required in the Great Hall. Especially you,' she shook the sleeping Robin, 'and you older visitors. Derwin, Conwenna, you can stay with me if you like, because you'd have to be as quiet as mice and sit still for quite some time up there. Their elder lordships aren't like Lord Albion and would expect you to behave perfectly, and they'll talk and talk 'til all hours. You'd be really bored, take it from me. The rest of you had best change into something clean and smart, if you have anything.' She looked at us dubiously. Derwin said he would like to come with us and promised to be very quiet, but Conwenna went off with Mrs Pea-Arge. I didn't feel quite right about this, but stupidly didn't say anything.

The only backpack that had survived the stampede on the plains was the one in which our silk gowns and the elegant boy's clothes from the Island of Creations, and our jewels from the Emperor's Island had been packed. We put the clothes, and realised we were leaner and more muscled from so much exercise. We made an effort to look respectable, and soon Robin, less sleepy now, came to get us. We would never have found our own way through this rambling mansion full of scientific instruments and endless rooms and corridors.

'Come on you lot,' he began. 'The masters have been waiting three days for you now. Shake a leg!'

'But we've only been here two days, well, one really,' Tandi corrected him. 'Give us a chance. How did they know we were even near here three days ago?'

'That's why people call them astrologers. Astrologers are supposed to know things like that.' So we followed him, and he continued, 'They understand the workings of the heavenly bodies, and the workings of the subtle centres of the soul, and how all things are related to each other.'

By this time we were at the doorway of the Great Hall. At the further end was a large log fire, and some fragrant wood was burning. There were lamps giving a soft light, and together with the flickering firelight the effect was comfortable and soothing. At the end of the room three men sat cross-legged on sheepskin rugs, facing each other. We hung back, and Robin went over and bowed low to them. We felt a coolness radiating from them, and a sense of peace, and saw their faces were serene and dignified. They indicated for us to sit down a little way back from them, as they were deep in conversation. Lord Albion came in and sat with them.

'Welcome to our summer observatory,' said the eldest of the three. He had a flowing beard and wore a brownish cloak trimmed with fur. His darkish skin made me think that he probably came from much further south.

'It's a great help to the fulfilment of our plans, that you've come this far,' said the second. This man was younger, wore a light green silken overshirt, and behind him lay a darker green cloak with golden embroidery round the edge.

'Do you want to go further, or are you content to stay here?' asked the third. He had a white woollen robe, and a cloak of bearskin was draped on the floor behind him.

'Sir, we want to go to the kingdom of Sasrar,' said Raynor. 'Is this the beginning of that land?'

'No,' replied the third man. 'But that's the right answer. Here you're safe, and can live in peace, but if you want to complete your quest, you must go on one more country.'

'I can show you the way there,' Lord Albion offered, 'but you must all want to go, and have the courage to go and you must go alone. One of you had a key to this country. It's helped you to get up here, and Robin tells me you've had and used others. Do you have any more?'

'Yes,' went on Raynor. 'Conwenna, who's not here tonight, has one still. It's gold, and shaped like a flower with many petals, with many different coloured jewels.'

'That is the key to Sasrar and she is going to have to be the one to use it. She should have been here,' said the man in the green cloak.

It did not seem right to go and hunt up Conwenna at this stage. There was a silence. Despite the last remark, we felt peace and inner stillness. After a time the three astrologers started talking to Lord Albion. Gone was his role as shepherd, and here were three counsellors advising their young king.

'Robin managed to bring this first group up from Chussan City. It was a near thing and they wouldn't have managed it without his help,' began Lord Albion.

'We can always rely on Robin,' said the first of the elders, smiling at him, and Robin modestly looked at the floor. He got up, put some logs on the fire and returned to his seat.

'There's a vast amount of turmoil in many countries,' said the man in green.

'It's definitely got worse since these young people activated the Temple of Support by using the key from there,' added the man with the white beard.

'That's bound to happen,' explained the man with the bearskin. 'The power of the Temple of Support is the urge within every human to find his or her eternal spirit within themselves. At this time the good men, women, and children will want that more and more. They'll want the tremendous joy and feeling of fulfilment when they become consciously aware of becoming a part of the whole of creation, and gain the ability to know absolute truth. That's why these young people have been the first to respond; they're not bothered about politics or power or money as an end in itself, or even knowledge used to dominate others. These are useless distractions.'

'The trouble is,' added the man in green, 'when this starts to happen, the forces of evil, both gross and subtle, will try to stop it working out.'

'That's just the point,' insisted Lord Albion. 'We've got to be patient. These young people may reach the mountain kingdom in a tired and even damaged state, mentally, emotionally or physically, but they can always be put right. If I go back to Chussan City and take up my crown, and the other kings and rulers who are not being given their due at present start to put things right, there will be so much trouble and war.'

'It's better we wait a bit longer, because in putting things right too quickly, we might not allow the seekers of Sasrar a chance to reach their goal. Too rapid change might cause more chaos. We must try to find subtler ways of creating a new world, and we can give help, as we have with this group,' said the man with the bearskin. 'Even though the portents are in the stars, we cannot be sure how things will work out.'

'I'm prepared to wait before going back to take up my kingdom,' agreed Lord Albion. 'Robin is training a lot of partisans, and everything will be ready for the takeover when the time is right.'

'Do you understand some of this?' said the man in green to us.

'Yes, sir, it makes a lot of sense,' Raynor answered for all of us.

'This is a natural growth process. Humanity is about to rise to another level and we're all players in this drama,' said Lord Albion.

Soon after this Robin suggested we leave, as the three astrologers and Lord Albion had other things to talk about. We tiptoed out, leaving Robin sitting alone on our side of the room, listening to the astrologers and Lord Albion discussing the fate of our world.

CHAPTER 14

CONWENNA'S FREEDOM

Nog needed a day or two more to recover before he could walk properly. We did not see the three astrologers again, but Robin told us they had left for their winter observatory, further west and away from the mountains. Lord Albion came and went as he was overseeing enormous flocks of sheep that were being brought from the high summer pastures to the valleys, before the snow came. We went gathering wild fruits and mushrooms of all sorts the next day, and some of us spent the one after that helping Mrs. Pea-Arge make jam from the fruit we'd picked. She also showed us how to prepare the mushrooms to be dried for the winter. We ate lot and slept a lot and it was all fairly laid back. That evening I found Conwenna sitting alone by the fire in the staff hall, after she had been talking to Robin.

'Hey, Conwenna,' I began. 'You look really down.'

'Robin told me that to get to Sasrar we have to go through a door into the mountain and it's like a tunnel or maybe a lot of caves. I can't do it. Asha, I've had enough. I can't take any more adventures; this last one finished me. I'm not going any further.'

'Oh come on! We're so nearly there now,' I looked at her worried expression.

'No, I'm telling you. This is it.'

'Maybe you can stay here for a bit and then join us later.'

'But I've got the key which opens the door through the mountain, and Robin told me that as I'm the youngest, and the key was given to me, it's me that's got to open it. It's not like Tandi's, where someone else used it, and anyway she turned up just when we needed it. And...'

'Don't worry right now, and don't tell anyone else, and maybe we can work it out by the time we leave.' Later in the evening, after Conwenna had gone to bed, I sat by the fire in the staff hall wondering what to do, when Robin breezed in. He had eaten supper with some friends in the nearby village, but came and sat with me, and noticed me staring at the flickering flames. The others were still round the table talking, laughing and playing a board game. Raynor came to join us.

'What's up, Asha? There's something on your mind, isn't there?' Robin said softly.

'Yes. Conwenna's had enough and doesn't want to go any further. For the first part of our journey she was so keen to get to Sasrar, but it's all been too much for her. She's so young, and in some ways not as strong as you'd think. She hides a lot and it's slowly been coming out. She's just said no way is she going on, and she's stubborn, that little lady.'

'I thought there was something wrong when I talked to her yesterday.'

'Any ideas?'

'Yes, but let's go up to the Great Hall, it's quieter there.'

Derwin and Lee disputed a point in the game, and Ahren told Derwin, with a lot of joking and more laughter, not to cheat so much. At this moment Tandi joined us too, as Raynor, Robin and I were leaving the room. We went along the echoing corridors and the moons' light streamed in the windows and lighted our way. We finally reached the empty Great Hall, where Robin lit a lamp and we sat on the sheepskins as we had the other night. The log fire was burning at the end of the room, warm and comforting.

'First we get into a more meditative mood,' began Robin. 'This room is a very good place for that, because those men you met the other night were very - wise? Spiritually aware? In touch with reality?'

'So?' I questioned.

'Can't you feel the atmosphere? Deep, still, powerful?'

'Yes, you're right, there's something very special here.'

'How do we get meditative?'

'Put your attention on the top of your head, and let the thoughts drift away. You'll start to feel that cool breeze, most probably on you hands but also maybe all over your body too. It's the same as you often feel when things are right and in tune with nature, and you'll most likely also have a sense of radiating joy coming from your heart.'

'I've done that sort of thing before, with a hermit in some mountains,' said Raynor.

'Sounds good to me,' I smiled.

'Me too,' said Tandi. So we did as he said for a short while.

'How do you feel now?' asked Robin.

'Pretty amazing - still joy,' I said.

'Tremendous,' agreed Raynor, his face shining.

'Absolute peace, and a wonderful sort of sunny-morning-in-spring feeling,' added Tandi, looking even more radiant than usual.

'That's the power of the spirit. It's in everything, everywhere. Great, isn't it?' Robin's face was also shining. 'Now I'm going to show you something which often works. You'll learn more about it in Sasrar, but this is how to put the attention of the all-pervading cosmic power on a problem. If you feel that joy and coolness, it means you are already in touch with that, and can tap into it whenever you want.

'You have something called the Tree of Life inside you, which in most people is sleeping, but in you seven, and some of the rest of us, it's awake, and can give you these beautiful experiences. It's like a road to the spirit, hidden away inside each of us.' Raynor and I looked at each other in delight. The prophecy! We said nothing though and listened. 'So what we've got to do, is to put our left hand on our knee, palm upwards, then make a circle, clockwise, in the air just above it, with our right hand, like this,' he did it and we watched, 'then you put your attention on the problem. Or, you can write it on your left hand with your right index finger, and circle it in the same way.'

'And then?' I asked.

'Forget it. If you ask the cosmic power to look after to the problem, which by doing this you just have, you mustn't go on worrying about it. Where's your faith?'

'Just curious,' I smiled. We sat for a few more minutes and I felt wonderful. If this was Sasrar, then I wanted lots of it. Soon Robin brought us down to earth.

'Right, that's it. That board game they were playing is quite good. Why don't I show you how to play it?' Robin led us downstairs again. He intrigued me from the first moment I met him; he was such an odd combination of mystic and man of action. I didn't have a chance to talk to Raynor or Tandi about what he had said, but felt a bubbling, peaceful, inner joy the whole of the rest of the evening. We never did get to learn the board game but just sat and watched the others playing it. We all felt too full inside.

That night I had a dream, one of my prophetic ones. Not only do I have dreams, but am often to be able to interpret them as well. In the morning I woke up and was vaguely staring at the painted designs on the wooden ceiling beams, working this one out.

'Asha, you awake?' Conwenna banged on the door and walked in without waiting for me to reply.

'I am now, that's for sure! Come and sit down, and open the shutters while you're near the window.' Conwenna opened them and the morning streamed in: sun, bird song and the distant sound of falling water.

'You know what?'

'What?'

'I just had the most incredible dream. So clear, you can't imagine,' she made herself comfortable at the bottom of my bed and wrapped herself in the spare duvet. 'I mean, you're the one who has important dreams.'

'All right, slow down. Tell me, and we'll try and understand what it's trying to say to us.'

'It started like this. There was this beautiful lady, like my mother used to be, with such a kind smile, but somehow not my mother, more like everybody's mothers all rolled into one. She was in what I thought must be the land of Sasrar, but somehow it wasn't this Sasrar.'

'Go on,' I realised this was the same as my dream, and was astounded, but didn't interrupt her.

'Then from her heart came a golden stream of light, and I felt this fantastic feeling of confidence and peace, and I was suddenly completely free from that sense of fear and panic I so often have. This golden light spread and spread and it came across all the stars from the place where this lady was, until it reached our world, and then it went into the hearts of all the people in this land of Sasrar on this world.

'Then the dream changed, and I saw us all as we were before we left home, back in Teletsia, and just one grain of that golden light came into each one of our hearts. It was this that made us find the prophecy, and started us wanting to come on our journey. Then I saw how this golden light was radiating from within all the people who have helped us: Stellamar, the Ganoozals, Uncle Mazdan, Luth and the others in that country, and even the tigers had it. Oh, I nearly forgot Nog, whose heart is pure gold. Then I saw it in Prince Roarke and Lord Albion, and the keys are made of pure golden light. That's why they could do such amazing things for us.'

Here she stopped, and looked anxiously at me, because she knew I had tried to put these extra sensory experiences behind me since the dreadful time I'd had in the Sea of Illusion, but I smiled.

'On this world, the power of this light was coming from Sasrar,' she went on, 'I heard this kind voice, even though very distant, telling me that I have to open the door and we all have to go there, because then this whole world can change. The people we've met who already have the light inside them are looking in on the drama. They've mostly come from somewhere else, maybe even some other planet, to help us all grow. They were very good people wherever they came from, and wanted to help our world get better, so their souls have taken a body here.

'If we can get to Sasrar, then it will open the way for ordinary folk like us, and the Tree of Life of many other people will be able to be awakened like ours are. That's why we've had so much help, to make it easier for us to get there.'

'You won't believe it, but I had more or less the same dream, but in my dream there was a lady saying that there's one problem. She said if you, Conwenna, didn't have the desire to get to Sasrar any more, then some other young people are going to have to go through all the stuff we've had to face to open the way. It'll be much easier for everyone else if we can get there, but we're free to choose. It's up to you.'

'You're not serious?' Conwenna didn't know how to handle this one.

'Dead serious,' and at this moment Nog came bounding in. His leg was fine now, and he went up to Conwenna, put a wet nose in her hand, grabbed her duvet in his mouth and started trying to pull it off my bed. 'He's telling you something,' I laughed. 'That dog's got more sense than all of us.' Nog lost interest in us and went off to find Raynor.

'Will you hold my hand when we're going under the mountain?' she said in a small voice. 'You know I can't stand the dark, and caves and all.'

'Of course,' I gave her a hug.

Later we were having breakfast, and Robin appeared. I waved at him and he came and sat by me.

'It worked, that thing you showed us.'

'I knew it would. It always does. It's called a bandhan.'

'Conwenna and I had almost the same dream, and she's all right to go on now.' I told him about our dreams in detail.

'So there you are.'

'There was one part of our dreams that maybe you could explain. We dreamt that these wonderful people who've helped us so much, like Lord Albion, are very evolved souls from another world, who've come here to help us all. Is that really the case?'

'Yes,' replied Robin, after a pause. 'The dream was right, but we're all here together now, even if some of the people you've met are somewhat different. They're working very hard for you, and a lot of other people. These spiritual guardians often take on the characteristics of whichever subtle centre they relate to. Lord Albion, the true ruler of Chussan, the seat of the sixth subtle centre, embodies humility, forgiveness and compassion, the innate qualities of this centre. That enables many who know him become better people, because of the example he gives them. By the way, I'm leaving today. Work calls.'

'How do we thank you for all your help?'

'You don't. We're all connected on a deeper level, so if something helps all of you, it's good for me too. You'll learn about that in Sasrar.'

'Have you been there?'

'Many times.'

'I thought so. There's something different about you.'

'We'll be seeing a lot more of each other, and everything will become clear in time.' Robin said good bye and left.

Lord Albion had to go in our direction and offered to take us some of the way. He was much loved here and everyone knew him. We climbed into a farm wagon pulled by two heavy horses and as he drove us through villages and past farms near the road, the people waved and smiled at him. We stopped at an inn where we sat outside and ate at wooden tables. The landlord brought us venison stew, fresh pressed fruit juice and mouth-watering pastries, and would not let us pay.

Afterwards we went on, and later in the afternoon, when Lord Albion had finished his business at two farms where he was arranging for winter grazing, we left the main valley. That went away westwards, and was now very broad, but still had high mountains at the sides. We went up a narrower valley which led north, towards the highest mountains in the area. After another hour or so, the mountains closed in, and ahead we could see a sheer cliff face with a river coming out of its base.

'I'm going to have to leave you now,' Lord Albion said to Raynor. 'I've got to go back to that last farm we passed. The farmer wasn't there earlier and I must see him today, because there's a flock of six thousand sheep arriving at his farm this evening or tomorrow, down from the high pastures. He needs time to get the pens ready. He knows they're coming, but he doesn't know when.'

It had all looked too easy, but we were going to have to do this one ourselves.

'How are we going to get past that?' asked Tandi nervously, looking at the cliff some way ahead.

'You've got to go through the mountain,' said Lord Albion. 'That's where you need your key. It will open the door which is near where the river comes out. The door is said to lead into a series of caves, and if you keep going north, the caves will open out into a valley. That's Sasrar.'

We were disappointed that he was not coming too, but thanked him, and off he went in the farm wagon, leaving us alone as the shadows lengthened. We walked through the meadows, and within another hour reached the cliff face. There was definitely no way anyone was going over the top of those mountains. They were high, snow covered, and much too steep to climb. We sat down to have a rest at dusk. I looked at Conwenna and smiled hopefully. Raynor, Ahren and Lee had found the door, which was old, smallish, and made of some dull golden coloured metal.

'It's going to be terribly dark in there, isn't it?' said Conwenna to me.

'Lord Albion gave the boys lanterns, so it shouldn't be too bad,' I reassured her.

'Can't we stay here tonight and go tomorrow morning?' Conwenna tried to get out of her dreaded task.

'There's one problem,' said Raynor. 'It might not be safe, plus it's going to be very cold quite soon.'

'I'd rather be cold outside than in a cave,' Conwenna was still thinking up excuses. Just then we heard a distant howl, followed by another one answering it.

'I didn't want to tell you,' continued Raynor, 'but Lord Albion warned me there are wolves around here. They don't usually attack people, but you can't be sure.'

'That noise was more than one, and not too far away either,' said Ahren.

'Let's get going,' said Tandi. 'I don't want to finish up as wolves' food, having come so far.' We all looked at Conwenna. It was getting very dark now, and we heard the howl again. She looked back at each of us in turn, and we all stared at her. Those howls sounded very scary. Conwenna didn't move.

'I'm not the youngest, but I'm nearly the youngest,' said Derwin. 'If Conwenna won't open the door, I will. Here, give me that key. It couldn't be worse than having dragons about to eat you up,' and he moved towards Conwenna. Before any us could explain to Derwin that it wouldn't work, and it had to be the youngest of us who opened the door, something changed in

Conwenna. Recently she and Derwin had stopped arguing with each other, and had become more friendly, but the thought that Conwenna was about to be shown up by Derwin did the trick.

She bit her lip, took a deep breath and got up and walked to the door. She took off her key, found the keyhole and opened the door, then took the key out of the door. We lit the lanterns, and once we were all inside she closed it carefully behind her, but didn't lock it. She said she felt that was right. The way was now open.

We saw a wonderful and totally unexpected sight as we looked around us. The rocks were nearly all crystal and jewels, and flickered and shimmered as we moved. Far from being dark, this first cavern was blazingly light, because like so many mirrors, the shining rocks magnified the light of our lanterns rather than swallowing it up. At the side of the cavern was the small river we had seen come out into the open. We stared in wonder.

'Look at my key!' Conwenna cried out. Her key was now radiating the strongest light of all. It lit up the moment we entered the cavern, and shone in all colours of the rainbow. She held it up on the end of its chain, and it swung round until it faced one particular direction.

'Just try something, Conwenna,' said Lee. 'Turn your key the other way, to face the left hand wall.'

Sure enough it righted itself, and the front of the key faced north. We tried it a few times, and then realised that this key was not only the best light we could have, but also our direction guide, because it always faced north. We started walking, and cavern followed cavern, each one lined with shining crystals. As the lanterns started to go dim, the key took over. Whenever there was a choice of ways, the key guided us by showing us the way north.

'See,' I whispered to Conwenna, holding the key up, 'your dream was right, and you didn't need to worry about the dark. The light is everywhere. Except the golden light has become all the colours here.'

After some time we felt tired and hungry. We fetched water from another underground river, this time flowing down towards Sasrar, and ate some more of the food Mrs. Pea-Arge had given us. Although it was hard and uncomfortable sleeping on the ground after some nights in beds, it was neither cold nor dark. We wrapped ourselves in our cloaks and buried the key under someone's pack. It still gave out a faint glow, like a glowworm in the night, but that kept Conwenna happy.

Later, and we presumed it had to be morning, we all woke up at more or less the same time and went on. We didn't say much, but I felt that sense of peace, joy and inner stillness like in the Great Hall at the astrologers' house. I noticed that everyone began to have a radiant glow on their faces. We had one or two differences of opinion about which was the right way to go, but the key was a perfect guide, and we didn't go wrong.

It must have been early afternoon when far ahead we saw a different sort of light. There was a crack, far overhead in the cavern and we could see daylight coming through. Later the path we were walking on through the mountain came to an abrupt end at a door set into the rock face. It was locked, but there was a keyhole.

'Try your key, Conwenna,' said Raynor. She put it in the keyhole and was able to turn the lock, but when she wanted to take the key out, it would not come, and was stuck in the lock. We pushed the door and it swung open away from us, and walked through into the bright sunlight, blinking in the glare. As we turned round to see the rock face behind us, the door swung shut and blended invisibly into the side of the mountain. Conwenna's key had been left in the door on the inner side.

Soon we were walking in a deep crevasse, then a deep narrow valley, and suddenly we were out of the mountains in a wide wooded vale. There was a track, which we followed to the end of the wood, and ahead of us were farmlands, with the mountains behind receding into the distance. There were many waterfalls coming off the mountains, and it was much warmer than the day before. Our way through the mountains had been downhill almost all the way.

'So, this is it,' said Raynor. We stopped to rest. It did feel wonderful: a light, overwhelmingly safe feeling.

'Now what?' said Ahren, cracking some nuts he had found and handing them round.

'I'm going to try something that Robin taught Raynor and Tandi and me the other night,' I said. I made the bandhan, circling my right hand in the air over my left hand, and thought, 'What are we supposed to do now, having crossed a quarter of the world to get here?' Nothing happened, and after a short while I said, 'Come on everyone, I'm sure it'll work better if we do this together.'

We all did so, and yes, this was the land of Sasrar. After we had been sitting and resting for a while, round the corner of the track came two girls of about twelve years old. When they saw us they ran towards us and welcomed us.

'You must have come through the mountain. There's a legend that there is a way through, from northern Chussan.'

'Yes, it's true – that's how we came,' said Conwenna.

'That's so wonderful!' They introduced themselves as the daughters of Mr and Mrs Channum, a farming family from nearby. We told them who we were, or tried to, but this bit of the conversation I won't forget:

'How did you know to come and find us?' asked Raynor.

'How do you think? We felt such a strong flow of vibrations. We knew some people must have come,' said Lalla, the younger girl.

'I'm sorry, what do you mean by 'vibrations'?' went on Raynor.

'But you must feel them too. You have them, that's for sure - the cool breeze that you feel from people, when things are going right,' said Mandorla, the elder sister.

'Oh, you mean the coolness? Yes, but we've never thought of that as vibrations,' I said.

'How did you know where to look for us?' asked Lee.

'Vibrations of course, how else?' said Mandorla, with a laugh. 'Come, you must be tired. We'll help you with your packs. Our farmhouse isn't far so you must stay with us tonight.'

'Visitors are a real treat,' said Lalla. 'Mum said she felt some people were coming at last, but I bet she didn't think you'd be so young.' That was our first taste of the land of Sasrar.

The Seventh Key: Unity with the Eternal Spirit

'Today we will go over the qualities of the seventh subtle centre: self realisation and integration, our conscious awareness of our relationship with the Eternal Spirit and the all-pervading power of divine love. Its seat and centre, as you well know, are here in Sasrar.'

Mr. Meeky, Village Schoolmaster, Gangaton, Sasrar

CHAPTER 15

THE CHANNUMS

We walked past harvested fields and orchards and in the hedgerows were autumn flowers: pink, white, yellow and red. It was sunny and warm, white clouds scudded overhead and a soft breeze blew. Soon we saw a grey stone farmhouse with its outbuildings and we entered the tidy farmyard. Everywhere were vines, heavy with fruit, and creepers and more late flowers.

'This is our home,' said Lalla. 'Come and meet mum. She's making chutney and pickles.'

We went into another large kitchen, and there was a woman who didn't look old enough to be the mother of the two girls. Her chestnut hair was tied back, her smiling face had not a wrinkle on it, and her skin had that same shining bloom that I had noticed on ours in the last day or so. In this kitchen, unlike Mrs. Pea-Arge's, it was a chutney and pickle making day, with a sharp smell coming from the large pots on the stove. We soon made our introductions and were seated at the table, quenching our thirst on more pressed fruit juices.

'Lord Albion said some people might be here soon,' said Mrs. Channum.

'Does he come up here?' asked Lee.

'Now and again, but these days he doesn't get much time,' she replied, clearing away the cooking.

'How does he get here?' asked Conwenna.

'On his horse. Didn't you see it?' she said nonchalantly as she tidied up. Ahren jumped up to help her with the big pot of boiled chutney. The dear chap had learnt some manners recently, I noticed.

'No, we only saw some ponies,' Conwenna went on. 'How does he get through the mountains?'

'He doesn't, he goes over the top. It's a flying horse. Didn't you know?' said Lalla.

'Umm, no.'

'My dad looks after his horse when he's here. He's called Tharmas. He's

255

white and he's got big golden wings and he's friendly if you've got good vibrations, but bad people have had it when he's around. He's really fierce then. Only Lord Albion can ride him, or someone Lord Albion tells him to carry, like Robin Markand. You've got to have an incredibly clear Tree of Life to ride one of the flying horses.'

'Our friends have come from a long way away,' said Mrs. Channum. 'They may not have any idea what you're talking about.' Lalla was silent, puzzled by our ignorance. I was fascinated. This was certainly a new world. I ate the delicious biscuits I had been offered and kept quiet, as there would be plenty of time for explanations later.

'You've arrived on the right day,' said Mrs. Channum, 'because this evening we have our weekly singing get-together, and it's at our place tonight. We take turns and go round the nearby farms. All the neighbours come and we sing and dance. Maybe you'd like to rest first?'

'Have you got room for all of us?' asked Tandi, because this was not a large house like the astrologers' rambling mansion.

'Oh, yes, if you don't mind sharing with the girls. You boys can go in the attic; there's a spare room up there. Just be careful of the low beams.' The boys went up to the loft and were soon a chorus of snores, and we girls shared with the Channum girls, who each had a room. I was with Mandorla, and Tandi and Conwenna were with Lalla, as her room was bigger. Mandorla pulled a spare mattress out from under her bed, and I was about to lie down and have a sleep too, when I noticed something on her desk, in the alcove under the dormer window. It was an open exercise book, and in it was a picture of a person sitting cross-legged, and superimposed on the body was the inner Tree of Life, similar to what I used to see. The other side of the book was hidden by a scarf that lay carelessly on top of it.

'Hey, what's this?' I asked Mandorla.

'That,' she said, with a sigh, 'is supposed to be my holiday project. You wouldn't believe how much Mr Meeky has given us this summer. We're going back to school next week and I haven't nearly finished it all. That's my geography assignment,' she looked sideways at it, not too happy with its unfinished state.

'Geography?' I looked surprised.

'Yes, I've got to do a map and show which countries go with which subtle centres. It's revision really; we've done it masses of times before, but somehow the weeks have slipped past and I haven't got around to doing it. Then there's the general knowledge one. That's Lalla's but I said I'd help her. It's easy, just making a diagram of the Tree of Life and putting in the qualities that go with the subtle centres.'

'Why is it easy?'

'It's common sense, isn't it? I mean, you feel it all within you, on your fingers, and in your own subtle centres.' She could see I was baffled.

'You mean you learn all that - at school?'

'Of course. Everything's connected with the Tree of Life: maths, science, art, literature and so on. What else is there to learn?' She looked at my lost expression again and went on, 'What do you do at school then?' She looked bewildered.

'Not that, believe me.'

'Your country must be a bit different to ours then.'

'Totally. We come from Teletsia.'

'I've seen that name on the map. That's the country attached to the first centre, isn't it?'

'Yes, I suppose so.'

'But it's half a world away. You're not seriously telling me you've come all the way from there?'

'It wasn't easy. Tell me more about this Tree of Life and how it fits with your geography.'

'All right, my story first, then yours later. Fair enough,' and then Mandorla, at least three years my junior, proceeded to explain to me a major part of the prophecy. It came to her easily and spontaneously, as simple as a recipe for apple and raisin chutney.

'I'm all yours,' I said as we sat at her desk, the afternoon sun flickering through the apple tree outside her window.

Mandorla took a pen and paper and made a sketch of some of the countries of the world. We didn't learn much geography back home at school in Teletos, but at least I recognised Teletsia and the Great Sea, or Sea of Illusion, and the northern landmass we were now on, from having travelled over these places.

'So,' she began. 'How much do you know?'

'Let's assume I know almost nothing.'

'Right. This is a picture of our inner selves,' she pointed to the diagram in her exercise book, 'and this is a map. First I'll explain the circles inside the person's body; the Tree of Life.' They looked remarkably like the flowers of our jewelled keys, each with a different number of petals, and each with different coloured jewels. 'Each subtle centre within us corresponds to one of the countries on this map I've drawn. This is because the Mother Earth is also a conscious, living being, with an outer body and an inner Tree of Life. Are you with me so far?'

'Oh yes, very much so,' I couldn't believe that my questions of ages were being answered, in this simple farmhouse by a young schoolgirl.

'This is the first centre, and it's at the base of the backbone in us. This is the root, the beginning. On the map, it's in the land of Teletsia. That centre within us has four parts or petals. Hang on, I must just look at my notes a moment,' she scraped around some loose papers. 'Mr Meeky said the power is concentrated in, um, what did he say?'

'The Temple of Support, an old stone circle,' I said without thinking.

'Yes, that's it. See, you must have learnt something at your school.'

'Go on.'

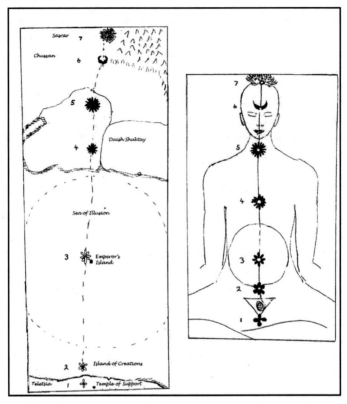

'The qualities of that first centre are innocence, and having the wisdom of a child. You know how little kids hit the nail on the head, when bigger people miss the point?'

'Oh yes!'

'The second centre has six parts or petals, and it is found on the Mother Earth in various places, but especially that little island off the coast of Teletsia. See that spot on the map.' I looked and remembered Ahren's six petalled key, which had turned into our raft. 'The qualities of this centre within us, which is in our lower abdomen area, are creativity and pure knowledge. Music, art, wisdom and all that sort of thing.' I remembered the extraordinary house, and the grounds, and the pond where our jewelled keys magically came from, on the Island of Creations. 'The third centre is this little island in the centre of the Sea of Illusion. Inside us it is in the abdomen. Its qualities are material blessings and around it is what is called the void or Sea of Illusion. Within us this governs our seeking, and our awareness of what is right or wrong. Mr Meeky says a lot of people get lost there.'

'Yes, that's for sure,' I laughed. Little did she know.

'Next is the heart centre, and it also governs the lungs and that part of the body. On the planet it's those countries just above the Sea of Illusion. Its qualities are courage, love, and knowing that we are really pure eternal spirit.

258

You know that lovely feeling you have when you meditate?'

'Yes, it's great, isn't it,' I said, truthfully for once. I realised that our brush with the tigers had something to do with the courage part, and the awareness of the spirit was perhaps connected to the hermit in the mountains.

'The next centre is in the throat, and governs all our senses, and also our feeling of universal brotherhood. Also, solving problems by being sweet and nice, and enjoying doing things together. On the planet it's to the north and west of the heart countries. In one place it stretches down to the sea, and it goes up to where Chussan begins.

'Within us, that subtle centre is quite complex,' here Mandorla was reading from her notes, 'it has sixteen petals.' I remembered Tandi's delicate sixteen petalled key, which turned into a lethal weapon when needed. It had certainly brought us all back together when we were dangerously divided! I wondered how much I could tell Mandorla of our journey. I still had that lingering reticence from so many years of having to hide my inner feelings, and experiences.

'The sixth centre is the country you've just come through. Did you come over those enormous plains?'

'Yes, days and days of walking until a nice couple lent us some ponies - but this is your story. Mine comes later.'

'This centre has two main qualities, forgiveness and transformation, or one could say resurrection into something more subtle and powerful. That's why the diagram shows two petals, in the forehead. The ego and all our conditionings are stored up there, but we have to overcome them to be transformed.'

'Yes, it was a beautiful key, with shining diamonds.'

'What?' luckily Mandorla went on speaking. It had just slipped out. 'Then last comes the seventh centre, here in Sasrar on the Mother Earth, and at the top of our head. It has a thousand petals. It doesn't in my drawing, but it should have,' she looked at her diagram critically, then went on reading. 'Its qualities are fulfilment, integration, and self-realization. That is, feeling the subtle system consciously, especially as a cool breeze on the tops of our heads and on our hands. Once the life force has risen from its coiled dormant state at the base of the spine, just above the first centre, to this seventh centre, then this becomes a living reality. We're all born with that, aren't we?'

'Some of us.'

'Mr. Meeky says most people in other countries don't actually experience all this, and that one day we must try to tell them about it, because life isn't really worth living until you've got that. I can't imagine life without knowing that when I feel a tingling on a certain finger, that someone around has got a problem. Imagine not knowing more or less what the poor person's problem is, by putting your attention on their inner system. I mean, how could you help them? How can you feel good if there are people around you who are not feeling all right? What would it be like not to be able to turn to that joy inside you?'

She lost me when she talked about the tingles on the fingers, and the coiled life force. Lalla came and told us the singers would soon be arriving, and could we help her move some of the furniture in the living room to make more space for the dancing.

I saw Raynor downstairs, and mentioned that I'd just had a vast slice of the prophecy explained.

'Who by?' he asked. 'Mrs. Channum appears to be more into chutney than the secrets of creation.'

'It's Mandorla's holiday project.'

'Come again?' Raynor assumed he'd misheard.

'Can you help me with these chairs?' interrupted Lalla. 'They're too heavy for me to move alone,' and that was that for the time being.

Mr Channum had by now returned from whatever he'd been doing outside, and eventually did most of the furniture moving. He was a tall, lightly built man with a lively face, which had that same easy smile and glowing complexion as everyone else here. His daughters knew exactly how to get round their dad and persuade him to help them.

Soon other people started arriving: whole families from grannies down to babies. Eventually there were about fifty people there, and everyone said hello to us. They assumed we had come from the other end of the vale of Sasrar, which was why they didn't know us personally.

After some time we sat down and Lalla explained that they would start the evening with a short meditation. Then they all did something rather strange. They put their hands in front of them at the base of the body, and moved the right one around the left one. Then they went on doing this, but raised both hands slowly upwards until they were above the head, at the place of the subtle flower at the top of the Tree of Life, above the fontanelle. They did this three times, then did something else I had never seen before. They put their left hands on their knees, with the palm upwards, then made an arch over their bodies with the right hand. They did this seven times. None of us knew what was going on, but some of the people present came and explained that when they were raising their hands up above their heads, they were reawakening the inner Tree of Life, and when they were making the arch they were making an arc, or bandhan, of protection around both our gross and subtle bodies – or in other words, the physical body and the inner Tree of Life.

Lalla, sitting next to me, told me it was one of the first things they learnt as children, and this bandhan of protection was done every day, at least once, by everyone in Sasrar. After this, everyone in the room did a meditation together, a bit like we'd done with Robin. It was simple, but we all felt relaxed and peaceful, and a coolness wafted over our hands even though I couldn't see any windows open. Then some people got musical instruments ready: a couple of stringed ones which were plucked, a keyboard one like a small organ and various drums and bells. Someone handed round some well-used books, which contained the words of the songs. They were tuneful and rhythmic, and had easy choruses, so by the time they got to the second or third verse we were all joining in. Some of them set your feet tapping and we found ourselves, and a lot of the people, getting up and dancing. The songs were all praising some aspect of the all-pervading power.

It was the last song that struck me most. As we sang it I felt a powerful sense of exultation, so strong that I could hardly bear it. The chorus was: *Waiting for her, the wind blows on our hands, and all we feel is joy.* As we sang that, there was a great gust of wind and everyone put their hands up to feel it. Where was it coming from? There were no windows or doors open and the room was warm, with a log fire burning at one side. Then I noticed a picture of a lady, seated on a golden throne, with a crown of stars above her head, and the moons at her feet. Her hands were in a position which suggested blessing and in front of the picture someone had put some bunches of flowers. I had seen it before, but didn't connect the cool breeze with it. Now I realised the cool wind was coming from that direction. The lady in the picture had a powerful smile, and her eyes followed you, but in a kindly, reassuring way, as if she was looking after you.

'Who is the lady in the picture?' I asked Mandorla later.

'Oh, that was given us by the Grandmother. She painted it, and it's of the primordial Mother of everyone. You'll meet the Grandmother in a few days. She lives at the other end of the valley.'

'How does the coolness come from the picture?'

'Because the subject is very holy, and the Grandmother radiates that caring motherliness so strongly that even the picture she painted is a source of all that's good.'

'Is she your granny?'

'She's a distant cousin, but in a way she's everyone's granny. We all love and respect her. I'll tell you more tomorrow. I'm so tired now, let's go to sleep.'

She didn't tell me about the Grandmother the next day, but she did tell us more about the Tree of Life. Raynor has never been an egotistical person, which is a good thing, because having parts of the prophecy explained to him by Mandorla, thirteen years old and not very scholarly, must have been quite a test for someone who had spent years swotting away at books. He was fascinated.

The day after that Mr. Channum was to take a lot of produce to the monthly farmers' market in Kedar, the largest town in the valley. When Lee asked him if it was the capital of Sasrar, he said uncertainly, 'Well, it depends what you mean by capital'. He said he would give us a lift in his large truck on condition Nog did not disturb the live chickens he was taking.

The truck was a self-powered machine and he tried to explain how it worked. 'It's the power in everything and we just channel it into the engine. It's being charged up now, in the barn. We usually get the power from the panels facing the sun on the roof of the house, but we also have a collector in the stream. Some farmers use the wind, but we're in a very sheltered spot here, so I don't bother.' We all got on well with Mr Channum. He was a down-to-earth, but highly intelligent man, who had a deep love and understanding of the world around him. The lamps which lit the house and the cooking stove ran on this same clean and natural power. Mr. Channum said it was easy to understand and run and everybody used it.

The following day we all wedged ourselves in the large truck between the crocks of jam and chutney, crates of fruit and eggs, and cages of chickens. We drove out onto the paved road that led north, up through the valley of Sasrar, past farms and small villages. The truck hummed along slowly and steadily. We passed other trucks similar to ours, and also some horse drawn carts. Although we did not see excessive wealth, there were no signs of poverty either in this well kept, fertile land with mountains in the distance, all around us.

By the evening we had travelled a long way but there was still no sign of the town. We stopped for the night with Mr. Channum's elder brother. He was also a farmer but was proud to tell us he went in for quality dairy cattle, rather than fruit, nuts and chickens. We all sat round the log fire after our evening meal, and this Mr. Channum wanted to know about the outside world. To begin with we tried to tell him about what was farmed in the various countries we had been through, and how people lived in that way. Nevertheless he was subtle and quick, and soon we had told him about the Sorcerers of Teletsia and how we had been forced to escape.

'What an extraordinary way to do things!' he said, referring to the repressive and fearful government of Teletsia. 'It'd never work here for more than half a day.'

'Who is the ruler in Sasrar?' asked Raynor.

'The vibrations. All of us do our bit, but it's the collective consciousness really. There is the Council of Elders, and we often ask the Grandmother for advice, but at the end of the day it's the all pervading power.' We looked confused.

'We understand about the cool and hot vibrations, but not how you could use them to help run a country,' said Raynor, grasping the flow.

'Don't you now?' Mr. Channum senior was surprised. 'I thought everybody knew about that. Oh well, it takes all sorts to make a world.'

'Have some more pears, dears. They're so good this year, and they don't keep,' urged Mrs. Channum senior, and went on with her embroidery.

'As I was saying,' went on Mr Channum senior, handing round the pears, 'you know that when you put your attention on a person or situation, or ask a question in your heart, and it's good, all right or whatever, then you feel cool flowing?'

'Yes, indeed,' said Lee.

'Well, when we want to decide something which effects us all, like who's to be on the Council of Elders, or whether to put a school in this village or that one, we just ask the vibrations. It's the all pervading power that is making the decisions.'

'And everyone goes along with that?' said Raynor. The Sasrar people looked at him as if he was a bit simple. Poor Raynor, he looked at the floor. It could have been any of us. Tandi came to his rescue.

'See,' she butted in as they were beginning to laugh, 'the country we come is not at all like this one. The very fact that we felt the cool breeze made us dangerously different, and our rulers would have tried to destroy us if they had known. Our ability to go into a state of inner peace where they couldn't hypnotise us was one of the reasons we had to run away.'

'You're right,' agreed Mr Channum junior. 'We just don't know what it's like to live in that sort of a society. Up here, if someone does get big headed and starts throwing his or her weight around, they themselves start feeling a pain in their head, the rest of us feel their pain too, and also a tingling on the right ring finger. All the subtle centres have a particular finger which corresponds with them and that one goes with the ego. It isn't very sensible to give yourself and everyone around a bad time, is it?'

'Well, no,' said Raynor.

'This all-pervading power is so strong in this country; it gives you hints, because everything, wind, rain, lightning, and all that, are under its control. So that's how things work in Sasrar,' explained Mr Channum senior. 'You know, even talking about that place you came from gives me a headache. Reckon you're much better off with us.'

Lee had been listening carefully to all this, and he later told me that while the conversation was going on, he recalled the vow we made so long before, on the island near Teletos: 'If I could devote my whole life trying to solve the nightmares of this country, I swear I'd do just that,' and he knew that now we were in a place where we could learn how to make this a reality. He realised that there was a tremendous veiled power behind and at the basis of this simple, friendly culture and country, which was being casually discussed during this informal conversation.

Chapter 16

Home at Last

The next morning Derwin and Conwenna were not around when the rest of us were packed up and ready to go. The truck was loaded and everybody was waiting in the farmyard. Mrs Channum senior had also disappeared and Mr Channum senior was chatting to his brother, who didn't appear to be too bothered about the delay. Finally Tandi went to have a look for the two youngest, and found them in a barn, sitting in a corner among some hay with Mrs. Channum. They were playing with some puppies.

'Derwin wants one,' said our hostess, 'and they're ready to leave the mother. What do you say?'

'Oh come on Tandi, say yes,' said Derwin, with one in his arms.

'We'd better ask Raynor,' Tandi cautioned him.

'He's got a dog, so why can't I have one? No one ever complains about Nog.'

'That's not the point. You've got to look after puppies, and they have to live somewhere and be trained,' said Tandi, kindly, but as always being practical. 'We don't know where we're going to be living, let alone a puppy,' but within moments she was falling for them, these little balls of fur. The mother was a friendly and intelligent looking sheepdog and soon the rest of us found Derwin and Conwenna and began playing with the puppies too.

We'd had a variety of animals back in Teletsia, and what always happened was Derwin persuaded someone to buy him a mouse or a rabbit or whatever, and I finished up looking after it. It warmed my heart to see him so taken, especially by one puppy which was black and white, more lively than the rest, and had a ridiculous little brown spot on the end of its tiny pink nose. I reckoned I'd be happy to look after that.

We heard Raynor talking with someone at the door of the barn. I looked round and to my surprise saw him walk in with Lord Albion. Mrs. Channum knew him, and jumped up to greet him respectfully.

'Hello, everyone,' he began, then to Mrs Channum. 'How are the puppies?'

'They're coming along nicely, My Lord. If they're as good at herding sheep as their mother, you'll have a fine pair of working dogs,' she replied. Lord Albion looked at Derwin, playing with 'his' puppy.

'We might as well take all three now,' suggested Lord Albion. 'If you can give us a basket to put them in, they can go up to Kedar on the farm truck. I'm sure Derwin will keep an eye on mine as well as his until you get there.' Naturally enough, from then on Derwin's puppy was looked after almost entirely by Raynor, Tandi and me.

When we went outside into the yard an extraordinary sight greeted us. The Channum brothers were still chatting away about farming matters, but there also was a large white horse, with the most beautiful golden wings, very long and shining in the sun. They framed his body like a swan.

'Come and meet Tharmas, my friend and steed,' said Lord Albion. We cautiously patted him and he stamped his foot and nodded his head by way of recognition. 'On this fellow, I'll get to Kedar long before you, but it's easier to put those puppies in the truck.' We finally left and as we drove Raynor asked Mr. Channum junior about the flying horse.

'He's a very special creature,' began Mr. Channum. 'There are herds of them living wild on the plains to the north of here. Lord Albion found Tharmas when they were both very young. He was a child of about your age, Derwin, and Tharmas a colt of about a year. Not all the horses develop wings, and in some they don't grow big enough for them to actually fly.'

'Lalla said a person has to have a very clear Tree of Life to ride them,' went on Raynor.

'Yes, Tharmas is more than an ordinary horse with wings, especially as

Lord Albion is so inwardly powerful. They grew up together, and although all the flying horses are special, Tharmas has also gained a lot from Lord Albion. The powers working through Tharmas are spontaneous and automatic.'

'What do you mean?'

'Well, for instance, when he began coming to our farm, which he often does, all our fruit trees started to give about twice as much fruit, and they never get blight, and we never lose the fruit to frost or wind any more. I mean, this is Sasrar, and our crops were pretty good anyway, but since Tharmas has been roaming around our paddocks, the farm is tremendous. I never stop him helping himself to the odd apple. If he's in the neighbourhood, what's good gets better, and if there is anything wrong it gets exposed and removed. You can imagine what would happen if Lord Albion rode him to some of those other countries you told me about, like your Teletsia, for example.'

'I'd just love to see those horrible Sorcerers running scared,' laughed Ahren.

'It's more that when he's around, things just start to happen to root out evil and set things right. Unless you knew you'd never connect him with the process. It's like his presence activates the natural world - weather, the Mother Earth, and so on.'

'Sounds just what we need in Teletsia, except we'd need a whole herd of them,' said Ahren, who always had a lot of faith in animals.

'If you put your attention on Tharmas's inner side, there's so much coolness coming from him, but he's still an animal. I had to be quite hard on him one time, when I found him with his head in the corn bin, gorging himself on the oats I'd been keeping for next year's seeds!'

In the afternoon Mr. Channum told us we were coming into Kedar. It was a smallish town nestling between two hills, and we were now at the north end of the valley. Ahead was a large mountain with seven peaks, and the vale with its now large rivers wound away to the left. Behind the mountain the rivers fell over great thundering waterfalls and flowed through treacherous gorges before the valley opened out into more plains, stretching away to the north, but we couldn't see any of this from where we were. The gorges made it very difficult for anyone to approach Sasrar from there, unless they knew the secret and well guarded paths through the mountains. All the way up we had seen waterfalls coming off the high mountains at the sides of the vale, one reason it was called the land of a thousand waterfalls. We turned up a track before the town of Kedar, and Mr. Channum told us he was taking us to see the Grandmother.

'It's better to take you there than to the Council of Elders. The Elders are very nice people, but you'll feel more at home with our honorary grandmother,' he said. At the end of the track was a long, low house, surrounded by gardens. In the gardens were various cottages. Mr. Channum explained that the house was where the Council of Elders met and the Grandmother lived in one of the cottages. Lord Albion came to meet us.

We unloaded our belongings, including the basket of puppies, thanked Mr Channum, who drove off to the farmers' market in Kedar, and Lord Albion took us to one of the cottages. A girl came out, saying she had been expecting us for some time, then Lord Albion left us and took his two puppies. We washed and changed into our silken garments from the Island of Creation.

Some time later Lord Albion came to find us again, and took us to the home of the Grandmother. We went into a comfortable room and sat on the floor covered with brightly coloured hand woven carpets. The girl we had seen earlier came in and asked us to wait. While we sat, not saying anything, we all had the same inner experience. We felt completely silent, serene and without any thoughts. The windows were open and outside we could hear and see the girl and some of her friends, sitting under a tree singing. The wind was blowing a little and the birds were singing, but in between we heard snatches of the songs. These are some of the words that came to us:

'You save us all from the dark,
Taking us inside your heart.'

'You are love, and blissful ease,
Giver of wisdom, giver of peace.'

'Eternal light, infinite bliss,
Transforming all our lives with this.'

Then the songs died away, and the coolness we were beginning to know so well flowed over us, from the tops of our heads, over our bodies and out through our hands. We heard footsteps as a lady came into the room. She had the dignity of a mature person, was of medium height, her greying hair tied back in a bun, and had a round, smiling face. She wore a long pink skirt and a loose jacket, both of which were embroidered with brightly coloured flowers. She radiated warmth, hospitality, compassion and friendliness. We stood up to welcome her and our hearts spontaneously exploded with joy, as if reverberating with some quality within her. Lord Albion came in too.

'Here are the young people from Teletsia,' he said. 'The first group have come to fulfil the prophecy. Raynor, introduce your friends to the Grandmother.' He did, and soon we were sitting at the feet of this wonderful lady. Her beaming smile glowed with love.

'You've come at last!' She began, and embraced us all in turn.

'Do you feel the coolness, and the joy?'

'Yes, it's wonderful,' we said, in our different ways.

'That is the power of creation, the love of the creator, and how She speaks to you. How do you feel?'

'Home and safe!' said Conwenna.

'Will you be looking after us now?' asked Derwin, holding his puppy in his arms. He had never quite got over having to abandon his family, despite the fact the journey had forced him to grow up enormously in other ways.

'Yes, the power of love, which is the universal Mother, will see to that. Like all of us who live in Sasrar country, She is very close to me inwardly, and radiates through my heart, although She is omnipresent. When you have been here for some time you will also feel that closeness.' We turned round as the girls who had been singing in the garden brought in a scrumptious spread of cakes and drinks.

'Here in Sasrar you all have to become a part of the joy, and the wisdom, and the peaceful power.' She took from a box by her chair seven golden keys, inlaid with many different jewels. They were all slightly different, just as every flower is unique, but similar to the one Conwenna previously had.

'These are Sasrar Keys of Wisdom,' she explained, 'symbolic of the compassionate power that heals the whole of creation. You will witness that power which flows so strongly, working its magic through all of us, and through all things that radiate vibrations. You will share it with many others, and through this the world will be transformed for the better. These keys have the qualities of all the seven combined.

'The name of this Mother Earth is Navi Septa, which means new seven, the seven subtle centres which exist in each of you, the earth herself, and everything in creation. The more you share the power of these vibrations, symbolised by your keys, the more that benign energy will flow through you.

'While you are here you will learn to use many healing powers. Not only will you show people how to heal themselves, you will show them how they can help heal the world around them. Some of you will learn to ride the flying horses, who are the embodiment of the force of change for the better. They are the power of positive destruction that will get rid of much that is wrong. You have to remember one thing: you are only the instruments of the all-pervading power, and then your lives will be full of joy. You will have many wonderful adventures and you will make many great and lifelong friends.

'Right now, just relax for a while and make yourselves at home. We've been waiting a long time for you. Welcome – children of the Teletsian prophecy!' At that moment we knew why we had made the great journey.

After we had eaten and drunk, we took our leave but Raynor stayed behind. He later told us that after he had spoken to the Grandmother about Teletsia and our long journey, she asked if we would like to live in the cottage in the garden for the time being. We assumed that was all, but there was another thing, something that had been in his heart ever since we had left the Emperor's Island in the Sea of Illusion. As I left the room I heard Lord Albion saying to Raynor, 'You must treat the Grandmother as if she were your own mother or grandmother. It's only right you discuss that with her.'

He wanted to ask Tandi to be his wife, and despite their both being so young, the Grandmother gave her full approval. As our lives had been so unsettled and our journey so dangerous he had kept his feelings to himself, so as not to distract himself and Tandi from the all-important task of helping to get us to Sasrar. Only Raynor could have the iron will to have kept that secret for so long! The rest of us laughed, and one by one gave both of them a hug of congratulations.

The Grandmother gave him another present: a beautiful ring which she told him to give to Tandi as an engagement gift. Tandi was amazed and delighted, because she too had long felt the same way about Raynor, but had concealed her feelings for the same reasons as him. He had hidden his emotions so well, that although when she had first returned to us in Prince Roarke's country she had suspected something, she later thought she had been badly mistaken, and had tried hard and unsuccessfully to put her feelings aside.

The next day Derwin and I were in the garden of the cottage which was our new home with the puppy. I overheard Raynor and Tandi as they came towards us across the grass.

'Will you ever forgive me for keeping you in the dark so long?' said Raynor.

'Of course!' she replied. 'I admire you all the more for doing so. You showed yourself a true leader when you put the interests of the group before your personal feelings.'

'That's a weight off my mind!' At this point they came up to where we were trying to teach Kootie, the puppy, to sit on command. It was a complete failure.

'Asha,' began Raynor, 'our new grandmother wants to see you, and also Conwenna. Where is she?'

'She's gone to Kedar to buy a collar for the puppy.'

'I think I'd better take over the task of dog training,' Raynor stroked Kootie. 'Go and see Grandmother, and I'll send Conwenna along when she gets back.'

'Come in, my dear, and sit down,' began Grandmother. 'Raynor has been telling me about all of you. He said you used to see the subtle centres inside people.'

'Yes, but I don't any more. I didn't realise it was perilous.'

'You mustn't feel bad. It enabled you to help your friends during that dangerous period when you were in Teletsia.'

'I'm happy you say that,' I breathed a sigh of relief, because I had never quite forgiven myself for what had happened in those days.

'There may come a time when we humans change and develop, so we can safely see the other realms of creation, but not now. Maybe one day we'll all be strong and centred enough to be able to see the regions at the edges of our present reality, but at this time we must just be aware of what we see with our five senses. We must trust the warm and cool vibrations, and know that as long as we put on the bandhan of protection, and go into the state of inner thoughtless peace in our meditation, we will be looked after. When we meditate we are asking for the attention of the divine power to be on us, and then that power protects us from danger. There are angels and many heavenly beings that we do not see, looking after each and every one of us. They see everything and protect us, but what is best for us not to see, we don't and won't, especially if you follow the advice we give you up here.

'And talking of angels, that little girl outside in the garden – she's almost an angel - go and call her, will you?' I never thought of Conwenna as an angel, but did as asked. She had bought a little collar of red leather for Kootie and put it on him. She was soon sitting down next to me in front of Grandmother.

'I wish I could have a puppy too,' she said.

'Puppies are quite a lot of work,' replied Grandmother. 'One is enough for the time being, and in any case, we must get you all ponies. You need to be able to move around, and if you want to go up in the mountains, ponies are ideal. So you will have an animal of your own, very soon.'

'Thank you,' Conwenna was beaming.

'Are you happy here?'

'Yes. I was always afraid in Teletsia, even at home, where I was with my aunt so much, because my father was often away – and I even discovered he was a spy.'

'There may have been some explanation for your father's behaviour. Come here and give me a hug, and if you ever feel the need, be sure to come and see me and together we'll put everything right.'

The following month, the wedding of Tandi and Raynor was celebrated in great style, attended by the nearby farmers and villagers, and our new friends in Sasrar. Tandi looked glorious in a red and gold silk dress, and some exquisite jewellery borrowed from our new honorary grandmother.

We all wore our new keys openly and with gratitude. I also had on the pearl necklace I had been given on the Emperor's island, as did Conwenna, and the boys wore their jewels too. There was music and dancing and wonderful food, and in the evening the first snow of the year, the first snow I had ever seen so close, fell softly out of a dark sky. We from Teletsia ran outside and let the snowflakes fall on our hands, clothes and faces, fascinated by their pristine-pure delicacy. Like people should be, each one was beautiful and unique, an expression of the love of the creator. The Council of Elders declared a holiday, Grandmother and all our new friends gave blessings and gifts, and everyone was full of hope and good will, not only for the young couple, but also for the new beginning it symbolised for young people everywhere.

However, that was indeed only the beginning!

Lightning Source UK Ltd.
Milton Keynes UK
UKOW021032221011

180760UK00001B/22/P